CLAIMED
Blood Ties Series

A.K. ROSE
ATLAS ROSE

R🌹S E

Copyright © 2023 by A.K. Rose

All rights reserved.

No part of this book may be reproduced in any form or by any electronic or mechanical means, including information storage and retrieval systems, without written permission from the author, except for the use of brief quotations in a book review.

For all trigger warnings please refer to my website here

For those who needs a beast of their own.

I have to say thank you to a few people for helping me get through this one. My alpha readers: Jess and Renee. You are both my rocks and this book wouldn't be what it is without you. To Kayla and Zoe, my little cheer team, fierce, *fierce* love for the both of you, and my group of Badass Authors. Without you *I* wouldn't be what I am, so thank you from the bottom of my heart.

And to you.

My readers.

My family.

You are...*everything*.

Love,

Atlas.

ONE

London

"Tell her..." Colt croaked in my ear, his voice lifeless and strange. "Tell her I lo—"

Then the line went dead.

The.

Line.

Went.

Dead.

"Colt?" My pulse boomed as I called.

But there was no answer from my son.

Just an emptiness from the phone that hit me like a bullet. Right in the middle of my goddamn chest.

"*Colt?*" I repeated, then slowly pulled the phone away.

The screen was blank. No call. No Colt.

"Where the fuck is he?" Carven barked, stepping closer. His eyes were wild and his skin gray. Colt was the only one who made Carven look like that. The only one who'd—*break him*.

I killed her...I killed Ophelia.

I shook my head as Colt's words returned. "Fuck...*FUCK!*" The hallway inside the house swayed. "We have to go." My voice was not my own, sounding distant. "We have to go right *FUCKING NOW!*"

Fear punched through me as I took a step, then another. Then pushed into a run, before I picked up pace, slamming my hand against the end of the hallway to catapult me toward the rear of the house.

Footsteps pounded in unison. They were a step behind, racing as I dug into my pocket and punched my way through the door.

I killed Ophelia.

The words slammed into me as I stabbed the button and unlocked the Audi. Agony ripped through my shoulder. I didn't have time to think about the bullet still lodged in it. A remnant from the shoot out in front of the restaurant. I ignored the pain and everything else as I yanked open the door and climbed in.

Bang.

Bang.

"Talk to us!" Vivienne yanked her seatbelt down.

"He killed her." I stabbed the button and started the engine. "He fucking *killed* her!"

My mind raced as I shoved the car into gear and punched the accelerator, spinning the wheels before they caught traction. I slammed forward against the wheel as we reversed back down the drive behind the house and hit the street with a brutal *jolt*.

I ground my teeth, swallowing the agony, using that cold, cutting pain to hold on instead.

"He...killed her?" Carven murmured, glancing my way.

Fuck...

His blue eyes looked almost black under the streetlights as I shifted gears and drove the accelerator all the way to the floor, working the gears as we took a corner and raced toward the city.

I couldn't answer. Because all I could hear was those hollow fucking words in my head.

I killed her.

My gut clenched at the words.

I killed Ophelia.

Panic made my mind race with the possibilities as we tore along the streets.

Hale's here. He's just pulled up in the drive.

Tell her...

Tell her I lo—

I clenched the wheel as oncoming headlights blinded me. The streets blurred through the roar in my head and reflex took over as I hurtled through red lights, pushing the car harder than I ever had before. I jerked the wheel, cutting across the traffic and drove down the wrong way on a one-way street, bypassing the clubs and the bars until I turned one last time.

I glanced at the clock. It'd been thirty minutes since I took that call from Colt...

The longest thirty minutes of my goddamn life.

"There," Carven growled, reaching for his door handle as I braked hard and skidded to a stop in front of her two-story townhouse. He was out of the car in an instant, drawing his gun as he charged toward the house.

I was a *second* behind, shoving my door wide and leaving the engine running. My focus narrowed in. All I saw was the empty drive and the dull light through the blinds from inside. "At the back!" I roared, pushing forward.

Carven grabbed the railing of the stairs and lunged, taking them two...then three at a time.

Boom.

Boom.

BOOM.

His boots thundered.

Until he slipped...and hit the stairs hard with a brutal *crack* of his knees, then surged upwards, pushing all the way to the top with a terrifying roar.

"Colt!" Vivienne screamed behind me as I raced upwards. "COLT!"

But her call went unanswered even as Carven barged through the door, leaving it to slam back against the wall with a *bang!*

Claimed

I was inside in an instant, tearing into the familiar entrance. Revulsion coiling in my chest like a wounded serpent. For one panicked second, I jerked my gaze to Vivienne as she stepped into the place I'd once shared with *that* woman.

The place I'd bought for us a long time ago to keep up that fucking charade of a marriage. Only I was never really here... and *she* refused to fucking leave, forcing me to come here.

To take care of her needs like a husband should.

I pushed that disgust aside now, tearing past Vivienne and the kitchen to the expansive living room that overlooked the city. Lights sparkled in front of us, spread out like a blanket of stars. But the fucking view wasn't why I was here.

Blood splatter marred the wall...the sight of that was a fist to my chest.

"The bedrooms." I jerked my gaze left. "Check the goddamn bedrooms."

We whirled and raced up the stairs. Carven had disappeared, the slamming of his boots echoed in the resounding boom in my chest.

"London," he called, his tone dull and lifeless.

I jerked my gaze to the sound and charged through the doorway of the master bedroom.

Through the murky light, I saw it.

A body slumped against the wall. Fear punched through me. But it was too small to be Colt. Familiar black strands of hair glistened with blood. "The light." I croaked, unable to tear my gaze away as I rounded the bed. "Someone get the damn light."

Click.

The room was filled with illumination, one that spilled over the...*mess* in front of us.

I stared...unable to tear my gaze away from the face that should've been familiar.

But not like this.

Carven was stopped in front of her. If I hadn't known better, I'd never know it was *her...Ophelia.*

One eye was fixed open. The dark pupil was blown. The whites were filled with blood. But it was the caved-in side of her head that held me transfixed. One where her brain should be. But it wasn't, was it? Because it was *everywhere.* Gray matter glistened on the midnight-colored hair, clumped with blood. Her head was crooked unnaturally to one side. Broken bones of one arm pierced through the skin. Shards of white smeared with crimson.

Vivienne turned away and retched.

This wasn't just a murder.

This was rage.

"He's not here, London." Carven turned to me. Those blue eyes were not the man in that second...they were the boy. One I'd saved before. One who needed me to save him again. "My brother isn't here."

Footsteps faded as Vivienne stumbled from the room. The soft *thud* of her hand slammed against the wall before she staggered down the stairs.

"We have to find him." The small shake of Carven's head broke my fucking heart. "We have to get him—"

"*NO!*" A shrill scream cut him off. One filled with torment. "*NOOO!*"

I jerked my head toward the sound and lunged. Carven charged behind me as I stumbled out of the bedroom and down the stairs, heading toward Vivienne as she stood outside the kitchen with her back to me.

I scanned the kitchen counter, searching for a body.

But there was none...

"What is it?" I roared.

She shook her head and turned away...

That's when I saw it.

Small.

Thick, pink, and severed.

I stumbled forward.

"That motherfucker...." Carven started. *"THAT GODDAMN MOTHERFUCKER!"*

My mind refused to accept what I was seeing. Still, I knew as I moved forward and reached out to grasp the cold, cleaved-off thumb of my son.

I closed my eyes as the room swayed.

Hale had what belonged to me.

Only this time, it wasn't Vivienne...

It was Colt.

"I'll fucking kill him," I whispered. My voice was nothing more than a croak of air before I roared. *"I'LL FUCKING KILL THEM ALL!"*

TWO

Vivienne

I jumped at the roar as London lunged, grabbed a glass vase filled with blood-red roses in front of him, and heaved it across the hall.

Crash!

It smashed against the wall next to the paintings.

His powerful chest rose with a harsh breath as he fixed that dangerous stare on the water as it dripped to the floor. With a guttural snarl, he strode forward grabbed the first painting, and yanked it from the hooks holding it in place.

"Touch MY fucking SON!" he bellowed, slamming it down. *"AFTER ALL I'VE DONE FOR YOU!"*

The wooden frame splintered instantly before he cast it aside, leaving it to clatter to the floor.

But his reaction was like a switch had been tripped...*in all of us.*

A ripple of rage coursed through me. Colder. Hungrier. More savage than I'd ever felt before. I sucked in the foul, fetid air of that place as he grabbed the next painting and wrenched it free.

Crack!

It shattered before he moved on, tore each one from the wall, and lunged forward. The soft, sheer blinds were next. Shredded in blind fury, they fluttered to the floor before the low-rise steel table was lifted into the air and heaved clear across the room.

Crash!

In a matter of minutes, the room was utterly destroyed. Broken, torn…

Still, it wasn't enough.

It wasn't *anywhere* near enough.

Hard muscles rippled under his white shirt as he spun. That incensed look of rage was darker than I'd ever seen it before. "I'll burn it." His husky words were the match he needed. "I'll burn it all to the goddamn ground."

He strode into the kitchen, then yanked open the cupboard and rummaged through until he pulled out a large bottle of kerosene and placed it on the counter. But his gaze moved to that thumb.

I couldn't look away as he reached out and grabbed it.

My gaze fixed on the touch I craved. To feel those callused ridges brush my tears away. But I wouldn't, not anymore. Tears threatened. But they weren't tears of sadness…they were of rage.

The kind that swallowed me.

London bowed his head as his fist closed around that shorn-off digit, his body quaking. "I promised him," he whispered raggedly. "I promised him when I carried the both of you out of that place, they'd never take him from me." There was a small shake of his head. "Now Hale has him. So I failed. I fucking failed."

I opened my mouth to answer.

But no words came, trapped behind that lump in the back of my throat. Out of the twins, Colt was the one he protected the most. The one beaten. The one tortured...the one scarred. I saw the weight London carried now. The weight of responsibility to a broken boy...and now to a man.

It rippled back to me.

Go to him, London's voice rose in my head. *Fuck him, Wildcat. Love him. Take care of my son...*

All the times London pushed me to Colt. Over and over again, as though he knew what Colt needed.

And he was desperate to put the son's needs before his own.

"No..." Carven snarled, striding forward until he was in front of London. His words were a growl behind clenched teeth. "*You* didn't. It was them. It was *all of them*. Fucking Hale and The Order. They take and corrupt and destroy. But they *won't* destroy us, London. Do you hear me? They. Won't. Destroy. Us.*" He grabbed London by the back of his neck, dragging him close until their foreheads touched. The sight of that raw, masculine need for strength drew me forward. "*Familia est omnia.* Isn't that what you've always told us, London? *Family... is...everything.*"

London shuddered, then reached out, grasped my hand and drew me closer. So close that I became part of the need for strength. Sparks collided in London's dark eyes as he turned his head and fixed that desperate gaze on me. "Familia est omnia."

Carven was the one who broke through his grief. The one who carried more pain in the absence of his twin than all of us combined. "We exist in a place they can't reach," he murmured. "No matter how many times they take us. We have something they will *never* have...we have *us*."

I turned my head, meeting those blue eyes. Eyes fixed on mine as he whispered. "So you can either stand here and carry the fucking weight of all of this, or you can be the father you've always been...and help me get my goddamn brother back."

With one hand gripping Colt's severed thumb, London unscrewed the top of the kerosene, grabbed the bottle, and strode around the counter.

Flick...

The image ignited that same fury in me. I turned around and started walking. I knew where I was heading...and was unable to stop it.

My hands shook.

My breaths panted as I strode into the bedroom she'd shared with the man I loved. This was more than jealousy now. More than a petty fucking pissing contest I'd spat in the restaurant. I reached out, grabbed the bedding from the bed and, with a burning roar, ripped it free. Once I started, I couldn't stop. I tore her clothes from the closet, dumping them into a pile in the middle of the room.

It wasn't enough...but it was a start.

The heavy thud of London's steps approached. I spun, my wild eyes moving to the bottle in his hand. One that was now half empty.

The pungent stench filled my nose as he handed it to me, his gaze moving to the body slumped against the wall. As he stared, I grabbed the bottle and upended the rest of the flammable liquid, splashing it over the clothes and the bedding.

"The match," I croaked, my throat raw. "Give me the damn matches, London."

He reached out and handed them to me without a sound. My fingers never trembled as I tore one free and spun around. One flick and a flame came to life. I tossed it, watching it fly through the air before it landed. Chanel burned just as readily as the bedding.

In a *whoosh,* the pile was engulfed. Flames rose, climbing up the bed and onto the mattress where they'd once laid.

"We need to leave," London urged.

I gave a slow nod, glancing over my shoulder. Through the reaching flames, I seared the image of her mangled face into my mind. There would be more like her by the time I had Colt back...*many fucking more.*

Carven flicked more matches, setting alight the rest of the townhouse.

"Guild," London snarled into the phone as we headed out. "It's time." His heavy steps thudded on the stairs as we descended. "Pay every fucking mercenary whatever they want. But I want this city torn apart. Find Colt and find him now."

"We're coming for you, Colt," I whispered as I raced down the stairs and lunged for the car. "Hold on, baby, we're coming."

"Where?" Carven demanded. He yanked the passenger door closed as London climbed in behind the wheel. "Where do we start?"

"In the center of this fucking nest," he answered as he started the engine and shoved the car into reverse. We backed out of the driveway before the Audi lunged forward. "We go to Hale."

I yanked my seatbelt down, driving it into place. The sharp *snap* of Carven's gun was loud in the car. "Do it," the son urged. "Take me to him."

"Vivienne." London started, meeting my gaze in the rear-view mirror.

"Give me a gun," I demanded. "I need to fight."

One careful nod of London's head and the memory of them bursting into Macoy Daniels' house rushed in. All I saw was my silent protector vaulting over that sofa, desperate to get to me. He would've killed anyone at that moment. Just as I wanted to kill now.

London reached into his jacket and pulled out a gun, handing it to me in the backseat of the car. I grabbed it, my fist curling around the patterned grip. Cold steel warmed under my touch. I shoved all fear aside and fixed my gaze on the streets ahead as we headed just out of the city, to where opulent houses waited. London was fixed on the road as he slowed, then turned into a driveway. A guard stepped out of a hut as we turned and pulled up at the towering iron gates.

But Carven was already moving, opening the passenger's door and climbing out, lifting his hand as he quickly took aim across the windshield of the car.

Bang!

The guard never had a chance, dropping where he stood. Carven moved fast, rounding the front of the Audi, bending low to snatch the two-way from the guard as he raced for the hut.

"Stay behind me, understand?" The words were a command, but one filled with fear as London glanced at me in the mirror.

"I understand." My words were dull and lifeless.

As Carven raced back to the open door and the gate slowly opened, I knew why. The Audi lunged forward, the engine roaring as London headed for the sprawling house at the end of the drive.

Shadows moved, coming for us. London slammed the brakes and pulled up hard...*and Carven was gone in an instant.* Doing what he was good at...being the cold, merciless killer as he hunted for his twin.

My breaths raced as I yanked the door handle and shoved, racing out after London.

Bang!

Bang bang bang! Shots fired in unison.

I lifted my gun, taking aim as a blur sharpened to one of Hale's guards narrowing in on London. *Breathe...breathe and squeeze.* My finger curled tighter and tighter.

CRACK!

The weapon kicked in my hand. I didn't have time to think, all I saw was the glint of steel aimed at those I loved and I reacted.

The guard stumbled backwards as the shot slammed into his shoulder. With my heart racing, I took aim again and fired as he took aim at me.

CRACK!

Only this time I hit him square in the middle of the chest. He sucked in a hard wheeze, coughed...then fell.

I watched him crumble. Flecks of blood flew through the air. But as I watched, I felt nothing at all.

A numbness clenched around my heart like an impenetrable icy fist. It was that fist I felt now. Not fear. Not disgust. *Only that fist.*

"*Vivienne!*" London roared. I tore my focus from the dying man and lifted my weapon again, took aim at the corner of the building, and rushed forward.

BOOM! Carven took aim and fired, blasting through the front door. I didn't even flinch or turn my head, just rushed forward and stepped into the dark, chilling air of a foyer.

This is Hale's house.

An icy shiver raced along my spine as I stepped inside the nest of my tormentor. I tried to catch my breath, but still it raced, clawing upwards as Carven's steps faded up the stairs.

"Basement." My words were cold and detached. "If he's anywhere...it'll be a basement."

The whites of London's eyes shone in the dark as the *crack* of a shot rang out from upstairs. But as we moved from the foyer and deeper into the house, with London leading the way, a wave of despair swept through me.

This place felt...empty.

Hollow almost.

And not just sparse. The light flicked on, illuminating what was the coldest, barest kitchen I'd ever seen. London scowled, turning around. Heavy steps moved overhead as Carven raced from room to room.

"Stay here," London commanded.

I shook my head. There was no way in hell I wanted to be anywhere in this place on my own. But I gripped the gun and took a step backwards, pressed my spine against the wall of the kitchen, and listened for my lover's resounding steps.

Hope filled me, then dread crept in.

He's going to be here. He's going to...he's going to be alive.

He had to be...he...had...to...be. That ache in the back of my throat grew. They took the Daughters back to The Order to sell us for sex. *But what did they do to the Sons? Where did they take them?* I didn't know. I didn't know anything, because I'd never known they existed.

Not until London dragged me to his house for the first time. My hand sank, the gun aiming at the floor as the dread grew inside me and the heavy thud of footsteps raced down the stairs, coming closer.

"He's not here," Carven barked. "HE'S NOT FUCKING HERE!"

"No one is," London added, coming out of the darkness. "The house is vacant."

"Vacant?" I whispered.

He inhaled hard, dragging his fingers through his hair. Carven's lip curled into a sneer before he turned and strode away, melting into the darkness. He just left...like that.

"What the hell?" I started.

It was like he knew. Like...Hale had fucking known.

Of course he had...he's been planning this for weeks.

He knew London would react. He was *planning on it,* wasn't he? Leaving him to be the cold-blooded assassin he truly was.

A roar came from outside. One filled with agony before a grunt followed as Carven dragged one of the guards he'd shot through the open front door and into the house. London scowled, then strode forward.

Carven threw the guard to the floor, then lifted his gun, pressing the muzzle to his forehead. "Where the fuck is he? Where is Hale?"

The pale, shaking guy shook his head. "I d-don't know."

But the Son didn't believe him, leaning down. "Answer me or I'll pull this goddamn trigger and splatter your fucking brains across this floor."

The guard's eyes widened. Still, he carefully shook his head. "I—"

"Tell us what you *fucking know!*" London barked, making me jump.

"N-nothing," he stuttered. "*I know nothing!* I was hired last fucking week, told I was to guard the place in case of looters. *I don't even know who lives here, for fuck's sake!*"

Carven glanced at London.

"Jesus fucking Christ." London met his son's stare.

The guard shook his head and unleashed a low, thick sob. "I don't even know who lives here."

They had no idea what they were involved in. No idea the kind of man who employed them—

BANG!

I jumped as his head flew backwards and he slumped to the floor. Shock filled me, an endless vacuum that squeezed my stomach until I tasted acid in the back of my mouth. But I didn't wretch at the brutality of Carven, and I didn't turn away. He looked down with an unflinching stare, then turned away.

He walked out, leaving both of us to stare at the mess he'd left behind.

"Vivienne—" London started.

"I'm not leaving." I gripped the gun and met his stare. "I'm in this now. There is no backing out, no leaving me behind. Let me fight for you, London. Let me do whatever needs to be done."

His brow creased. There was a tortured look that tore across his gaze. "I wanted to protect you from this. I wanted—"

"They will *never* allow that, not while they exist."

He knew that.

I knew that.

Maybe more clearly at that moment than I ever had. London wasn't going to be predictable...not anymore...

This was personal.

"You stay close to me," he added. "You hear me? You. Stay. Close."

I gave a nod as he turned. We left the busted door to Hale's house open as we climbed back into the Audi.

"We start at the clubs," Carven demanded, his gaze fixed ahead. "Someone has to know where Hale is. We're going to find them and when we do, we'll find Colt."

London never spoke, just shoved the car into drive and punched the accelerator all the way to the floor.

THREE

Carven

EMPTINESS. THAT'S ALL THAT FILLED ME NOW. NOT THE sharp stench of flames, or the tang of blood that clung to my nostrils. I was a vacuum of violence as I climbed back into the Audi outside Hale's empty house. A void. One that stared straight ahead as London started the engine.

"The warehouse." I heard myself mutter. "Take me to my warehouse."

Colt's face came to me. Dark, intense blue eyes that bored right through me.

But out of the millions of snapshots I had of him, one came blazing back. It was the moment with Vivienne, when he saw me hurting her.

His fists were curled, pulled back, ready to unleash as he grabbed me by my shirt, that careful stare full of rage.

He would've punched me then. Would've laid me the fuck out...for her.

I closed my eyes as the floodgates opened and the flickers of him and her came rushing back, rushing to me so fast I couldn't catch my breath. Them on the chair in London's dark room, them in the shower as he fucked her against the wall.

Them holding hands.

Kissing.

Loving.

"Faster." I opened my eyes. "Drive faster, London."

The Audi surged and the speedometer rose. I gripped my gun and reached for the door handle as the glinting fence of my warehouse came into view. Tires squealed as the car pulled up hard. I was out before I knew it, slamming the door behind me, and racing for the locked gate.

My fingers shook as I punched in the numbers. The sound of London's growl inside the car as he fought with Vivienne tried to push in, but I had no time for them now. All I had was that savage, desperate need of purpose.

One I'd use to find my brother.

I raced for the rear door of the compound, punched in the code and pushed in. Lights flicked on, catching my movement. I didn't look at the wall of faces, didn't care about strategic goddamn moves. I was beyond that now.

I grabbed the duffel bag from under the counter and started packing, loading guns, ammunition, and grenades inside before I grabbed the handles and turned.

The black Chevy waited, gleaming under the overhead lights. My brother's favorite car. One I'd use to get him back. I crossed the floor of the warehouse, but sensed movement behind me.

Claimed

Hinges squealed as I pressed the button and the overhead door rose. My pulse was racing as I yanked open the door, tossed the bag into the back, and climbed into the driver's seat.

But I wasn't the only one.

The passenger door opened, and Vivienne climbed in.

A nerve pulsed in the corner of my eye at the invasion. I didn't turn my head. Didn't look at her. "You sure you're ready to see this?" I asked, knowing what I was about to do.

She just lifted the gun in her hand. Her focus was dead ahead, mirroring mine. "Wouldn't want to be anywhere else."

My chest tightened at the unflinching tone of her voice. Still, I shoved the car into gear and punched the accelerator, tearing out of the warehouse until I left it behind. The automatic doors would close. The security would engage. But that was the last thing on my mind as I turned my focus to the Hale Club.

If his rats were going to be anywhere, it was there.

No doubt by now they would've heard about the attack outside the restaurant...and Ophelia. I was betting they'd close ranks—I pressed the car harder, peeling out of the open gate—or, they'd run. If they did that, I'd lose Colt for good.

Get to them...

I punched the accelerator harder, glancing sideways to find London's Audi now gone.

Just get to them.

Vivienne was silent in the seat beside me as I worked the gears. Her eyes were wide. Her skin was pale. But her hand clenched around the gun's grip didn't tremble, not as far as I could tell anyway.

In an instant, the image of her lying over my brother in that shopping mall came rushing back. She was savage then, slashing the air with the shard of mirror in an attempt to protect him.

She'd need that savagery now.

No.

Colt would...

I yanked the wheel and tore through the streets, heading for the foul fucking place filled with dark corners and darker deeds. The place where these bastards hid. Where they schemed. Where they spewed their filth.

"Shoot to kill, Wildcat," I muttered as I turned a corner. "And whatever you do...don't fucking miss."

The tires squealed as I yanked the wheel once more and wound down the window of the Chevy. Black sedans waited ahead, the bodyguards sitting inside. They weren't waiting for me, which meant maybe word hadn't yet reached them?

I should be so fucking lucky.

"Behind me, baby," I growled and punched the brakes, swung the wheel, and skidded wide.

I slammed sideways, then yanked the handle and shoved. I was out of the car in an instant, lunging across the hood as the V8 engine throbbed underneath, and took aim as the first guard climbed out.

Crack!

I fired, taking him out, and swung my weapon.

I expected shots from behind me. I expected her screams of rage. But Vivienne was silent...until I fired again, then risked a glance over my shoulder....to find her running hell for fucking leather for the club.

"*Fuck!*" I roared as I fired again, but missed the asshole, who lifted his gun and fired back.

I stumbled backwards as the asshole's shot hit the windshield of the Chevy, putting a neat fucking hole right in the middle of the thing. I unleashed a snarl, took aim again, and squeezed off a shot, hitting him in the chest. I needed to be that cold killer... but that goddamn woman was making me fucking panicked and full of white-hot, impulsive rage.

That I didn't need...not here...not now.

I spun, driving my boots against the asphalt as I raced after her. But the moment I neared I caught sight of a massive bouncer standing outside the door.

She never missed a beat, just dropped her hand low to hide the gun behind her thigh as she screamed, "Please help me! My boyfriend has a gun! He...he attacked me!"

Of course, the asshole jerked his gaze to me, a savage glare narrowing in.

All she needed was to take the focus off herself. The moment she was close enough, she lifted her gun and pressed it against the big bastard's side. "I don't want to shoot you," she urged, breathlessly. "Just let us inside."

Stupid. Goddamn. Woman.

The asshole just lowered his gaze, narrowed in on her, and shook his head. "No—"

Bang!

The sound was muffled against his body. He jerked, then stumbled backwards and looked down.

"I gave you a choice," she murmured as she stepped closer to reach out and snatch his passcard from his belt.

He stumbled, then fell to his knees. I lifted my gun and took aim. Crack! The bullet found its mark right in the center of his forehead before I met her gaze. "I said *with me*, Wildcat," I snapped.

But she was already turning and pressing the card against the sensor. Locks opened with a click before she pushed through.

The woman was going to get herself fucking killed.

Only, she didn't look so vulnerable stepping through the automatic doors with the gun in her hand. She looked like...*one of us.*

I followed her inside, sinking into that hunger. *Click.* A switch flipped inside me. As she strode through the entrance and out into the main bar, I knew exactly how this was going to go down.

Most of the tables were empty in the exclusive club. But it wasn't the front of the club she wanted...it was the rear. I lengthened my stride, catching up instantly. "Wildcat."

She sucked in hard breaths and turned that savage stare my way as I pushed ahead, lifting my gun and taking aim.

Claimed

Crack! The guard standing outside the rear door dropped to the floor.

I'd wanted to go in through the back, the way I'd snuck in before when I'd killed the piece of shit who'd hurt her. But the woman was a force of raw chaos right now. One that consumed everything in its wake. I stepped around the guard and pushed through. One step and I took aim, driving myself toward the discreet tables and the filth who sat around drinking top shelf Scotch.

I lifted my gun, taking aim at the first bastard who held the rim of a glass to his lips.

"Where is Hale?" I growled.

His eyes widened, glancing from me to Viv. "I don't—"

Bang!

But my hand hadn't moved, my gun still aimed at the spot where his face had been.

Now her gun trembled. Her eyes were wide, that incensed look of horror and rage swinging to the next one. "*Where is HALE!*" Vivienne screamed.

But the asshole was already moving, shoving back from the body of his former friend as he lifted his hands. "Wait...wait! I-I can give you *m-money!*"

Bang!

The gun shook as she fired, hitting him in the side of the neck instead. Blood spewed from the severed vein and splashed against the back of the seat.

"Wildcat," I called, lifting my hand for the gun.

She jerked her gaze my way.

"Easy," I urged.

She was close to breaking, one squeeze of the trigger away from us losing my brother.

"We can't find him if you kill them all." I took a step closer, just enough to run my hand along her arm.

Her muscles trembled as goosebumps raced with my touch. Movement caught her eye, making her swing the gun around.

Two bartenders ducked behind the bar, their hands raised in the air, panic blazing across their faces. She spun around, aiming her gun through the club as hard, panting breaths consumed her. I saw them the moment she did...three of the bastards, edging toward the rear of the club.

My lips curled at the sight.

But she was already moving, lunging like the wildcat she was to scurry over the plush black leather sofa that divided the space.

"*YOU!*" she screamed.

They ran. The motherfuckers...like cockroaches exposed to the light. I unleashed a snarl and went after her, sidestepping the tables before vaulting the sofa two goddamn seconds behind her.

But the three roaches didn't make a run for the exit. Instead, they headed toward the rear where there was an office and the secret door of a panic room behind the wall.

"The fuck you do!" I barked, moving faster as we hauled ass through the rest of the club.

But it was Vivienne who dropped her shoulder and barged through a second after they shoved the door wide and careened inside.

"WHERE THE FUCK IS HE!" she screamed. *"Where the fuck is Colt!"*

Three white men wearing the same fucking steel gray suits.

That's all I saw when I pushed inside and lifted my gun. "You will answer her," I urged and took aim. "You will tell her exactly what she wants to know."

But they never had a chance to answer. Vivienne surged forward, grabbed the first asshole by his jacket, and screamed in his face. *"TELL ME WHERE YOU TOOK HIM!"*

They didn't know. That was easy to see. Left out in the cold, the foul fucking captain had abandoned ship and left his crew behind.

"Look, just calm down," one of the assholes snarled as he stared at her. "We might be able to figure out who the fuck you're talking about."

Calm down...calm down? Condescending, fucking prick.

"We can help." Another one glanced at his buddy, then me. "If *you* tell us who you're looking for."

"Tell. You. Who. We're. Looking. For?" I took a step closer, herding them further into the office. *"Tell you who we're* LOOKING FOR?"

One of the guys glanced at a section of the wall behind them. One I damn well knew housed the safe room. They thought they could scurry for safety, call the police, and wait us out.

I swung my gun toward him. "Take a step toward that door and I'll put a bullet in your head."

He flinched, paling instantly as he shook his head. "I don't know what you're talking about."

Bang! I squeezed off a shot, one that hit the wall next to him. "I know more about this place and your kind than you *ever* will. Now, we're going to ask one more time. Where is Hale, and where the fuck has he taken my brother?"

"Hale?" The asshole who'd looked to the panic room muttered.

I took a step closer, so close I stared into his eyes. "Yeah, Hale. Tell us where he is...and we'll let you live."

The one next to him shook his head. "We...we don't know."

I swung around. *"You. Do. Know!"*

He trembled, wide-eyed, his knees shaking until he finally fell to the floor.

"Tell us!" Vivienne screamed. *"Tell us where he is!"*

But the asshole ignored her. Instead, he turned my way, sizing me up. "I can help you. Just you and me." He even shifted his body, giving Vivienne his back. "Let me make some calls. I'll try to get a hold of Mr. Hale. I'm sure we can get to the bottom of this."

Mr. Hale...

This fucker wasn't even important enough to call him by his own name...and yet—

Wildcat shook her head. Her hand clenched around her gun. "Look at me, asshole."

We both stood here with guns pointed at them. Yet in that guy's view, there was only one threat here and it sure as hell wasn't Vivienne.

"LOOK AT ME!" she screamed.

He flinched, his jaw flexing. "Fucking women, right?" he forced through clenched teeth, shooting me a glare. "Every one of them, attention seeking whores. I bet you she roped you into this, right? I bet she fucking did. It's okay, I get it. I know exactly what good pussy can do, but there's plenty of cunt around here. You don't need to do this for one decent ride."

"One decent...*ride?*" Vivienne repeated slowly. "ONE DECENT RIDE?"

She stepped closer, lowering her gun until she pressed it against his cock. "Is *that* what you think of me? All kitten and no FUCKING claws? Not dangerous enough to look at. Not fucking important enough for you to see until you're fucking me, that is..."

Bang.

Her hand flinched. He screamed as he fell to his knees and grabbed between his thighs. Bright blood seeped between his fingers as he clutched his bullet-mangled cock.

"I'm not the goddamn kitten, asshole." She lifted the gun to his head. "*I'm the fucking lioness and you took my mate.*"

"*Fucking BITCH!*" he howled, writhing.

Only the third guy, who'd stood quiet through all of this, didn't look down at the scumbag next to him...no, he watched her... then reacted, lunging with a roar to grab the gun from her hand.

The moment he moved...so did I.

But it wasn't my gun I reached for...I dropped my hand to my waist, palming my knife in a second. My thumb pressed the button, releasing the blade as he grabbed her wrist with one hand and swung her against the wall.

She hit hard, unleashing a roar, and squeezed the trigger. *Crack!* The bullet slammed into the ceiling.

"You fucking bitch!" he screamed, wrenching her against him to growl in her ear. "I hope Hale has whoever you're looking for...and I hope he returns him fucking destroyed."

With a savage snarl, I moved.

A bullet to the brain was too easy for men like this.

Too quick.

Too simple.

I pressed the knife against his neck, letting him feel the sting as the blade bit his skin. "You'll release her now. Do you understand?"

Hard breaths consumed him as he slowly eased his hold. Vivienne jerked out of his grasp. Her hair swung wildly as she turned on him and unleashed her fist, driving it into his face.

His head snapped backwards.

"Easy now, baby," I urged, my gaze never once moving from the piece of shit.

I hope he returns him fucking destroyed...

That cruel fist tightened around my heart, squeezing until I could barely breathe. All I could see was my brother's fucking severed thumb on the counter in that townhouse. The Hale

Order almost destroyed my brother the last time…this time they might just succeed.

"In that case, we'll need to send Hale a message." I tightened my grip on the knife and lowered it, before I plunged it deep into his gut, then jerked upwards, disemboweling him where he stood. *"We're coming for you."*

FOUR

London

"Vivienne..." I lashed out, grabbing her arm as she reached for the door handle. "Carven's dangerous."

Those beautiful brown eyes that always sparkled with excitement were dull and lifeless as she answered. "London." She looked at my hand on her arm. "Right now, we're *all* dangerous."

I could do nothing but let her go as she climbed from the car, then pushed into a run after Carven, following him into that warehouse he shared with his brother. My heart boomed as I watched her disappear. She'd follow him into the bowels of Hell to get Colt back. She'd hunt. She'd kill. She'd do whatever it took to keep those we loved safe.

Finally, our Wildcat was one of us.

Now all we needed was Colt.

I'd failed...

I'd. Failed.

The words lashed like a whip. I would beat myself to death with them if I thought they'd bring my son home. But they wouldn't...*power would.*

I tore my focus from the warehouse, shoved the Audi into gear, and punched the accelerator.

In my mind there was only one place to start. Hale's fastest way out of the city, his private jet. I swung the wheel and drove my foot against the accelerator, driving to the outskirts of the city to where the private hangar sat.

I knew the road well. My Gulfstream was tucked away in the same complex. My pilot was on standby, the jet fueled and ready to go at a moment's notice.

If Hale was running...it'd be fast and under the radar. So this was perfect. I gripped the wheel and focused on the road. But it didn't matter how hard I stared at the flashing white lines as they passed me. Vivienne's words rose to haunt me.

Right now, we're all dangerous...

I clenched my jaw as the sparkling lights from the hangar shone in the distance. She couldn't be more fucking right. I never slowed, even when the road veered to the left and away from the private area. The place was illuminated by security floodlights, hidden behind a high eight-foot fence topped with razor wire. But that didn't stop me from jerking the wheel and hurtling the Audi toward the gates.

Thanks to Vivienne, I knew the car could withstand the impact.

I clenched my grip, ground my teeth, and braced for impact as the Audi hit the gates with a brutal *bang*. The locks on the gate shattered as I flew forward, hitting the steering wheel hard enough to knock my breath free in a whoosh. Steel scraped as I burst in and tore toward the far end of the massive steel building. Lights were on in the hangar Hale owned, the shine spilling under the door.

I fixed on that glow as I pumped the brakes and wrenched the steering, skidding the car to a stop just outside the cracked open roller door. There was no room for thinking now. I acted on emotion alone as I stabbed the seatbelt and shoved out of the door.

My boots thundered as I yanked my gun from the waistband of my pants and ran. I *ached* to put a fucking bullet in Hale's brain, right after I got Colt back. Then I'd wipe that motherfucker from this world...forever.

I focused on that feeling as I grabbed the open roller door and shoved, striding into the private hangar. Hale's Boeing 767 was still there. Gleaming. Perfect...and silent. I scanned the space, searching for Hale or his pilot. Maybe I caught them before they geared up?

My footsteps were quiet as I lifted the gun and took aim. I'd take out his pilot, Ulrich, if I could. He had another on standby, but if it cost him time before he fled the state and the country, then I'd fucking take it. Anything to give me a few more precious moments to track Colt down.

But the moment I stepped around the front of the jet, I realized something was *off*. There was no pilot, just a worker sweeping the concrete floor of the hangar like it was a normal fucking day. He worked with his back to me, earphones on, humming away, oblivious to me standing behind him with the gun in my hand and murder on my mind.

My mind raced as I glanced around the space. I'd thought for sure he would be here...but he wasn't. I took a step backwards, moving without a sound, until I stepped around the nose of the plane and kept on moving.

Hale wasn't flying.

That meant only one thing.

He was still here...

I strode out of the hangar and climbed back into the Audi, ignoring the cracked headlights and deep gouges at the front. My thoughts turned to the many dark corners that cockroach could hide in and, as I backed out and drove forward, one pushed to the front of my mind. If he wasn't at The Command Room, then he wouldn't be far away.

After all...it was where he enjoyed watching the Daughters ply their skills.

I flew past the open gates of the hangar area and kept driving.

Thoughts pushed in...*I killed her...I killed Ophelia.*

"Jesus, Colt," I murmured. "What the fuck were you thinking?"

My gut clenched at the thought of my son being pushed to do what he had. Blood-matted hair, a smashed in skull. Ophelia had looked like she'd been in a car wreck. But it wasn't a car that had done that...it was *my son*.

The kind of rage that came from someone broken.

I fixed my gaze on the lights of the city and turned along the built-up streets, heading to the whorehouse that doubled as a nightclub for the elite. The place where Hale came alive. I jerked the wheel and pulled into the small backstreet that led to the club, then braked at the entrance.

Cars packed the small parking lot. I braked behind a sleek black Bentley and climbed out. The faint thud of a heavy beat reverberated in the air, growing stronger as I headed for the rear door. There was no downtime in this place, just a constant, steady stream of Daughters from The Order and men who paid well to use them.

I swallowed hard as I punched in the code for the rear door. A code I'd used enough times to commit to memory. A code I'd never wanted to use again. That heavy beat vibrated through the handle. I turned, pushed through the door, and stepped into the darkened hallway.

There were already Daughters waiting.

One knelt on the floor just inside the doorway. The sheer red lingerie drew my gaze as I closed the door behind me. She was posed for that act alone. Just inside enough that I had to look down on her...

I imagined what that image might invoke in another man. It'd make him feel...superior, powerful...*dangerous,* for her, that is.

I swallowed hard, my gaze moving over her bowed head and parted thighs. Shaved and clean. She wore suspenders hanging lose and nothing else, leaving her bare and open to view.

My cheeks burned as I looked away. But there were five more of them waiting. Barely dressed, conditioned to be used.

"I like pain," a blonde with bright blue eyes murmured as I stepped close.

"I fucking doubt that." I kept moving. "Very much."

These women didn't know what the fuck they liked and Vivienne could easily have been one of them. That fucking nerve pulsed at the corner of my eye as the image of her held down on Daniels' desk flooded my mind.

They would've all taken turns with her that night.

They'd have left her fucking brutalized...then they'd have sent her here. To be whored out and eventually sold. This was where they brought all the problem Daughters, wasn't it?

I felt sick at the fucking thought.

And goddamn dangerous.

I lifted the gun and moved along the hallway to where rows of rooms and Daughters waited. Because why have one when you can fuck your way through a whole breed of them? Only I wasn't here to fuck. I was here to hunt.

Movement came from the far end of the hall as a bouncer stepped out from one of the rooms and reached for his fly. One yank and his zipper rose as he snarled. "Next time, you'll learn to say yes, won't you?"

I was already lifting my gun, already taking aim as he jerked that cruel gaze to mine. "What the fuck?"

I grabbed his shirt and drove him backwards, all the way until he hit the far wall. "Where the fuck is he?"

He glanced at the doorway behind me. Still, I already felt her slinking from the room and out into the hall.

"Eyes on me, motherfucker. She's not going to help you now."

From the corner of my eye, I watched the Daughter come near. The shine of blood drew my focus, making me turn my head for just a second. Her lips were busted, the red mark of a handprint bright on her cheek.

"Please don't hurt him," she whispered, fear etched into her tone.

I turned back, shoving my gun hard into his stomach. "Not if he tells me what I want to know. Where is Haelstrom Hale?"

There was a scowl from the bouncer, then a cold fucking smirk. "Why? Did he take your bitch?"

"London," came the deep, careful tone behind me, accompanied by the heavy thud of boots. "Why don't we take this into my office?"

The corner of my mouth twitched. And just like that, the cockroaches come...with the right motivation. I fixed on the berating piece of shit and shoved the bouncer hard against the wall. "You like to hit women?" I lifted the gun, then pressed it to his wrist before I pulled the trigger.

Bang!

Making sure the bullet shattered the bones and shredded the nerves. "I'll make sure you never hit anyone...ever again."

He unleashed a roar, grabbing hold of his arm. I left him in agony, took a step backwards, and turned.

Atwood stood behind me, not once glancing at his ruined bodyguard.

"Fuck you!" The bastard screamed.

"You did us a favor." Atwood turned around and started walking. "It was time to fire him, anyway."

Claimed

I followed as men stumbled from the rooms, some partly dressed, others buck naked with softening hard-ons. I never glanced their way as I left the whorehouse behind and followed Hale's pimp toward the nightclub. A massive guard stood sentry at the door. One nod from Atwood and he stepped to the side, opening the door for us to walk through.

That heavy beat reverberated, pulsing through my body. I gripped the gun and skirted the barely lit dance floor, sidestepping the dancers. Atwood slipped away, disappearing for a second between the gyrating bodies before I stepped through.

Then he climbed the steps that led to the office and security room on the floor above. I never looked over my shoulder at the packed club, just focused on the man in front of me...a man that'd give me what I wanted...or else.

His fingers moved over the keypad outside the door before he pushed in. The door closed with a heavy thud behind us, instantly blocking out most of the music. Still, I felt it shuddering the floor as we headed past the security room to the office in the back of the place.

Atwood never once faltered, just stepped inside his office and waved to the plush leather seat on the near side of his desk. "You know your way around." He flopped into the well-cushioned chair behind him and lifted his gaze to mine.

I didn't sit, just stood on the other side of the desk and looked down at him. "Where is he?"

Atwood gave a shrug. "How the fuck do I know? He hasn't answered my calls in days."

I leaned down, gripping the edge of the desk with the gun in my hand and stared into those unflinching eyes. "You expect me to believe that?"

"Believe what you fucking want." He exhaled slowly. "I thought you were here to clean house."

I almost believed him as he slowly opened the top draw of his desk and carefully pulled out his phone. His fingers moved across the keypad, unlocking the damn thing before he pulled up his call log.

There it was...

A screen full of missed calls to Hale.

Atwood gave a nod. "I'm not lying. I thought Hale sent you here to fucking kill me."

Hale's empty house was one thing...but no communication with his money maker was a whole other thing all together.

"When did you hear from him last?"

He licked his lips.

My gut clenched at the movement.

"Two weeks ago," he answered.

He's lying.

I searched his gaze. "What happened two weeks ago?"

There was a scowl before his gaze flicked to a cupboard on the right-hand side of the room. "Y-you tell me, London. What the fuck is going on with you? You take the bitch that was contracted to Daniels, then you fucking kill him? Jesus Christ.

Claimed

Everyone says you're gone in the head, that you're a dog to be put down."

"A dog, huh?" I repeated. "And what do you think?"

He glanced at that cupboard again...for the second time. I slowly rose as his cheeks flared red.

"I think you have your reasons. But I'm not part of this. Whatever you and Hale have, it's between you." He shook his head, his tone faltering as I took a step backwards and moved to the cupboard that seemed to hold his interest so much.

"St. James," Atwood urged as I stopped at the red cedar door. The paneling on the front was a jar, as though someone had tried to stow something inside...in a hurry.

I pushed the door aside, to find papers shoved sideways just inside. I reached in, grabbed them, and pulled them free.

Contract for London St. James.

That twitch flared at the corner of my eye as I quickly scanned the first paragraphs. "A million dollars, huh?" I muttered, stopping at Hale's signature at the bottom. "Seems a little low to me."

I lifted my gun at the same time I turned my head. My finger was already squeezing the trigger as his eyes widened.

"No! Wait—"

Bang!

His head flew backwards. Blood bloomed. I was already swinging the gun toward the door as the heavy thud of boots came. The moment the door opened, I fired, hitting the guard in the middle of the chest. Then I moved, taking out three more guards as I moved to the door of the nightclub.

By the time I made my way downstairs, they were all dead.

Still the dancers kept dancing.

People kept partying.

I made my way through the crowd, meeting the bouncer at the door that connected the rooms out back. He scowled, glancing behind me. "Mr. Atwood?"

His words barely reached my ears as I lifted the gun, took aim, and fired.

Crack!

The sound echoed. Then came the screams. But I didn't look behind me, nor did I care. My focus was on the contract in my grip as I pushed through the door and fired, taking out two more guards as they rushed toward me.

The Daughters would run...if they were smart.

My phone was in my hand before I shoved through the rear door to The Command and stepped out. One press of the button and it was answered instantly.

"Guild, it's time to call in every favor I'm owed. I don't care who it is. I don't care how hard you have to push them. I want them all to know that after tonight, they're either on my side... or in my fucking way. From now on, there are no sidelines." I strode toward the Audi, my focus on the paper in my hands. "Let them all know there's three million dollars to the person who brings me Haelstrom Hale alive."

"Three million?" he muttered. "That's a lot of fucking money, London. You sure you want to bid that high?"

"Believe me..." I yanked open the driver's door to the car and climbed in. "That's just for starters. Call Harper, tell him to send out the calls. I'm on my way to see the Rossis...then I'm going to Wolfe."

"Whatever you need. Consider it done."

"Just find my son, Guild. That's all I want."

Tires howled in the background. The engine of his car gunned as my best friend drove hard. "Believe me...that's what we *all* want."

I ended the call and stared at the crumpled pages in my hand. "A million fucking dollars? You always were a cheap motherfucker."

And I was the money man...only now I needed a lot more of it.

I shoved the car into gear, wincing at the hard glare of the sun as it peeked over the horizon. The night was over and still no sign of Colt...that alone made me feel sick.

"I'm coming for you, son," I muttered as I leaned down on the accelerator. "Just hold on...I'm coming."

FIVE

Vivienne

"Where the fuck is he!" I gripped my gun with both hands and took aim.

The bleeding piece of shit didn't answer. Those wide eyes fixed on the muzzle as it bounced from one side of his head to the other.

"I...I don't fucking *know!*" he screamed. "I don't know any fucking Son, *or where Hale is!*"

I sucked in the dust-filled air, remembering to breathe. Slowly, that rage-filled haze eased, just darkening a little, leaving the biker to look to his buddies for protection. I didn't need to follow his gaze to know they were all dead...

Stabbed and shot. By Carven's hand and my own. I glanced at the bloodied strands of someone's hair hanging from the butt of the weapon in my hand, faintly remembering me driving it down over and over...and over.

We'd come for Hale...but we'd take their vile lives instead.

Leather smeared with blood was all around me. Their screams rang inside my head.

Or was it my own?

I couldn't tell anymore.

"Tell. Me. Where. He. Is." My voice was husky and cold. "Or I'll kill you."

He shook his head, unleashing a low moan as he pressed his hand against his side. Blood still spilled between his fingers from the bullet in his side. It didn't matter. He was dead anyway.

Metal on metal squealed from the open doors of the warehouse.

"You're like that other fucking bitch, aren't you?" he groaned. "The one the Banks brothers were after."

I flinched. The words tried to push past the murderous haze inside my head. "Y-you know Ryth?"

My sister.

I remembered now. Remembered it wasn't just my Colt they wanted. They wanted all of my family. *They wanted me.* I surged forward, dropping on top of him and drove my knees into his chest as I shoved the gun into his mouth. "You fucking bastard. You took her, didn't you?"

He unleashed a moan, trying to push me off, but his blows were weak now as he groaned. "We did what we were told."

That white haze pressed in, narrowing my vision. All I saw was that severed thumb on the counter. And rage followed, the kind that made me feel savage. I shoved the gun against his lips and aimed upwards. "She's my family. So, you take from me, motherfucker...*and I take from you.*"

All I needed was a twitch of my finger. One tiny...*squeeze.*

Boom!

His body kicked under me as his head flew backwards.

I felt nothing as I rose. Not disgust at what I'd done. Just... empty. There weren't enough bullets in the world to fill that hole inside me. Still, I'd kill and I'd keep killing until they gave Colt back to me. My knees shook as I pushed away from the body.

A man's scream came from inside the warehouse. I sucked in a hard breath as I glanced at the open door. Movement came from beyond. Dark. Murky. Shadows gathered around Carven as he strode out, clinging to him like a cape. He was born anew from the violence within those walls. A god of wrath and vengeance.

If he was a god...what did that make me?

Damned by love.

One glance at the dead man at my feet and he murmured. "We need to go...now, Wildcat."

I tried to move, but my body no longer obeyed my commands. My knees shook so hard, they buckled as Carven reached me. Strong hands caught me, pulling me hard against him.

"Easy now."

BOOM!

I jumped at the deafening sound. Behind us, the warehouse exploded. Walls blew out. Windows shattered. They were all dead, and still we had nothing. No Colt and no Hale.

My throat thickened as I clutched Carven. Black smoke followed, spewing into the air. As I watched the building crumble, I felt the city quake and it wasn't just from the detonation. It was in fear. Fear of what we'd done...and what we'd do.

"I'll k-kill them." The words burned like acid in the back of my throat. "I'll kill them all."

"I know you will, baby." Carven stared at me as I watched the ruined building collapse.

Still, my body shuddered and shook, unable to even stand upright.

"Just not right now," Carven murmured. "I'm taking you home."

I shook my head, lifting my gaze to the brightening sky. "No."

"Vivienne."

"I said no!" I roared as tears filled my eyes. "I can't, Carven... not until we find him."

He never flinched, never scowled. Never reacted to the shrill sound of my voice at all. But my knees gave way, even as I held onto him. He grabbed me, then bent. Those strong arms trembled as he cradled me against his chest.

He was exhausted, blood-splattered. stained by evil. Still, he gently carried me back to the open door of the car. Carven was the savage son. The cold, unflinching animal created to destroy and yet his body quaked with the effort as he lowered me gently into the car and snapped the seatbelt in place.

As he rose, I caught the smear of fresh blood on the side of his shirt. He was hurt, too. Cut deep from the shorn metal in that place when he'd fought the Son who'd tried to abduct me.

He knew they were chasing me…and he'd said nothing.

I shut my eyes as he closed the door with a *thud*.

BOOM!

Something exploded in the warehouse. I didn't open my eyes at the sound and barely flinched. I didn't care anymore. Not about them or about what I'd done. There was no going back for me anyway. The Order had made sure of that.

It was kill or be killed.

And those who I loved would make sure I wasn't the latter.

Carven opened the driver's door and started the engine with a growl. One glance at the smoke billowing into the air from the warehouse and he shoved the muscle car into gear and tore out of there. That black smoke filled the side mirror as we left the biker club behind.

You're like that other fucking bitch, aren't you?

I closed my eyes as those words hit home. It wouldn't end. The breeding. The destroying. The controlling. Not until now. I opened my eyes and turned my head as Carven pressed the button on his phone. These men will burn The Hale Order to the ground. It was the only way to stop this once and for all.

"Guild, it's me. No, nothing. You?"

I saw hope die in his eyes as he drove with harsh jerking movements. We were far too tired to care.

"We're going home." He cut me a steely look. "Call me the instant you hear anything. I mean it...yeah." He glanced my way. "Wildcat has done well, real well..."

He lowered his phone and hit the button.

I didn't fight him this time as he nosed the car to the expensive suburb neighborhood where we lived. Instead, I hit the button on the seatbelt and shifted closer to him, leaning my head on his shoulder. He lifted his arm, wincing with the effort as he pulled me close.

By the time we turned into our street, sleep had all but given up on me. I tried to blink the sting away from my eyes as we pulled into the driveway. A pang tore across my chest as I stared at the empty spot where Colt's four-wheel drive had sat last night.

I wanted him back.

Now.

Every second he was with them was a second longer they'd hurt him. I tried to not think about it as Carven killed the engine and I climbed out. Tried to push away his screams that resounded in my head as I made my way to the back door.

A guard stepped out from the side, carrying a sniper's rifle in his hand. He stared, wincing as I passed.

"Turn your goddamn head," Carven snarled. "Don't fucking look at her like that. What the fuck do you think this is, a *goddamn playdate?*"

The guard's eyes widened before he turned away. I didn't need to see the horror in his stare. I knew exactly what I looked like.

I'd seen it all in the reflection of those I murdered. As I yanked open the door and stepped into the hallway, I realized I was past caring.

The devil could take my soul if there was a deal to be made. I'd gladly hand it over, wrapped in a bow and all...

As long as he gave me back to those I loved.

My steps were slow. My body, heavy. I barely saw anything as I made my way to our wing and stepped into my bedroom. The bedding was still a mess, the sheets rumpled from where Colt had lain. I stopped at the foot of the bed, listening to the thud of the bedroom door further along the hall, and in a brutal wave, it all hit me.

I crumpled, grabbing hold of the soft comforter as I sank to the floor.

He was gone...

Just like that...

I shook my head as a sob ripped free. But it wasn't tears I wanted. I strangled the softness as a scream ripped free, searing and bloodied, unfurling like a demon inside me. My hands shook, yanking and tearing the sheets until the momentum consumed me and shoved upward.

"YOU FUCKING BASTARD!" I screamed. *"I FUCKING HAAATEEEE YOOOUUU!"* Each breath was like swallowing shards of glass. Still, it was all I had. One after another, cutting and slicing, shredding me apart on the inside. I licked my lips and tasted blood.

What they'd done to me was one thing.

But to do that to someone pure like Colt...it was *inhuman*.

I stared at the ruined bed. That's exactly what Hale was...*a beast...a monster.*

Only now, he'd just created a new breed of monsters just like him. Ones who'll hunt him down.

And I was one of them.

I unfurled my fists, letting the soft comforter fall to the floor before I turned away and headed to the bathroom. A numbness moved in. Not cold. Not *anything*. Still, that blistering burn stayed in the back of my throat.

The bathroom filled with the hiss as I turned on the water, then slowly undressed. By the time I stepped into the shower, I'd lost all sense of myself.

I couldn't feel the cloth as I dragged it across my skin. Nor could I feel the heat that made my skin glow bright red. I tilted my head back, losing myself in the robotic movements as I washed my hair, then conditioned and rinsed.

You're like that other fucking bitch, aren't you?

The words echoed as I stepped out and grabbed the towel, drying myself with slow mechanical movements before I placed it back onto the railing. Sleep...that's what I needed. Sleep, then I'd go again. We'd start somewhere, *anywhere...*

Movement came from the doorway as I turned toward the bed. Carven neared, his hair glistening from the shower, a towel wrapped around his waist. Those blue eyes were almost black as he yanked the edge of the towel, letting it drop to the floor.

A flicker of familiarity fluttered inside me as he stepped close. His hands slid along me, his fingers finding every sting and ache as he pulled me against him.

"I need to fuck you," he murmured. "I need to feel...*something*."

Something other than rage.

I knew that hunger well.

One slow nod and I lowered myself to the bare bed and slid backwards, then lifted my feet to the edge of the mattress and parted my knees. I needed this as much as he did. He stared hungrily as he crawled along the bed. His hand slid to the inside of my thigh and pushed, opening my legs wider.

There was no softness here.

No time to be gentle.

Just two fingers sliding down my pussy before they shoved in deep. "You wish this was him?" He fucked me, making me squirm.

I shook my head. "No."

There was a twitch in the corner of his eye before he pulled out, grabbed me around the waist, and flipped me over. My palms landed hard against the mattress, my nails stung as I clenched. This wasn't the Carven I knew. This was the old him, the one who didn't care. The one who wanted me to hurt, just like he was hurting. I didn't fight as his hands gripped my waist and yanked me backwards against him.

That flutter pushed through all the rage trapped inside me.

"I love you," I whispered.

He stilled, that cruel grip easing around my waist.

Then there was nothing. No movement, no fucking, and no pain.

I flinched at the slow slide of his hand down my spine before he cupped my ass. "I'm sorry," he murmured. "You deserve better than that."

I turned around, finding those darkened eyes filled with desperation, and that flutter in my chest rose once more. My pulse sped at the sight, causing me to reach out and take his hand. My fingers curled around his and cupped it to my cheek. "You don't have to be sorry, Carven. I'm here, any way you need. You want to use me, then use me."

He scowled, then shook his head. "That's the thing...I don't. But I can't...I can't find my way. I can't feel anything other than..."

I lowered his hand and pushed upwards as purpose filled me. I could fight. I could kill. I knew that...but this...this is what they needed most of all.

I was their anchor in this violent, terrifying storm.

It was his cheek I cupped as I rose on the bed. "Then let me show you."

He never moved when I leaned close, just closed his eyes as I kissed him. He smelled of violence and rage. The smell of gunpowder clung to his body as though he were made of it. I guided his hand to my breast and gently kneaded.

Callused fingers brushed across my nipple, making me tremble. He broke away, staring into my eyes, then looked down. He liked the way my body reacted, brushing his thumb over the sensitive skin once more before he lowered his head. Warmth closed around the peak. My fingers were in his blond hair, combing through the sodden strands.

He needed this.

I needed this.

It was the one thing I could do.

With a low moan, he bent, slid his hands under my thighs, and lifted me.

"I want to feel you, Wildcat. I want to...remember how it was with the three of us."

You want us both?

Those words filled me as he eased down onto the bed. Those hard lips were soft against my skin, kissing down my breasts, then over my ribs and my stomach before he lingered at the top of my slit.

"Open your legs for me, baby."

I did as he wanted. Cold air moved in. But I didn't have time to shiver as he pushed his tongue into my warmth.

"Oh, fuck." I lifted my head, watching beads of water fall from his hair to hit the bed underneath me. "Yes." My hips moved as he sucked my clit. Those strong fingers that were so at home around a trigger now slid down my lips and opened me wide. "Harder, Carven."

With a guttural sound, he moved lower, sucking and probing as he stroked along my lips, running all the way to my clit. I jutted forward, my hand moving to the back of his head.

"More," I panted. "Christ, I'm going to come."

My body bloomed, pulsing slowly as he sucked, then pushed those fingers inside. I unleashed a moan, my head tilting backwards. "If you don't fuck me right now, I think I'll die."

He moved faster. Making me jerk my eyes open as he pushed me against the bed and rose upwards, settling between my thighs. "Well, we can't have that. Can we, Vivienne?"

He only used my name when I forced him.

But he used it now.

His tongue snaked out, licking the remnants of my desire as his cock thrust between my legs. I wanted to take my time. Wanted him in my mouth. But we were too far gone for that. I fisted the half-torn-away sheet, bracing myself as he thrust deep.

"My fucking *Wildcat*," he grunted, driving his cock inside all the way to the hilt.

I writhed underneath him. Opening wider, aching for one more precious inch. I wanted his cock to stretch me, wanted him to fill me until it was all I could feel.

"Fuck. Me," I growled.

He lifted his hand. Those strong fingers grasped my throat. Fingers I'd seen drive a blade through a man's belly last night. Fingers I'd seen gouge and puncture...and *squeeze*.

"Tighter," I whispered, holding his gaze.

Danger flickered in those eyes. His jaw flexed as the muscles on his arms corded. I reached up, closing my grasp around his forearm. "Now fuck me like you want me."

His hips slammed home, tearing a whimper free.

Air forced out with every savage thrust as he drove home again...and again...and again.

This was the Carven I needed.

This was the man who'd found his way to me.

"Th-a-a-t's my k-killer," I whispered as he fucked like his life depended on it. "This is wh-ere you b-e-long. R-right h-here."

A dangerous sound coiled in the back of his throat and slithered between his lips. "You. Belong. To. Us."

"I belong t-to you." I grunted as that wave rose, unleashing with a savage force inside me.

My body clenched tight, causing me to thrust and shudder and moan as I came hard.

"Damn right you do." He eased his hold, sliding his hand around the back of my neck while he kiss me hard.

This was our anchor.

This was our home.

While all four of us had this...we would be okay.

I closed my eyes and thought of Colt as his brother gave a grunt, and warmth filled me.

I'll find you, I whispered inside my head. *I'll save you, just like you saved me.*

SIX

Vivienne

WHERE IS COLT!

I jerked awake with the roar howling in my ears. The sting in my eyes was instant as I blinked, staring at the walls of my bedroom. For a second, there was nothing but the booming of my pulse and the lingering scream...until slowly, the events of last night came rushing back.

He killed her...he killed Ophelia.

The severed thumb on the counter. Bloody and pale. A thumb I'd stared at, instantly knowing whose it was.

Bang! The echo of a gunshot followed and my hands shook, remembering the harsh pattered texture of the grip and the way it had kicked in my hands.

You take from me...so I'll take from you!

I killed him. I closed my eyes. I killed all of them. Their faces rushed back to me. Wide eyes. Pale skin. The way they'd looked at me...like I was evil.

A sob tore free.

Maybe I was.

Maybe that was what it took to live in this world.

Maybe that's what it took to love.

I opened my eyes as Colt's face rushed back to me. His beautiful thick curls, so soft against my fingers. Those dark blue eyes filled with so much innocence. I lifted my head to see the bottom of the barren bed. I'd give anything to see him sitting there with a gun in his hand and desire in his eyes...my silent, sweet protector.

But he wasn't here...and neither was Carven. I pushed upwards as the realization took hold. Carven was gone...had he left without me? I shoved against the mattress and scrambled out of the bed, hurrying to dress. Was there some news he didn't tell me about?

Maybe they'd found him? Maybe they'd found Colt.

I yanked on a bra, panties, clean black jeans and a t-shirt before I tugged on the same filthy boots I'd worn last night. Boots splattered and stained. I didn't want to look at that. Instead, I lunged around the bed and hurried for the door.

By the time I hit the hallway, I was running, tearing along the hallway to Carven's room. One shove of his bedroom door and I found the room empty. The bed was made. The scent of his soap lingered in the air. He was gone...*he was gone without me.*

"You fucking promised." I spun around and ran, heading along the hallway to the main part of the house.

"What do you mean you can't get involved?" London's threatening tone reached me as I neared his study. "If you stand with Hale, then you stand against me. What the fuck do you mean you have problems of your own? Dante...*Dante! FUCK!*"

I slowed at the entrance of the study as movement came from the rear of the house. The door opened and Guild walked in, dressed completely in black, carrying two sniper's rifles in his hand. *That's what a contract killer looked like.* He lifted his head, those kind eyes flaring for a second before he scowled.

He didn't like me seeing him like this.

Didn't like me knowing what he truly was.

I guess we'd all shed the masks now, revealing our true faces.

"Vivienne," he murmured carefully. "Is there anything you need?"

Even now, amongst all of this, he wanted to take care of me.

I glanced behind him as another male followed, dressed the same, carrying the same weapons. "Carven," I murmured.

"Right here, Wildcat." Came the croak behind me.

I spun, finding him standing here, freshly showered and dressed in a t-shirt and black cargo pants, holding two cups of coffee in his hand. "Figured I'd let you sleep for as long as I could."

I lifted my gaze from the steaming cups. "You did?"

His brow tightened before he stepped forward, handing me a cup. "Yeah."

"Guild!" London boomed, drawing every focus to the open door.

Our butler-slash-mercenary moved, stepping around us to enter the study. Others followed, men I didn't know. Still, they seemed to know me, giving me a gentle nod as they passed and stepped into the room.

"Ares is out," London snarled. "I don't know if Hale got to him, or what."

I turned at the name and moved in.

"Baby..." Carven called, his tone full of worry.

But I was too far gone to not be a part of whatever they were planning. I had blood on my hands...a lot of blood. And I was prepared for more.

London glanced my way the moment I stepped through the door. Those hard eyes never widened, nor did they show any concern before he looked away. A flare of pain tore through me. Did he just...dismiss me?

"I have someone already intercepting his calls." One man who'd followed Guild into the room murmured. "If he's with Hale, then we'll know soon enough."

London shook his head. "We can't wait that long. If the others are involved, then we'll have no choice but to take them out too."

"Kill them?" The words slipped out before I realized it.

The room went quiet. All heads turned my way.

"Yes, Vivienne," London said carefully. "If they're not with us—"

"They're against us," I finished for him.

Meredith's face rose. A face that was faintly familiar. One I'd seen in *that* place, and a cold shiver of fear rose. Something was happening at the Ares house. Something dark. Something dangerous...and London was about to make it even more deadly.

"We need to track down the others, as well. Riven, Kane, and Thomas Cruz. They have to be close. They can't have gone underground. There's no way Hale would let them. No, he'd hold them close. There's still value in doing his dirty work. There's still work for The Principal, The Teacher, and The Priest. We need to know exactly who we're dealing with before we go in."

I flinched with the names. I didn't know their real ones...just *The Principal, The Teacher, and The Priest.* Those I knew. A shiver ripped through me as it hit me. "Go into *The Order?*"

Only this time there was no explanation, nor did London meet my gaze. He just looked down. "We have no other choice."

Carven placed his coffee on the desk behind me, then stepped around, grabbed the bottom of his shirt and tugged it over his head. The same black shirt the others wore settled over his black pants. *What the fuck was happening?*

I shook my head as I realized. "You...you're going in there?"

"We have no choice," London answered.

I spun as that howling terror crawled upward inside me. "No...*no no no no no.* You don't want to do that. You don't want to go into that place."

The *thud* of locks sounded in my head.

And the slow, careful steps of the guards followed.

You going to be quiet for us this time? Or are you going to kick and scream?

"Not in that place, London, not in that hell."

Only then did London look at me, pushing off the desk to step close. "It's the only place that makes sense, pet. The only place someone like Hale would take him, knowing full well we couldn't get to him."

His face blurred under my tears. "They'll be safe, and in and out before anyone even suspects," he assured me.

"You don't..." I forced the words around the lump in my throat. "You don't understand the things they do there."

London's eyes darkened. "I think I have a fair idea."

"No." I shook my head. "You don't. You see what they wanted you to see. You only see the things they do in the light. But at nighttime...when they take you down to the secret rooms, they do things to you that torment you for the rest of your life."

"Secret rooms?" The man who'd followed Guild into the room repeated. "What secret rooms?"

"The kind only the guards know about...and some of the Daughters."

London's scowl deepened. "And are you one of those Daughters, pet?"

For a second, I couldn't answer. But he knew even before I nodded. "For a while, yes."

Shh...my own words echoed back to me as I pressed my hand over Ryth's mouth. *You can get out of here, can't you? I mean, not right now...but soon. Soon they'll come.*

I'd been so desperate to get out that night. Desperate enough to find Ryth the moment she was dragged into that place. Desperate enough to do anything but to be a plaything for the guards for one more night. But as that memory came back to me, I saw, from the corner of my eye, the looks of concern from the men in London's study. I knew exactly what I had to do.

"You won't be going in, London. You can't. One wrong move, one wrong hallway and you'll kill Colt if they have him. You won't be able to go in there...without me."

"No," Carven growled. "*Fuck no.*"

It was London who understood what was at stake here. And London I fixed on. "If you know anything about that place, you know I'm not lying. You won't find him, not alive anyway. Not without me."

"I swore you'd never go back there."

"And you've held onto that oath." Revulsion burned in my belly. "But the game has changed now. This is far beyond contracts and loyalties now. This is—"

"War," London answered.

"Yes," I whispered. "This is war."

"*If* we do this." London raised his hand as Carven unleashed a snarl. "We do this our way. If you go in...you go in with Carven."

I swallowed hard, knowing the bloodshed that waited to be unleashed. "Fine."

"Fine," Carven growled, coming closer.

The dangerous Son grabbed my chin and turned my gaze to his. There was panic, pure, bloodcurdling panic. "You will not move from my side. Do you understand that? Because...I *cannot* lose you too."

That lump in the back of my throat only grew in size until it was all I could feel. "You don't have to worry about that. You'll be so close you'll be my second skin."

"Good." His hold eased before he released a hard, slow exhale. "Good."

"So that's settled then." I glanced at London. "I'm going back in..."

SEVEN

London

FIFTEEN DAYS...*I'M GOING TO ENJOY STRETCHING YOU OUT, Vivienne. Very much.*

Those words came back to me as I stared at the pain in her eyes. They were the words I'd told her that day outside the classroom in The Order, when the need to both protect and own her had overwhelmed me. If only I'd gotten her out of that place fast enough. If only...*Hale had given me the goddamn contract.*

She wouldn't have stayed there a second longer. She wouldn't have been subjected to whatever hell those guards had put her through. She wasn't raped, that I knew. I'd seen the evidence of her virginity on the stained sheets in Colt's room, after their first time. But penetration wasn't the only way you could terrorize a woman...

No.

I knew better than that.

I like pain.

I winced at the memory of that Daughter kneeling inside The Command Room, just waiting for me to unburden every sick, debased desire on her body...and savage her soul just a little more than it already had been.

No.

The guards of The Order wouldn't have penetrated her. They would've been careful not to leave something evident. But they would've done other things. Degradation. Pain. Humiliation. I tried not to imagine the welts they would've left on her body and clenched my fists instead, aching to touch her.

I was too late to save her.

Please God, don't make me too late to save Colt.

"We'll get everything together," Harper murmured. "I'll make sure they're safe as they can be going in."

As safe as they can be going in. That was the kicker, wasn't it? Once they were inside, there was no telling what waited for them.

They could be walking into a trap for all I knew.

That twitch came in the corner of my eye.

That was it.

For all I knew.

I didn't know.

I scanned every face in the room. Harper, Carven, Guild. Men who were highly trained and good at what they did. Men who would go to the ends of the Earth for those I loved. Men who'd put their own lives on the line.

And it'd all be for nothing if we didn't know what they were walking into, or even if Colt was there. They would be going in blind. I couldn't have that. I would not risk another of those I cared about.

You don't get to think, DO I MAKE MYSELF CLEAR? Your job is to DO!

Hale's roar filled my head as I narrowed in on the one person who could tell me everything I needed to know. The one man Hale had all but thrown out of his office the last time I saw him...

Riven Cruz...

The Principal.

If there was a divide there, I'd exploit it.

If there was even a hint of a crack, I'd blow it wide open, enough for the truth to come out. I turned my gaze to those haunting brown eyes. Then maybe they wouldn't need to go in there at all. Maybe I'd turn Hale's hounds on him and get Colt out myself.

"Get everything ready." I turned and snatched the keys from my desk. "But don't make a move until I say so."

"Where are you going?" Vivienne snapped.

I stiffened. Only she would dare talk to me like that...and I'd let her. "To find out just how far loyalty will go...then to my bank. I'll need a rather large withdrawal."

I was already heading for the door when she called out. "Can't you just call them?"

I stepped out, lengthening my stride as I headed for the back door and pushed through. "It's not that kind of bank."

By the time I'd backed out of the driveway, I had Riven's last known address on my GPS screen. It was a penthouse in one of the upper-class towers in the city. I glanced at the time and pushed the Audi harder as I headed toward it.

Only, as I passed the opulent street not far from my own, my thoughts turned to Dante Ares. The man hadn't sounded right when I'd spoken to him. His tone wasn't just cold. It was empty, distant. Fucking scary if I had to make a finer point.

I've got problems of my own, St. James. Your fucking mess is your own. Keep me and my family the hell out of it.

"You're in it though, aren't you? One way or another, you're in it up to your fucking eyeballs."

I tore my gaze away and focused on driving, passing streets at a blur and turned into the heart of the city. Riven lived here, Kane lived further out of the hustle...but The Priest, Thomas. There was no record of where he lived.

That alone unnerved me as I pulled into the parking lot and braked. Heads turned my way as I climbed out. But they were more interested in the dinged-up front end of the Audi than they were in me as I headed for the expansive automatic doors of the foyer.

I walked in, adjusted my jacket, and headed for the front desk. The young woman seated behind the desk lifted her head, and her wide brown eyes grew wider. My lips curled, the smile automatic. They got the outside versions of me. The surface one where I kept calm and careful.

"Hi there," I murmured, narrowing in on her.

He cheeks flushed and her eyes twinkled. "Ah, um. Hi."

"I have a meeting with Riven Cruz and I seem to have forgotten my phone to let him know I'm down here waiting."

"Mr. Cruz?"

I widened my smile and nodded.

"Um..." she stuttered, rising from her seat. "I'm not sure."

"You're not sure I have an appointment, or you're not sure about Riven? He has the penthouse and I think he owns a good stake in the building, if that jogs your memory."

She jerked panicked eyes toward the doorway, then to the phone sitting on the desk.

Call, I urged. *Just so I know the piece of fucking shit is even here.*

I focused my attention on the gun tucked into my waistband. If the bastard was here, then I'd force my way in. Tie him up. Force him to give me the information I wanted...but I wouldn't take him out. Not yet. Not until I had Hale on his knees in front of me.

Then they'd all meet their fates.

The image of that filled me as the young receptionist glanced my way, then carefully reached out and picked up the phone. The automatic doors opened behind me and the heavy thud of a male's steps followed.

"Jessica," the asshole called. "Everything okay?"

I ground my teeth. *Just fuck off.*

But the insistent asshole never left. Instead, he stopped this side of the counter as the receptionist stuttered. "Mr. Grayson. This gentleman, Mr..."

"St. James." I answered, turning my focus to the guy beside me. The one dressed in the neat, two-piece suit and who looked every bit the part of an overpaid doorman.

"He was asking about Mr. Cruz," she added.

The smile he gave was every bit as fake as the goddamn Rolex on his wrist. "I'm afraid we don't give out information on our residents."

"I wasn't asking for information. Just to call him and let him know I'm here for our appointment. I seem to have forgotten my phone."

The asshole stared right through the lie. "I'm afraid we can't."

"Can't, or won't?" I forced the words through clenched teeth.

All he had to do was stay the fuck away for five more minutes and I would've had all the information I needed.

"Can't," the asshole added finally.

Can't.

If I had to take a guess, I'd say it was because Riven wasn't there. I glanced back at the receptionist. She gave me a wince that tried to double as a smile. "If he's not here, then maybe he's coming."

There was a slight shake of her head.

"No, he won't be," the manager finished. "I'm sorry your time has been wasted, Mr. St. James."

My stomach tightened, and panic rose. "Not half as I am."

I turned then, not bothering to give the receptionist another look and headed for the door. This was a total waste of my time. A total fucking waste—

Rage moved through me as I strode out and headed for my car. But the moment I neared the driver's door, I caught the sound of panicked steps hurrying toward me.

"Wait! Mr. St. James."

I stopped, then turned, finding the receptionist rushing toward me. She was sucking in hard breaths by the time she reached me. Her hair was windswept as she tried to smile and compose herself.

"Um, I thought you might need my number...you know...in case you need anything else."

I stared at the curled edges of the purple sticky note in her hand. "I don't think I do," I answered coldly.

She stepped closer and grabbed my arm. "He's not there. Mr. Riven, I mean. He's not there, and he hasn't been for weeks. His things are still there, but we were told not to give out information to anyone."

"I see," I answered as she pushed the note into my hand.

"Just in case," she urged.

I closed my hand around the crumpled piece of paper and turned away, climbing back into my car. She was still there when I started the car, stepping out of the way as I reversed out of the parking slot. One stab of the window control and it rolled down so I could crumple the note into a tight ball and hurl it out the window just as I hit the driveway.

The thought of holding another woman's cell phone number a second longer made me feel fucking sick. Thoughts of Ophelia rose as I turned the wheel and headed to the other side of the city, where the expensive buildings were surrounded by high fences and carefully controlled by armed guards...well, one building in particular.

"The bank," I murmured as I pulled the car into the driveway and stopped at the guard hut.

I rolled down the window again and grabbed my ID. My name wasn't enough to get me inside this place. No, it was locked down and guarded with better security than the president had. It should be...it was worth more.

"Mr. St. James. You're cleared for entry." The guard handed me back my ID and took a step back so I could put the car into gear and nose into the driveway.

The parking lot was almost full. I caught sight of the matte Black Badge Ghost sitting in the parking space marked President.

"Good. Saves me having to chase the sonofabitch down," I muttered as I parked five spaces away and climbed out.

I couldn't help but glance at the sleek bespoke machine Baron drove. It was new...very new. A gift he given himself to celebrate that harpy of a fucking ex-wife finally leaving him, although not without drawing blood on her way out.

I grabbed my wallet and pulled out my ID as I stepped through the doors and inside, stopped at the security gate and lifted my arms.

"Mr. St. James," the guard murmured as he stepped close.

"Bernie." I gave him a nod and lifted my arms as he waved his wand over my body.

"No electronic equipment?"

I handed him my phone. "There's no porn, so no sense in searching."

He just grinned and shook his head while I tucked the phone back into my pocket as he glanced at the two other guards waiting in the foyer and nodded, giving me the all clear. I left them behind and headed past the foyer with its lush gardens and expansive waiting area before I headed to the elevators. Black brushed steel gleamed, distorting my reflection as I pressed the button and the door opened.

My thoughts turned to the contract Hale had taken out on my life.

A million dollars.

I gave a chuff as the doors closed and the elevator rose, taking me all the way to the fourth floor. A floor for executives of the company only. Lights flashed before the doors opened.

Lawlor Diamonds.

The sign sparkled as I stepped out and turned, heading to the reception desk.

"Mr. Baron Lawlor."

I caught the voice of a woman standing on this side of the counter.

"My name is Cloe Woods. I have an interview for the position of Mr. Lawlor's personal assistant?"

I lifted my gaze as I came closer.

"You sure you want that?" The receptionist gave a careful shake of her head. "The job of his assistant, that is. He's...how shall I say it? *Difficult.*"

Harmony, that was her name, I think. They all looked the same to me. Hair slicked back into a neat bun, their makeup perfectly applied. The dark, midnight blue chiffon blouse embroidered with a diamond above her breast.

One look at the awkward woman standing in front of me and I knew she was in the wrong place.

My gaze lowered to the run in the back of her sheer black stocking. *Yep. Definitely in the wrong place.*

"Yes." She jutted her chin in the air, her voice trying its best to be forceful. "I am sure. I *need* this job. Here's my credentials." She shoved a folder over the counter, pushing it toward the receptionist...and knocked over a cup of coffee in the process.

"Oh *shit!*" she barked and lunged, tearing around the end of the counter to grab the cup and made the entire situation worse.

I just watched. If I wasn't so riled, I might've found it amusing.

"Just *stop!*" Harmony barked as she shoved backwards, grabbed a wad of tissues, and tried her best to stem the flood. "Leave it...*please, step away.*"

The temp dropped her hands and stepped backwards. "I'm so sorry."

"Don't..." Harmony jerked her gaze toward the black steel door across the room. "Just go through there. It's not like Baron's going to notice you anyway."

She was a rabbit amongst wolves here. She turned her head and glanced toward the door marked *Baron Lawlor*. A frightened little rabbit who was about to become a meal. Still, the rabbit had guts as she inhaled a hard breath, straightened her shoulders, and with the file in her hand, made her way across the floor.

"Wait," I muttered, stopping her instantly. "I'm first."

Harmony lifted her gaze, finally seeing me. She flinched, straightening instantly. "Mr. St. James. I...I didn't see you there."

She swallowed as the temp settled sage green eyes on me... before she scowled. I expected surprise, maybe even that glaze of lust...one just like Harmony was giving me. But this one didn't. She just lifted her hand, glanced at the cracked old watch on her wrist and said, "Sorry, I'm before you."

"Excuse me?"

Defiance blazed in her eyes. "My interview...is now. So that makes Mr. Lawlor's time mine...first."

I clenched my jaw, not in anger but to stop it from falling open. Maybe she wasn't a helpless little rabbit at all...maybe this one *had teeth*.

"Um. I don't think you—" Harmony started.

I stopped her with a wave of my hand. "By all means," I murmured to the temp. "I'd hate to make you late."

The feisty temp turned on her heel and walked across the open floor to her fate. I lowered my gaze to the run in her stocking and shook my head. I glanced at my own watch. It was three in the afternoon and time was ticking. I glanced at where she knocked on the door, then opened it and stepped inside.

It didn't matter, anyway.

She wouldn't be in there long.

Any moment now the door would open and she'd storm out, red faced and angry. Maybe there might even be tears in her eyes. I hoped not. *Don't be your usual asshole self, Baron...*

I glanced back at Harmony, finding her staring at me before I winced and started strolling toward the office. The door opened abruptly as I neared...and the poor rabbit stepped out. One glance my way. Those dull green eyes shone with satisfaction.

"I'll see you tomorrow then, Mr. Lawlor. Bright and early."

"Whatever." Came the mutter from inside.

She stepped around me. "Mr. St. James." Then she hurried away.

Surprise widened my eyes as I glanced into the expansive office with the stunning view of the city and stared at the man behind the desk. The man most people knew very little about...until last month that was.

I stepped inside and closed the door behind me.

"Did you see this goddamn shit?" Baron snarled, lifting his gaze and his phone into the air.

Lawlor's Blood Diamonds - the Inside Scoop by Jacqueline Lawlor. The headline was bad enough, but that Baron's face was front and center of it made it that much worse.

"That fucking bitch," Baron snapped. "What, a five hundred million payout wasn't enough for her? She had to do this shit?"

I stared closer, staring at the wording in the article. "She's in breach of her contract. You can sue her for that."

"Fuck sue her? It's not the money I give a shit about. You know what kind of attention this can bring down on us? The kind we don't need..."

The kind that could bring every fucking headhunter and greedy motherfucker to his door...*no...to our door*. Because I had a ten percent stake in whatever shitshow was about to be unleashed.

"About money," I started, then remembered the little rabbit. "Wait, you know there was a woman here, right? A temp."

"From the agency. I fired that double-crossing liar Brittany. Caught her feeding Jackie important company information. She's gone."

Brittany? Barron's right-hand woman. Christ, no wonder the guy was pissed. "Well, I hope the new one works out."

"She won't. But as long as it keeps the others off my back, I don't give a fuck."

"They're here?"

He gave a shake of his head. "Royal's in Dubai, Loyal is at the country estate dealing with the rest of dad's goddamn paperwork and Crew..." he met my gaze. "Who the fuck knows where he is? Why...what is it about, money?"

"I'm going to need an advance on next month's payment."

"An advance?" He rose from behind the desk. "We paid you two million last week."

"Hale has my son."

He flinched, that dark scowl deepening. "What's Carven done this time?"

I shook my head. "Not Carven. Colt...and he left this behind." I reached into my jacket pocket and pulled out the handkerchief holding his thumb.

I barely had to open it before Baron flinched. "What the fuck..." he exclaimed as he met my stare.

"Ophelia is dead. Colt killed her in retaliation for the attack."

"She was the one who organized the hit outside the restaurant?

I gave a slow nod. "It's too far gone, Baron. There's no going back."

"Jesus." He glanced at the bloodied handkerchief in my hand. "You're going to war, aren't you?"

I gave a slow nod. "And I'm going to need money to do it. Lots of it. Now, about that advance."

EIGHT

Vivienne

I TRIED NOT TO LOOK AT THE CLOCK, BUT IT WAS HARD. Especially when the entire room went deathly quiet, then one by one turned their heads to the ticking time bomb in the room before glancing at the empty doorway. I grabbed the lightweight Kevlar vest Guild had found for me and pulled it on, securing it at my sides.

Carven walked over and checked the fit, his fingers grazing the side of my breast in the process. That ravenous stare found mine before he licked his lips. "You trust me, right?"

I flinched. "Of course."

He gave a slow nod.

"Hey."

He lifted his gaze.

"There is no one else I'd go in there with. I need you savage, Carven. I need you so fucking savage that there is no way we can't come out of that hell without him."

"And you..." he added.

*And you...*I swallowed and turned away. But I couldn't escape. He stepped in my way, gripping my chin and forced my gaze to his. *"And you,"* he demanded.

"And me," I whispered, knowing deep down that if it came to me escaping or Colt, that it'd always be him.

Strength filled me. No, not just filled me, it *consumed me*. I knew I'd survive. I'd done it once. I could do it again. Still, I couldn't let Carven know that. I needed him to fight, because that was the only thing that'd save us.

"We go in quiet, find him, and bring him out, okay?"

I searched his eyes. "Okay."

He nodded. "Okay." Then he glanced at the clock on the wall, the one which said it was well after four in the afternoon. "We can't wait around." He stepped toward the heavy duffel bag filled with weapons. "We need to leave and get ready."

"You heard what he said, Carven." The unknown leader shook his head.

"Harper, if I waited around for London every time he asked me to, I'd constantly have my dick in my hand."

"Is that so?" London muttered as he walked into the study, his arms full of large boxes. "Then I guess you won't have room in your hands for these."

Carven spun, eyeing what he was carrying. "Jesus. Is that?"

"Fuck me, London." Harper moved forward, grabbing the boxes from his arms and turning them over. "These must've cost you a fortune."

"One hundred thousand for all four actually," he muttered, glancing my way.

A look crossed his face. One filled with desperation and disappointment. The others were oblivious, their focus on the night vision goggles he'd handed out like they were candy. But I saw him. I saw the man under the mask. The one he hid from everyone else. The real him.

"These are *nice*." Carven yanked a set on and pressed a button.

Harper and Guild were both consumed by their brand new toys, so much they didn't even see London as he turned and strode from the room. But I couldn't look away. I followed him to the kitchen. But he wasn't interested in anything to eat or drink.

No, he stood at the sink and stared out the window.

"I'd hoped to save you from this," he said.

I moved behind him, sliding my hand down his powerful forearm as he gripped the edge of the sink. "You can't," I answered, and that knowing feeling unfurled inside me. "No one could. This was inevitable."

He turned, looking down at me. "It didn't have to be."

I lifted my hand and caressed his cheek. "I think it did. I'm going to go in there with a Son by my side and we're going to tear the place apart. That sounds like justice to me."

He scowled, then gave a soft smile. One that didn't last long before his brow suddenly creased as he reached up with both hands to cup my face. "Come back to me. Do you hear me? Come back or there's no telling what I'll do to get you back."

He means death, right? *His. Own. Death.* Would the cold, detached, savage London St. James do the unthinkable to come for me? I searched his gaze as the answer rose. Unthinkable for me...but not for him. I was sure he'd thought about it more than once.

Agony ripped through my chest, tearing me open as that realization hit me. "I'll come back," I promised. "Whatever it takes, I'll come back."

"Good," he murmured, lowering his hand as he pulled me close.

I closed my eyes as my arms slid around him and inhaled his seductive scent one last time. It was not anywhere near long enough when the heady thud of footsteps headed our way. Anger burned inside me as Guild cleared his throat, shattering the moment with two simple words. "It's time."

London released his hold, turning his attention to the intrusion. "Looks like it's time to shine."

"And be shot at," I muttered.

"Not before you shoot at them," London added. "Carven told me you held your own yesterday."

"Held. My. Own." I stepped away, shaking my head. "Only you would put it like that, London."

I was pure rage. Brutal and deadly...and just like one of his sons.

London strode for the door, leaving Guild and me to follow.

I tried not to think about the haze of rage. But the moment I stepped out into the hallway and found the others waiting for me, that same bloodthirsty need lifted its ugly head and this time, the beast inside me smiled.

Without a word, I followed them out the rear of the house and climbed in to the mysterious black Hummer that took up most of the driveway. Doors closed with a series of thuds. Still, no one spoke as the deep snarl of the engine filled the space and we backed out of the driveway.

It wasn't until minutes later when everything outside seemed to blur that Carven touched my hand and drew my focus.

"You okay?"

I met his stare. "Yeah."

"We're going in quiet, okay? I'm going to be right there with you. I won't let them touch you."

My breath caught as I envisioned the hell we were about to walk into. "I know."

"Just stay with me, Wildcat. No running away this time. Promise me."

There was a tremble in his voice. A kind I had not heard before. I met his stare before he flinched and looked away. A seed of fear sprouted deep inside me. Carven was worried. No, he was more than worried. His hand clenched around the gun. *He was scared.*

My pulse stuttered at the knowledge. If he was scared, then I should be terrified. "We're going to survive this," I whispered. "We're going to find Colt and get him free."

But Carven didn't turn to me.

He just slowly nodded his head as he stared out the window.

I sat there and watched the streets pass as we slowly made our way out of the city and back to hell. I'd escaped this place once before. I'd escaped, and I'd survived. I shifted my gaze to the black Explorer London drove in front of us. London had been the one to risk it all and rescue me once before.

Now it was our turn to do the same...*if Colt was still alive.*

NINE

Carven

I sat at the base of a towering pine, watching the others in the dark, and suppressed a shiver. It was cold...*damn cold*. My breath blew white in front of my face. I was sure it was about to snow. *That's all we needed.*

The faint green glow of Harper's live satellite footage was the only light source the five of us had while we waited in the forest two miles from the compound which held The Order.

London had left my black Explorer at the base of the dirt road on the other side of the clump of trees. He wanted more than one vehicle to get out of here...if things went bad, that was.

Which was a little more than probable.

It was a fucking certainty.

I didn't care either way, as long as I got Colt and Vivienne out of there...

Right now, that was all I focused on.

Vivienne sat inside the open rear door of the Hummer. I barely made out her darkened silhouette as we waited for the go-ahead. The aching knot in my chest flared, making my breaths tight and shallow. I knew what that was now. What this panicked, out of control fucking feeling was that hit me harder than a damn shovel. It was fear...it was love...*it was everything.*

My brother.

I closed my eyes as agony swept me away.

I have to get him out.

I opened my eyes, watching Vivienne as she moved. No, *we* had to.

There was no stopping this for me. No turning away, even if the plan went to hell. She knew that. I'd seen that same self-destruction in her eyes last night. That same...limitless rage. It was a rage that'd help us now. It was a rage that'd bring Colt home.

"There's the patrol," Harper murmured, drawing my focus. "It's a...little light."

Twigs cracked as shadows moved. I hadn't even seen London standing that close to me before he moved. "Is that a problem?"

"For us?" Harper answered, the green glow catching the side of his face as he looked up. "No...it's just...*unusual.*"

Silence closed in as I pushed up from the cold ground to stand. No one liked *unusual* when they were about to storm a building full of highly trained mercenaries that doubled as patrol guards.

No.

We needed predictable.

We needed familiar.

"It doesn't matter." I lifted my knife, turning the blade to catch the faint glow of moonlight. "We're going in, either way."

Thud.

The sound of boots hitting the ground followed. "Yes," Vivienne whispered. "We are."

I found her stare in the dark as she moved closer and stepped into that faint green glow. Her stare was only for me. She didn't need convincing.

"You ready?" I asked.

One slow nod as she adjusted her grip on the gun London had given her. "Yes."

Twigs snapped once more. London neared, gripping me by the shoulders, just like he used to when we were just kids. "Be safe in there, the both of you. But if...if there's even a chance you can't get out without either of you being captured, or if there's... if there's no point in rescuing him, then I want you to haul ass out of there. Do you hear me?"

I heard him...loud and clear.

He meant if Colt was already dead. That's what he meant.

"Just come back," he finished, giving me a gentle squeeze before releasing his hold and stepping away.

"We'll be back before you know it." My voice was lifeless, but the words were more for Vivienne than anyone else.

She barely seemed to hear me anyway, shifting her focus to London as he stepped close. "I'll be right here," he murmured. "Right fucking here."

They melded together in the dark. I turned away, unable to watch them kiss. My desperation boomed in my fucking head. But I didn't need to look elsewhere for long before she broke away.

"We'll bring him back," she whispered, her teeth chattering. "One way or another."

She turned then and started walking, never once looking back. A wave of love slammed into me as I watched her. I'd never felt this way before. Never felt so...indebted to someone other than London in my entire life.

I'd never needed anyone.

Not like this.

But I needed her now as I followed her through the trees. I needed her more than I needed to breathe. I turned to her as we cut through the trees toward the fence line. That ache of love filled me, making me feel violent and desperate all at the same time.

I shifted my focus to the terrain in front of us, stepping ahead to lead the way. The last thing I wanted was her falling into a damn ditch and twisting her ankle.

She followed, the quiet thud of her steps haunting mine as we eased closer.

The Patrol is a little...light.

Harper's words filled me now as I turned my attention to the compound. It felt like minutes before the glint of steel came through the tree line up ahead. I slowed, almost stopping, and reached behind me to grab her arm.

Instinctively, she knew, her gaze following my nod to the shine of razor wire. I met her dark eyes, finding her careful nod.

The plan was simple; we get in and get my brother out without being seen...

But if that plan put me anywhere near anyone of those motherfuckers, you can bet his fucking life I'd take the bastard out. I gripped my knife and lowered my other hand to the wire cutters in my pocket, then pulled them free as I stepped close to the wires.

Snip.

Snip.

Snip.

I worked fast, cutting an area large enough for us to get past, and yanked the strands upwards. Vivienne moved, dropping to her knees before she scurried through.

That's it, Wildcat.

I followed her inside the compound.

"You're clear," Harper's murmur was in my ear. "Switch to night vision."

I reached up and tugged down the expensive goggles London had brought back with him. Vivienne's eyes shone neon in the dark. But she didn't want the goggles. Instead, she followed me as I moved low and headed toward the hulking building in the distance.

I pocketed the cutters, then sheathed my knife before I lifting the sniper's rifle equipped with the silencer. At this distance and in this light, I'd see them well before they even knew I was there. And they'd be dead in an instant. Just like they were yesterday.

Tobias Banks and his damn brothers might've taken Amo and several leaders of Death Valley Motor Cycle chapters, but they hadn't taken out all of them, leaving just enough of the assholes behind to gather two more chapters.

They were bad news.

And they handled a lot of Hale's dirty work.

The kind of work that would tarnish his image. If only they knew the vile fucker like we did. I pushed into a run, leaving Vivienne behind to catch up.

"Two coming up on your three o'clock," Harper's voice was in my ear.

The low sound of a vehicle came a second later. Vivienne slammed against me as we hit the corner of the building. I grabbed her, held my hand across her mouth, and turned my head as the patrol came to a stop around the corner.

"Wait here," I whispered.

"Carven—" she hissed, but I was already lifting the muzzle of the gun as I stepped around her.

I took aim as the first asshole stepped out, leaving just enough time for his buddy to follow and give me a clear line of sight for both of them before I fired.

Pfft!

Pfft!

Both hit the ground as I stepped out, taking aim and searching for movement. But there was none...

I glanced over my shoulder at Vivienne, then toward the building. *This is too easy...*I shoved the whisper aside and hurried back to her, leading the way further along to the set of automatic doors we had an access card for.

In and out, remember? It was supposed to be that easy. It was supposed to be that silent. Still, that unseen fist around my gut clenched tight. Something felt wrong.

I pressed the access card against the sensor and waited for the light to turn green before pushing through and held it open. Vivienne was inside, frantically searching the dark as I secured the door.

"You point and I'll clear the way," I murmured, stepping around her.

She jerked her head back to me, then slowly lifted her hand. "I think this way."

I gave a nod. Not that she'd see. But she followed as I moved through the room, stopping at the door long enough to ease it open and step out into the hall.

Instinct rose to the surface, taking me back to the default setting of a killer. It was where I felt most at home. I eased my rifle across my body and grabbed my knife. Vivienne pointed, and I advanced, rolling my steps as we moved.

The Daughters' rooms were east of here, that I knew. The place was almost like a hexagon, each wing branching off. Memories slammed into me. Unwelcome memories of crowded rooms filled with children's screams and the cruel guards whose brutal blows broke us.

Sons.

Daughters.

One bred to kill.

The other bred to be fucked.

But both would break, it was inevitable. Unless they had someone like London. I clenched my grip tighter as Vivienne pointed through the doors, then jerked her thumb right.

I gave a nod, moved to the side, and pressed the card against the sensor. Red flared, turning green before the lock gave a *click*. I pushed through, holding it open, then eased it closed.

"Status?" Harper murmured.

I reached up and pressed a button on my headset. One that told him we were still alive.

"Copy," he said before falling silent.

I sucked in a hard breath as Vivienne stopped walking. I jerked my gaze to her. Her wide, unflinching eyes were fixed straight ahead. She was shaking...I could see it clearly. I moved closer, brushed my finger along her jaw, then turned her gaze to mine.

She could barely make out my face, but she gave a nod. She was okay...for now.

I pushed on, moving further ahead, and turned right. Still there were no guards. Not patrolling the hallways, not anywhere I could tell. The icy breath of fate breathed down my neck, making me do something I didn't really want to. I pressed the comm button on my headset and spoke carefully. "Status?"

Harper's response was instant. "No more patrols, you're all good."

I scowled, then glanced behind us to the glass windows in the double doors we'd just passed through. *You're all good*...but were we? That nagging feeling wouldn't leave me alone. The place was silent. *Too fucking silent.*

It felt...*empty.*

"Carven?" Vivienne whispered, drawing my focus.

"Stay behind me," I whispered, moving in front of her.

If we were to come under attack, I'd make sure I took the first hit. I reached out and gave her the access card. "You hear shots, you run. Got me?"

She just nodded and took the card.

For that, I was thankful.

I grabbed my Sig, held the knife in one hand and the gun in the other, and I moved forward.

The Daughter is coming with me...

The dead Son's voice rose right at the perfect time, right when I was fucking jumpy enough. I pushed it aside, sucked in a hard breath, and kept moving, heading along the hallway as Vivienne pointed ahead. We reached halfway along before she held up her hand. *Stop.*

I turned as she pointed to a door that looked like the entrance to a closet. But it wasn't a closet, was it? The night vision picked up the words *Room 0.01. Be aware of steps.* It was some kind of...*service way?* One that hadn't been on the goddamn map. I met Vivienne's terrified stare. She was still shaking, maybe harder than she'd ever been.

This was definitely it.

My lips curled into a sneer as I lifted my rifle. Three steps and I reached out and grasped the handle. My body trembled and my muscles tightened, ready to fight to get my brother out. I glanced back at her and gave her a gentle jerk of my head. She obeyed and stepped out of harm's way as I turned back to that closed door.

He's in there...he's in there, and he's waiting for us.

I turned the handle slowly, then yanked hard, aiming the muzzle of the gun into the darkened space.

But there was no team of guards waiting to open fire, no roars of the dead men I was ready to put to rest. There was just...*nothing*.

I scowled, then glanced at the darkened smear along the doorframe in the night vision goggles...a smear that looked a lot like...*blood*.

"Behind me, Wildcat," I growled, not giving a shit if anyone heard me now.

I wanted them to...

I wanted them all to.

That lethal desire drove me into the solid darkness as I scanned the floor, seeing the section at the back fall away. There were stairs, narrow stairs.

"Status?" Harper called in my ear.

But I couldn't answer.

My instincts were screaming as I pushed forward to where the floor fell away into what looked like the pit of hell. I sensed Vivienne behind me, but I couldn't turn around. My gut clenched and my breath left me as I stopped at the top of the stairs.

The night vision picked up the stairs, as I sank down onto the first, then the second. The moment I saw movement, I'd open fire. But there wasn't movement. Just an eeriness that stood the hairs on the back of my neck. Halfway down the narrow passage, the sickening stench hit me. Foul, rotting...*metallic. Blood. And a lot of it.*

My throat clenched. My knees trembled as I hit the bottom stair. I scanned the dark...but my mind couldn't work it out. Not the vague outline. Not the mess along the wall.

"Carven?" she whispered. "I can't."

The moment it hit me, I knew it was far too late.

I saw blood...

So much fucking blood...

And a hand...lying close to my feet.

"*NO!*" I roared, spinning around as the *click* of the overheard light came.

I was already yanking the goggles upwards from my eyes as I lunged for her.

Her eyes widened, fixed on me as I barrelled toward her. Every cell in my body was howling. *GET HER OUT OF HERE... GET HER THE FUCK OUT!*

But her focus shifted behind me as I hit her midway down the stairs, grabbed her around the waist, and lifted before charging upwards.

"Carven, status," Harper asked again, this time insistent.

PLEASE NO! NOOO!

FUCK!

"No!" Vivienne stiffened in my arms. "*Carven NO! That's blood...THAT'S BLOOD!*"

"*Carven, for fuck's sake!*" Harper barked.

But I didn't care about them.

All I cared about was getting her out.

And getting her far away...*from this.*

TEN

Vivienne

"NO!" I KICKED AND SCREAMED, BUCKING IN HIS arms. *"NO!"*

But Carven wouldn't let me go, dragging me back up the stairs, one at a time. Still I saw blood. It dripped from the ceiling and smeared along the walls.

That was Colt's blood...

That was COLT'S BLOOD!

"Let me go, Carven!" I slammed my hands against his shoulders until I broke his hold. My head impacted the wall with a *crack* as I fell. White sparks of agony detonated, but still I pushed upwards, then lunged, slamming into Carven's hard chest.

"You're NOT looking. DO. YOU UNDERSTAND?" he roared, bending to grab me around my thighs, then heaved me up over his shoulder.

We were out of those stairs before I knew it, charging back into that tiny room that still haunted my dreams. *"He's dead. HE'S FUCKING DEAD!"*

Carven stilled, sucking in hard breaths until a wounded sound tore free and he yanked me against his chest. "It's not him, Wildcat. You hear me? It's not him."

I froze, unable to process what he was saying. All I could do was stand there as he crushed me against his chest. *It's not him...it's not him.* But there was blood. So much blood. It was all I could see as I whispered. "It's not?"

"No..." he whispered. "No, baby, it's not."

My body trembled as the faint voice came through his headset. "Carven, answer me, or we're coming in."

He pressed a button on his headset. "We're here. But you need to get here...*now*."

I looked past him to the darkened stairs. The horror in that room pulled me toward it. Like I was no more than a puppet on a string. One wrapped around my neck, determined to drag me back into the past.

Back where they took me and the other Daughters down there for another reason.

Fucking beg me to stop, bitch.

I flinched with the memory.

My shoulders curled as phantom pain tore across my nipples.

The cruel pinch of their fingers was so close to the surface of my mind. It was this place. This fucking place.

Go on, show us what you learned with The Teacher. Open your goddamn mouth.

The foul tang rose in the back of my throat, just like it had then when they'd forced me to my knees in that cold, dark dungeon.

"We're going to do a sweep," Carven spoke into his headset. "We'll meet you at the entrance."

He stepped closer, grasped my chin, and forced my gaze away from the entrance of that room to him. "We need to check the rest of the building. You with me, baby?"

I dragged myself away from that hell and gave a nod.

"Got your gun?"

I nodded again.

"Good. Let go."

I didn't think I'd be able to move, but Carven sheathed his knife, then grabbed my hand and pulled me with him. I looked over my shoulder as we left. "Who," I whispered. "Who is it?"

He just shook his head and adjusted his goggles, turning his attention to the hallways. He released my hand and headed back to the double doors. Red lights flared green before we pushed through. We moved faster this time, sweeping through one section as we moved to where the rooms were.

Not rooms.

Cells.

Because this was a prison.

My hand trembled, but I still gripped the gun, aiming it at the doors when Carven pressed the card against the scanner and the locks opened again. My heart was booming, filling my head as I waited for the onslaught of guards that'd come any moment now...

Any damn moment.

But as we passed through one set of doors to the wing where the bedrooms were, I felt it. The *hollowness*. "Carven," I whispered. "Something's wrong here. Something's really...*really wrong*."

The first door to the bedrooms was open up ahead. I shifted my focus to the next, then the next, and I saw the same...*they were all open*.

"We're here," Harper's faint voice came through the headset as Carven stopped at the open door to the first bedroom.

Carven scowled and glanced ahead to the rest of the rooms. He wanted to keep searching, to find out why the fuck there were no guards and no Daughters, but he muttered instead. "Come on, Wildcat. Stay with me here."

We headed back to the side entrance and opened the door for Harper and Guild, and finally London to step inside. I caught a shake of Carven's head as he glanced at the others. But whatever silent conversation they had, it didn't involve me.

"The bedrooms are open," Carven said finally. "There's no one here as far as we can tell."

"We need to do a complete sweep." Harper glanced at the hallway. "Guild and I will take north and west. London, you have south. You keep pushing along the east wing, checking the rest of the bedrooms. Signal if you make contact."

Carven nodded and glanced my way. "You ready, Wildcat?"

Claimed

Anger burned inside me. The moment he moved, I lashed out and grabbed his arm. *"Hey!"*

He shifted his gaze to me.

And in an instant, that fire in me died, buried under the weight of the horror of this place. "Don't shut me out," I hissed. "I need to know what's going on. Who the fuck is down there?"

Even in the darkness, I caught his flinch. The others left us behind as they spread out. London was the last to leave, glancing at Carven, then me over his shoulder.

"You trust me, right?" The son slid his arm around me and pulled me close. "You trust I'd kill for you. That I'd protect you any way I could."

The image of him and Colt rushing into that room in Macoy Daniels' house filled me. "Yes."

"Then I need you to trust me now, Wildcat. I need you to understand that this is me protecting you. Can you do that right now? Can you put your faith in me?"

He pushed the night vision goggles from his head. Those blue eyes looked black in the darkness. "Baby?"

"Yes," I answered. "Yes, I can trust you."

He gave a nod. "Good. That's good. I promise, when this is all over, I'll tell you everything you want to know. Everything, baby. But right now." He glanced at the doorway. "Right now, we need to move."

"Fine," I answered.

I was starting to understand Carven now. All the looks that I'd taken to be cold anger were instead...fear. He showed me that now as he moved away, lifted his gun, and stepped through the doorway.

Trust me...

Those words resounded as I lifted my own gun and followed him. That tight knot in the middle of my chest throbbed. I sank into the ache as we made our way back to the rooms once more. It wasn't Colt in that room.

It wasn't Colt...

Then who the hell was it?

Carven swept the barrel of his rifle along the hallway, checking the first lot of cells we'd left only minutes before, and then moved further along the hall. But every room was the same. Empty. Abandoned.

The heavy thud of his boots echoed along the hall as I stepped into the room that'd once been mine. My cell. My *hell*. At first, my feet refused to move, until I forced them to move from the doorway and head for the bed.

Nights.

Weeks.

Months...

Years.

That's how long this place had been my prison. I suppressed a shiver as I glanced from the messy sheets that'd been ripped from the bed in a hurry to the open top drawers in the dresser. It was those open draws which drew me deeper into my one private torture.

Step by step. I stared into the darkened edges of that void until I stood over it, staring at the messed up white lace panties that'd once been there. *They'd left in a hurry.* That was easy to see. I looked over my shoulder, mapping out the frantic movements.

She'd been dragged from the bed, no doubt by the guards as they stormed the room. Did they scream at her to grab her clothes? Or did they wrench open the drawers, or did...*no, she did. In her last frantic moment, she'd grabbed the only thing she had, even if it was a symbol of power over her existence...she'd tried to, at least.* I looked down, seeing all of her things there. White filled the space.

"It's all clear," Carven's voice in the doorway made me flinch. In the murky light, he watched me standing there.

"Did they take anything? From their rooms, that is. Did they take their belongings?"

A look passed over his face. Sadness. Anger. He gave a gentle shake of his head.

No?

"We need to meet up with the others."

He meant they wanted to go back to that dungeon under the ground. For a second I didn't want to move. The entire room...*no, the entire world shifted.* Like I stood in the middle of some terrifying kaleidoscope, one twist of the wrist and my world would change. I fixed on Carven, knowing it wasn't a twist of a wrist I needed to worry about.

Whatever was down those stairs terrified him.

Enough to haul me over his shoulder and drag me kicking and screaming out of there.

Part of me didn't want to know.

The naive part.

That part who wanted to believe this was all just one sick, crazy dream. But here was the thing about dreams...they soon turn into nightmares. Fuck if I wasn't going to be prepared for whatever came my way, nightmare or not. I stepped toward him. "Then let's go."

He stepped away, leading me back to that dungeon. By the time we pushed through the last set of double doors, I felt them standing outside that room, filling up the hallways with their energy and their strength. But there was only one of them standing there. "Anything?" Harper asked as we neared.

"No." Carven glanced at the stairs. "The rooms are...empty."

Empty.

Not, the Daughters are gone. Not, everyone has disappeared. Just...the rooms are empty.

Movement came in the dark as London stumbled out from the stairway and kept going until he slammed his hand against the hallway wall, bracing himself.

"London?" I stepped close.

But he stopped me with a shake of his head. "No...not yet."

"Not yet?" I jerked my head to where the silence waited.

Guild...Guild wasn't here. He was down there...in the dark. In all that blood. I shoved forward.

"Vivienne! WAIT!" Carven roared.

But it was too late.

I didn't slow, not when I hit the first stair and my knees nearly buckled with the impact. I grasped the banister and held on as I hit halfway and all but fell the rest of the way until the bottom.

That's when I saw him.

Guild, with his back to me, staring into the darkened room.

All I smelled was blood.

But I *knew* there was more.

I reached up, knowing there was a cord for the light switch...

My fingers grasped *something*.

Click.

The dull yellow light seemed to *ooze* into the darkness, eating at the edges of the emptiness...spilling around the mess.

Then I saw it, even as thunder came on the bottom of the stairs...and Guild jerked his goggles from his head then spun. There was blood...so much blood. It arced across the wall, slipping out of the bullet holes that peppered the wall and pooled on the floor, around the bodies.

All the...all the...all the...*Daughters*.

They'd fallen in piles. Arms and legs wrapped around each other. Some missing half their heads, others half their faces. Some...some facedown on the edges of the piles as they'd tried to run.

That same tilt came back to me now.

Sweeping my feet out from under me.

Strong hands grabbed me.

"I got you, sweetheart," Guild murmured in my ear, until more hands grabbed me. "I got you. You shouldn't be here. You shouldn't see...*this*."

But it was all too late. I *had* seen...*I had seen*.

"They killed them." I lifted my head, and through the blur, I saw their faces. "They killed all of them?"

Carven looked away.

So did Guild and Harper.

Only London didn't turn away from me. Those dark, merciless eyes were deeper and blacker than they'd ever been before.

"*Why?*" The word was a wounded moan.

London shook his head.

"WHY! WHY KILL THEM? THEY DID NOTHING, LONDON! THEY. DID. NOTHING!"

"Because this is what they do," London answered. "This is who they are."

Torturers.

Murderers...

Beasts.

"He's not here," Carven croaked. "My brother isn't here."

Then where was he?

ELEVEN

Colt

"Again." The command came from somewhere in front of me.

Synapses fired as my brain sent its commands; tense my stomach, clench my grip.

But did I move?

Did I do anything but hang suspended like a slab of meat trussed on a hook, watching my blood slowly fall to the floor in front of me?

Drip.

Drip.

Drip.

I didn't feel the warmth slipping away, nor did I taste the metallic tang I knew had to be there. I felt nothing. Not the killing ache in my shoulders from muscles strained far beyond their limits or their savage blows...not anymore.

I was numb.

Lost.

Not lost, a husky voice whispered from deep in the void. *I'm right here.*

And a shiver broke free.

I was scared of that voice in the darkness, that *lure of insanity.* Maybe even more than I was scared of *them.*

"Your fists don't seem to be effective," Hale's voice tore me away from the beast waiting for me in the deep recesses of my mind. "This time we go...*electric.*"

I jerked my head upwards and squinted into the dark. Shadows moved as my pulse kicked in my chest. Sparks of neon white flared from the thing in his hand, illuminating the big bastard in front of me.

It wasn't steel knuckles this time, or the baseball bat they'd used before.

This was worse...

I shook my head as panic howled inside, and I bucked, making me jerk in the chains that hung me from the ceiling.

My tormentor swung his hand and upended a bucket of icy water all over me. But I couldn't fight. I couldn't even move, not even when the empty bucket hit the floor and that sonofabitch stepped closer and drove the prongs into my side.

Agony ripped across my stomach, driving through muscle and bone into the very center of me. My body took over and threw my head backwards, my body tensing until the links on the chains gnashed loudly.

It came.

The blinding white.

A white so bright I saw nothing else.

Not the darkened cell they'd kept me in.

Not their faces.

Their cruel fucking faces.

LET ME TAKE IT FOR YOU! the beast howled.

My jaw was so tight my teeth cracked.

Brown eyes. Brown eyes. *Hold on. Please, hold onto her.*

Browneyesbrowneyesbrowneyes...

I couldn't let go of her.

YOU'RE GOING TO DIE! The beast slammed against its cell. *DO YOU HEAR ME? YOU. WILL. DIE HERE!*

I held on to the memory of her tighter than I held onto the chains.

The warmth of her fingers.

The throaty sound of her laugh.

Colt, she whispered in my mind. *I love you.*

"WHAT IS HE PLANNING?" Hale's roar followed.

Let me take it, the beast demanded. *I can do this. I did it before when you needed me. I can do it now.*

But that was when I was a kid, when I didn't know better. Now I did. I'd lost myself when he came. Time. My memories. Those brown eyes filled my mind. I closed my eyes, remembering the scent of soap on her skin.

If I let him take over, I'd lose again...only this time I'd lose her. My...*Wildcat*.

Agony stabbed deep, finding a nerve somewhere inside that made my legs dance and my spine bow backwards.

LET ME TAKE IT FOR YOU! The beast slammed against the confines of its cell.

I shook my head.

Drip.

Drip.

Drip.

The falling blood blurred.

"I *know you can talk!*" Hale bellowed. "I *don't care that everyone calls you a dumb mute bastard, you'll tell me what I want to know.* WHY DID YOU KILL OPHELIA!"

Drip.

Drip.

Drip.

"*AGAIN!*" Hale roared.

The pain came once more, driving deeper. My right leg trembled violently, until I couldn't hold on. With the mention of her name, it all came rushing back to me. The phone call to London...the panic in my voice.

London...I...I killed her.

NO! I jerked as Ophelia's scream shattered the moment. *You were mine when you were conceived, she screamed. Mine to torment. Mine to destroy.*

CRACK! Something broke inside of me.

Something...crawled free.

"That's enough. He's out."

He's out.

He's...out.

"Not yours."

"What?" That far away voice called. "What did you say?"

I forced my eyes to open. Through the cracks and the sting of the sweat, I saw them. "I'm not yours. I never was. I am... *Wildcat's.*"

"What the fuck is he saying?"

Hale's voice came clearly now. "Untie him. Leave him here. We'll try again later. I want to know what that bastard is planning. I need to be one step ahead. If it's a war London wants, then it's a war he'll get...*my way*. First, we need the bitch. We take her and they'll come. We take her and they're all dead...every single one of them."

I forced myself to hold on.

To push that emptiness away for just a little while longer. I lifted my head, but my bones were heavy as lead. Still, I found him in the gloom. I found his face. I found his eyes. "You touch her...and I'll kill you."

He took a step closer, lifting his gaze until he stared up at me. I jerked my body, trying to free my hands. But my feet swung free. There was no ground for me to grasp onto. Not up here. There was just *pain*.

Hale's lips curled at the edges as he looked down, past my bare chest, my body bruised and bleeding from their fists and their boots, then up again to meet my stare. "Son...you're already dead."

He gave a hard chuff, then turned around and left.

Already dead.

I don't think so...

But it wasn't my voice that came back to me.

It was *his*.

The *beast*.

I tried to push him back into his cell, tried to tether him to the past. But I couldn't...not anymore. My chest trembled as a dark, demented chuckle tore out of me. Metallic and hollow, tasting like blood and murder. That sound grew and grew and grew, until it bounced off the walls of this prison. Laughter reverberated through my body, turning into a roar.

It had no place in this horror.

Yet, here it was.

Here I am, the beast whispered. *Finally.*

Hale stopped cold in the middle of the darkened room, then turned around. There was a spark of fear in those beady fucking eyes, stilling that unhinged sound that had somehow come from me.

"*I KILLED HER!*" I screamed. "*I KILLED THAT FUCKING BITCH!*"

He jerked as though I'd slapped him and those cold eyes grew colder, pinching at the edges until they creased.

"*I caved her head in.*" I sucked in cold air. "Until there was nothing left but a mess. But that's *nothing* compared to what London will do to you." I looked at my tormentor, in front of me with that thing in his hand. "That's nothing compared to what he'll do to all of you. Even if you kill me...even if he *never* finds my body, he'll kill you all. He'll kill and kill and kill. He'll be the shadow you'll never see coming. He'll become wrath."

Hale swallowed hard with those words.

And I smiled.

It wouldn't matter how many men Hale surrounded himself with.

They still wouldn't stand a chance.

Blood dripped down my face from the fresh gash on my head, the warmth raced along my cheek and over my lips as I smiled. "He'll be seeing you, motherfucker. Real fucking soon."

TWELVE

London

"Aren't you coming?"

I stared straight ahead, gripping the steering wheel of Carven's Explorer, trying to keep the rage out of my voice. "No, pet. You go on inside with Carven."

He'd slammed the door behind him and stormed toward the back door of the house. If I stayed, it'd be bad. If I left, it'd be bad. Either way, this went down, it wouldn't be good, not after what we'd just witnessed. It was better if I left them. It was better if he...

Go to the Son, Vivienne.

The words were on the tip of my tongue as I turned and met her gaze. Wide, unblinking eyes stared back at me. Flashes followed, like flickers of a camera. Hands reaching for me. Blood...so much blood. I pulled away from the memory and from her, shifting my focus to the street. "There are things I need to tend to."

"Tonight?"

There was need in her tone.

Need to be around me.

Need for me to be strong.

But I didn't just want to be strong. I wanted to be *lethal*. "He needs you, Vivienne," I said, hating how cold I sounded.

She straightened as she stood outside the car. "Sure," she muttered before shoving the door closed and striding away.

You. Idiot.

I winced at the words. Still, they didn't stop me shoving the car into gear and slamming down on the accelerator. They didn't stop me from pulling up my phone to an address on the screen. The address of the pain in the ass that'd refused to give me what I wanted before...*now, he would.*

I drove through the city, my mind numb, frozen on the horror we'd just seen.

All of those Daughters...

All of those...

I jerked my mind away, glanced at the address on my phone, and turned down a street that just looked sad. Potholes eroded the pavement. Clapped out, rusted cars parked nose to nose along the street. Townhouses that were either boarded-up or had bars on the windows. I glanced at the street numbers and pulled the four-wheel drive over to the side of the road. Headlights flared further behind me. I lifted my gaze to the rear-view mirror and watched a car creep past the turnoff and keep going.

The two-story townhouses were in darkness. I glanced at the clock, finding it close to midnight. Hours it'd been...just hours since we'd stumbled from The Order carrying nothing more than the weight of all those deaths on our shoulders.

My shoulders, you mean?

Because no matter how you looked at it. This was *all* my fault.

If I hadn't killed Macoy. If I'd taken out Hale first...

If I'd...

If I'd...

If I wasn't so fucking obsessed with her.

I might've been able to keep my fucking head when they took her. But I hadn't...I'd easily stepped back into my own selfish need.

I needed to fix this. I clenched my jaw as that nerve pulsed at the corner of my eye. I needed to end this. But first...first, I had to find my son.

I killed the engine and watched as faint flecks of snow fell from the sky. *Jesus*...as if this night couldn't get fucking worse. I climbed out and closed the door gently behind me. The December wind howled, tearing right through my black cargo turtlenecked sweater and military vest I wore. I started walking, scanning the houses before I slipped down the side of one and watched for dogs.

That was the last thing I needed.

My boots were silent as I grabbed the top of the gate and vaulted over, hitting the ground with a *thud*. Barking started three houses over. I glanced toward the sound and kept on moving, making my way to the rear fence, then grabbed the top with both hands and heaved upwards.

Thud.

I hit the ground and scanned the rest of the houses. The wind howled, snatching away any sound I made. That's just how I wanted it as I moved, climbed the rear stairs, then pulled the multitool from my pocket and found the pick. Cheap locks made little work. One hard *thump* in the right place and the door popped open like a jar.

I was inside in an instant.

One glance over my shoulder and I caught the flare of headlights in the street behind me where I was parked...and that same sedan slowly rolled past. I scowled as I closed the door behind me. Someone was following me. Someone I needed to take care of.

Just not right now.

I turned around, glanced at the darkened room, and made for the closed door of the single bedroom in the place. One careful turn and I was inside, looking down at the sprawled-out asshole.

The fake Rolex sat on the dresser beside him. I was sure it was his prized possession. It made him feel important. Made him feel...*powerful*.

I stepped closer, then reached into my pocket and pulled a black zip tie free. It didn't take long. One gentle shift of his foot and I wrapped the plastic around and fed the end through.

Ripp...

He barely moved as it tightened.

"You have a nice house, Walter," I murmured, feeding the end through the other tie and stepped closer, looking down at the man in the middle of the double bed. "It would be a shame to make a mess of you in it."

His eyes snapped open as I pounced, grabbed one hand, and shoved, rolling him over to grab the other. He was bound before he knew it.

His hands behind his back.

His ankles wedged against each other.

I'd snapped them tight before he even knew that was happening. Before he could start to cry, that was. But he was crying now, his tears shimmering in the moon's glow that spilled through the bars on the window.

He didn't have a nice house at all. It was a shitty one-bedroom hovel, to be exact, on the upper east side of the seedy part of the city. It was in a shithole. One this asshole deserved.

"*No!*" Walter cried out and slammed his eyes closed. "*Take whatever you want! Just don't...kill me.*"

"Take whatever I want," I repeated slowly, breathing in the cool rush of faintly musty air. "What I want is what I wanted before...when you rudely interrupted me. I want information on Riven Cruz, and I want it now."

Walter's breath stilled as he opened his eyes. Confusion made him squint as he peered at me, then in an instant he understood. "You?" He hissed.

I didn't answer, just lifted the silenced gun. "So, this is what's going to happen," I breathed. "First, I'm going to release you, then you're going to log into the building records and give me every forwarding address you have on Mr. Cruz. You will not scream for help. You will not cause a scene...because if you do..." I lifted the gun as the memory of that room assaulted me. Wide, unblinking eyes stared up at me from the piles of bodies against the wall. A wall where their killers had lined them up and massacred them. Rage rippled through me. The hunger so raw I could taste it. "If you do, that will piss me off...and right now you don't want to do that." I fixed my gaze on Walter. "Do I make myself clear?"

He nodded furiously.

"Good. That's very good." I grabbed the tool and used the pliers to cut the ties.

He let out a moan, rubbing his wrists as I gave a jerk of my head, motioning to the living room. He followed, turning to keep me in his sights, before he scurried to the single sofa and plonked down.

"I could lose my job for giving you this."

"You could lose your life if you don't."

He jerked his gaze up as he opened the laptop. I stood over him, waiting for him to return his gaze to the screen. He did, logged into the database, and pulled up the files. One rip from the notebook beside him on the small desk and he scribbled furiously, writing not one address, but three.

"Here." He shoved the torn page at me. "I've done what you wanted."

I took the addresses, scanning what he'd written. "I don't need to tell you what will happen if you cause a problem over this?"

His cheeks burned. "No, you don't."

I have a nod, then turned away and strode for the door.

"You're going to kill him, aren't you?"

The question stopped me as I reached the door. Hale's fucking face burning in my mind. Riven was just a way for me to get to him. "Yes," I answered. "I'll kill them all."

I left him with the truth and walked out the way I'd come and headed down the stairs. Minutes. That's all it took for me to get back to the Explorer. By the time I did, I was sucking in hard, ice-cold breaths. They burned all the way down as I unlocked the four-wheel drive and climbed inside.

The heater on full blast didn't help a damn.

Still, I leaned close, warming my fingers in the heat and pulled up the first address on the list. It was a goddamn exclusive golf estate outside the city. That was out, so I turned my focus to the second on the list. Only the address didn't look right. I punched in the details on my phone and stared at the subway line that ran clear through the city.

"Sonofabitch," I swore, and looked outside the car.

Still, the address brought me back to the map of the railway. Riven wouldn't give a fake address, so there had to be something here. I put my faith in that, pulled into the street, and headed to the heart of the city.

The closer I came to the address printed on the torn piece of paper, the more I realized it wasn't *on* the subway line at all...it was *under* it.

I drove past the address, noting the dark sedans parked outside and pulled into a side street. A homeless man lifted his hand as I killed the engine, shielding his eyes. The alley was filled with homeless. They'd hung sheets of plastic, the only barrier as they huddled against the winter chill.

I pushed the door opened and climbed out. Death haunted me, my past, my present. But it was the future where it truly waited, lingering in the shadows, watching me. I walked back to the sedans, peering through the darkened windows before I turned to the building.

Thunder boomed as the midnight trains raced overhead. I winced, waiting for the roar to pass, and lifted my gaze to the apartment building directly under the tracks. Headlights blinded me instantly. Through the haze and the blur, I saw the hunched over figure behind the wheel of the same car I'd seen before.

It was a woman.

One who stared straight ahead as she drove past. I fought the urge to chase her and turned my focus to the building as I reached for my gun and worked the silencer free.

You don't get to think, DO I MAKE MYSELF CLEAR? Your job is to DO...you should've killed your fucking conscience when you had the chance, Riven, now get the fuck out!

Those words resounded, coming back to me clearly now. They were the same words I'd heard standing outside Hale's office at The Order.

Did The Principal have a goddamn conscience? I didn't think so...then again, that's what others thought of me. I stepped up to the door, glanced over my shoulder, then stared at the heavy lock. A lock that couldn't be picked, so I moved, stepped along the side of the building, and made my way to the rear, scanning the windows overhead.

The lights were on inside.

Riven was here?

He had to be. I searched the back door, but found the same unpickable lock. The only way in would be to break the door down, and that would take more strength than I possessed. I lifted my gaze to the balcony overhead, then to the six-foot fence.

But that...

That I could do.

I holstered my gun, then reached up and heaved myself upwards. Using muscles I hadn't used in a while, I lunged, slamming against the steel banister with a grunt. Rage drove me over the edge and I tugged on the door and found it open before I slipped inside to a bedroom.

I heard them instantly.

Low murmurs in...*what kind of language was that? Was that...Albanian?*

I scowled, then moved out into the hall. Cold. That's all I felt as I pulled my weapon free and made my way down to the first floor.

The sound of a shredder hummed and buzzed, fighting their panicked voices. They didn't lift their heads as I stepped around the entrance to the room. I counted three, but there could be more. They didn't even know I was there, until one of them jerked his head up and tensed. Heavy black tattoos reached all the way up a thick, muscled neck, an insignia was that was most definitely Mafia.

They looked like they were cleaning house.

"Going somewhere?" I growled, and lifted the gun.

One of them moved, easing his hand upwards. I swung the muzzle, barely taking aim. *Bang!* He dropped where he stood, missing half his head. The other two moved fast. One of them came for me, charging low, as the other reached for his gun.

With a guttural roar, the first bastard slammed into me, lifting me from my feet and throwing me backwards. But I was ready...and full of retribution. I swing my fist, connecting with the underside of his jaw. His head snapped back before he stumbled to the side.

"Where the *fuck is Riven!*" I roared, charging forward. *"TELL ME WHERE THE BASTARD IS!"*

A roar came from my right, deep and guttural, as another of them charged from what had to be the kitchen...with a goddamn carving knife in his hand.

Instinct took over. I wasn't the man anymore. I was the killer, the mercenary. The man I'd tried to leave behind. I lifted my gun and squeezed off a shot. But he was fast, only giving me enough time to hit him in the thigh. It didn't stop him. He lunged forward and lifted the knife high in the air...too high.

Jab.

Jab.

Jab.

I drove all my rage into short, fast punches, right at the edge of his ribs, and heard a *crunch*. It was all I needed as I grasped his wrist with the knife as we stumbled to the side. With a roar, I drove his hand over his head and hard against the wall.

Hate burned in his eyes.

Hate I knew.

Hate I breathed.

My fingers closed around the thick wooden hilt of the knife before I yanked it free. *"Do you know what they did in that place?"* I bellowed in his face.

He didn't know.

He didn't even care.

With a merciless snarl, I plunged the blade deep into his side and watched his eyes widen.

WHY! Vivienne's screams resounded in my head as he unleashed a cough, then crumpled to the floor. *THEY DID NOTHING, LONDON! THEY. DID. NOTHING!*

Movement came behind me, making me swivel around and lift my gun. There was blood on my hand, smeared all over my thumb and dripping to my wrist. I sucked in a hard breath and levelled the muzzle in the middle of the first asshole's forehead, then swung it over to his friend. "Now, I'm going to ask you once more...then I'm going to kill...and you won't be the only ones I visit."

They looked at each other, then back to me.

"Riven..." I glanced around the mess. "Where is he?"

"I don't know," one answered, his accent heavy. "He told us to clean, so we clean."

"You clean," I repeated, as hate and revulsion filled me. "Did he know?" I met each stare. "Did he know what they were planning?"

The question hung in the air.

"You know what? It doesn't even matter." I lifted the gun and took aim.

Bang.

Bang.

They both fell to the floor, just like the asshole at my feet. It didn't matter if Riven knew what Hale had been planning. His hands were still stained with their innocent blood. I stepped over the bodies as the shredding machine whirled and vibrated.

If I couldn't find Riven, then I'd find his brothers instead.

I'd hunt them down...

And kill them all.

Before this night was through.

I left that place, strode out the front door this time, and left it unlocked behind me. Blood cooled on my hands as I made my way to the four-wheel drive parked in the alley.

Colt would freeze out there.

The words hit me as I pressed the button and climbed into the car. No doubt they'd torture him and make him break. They'd do all they could, knowing every fucking blow they delivered would hurt me...

I yanked the door closed and gripped the wheel, staring through the windshield. "You motherfucker. You *goddamn motherfucker.*"

Hard breaths burned as I stabbed the button and started the engine, backing out into the street. I didn't bother to look for the woman intent on following me. I just punched the accelerator and spun the wheel.

"You want to fucking run from me?" I snarled. "You want to hide like a goddamn rat, you piece of shit? Then I'll make you come to me, asshole."

I headed deeper into the city and pulled up outside a small, plain office with wide glass windows and a small brass plaque that read *Kane Cruz Ph.D. Clinical Psychologist.*

Headlights bounced against the glass front of the office, blinding me.

Hurt my fucking family!

I gripped the wheel, aimed the car dead on, drove the accelerator all the way to the floor, and felt the Explorer respond as it mounted the curb and hit the glass window.

Crunch.

My head snapped forward with the impact. But the airbags remained intact, allowing me to lift my gaze to find the shattered front window. The glass was more than cracked...it was missing. I shoved open the door, leaving the engine running, and stepped out.

The smashed window led to an office. *His* office. The one I wanted. Only I had no information on Kane Riven. No one did. He was secretive...and dangerous. A psychologist by degree, he'd learned how to break a person's psyche...and rebuild them into the thing he wanted.

No.

The thing Hale wanted.

Jesus, the lessons he gave made the strongest male sick to his stomach. I stepped over the broken shards, went straight to his desk, and yanked out the top drawer. Papers fluttered to the floor. But amongst them was a black and white photograph. One bent and creased at the corners. I leaned over and picked it up, then lifted my gaze to the Explorer with the engine running outside the shattered window. I needed to find what I'd come for, and I needed to find it now.

Instead of staring at the photo, I shoved it into my pocket for later. Anything that worn was worth something. The rest of the papers were case files...but buried under them was an electric bill...one not in his name. I stared at the details.

"Margaret Roth?" I mumbled, staring at the address. One that wasn't familiar.

I glanced around the rest of the sparse office with its tan leather sofa and imagined the poor bastards who came to this sick fucking snake for help.

They'd leave more fucked up than they came in...

That was guaranteed.

I turned around and took a step before stilling and lifting my gaze to the red blinking light in the corner of the room. He was watching. *Good.*

"I'm coming for you," I mouthed, staring into the camera.

Then I turned away and stepped out of the ruined office before climbing back into the car and shoving the vehicle into reverse. I tried not to look at the blood on my hand as I drove, swiping it on my cargos instead.

I followed the GPS to the address on the bill. But the moment I turned into the area where it led me, anger burst out. *"FUCK!"*

It wasn't a goddamn subdivision. It was industrial, with towering fences and old, darkened warehouses. It was nothing...*NOTHING!* I punched the steering wheel as I turned down the dead-end street. The GPS marker flashed red as my headlights splashed against an old, faded sign: *Hazard – Keep Out.*

The towering old gate was padlocked. But the track was well worn, leading through the entrance to some kind of building at the back. Whatever this place was, it was well used...

Just not tonight.

I turned the car around and headed back. It wasn't enough. It wasn't anywhere near enough. Not enough blood on my hands, or enough answers. That gaping hole in my chest only ached deeper. I wanted my son back...I wanted Colt.

I pushed the four-wheel drive harder, then harder still, until all I heard was the roar of the engine and the thunder in my ears.

WHY! Vivienne's screams resounded in my head.

But it wasn't her face I saw...

It was Colt's at ten years old as I carried him out of that place. That fucking place...

Those fucking bastards.

I wrenched the wheel, skidding the vehicle sideways, and overcorrected. The lights spun as the rear of the vehicle whipped around, coming to a stop with a *bang* against the curb. Headlights of cars were visible in the distance, but they weren't near...

They weren't...

I sucked in the cold air, trying to still the booming of my heart.

My phone came alive, the screen illuminating as it became active. "Jesus fucking Christ," I moaned, and reached for it with trembling hands.

Benjamin Rossi.

I scowled, then hit the answer icon. "Rossi, a little late for—"

"Is it you?"

I clenched my jaw. "Is *what* me?"

"Don't fucking play with me, St. James. Someone's after Ryth and the boys. So, I'm going to ask again...*is it you?*"

My guts clenched. "No, it's not me."

"Then it's someone. There's word on the street a team has gone after them. You're telling me you know nothing?"

"That's right," I answered. Now I thought of Vivienne...and her face when I had to tell her...that her sister was dead. "Can you intercept?"

"I have Freddy and the guys on it, but they may already be too late. Lazarus is calling Tobias now. Let's hope they're as ruthless as they were before."

I lifted my gaze as I sat sideways against the edge of the gutter to stare at the glow of the amber lights. "Yes, let's hope. Will you keep me updated if you hear anything else?"

"Yeah."

I fixed on the building in front of me...the towering chapel and bell tower of the old sandstone church. "I appreciate it."

"When I find out who it is..."

"It doesn't matter," I answered. "Take them out," I snarled. "Take them *all* fucking out. Leave no one behind. Make them fucking know, they go after Ryth, or Vivienne...or any of these goddamn Daughters, there *will* be consequences."

I couldn't stop the rage from spilling out.

"My thoughts exactly," Rossi answered. "I'll keep you informed."

Then he was gone, leaving me staring at that fucking amber light glowing like a damn beacon, until movement caught my eye. Headlights flared up ahead and a white van pulled over and parked outside the church.

I glanced at the clock. It was almost three in the damn morning. What kind of service—

The driver's door opened and a figure dressed in black stepped out.

He glanced over his shoulder at my car, parked sideways with the engine running and the headlights still on. The moment the Explorer's glow spilled over him I unleashed a savage sound. Black shirt. Black trousers...and a white clerical collar...

Thomas Cruz turned around and headed for the church, slowly climbed the steps, then he disappeared inside.

"Fuck me," I whispered, unable to comprehend what I'd just seen.

But one look at that familiar white van and I realized this wasn't a figment of my imagination...

It was The Priest...here.

Claimed

My hands no longer shook as I eased my foot off the brake and pulled the Explorer alongside the curb and parked. They barely even trembled when I killed the engine and climbed out.

My gun was in my hand in an instant as I headed for the stairs to the church.

There would be no sanctuary here tonight.

Or any night to come.

Not for them.

Or for me.

Until this was done.

THIRTEEN

Vivienne

The *BANG* of the back door resounded in my ears. But it was the crunch of the tires and the sound of the Explorer backing down the drive I held onto. London was gone. Just like that, leaving us alone.

There are things I need to tend to, he said.

Sure there were. Things that were more important than his family hurting right now.

I clenched my jaw at those words, hating him in that moment and hating myself.

I hated that I needed him, that I felt out of control when he wasn't near.

BOOM!

A fist impacted a wall inside the house as I followed Carven inside.

Headlights flared across the window at the front of the house before they were gone. Only, it didn't matter what we needed. As always, London did what London did...and the rest of us survived.

"MOTHERFUCKERS!" Carven screamed. "GODDAMN MOTHERFUCKERS!"

There was a squeal and a scrape as something heavy shifted in the living room and as I neared the entrance, the heavy as hell leather sofa sailed clear across the room. It landed with a *thud*. I dared to step into the doorway. But it didn't matter. I was invisible in that moment as Carven charged past me and out of the room, heading for our bedrooms.

But he didn't disappear into his room. He strode past to where the massive, fully equipped gym waited. I flinched with each thud of his steps, my own rage desperate to be unleashed as the lights flicked on and the first brutal *smack* of the boxing bag sounded.

"Carven," I called as I followed him inside.

He didn't hear me, his focus directed at the red leather target that hung suspended from the ceiling.

Smack.

Smack.

SMACK!

The bag bounced and trembled. His head was down, fists ruthless as they landed time after time. He didn't want to talk to me. He didn't even want to acknowledge I even existed at that moment. All he wanted to do was take out his rage and frustration on the goddamn punching bag.

Thud...thud...THUD. The last punch bounced the bag so high the chain that tethered it to the ceiling rattled. I turned away and glanced at the door across the hall. *Colt's room.* I stepped closer, drawn by my own fucking torment.

I swallowed more than breathed. The cloying scent of blood clung to my nostrils. It was that smell that came back to me as I turned the handle of his door and pushed it open. I didn't want to smell that place...*not here.*

I wanted to breathe in some trace of him, to sink into the feel of his touch and the warmth of his body. I wanted him, any way I could get him.

Shadows crowded his room as I stepped inside. I stopped at the foot of his bed, remembering that first night when the storm overhead had boomed and I'd woken up screaming.

He was there, sitting against the wall of my bedroom, fighting his own demons from our past. Yet he'd pushed that beast aside...for me.

I sank down on his bed and rested my head on his pillow. The trace of him was faint here. Because he spent most of his nights with me. A sob tore from my chest. *He spent most of his nights with me.*

"Where are you, Colt?" I cried, burying my face in his bedding.

I fisted his comforter as the image of that severed thumb slammed into me. I shuddered violently, my own rage howling inside me. All I could do was scream, muffling the sound of my torment. I beat the bedding, driving my anger into the downy softness over and over again until my tears stained the fabric and I couldn't feel anymore.

I was empty.

And numb.

I knew I couldn't stay here.

I shoved upwards and stared at the rumpled bedding. It was too real, too raw and too goddamn lonely. That's all I felt as I hurried from the room, the tears in my eyes blurring the way, and barged through my bedroom door. It hit the wall with a *bang* as I ran for the bathroom.

Rage filled me.

The kind of rage I'd felt before.

I flicked on the lights and all but lunged for the vanity, grabbing hold of the corners. *No! NO!* Screams sounded in my head. My own screams as I'd stood in that room at The Order, and those of the man I'd killed with my own hands.

I'd killed.

I lifted my gaze to the mirror.

I'd killed like it was *nothing*.

"Not nothing," I whispered, not even sure who I was speaking to anymore. "It's called retribution."

Retribution. That's what I felt like and it wasn't just for Colt now. It was for all the Daughters, all those women they'd forced down into that room. I shook my head.

Head up, Vivienne. Look them in the eye and never give them a reason to think you're weak.

London had always made me look strong, always made me be on guard, a force to be reckoned with. Now I was. I shoved away from the vanity and swiped my tears away.

I pulled my holster free, then Carven's black turtleneck shirt I wore for camouflage, hurrying to strip off the rest before I stepped into the shower. I needed the stench of tonight off me...desperately.

Hot water scalded my skin, turning me red. I scrubbed furiously, then stepped out. But I still felt just as dirty as I had when I'd stepped in. There wasn't enough water to scrub murder from my soul. Not anymore.

I grabbed a towel and dried my body, made my way into the bedroom, then froze in the doorway.

Carven was standing there...waiting for me, his chest heaving with commanding breaths as he swung those murderous blue eyes my way.

Fear tore through me, cold...*chilling*.

We said nothing, just stood there staring...until some unspoken need shattered the moment. We both moved, striding toward each other. I released my hold on the towel wrapped around my body and let it fall.

His hand fisted my hair, yanking my head backwards, exposing my throat. I unleashed a moan, staring into that soulless stare. He was soulless at this moment...*but so was I*.

His lips trembled, then curled, exposing his teeth as he lowered his head to my neck. The pointed tips of his canines grazed the length of my vein.

"I want to tear you apart." His breath was hot against my skin.

"Do it," I moaned, and closed my eyes. "Do whatever you want with me."

He jerked my hair harder, bowing my spine, making sure I knew exactly who I was dealing with. There was no softness... no comfort. Only the warmth of his tongue sliding along my throat, leaving me weak at the knees. Carven wasn't just desperate. He was also dangerous.

He jerked his head upwards and released his grip on my hair before he grabbed my shoulders and shoved.

I flew backward and landed in the middle of the bed, naked. Panic punched through me, driving me upward as I turned and lunged away from him.

But Carven was on me in an instant, grabbing my ankles, yanking me against him. I fought, just like he knew I would. He needed this...*he needed a release.*

"You want to run from me, Wildcat?" he growled, shoving his body between my legs.

Hard fingers gripped my ass and spread my cheeks wide.

"No." I bucked and kicked out as I tried to get away.

But his face was there, his tongue running along the crease of my ass before licking around the tight ring of muscle. "You run from me and it'll only make this worse."

I twisted, thrashing to get away. Those hands went to my hips, his fingers bruising as he jerked upwards. "I warned you before how it would be between us." He threw me sideways, manhandling me until I landed on my back.

Only this time, I was ready. I lifted my foot and kicked, hitting him square in the middle of the chest. It wasn't hard enough to hurt him, but hard enough to knock him backwards. This was no cat-and-mouse game between us, no predator and prey. We were both just as deadly now. Each just as debased as the other.

He tumbled backwards, unleashing a roar as he caught the fall. Still, it gave me enough time to lunge across the bed and race for the door.

"Where the fuck do you think you're going?" he roared.

He wanted me to fight, he *needed* it.

I flew out the doorway, knowing instantly where I was running.

"VIVIENNE!"

I never stopped, never slowed, just raced naked for the gym once more. My chest was so tight I could barely breathe as I tore through the doorway and scanned the massive space. A boxing ring on one side. A rack filled with guns, knives and other weapons on the other.

"What the fuck are you doing?" he demanded behind me.

I spun, and found him stalking toward me. "You want to fight?" My anger was entwined with desire. "Then we fight."

There was a twitch in the corner of his eye. He grasped his black t-shirt and yanked it over his head. "I don't want to fight you, Wildcat. I want to fuck you. I want to drive my cock so deep into that tight cunt of yours, you'll scream my goddamn name."

My body clenched with the words. Still, I gave a chuff. "You think so, huh?"

One brow rose. "Oh, I don't think, I *know*."

He came closer, forcing me backward toward the boxing bag suspended in the middle of the room. His gaze went to my breasts. "I'll force your legs open if I have to. Either way, I'm in that pussy."

Christ, the thought of that made me tremble.

My body reacted, tightening...and he saw. "You like the thought of that, baby?" He grazed his lips with his teeth. "Want me to bind your hands so you can't fight me? Want me to spread open your legs so I can fuck you whenever and however I want?"

I swallowed hard, shaking my head. "No."

He smiled, giving a chuckle. "Stand still, let me finger you, and I'll know if you're telling the truth."

I shook my head, stepping backwards. The bag was just behind me. I knew it was there...somewhere. "No."

"No?" His long, careful strides were deceiving, bringing him far too close.

I risked a glance behind me, knowing instantly it was the wrong move...*or was it?*

He pounced, grabbing my hands, his deft fingers circling my wrists as he pinned them behind my back. "No, you said."

I struggled, rubbing my breasts against his chest. "That's right, *no.*"

That twitch came at his top lip. He forced me backwards, making me stumble. But he did it on purpose, shifting both my hands to his one.

That allowed him to pull his free one away...and push it between my legs. I bucked, hitting the punching bag he'd all but destroyed earlier. "So, you don't want me to hold you down and force myself in here."

He pushed his fingers inside. I stiffened, catching my breath at the invasion.

"And this." He pulled his fingers away, staring at the glistening tips. "Isn't you being turned on by the thought of me using every fucking hole you have?"

Unable to speak, I shook my head.

His touch returned, forcing its way inside. "Wildcat," he breathed huskily. "You're gonna be the fucking death of me."

Only my body didn't fight so hard now. My hips jutted forward as he pushed inside.

"Spread your legs," he demanded, driving his fingers deeper before easing out.

My foot eased to the side.

"That's the good little kitten," he smiled, sliding all the way inside.

A moan slipped free at the aching and throbbing in my chest.

"Listen to you purr." His smile was cruel.

I struggled.

"Reach above your head, grab the top of the bag," he demanded, lifting his gaze. He never stopped touching me, slipping free to circle my clit. My hands shook as I rose to the top of my toes, stretching my body to grasp the chain secured to the top of the bag. His breath caught, looking down at me. "Fuck me, you are gorgeous."

My taut muscles trembled with his words. He moved, reaching for the button on his pants. I couldn't look down, couldn't see what he was doing. But by the savagery in his stare, I had a fair idea.

"You want to run from me?" He bent down, grasped my thigh with one hand, and reached up with the other, pinning my hands against the steel links. "I'll show you just how far that will get you."

With a brutal thrust, his cock drove all the way inside. I bucked as he filled me, the links on the bag rattling overhead.

He dropped his head and moaned into my ear. "Jesus fucking Christ, I missed this."

A hard thrust and the bag bounced.

Again.

And again...

"I told you I was going to use you," he groaned, thrusting so hard it drove the air from my lungs.

That fight turned into longing, one that stoked the fire inside. I didn't care. I needed him too.

I wound my hands around the chain and lifted my other leg. He took my weight against the bag. Hard thrusts drove deeper, so deep he was all I could feel until that rush of need swept through me.

I'll protect you...

Colt's voice drifted, making me cry out.

Carven stopped deep inside me. "Baby?" Concern filled his eyes.

"Take me...take me down," I whispered.

He did, holding me steady until my ass hit the hard blue covering. I wound my arms around his neck and held onto him. He seemed to understand, knowing I needed this as much as he did. One surge of his hips and he made me jolt. I closed my eyes, picturing both of them. I needed Carven...I needed the feel of his body and the scent of his skin.

Because he wasn't just him at this moment.

He was also my connection to Colt.

I opened my eyes to find him looming over me. Strong arms caged me in as he drove his lips against mine.

"I love you," I whispered. "I love all of you."

He lowered his head and deep, purposeful thrusts replaced the frenzy. "I love you too, Wildcat."

I unleashed a moan, driving my nails into the back of his neck. But the Son...he loved the pain, using it to drive deeper. The peak rushed toward me. But it wasn't beautiful and perfect. It was a drug...a drug I craved.

My pussy clenched as that euphoria hit me, giving me a blissful, poisonous taste of oblivion.

I unleashed a moan, dropping my head backwards.

I'm right here, Wildcat, Colt whispered inside my head.

Carven gave a hard grunt, then stilled as he filled my body with warmth.

Hard, panting breaths filled the space between us.

When I opened my eyes, I thought hope waited. But it wasn't... instead there was still that void. That gaping fucking hole where my protector had been. But he was there...in that second, before my climax hit. He was right there...waiting for me.

I lifted my gaze to Carven's.

But there was nothing to say as he eased out of my body...and slowly rose.

He reached out his hand for me. I took it, knowing I needed more.

Just to touch Colt one more time.

I rose from the floor and followed him to his room.

As I climbed into Carven's cold bed, I knew how to reach Colt...

I'd let them fuck me...as many times as they could. Just so I could reach him...

One. More. Time.

FOURTEEN

London

He was here...the goddamn Priest. I took a step toward the church before fate took over, lengthening my stride until I pushed through the massive wooden door of this place of worship. Hinges squealed as shadows descended, moving between the pews...until I realized the shadows were me. Ominous and dark, they reached over the rows of hard wooden seats as I headed for the massive statue of Jesus hanging from the cross suspended at the front.

There he was.

Thomas Cruz.

The one they called *The Priest*. He paced the floor in a frenzy before suddenly turning and sinking to his knees. I watched his head bow, my boots a heavy muffled *thud* against the hard wooden floor as I came up behind him.

But he didn't seem to hear me, lost in his own torment he clasped his hands together, not quite in prayer, more like in distress. I swallowed the tang of rage. His distress had only just started.

"Thomas," I growled his name. He whipped his head toward me, his gaze narrowing as I lifted my clenched fist into the air. "Your God will not help you tonight."

I unleashed the blow with a *crack!* His head snapped backwards, but if I thought the goddamn lying bastard was going to go down easy, I was mistaken.

He shoved upwards from the floor. "London." He started, his gaze moving behind me.

Was he searching for the sons?

Was he expecting Carven to follow, full of fury and rage, determined to exact revenge for his brother? But there was no Carven...and there was no Colt. There was only me.

"*Wait!*" he roared as I lunged, driving my fist against the side of his head.

The blow hit with a *crunch*. He stumbled sideways and slammed into the tiered rows of dozens of candles alight and glowing. Some spilled, their flames hitting the white fabric covering.

"Fucking wait?" I barked, lunging once more to grab him by his black shirt. "*You. Fucking. Bastard! Where is he...*WHERE IS MY SON!"

He shoved, kicking out with a foot to catch me on the side of the knee. My stance buckled as pain shot straight into my thigh. The bastard was fast...and strong, tearing out of my grasp to stumble backwards. "I don't know, *okay!* I don't know about Colt...*I don't know anything!*"

"*LIAR!*" I rushed him.

But he swung his fist, arcing high in the air, aimed for my head. I ducked and drove my own upwards, hitting him under the jaw. Once I started, I couldn't stop. My knuckles burned as they made impact. I unleashed the darkness inside me, driving it down into his face.

There was no hope for him.

No going back now.

Thump!

My son was all I saw. His bright blue eyes filled my mind. A montage of moments as that scared, broken boy slowly learned he was safe.

I'd made him safe.

Thump!

I'd made him strong. *I did that,* pouring my heart into those boys, teaching them how to fight...and how to kill...and finally... how to be a man...and a lover.

Go to him. Those words haunted me now. *Go to him, pet.*

I grabbed The Priest with one hand, holding his body off the floor as he slumped. His eye was a mess...bloody and bruised. His mouth was no better. Blood slipped between the cracks of his teeth and stained the enamel. I sucked in hard breaths, remembering the last moment of Killion Dare...as I'd severed his thumb and sent it to Hale.

Now *I* had caused my son pain.

A roar tore free as my mind morphed it into Colt's severed digit on Ophelia's kitchen counter.

I'd done that.

I'd done that.

I sucked in a hard breath, seeing the blood splatter on my hand. "Someone has to know where Hale is." I settled my gaze on those blood-filled eyes. "Because he has my son."

His head rolled backwards, as did his eyes...until he was out and I lifted my head to the carnage. Flames from the broken candles grew bolder, eating away the corner of the cloth. I heaved Thomas upwards, dragged him over to the destruction, and slammed his body down on top of the fire...snuffing the flickers out instantly.

A low, throaty sound shattered the silence.

Shadows shifted behind me, drawing my gaze.

I swung around and found a woman standing at the edge of the pews...watching me. Not just any woman...her...*Helene King*.

"One way to put out a fire, I guess," she murmured, unfazed by what she was seeing.

I dropped The Priest.

"Uh-uh." She shook her head and lifted the gun in her hand. "I'm not here to fight with you, London."

I didn't care what she said. The fact she was here was more than telling. "Really?"

"I'm here to offer...my support." She glanced at I Priest.

"Fuck your support." I surged forward. *"Give me King!"*

She stepped backwards, but there was no fear in her eyes. Just pure determination as she aimed the gun at the center of my chest. She'd do it, too. She'd pull the trigger. That stopped me.

"My father isn't who you need right now. Focus on your family, London, and I'll focus on mine." She eased her grip around the gun, handing me a card instead.

I took a tentative step forward, finding an address scribbled on Kane Cruz's business card. "What the fuck is this?"

"You wanted to find The Teacher, there he is."

I lifted my focus. "Why are you helping me?"

She turned to The Priest once more. "Let's just say, if we don't find your son, Hale, and the rest of the splintered Order, we have option B. One I'm hoping we don't have to use."

"Option B?" I shook my head, glancing at the card then back to her. "What fucking option B?"

But she was already stepping backwards, sinking back into the shadows and not giving me her back until she was sure I wasn't following.

"*What option B!*" I barked.

The Priest behind me gave a moan and mumbled, "What?"

I spun around, finding him trying to push up from the floor. Fuck, his face was a mess. I clenched my bloodied knuckles, my gut clenching with what I'd done. *Jesus.* Revulsion gripped me as I reached into my pocket and pulled my phone free.

I swiped my thumb across the screen, leaving a bloody smear in its wake as I pressed Harper's number.

"Yeah?" he answered instantly, sounding tired.

"The church on the corner of Heist Street and Malibu... Thomas Cruz is waiting."

"The fucking Priest?" He sounded awake now.

"Yeah." I lowered my head to the card in my hand. "If Riven doesn't want to answer my goddamn messages, then the Therapist will be joining him."

"You don't know what you're doing." The Priest tried again to push up from where he lay.

"Oh, I think I have a very good idea," I answered.

"I'll be there in five," Harper said.

"We'll be waiting," I added before I hung up.

Thomas didn't look priestly as I stepped forward and aimed my phone's camera at his face.

"Fuck you," he spat as the flash brightened the blood on his face.

I attached it to a message to The Principal before I stepped closer, standing over him. "Let's see if your brother wants to answer my messages now. I have no problems spilling more blood. As much as it takes to get the answers I want."

"We're on the same fucking side here," he growled, spitting more blood.

I lifted my stare to the statue of Christ hanging over the beaten priest. "Oh, I doubt that...very fucking much."

FIFTEEN

Vivienne

"No!" Carven bucked and roared beside me, thrashing against the sheets.

"I'm right here," I soothed, rolling over to stare at him in the dark. "Carven, I'm right here."

I pressed my body against him, comforting without using my hands to touch him. The last thing I wanted to do was shock him while he was deep in whatever hell he battled. It was the third time he'd screamed in his sleep. The third time I'd talked him down from whatever terror gripped him tight. He was more like Colt than he realized.

"Vivienne?" he mumbled, his voice husky.

"I'm here."

"Maybe it's better for you to sleep in your own bed. Don't want to hurt you."

I flinched, keeping it from my tone. "Okay."

I wanted to stay and fight, but I just didn't have the energy. We were all just doing the best we could, protecting each other, hiding our own demons. My movements were slow as I rolled and kicked the sheets away. Exhausted and just *done*, I made my way to my room, pulled on silk pajamas from my dresser, and crawled under the blankets, shivering against the cold sheets.

This wasn't right.

Us here without him.

I closed my eyes and rolled over in the bed, but I suddenly jerked them open. Something nagged me. A sound...a *feeling*. I slid out of bed and made my way into the hallway in time to catch the fleeting flare of headlights, then the crunch of tires.

London.

I followed the sound to the rear of the house, listening to the *thud* of the back door before heavy steps faded into the weapons room. He didn't hear me, didn't even see me, even when he flicked on the overhead light and stepped further inside the small room.

Rows and rows of weapons, from Glocks to SIG Sauers, to some kind of gun melded with a wicked-looking knife. I no longer flinched at the sight of them. Now I felt their edge...their brutality. Now, I knew how to hate.

He stiffened, suddenly realizing I was there. "Pet." His voice was quiet...too quiet. "You don't want to look at me right now."

"Don't I?"

He shook his head.

"Try me?"

He turned around, those dark eyes boring into mine. He was covered in blood. Flecks splattered his cheeks and there was a drop at the edge of his jaw. But that was nothing compared to his hands. I lowered my gaze, feeling my heart stop. Busted knuckles crusted with blood clenched, then dropped away as I stared.

My pulse boomed as the energy between us crackled, until we both lunged, slamming against each other. Teeth gnashed as we kissed, hands grabbed, tearing what clothing we could.

He still wore the tactical black vest...still wore his weapons, bloodied from whatever he'd been up to. But none of that mattered right now. I cupped his cock, gripping the hard length under black cargos.

"Jesus, pet," he groaned.

That primal sound triggered something just as ferocious in me. I reached up, grabbed the webbing around his shoulders, and yanked him harder against me. "Fuck me," I demanded. "Fuck me like you've fucked me before."

He stilled, that stare pure predatory. "You don't want that."

"Like I said...*try me.*"

With a wicked curl of his lips, he lashed out, grasped my wrists, and drove me backwards. I hit the wall hard, knocking my teeth together. Then he kissed me so hard he bruised my lips against my teeth. I moaned, driving my body from the wall to press against him. I wanted to feel that bulge in his trousers, needed to rub myself against him.

"Uh-uh." He pulled his hips away. "This is for me. You want to be a good little whore for me, pet?"

I trembled as I released a moan. "Yes."

"My wet cunt," he moaned. "That's what you are, aren't you? I bet you're fucking dripping." He lifted his gaze to my hands, then reached up, grasped the webbing of a shoulder holster hanging on the wall, and he wrapped the straps around my wrists. "No pulling away now," he ordered as he secured my other hand.

I twisted my hands and grasped the hard weave as he slowly sank to his knees.

The overhead light shone against the steel of his gun, still snug against his hard chest. But this man didn't need the damn Sig... he was a weapon all on his own. Those bloody knuckles moved as he reached under my long silk nightshirt and dragged down my panties.

"Look at this..." He lifted the blush pink fabric, then crushed it in his fist and pulled it to his nose. "You're goddamn soaked," he groaned, then pushed them into his pocket. "Mine." He lifted his gaze to me. "All fucking mine. I'm going to use them later. I'm going to fist that lace and rub it over the head of my cock. I'm going to imagine it's your sweet cunt as I'm fucking it. What do you think about that, pet?"

A tremor quaked through me as he shifted his focus to my buttons, then reached up. "I'm going to use them, just like I'm going to use you."

He worked the buttons, opening one after another slowly until he reached the end. One sweep of his hand and he parted my shirt, letting it slip to the sides of my breasts.

"Fuck me, you are perfect," he moaned, slowly taking in every inch of me.

My body tightened as he brushed his thumb across my nipple, then leaned close. I closed my eyes and clenched the tactical vest tighter as his warmth closed around the peak. The graze of his teeth had me moaning, then a sudden lick and he pulled away.

"Not for you, pet," he growled as he ran those bloodstained fingers down my stomach and my abdomen, then over my mound.

He met my gaze. "Open."

I swallowed, doing as he demanded and widening my stance. A surge of excitement and fear tore through me as he narrowed his gaze between my legs.

One brush of his thumb over my mound and he murmured, "Look at that pretty pussy. Did Carven use you?"

I licked my lips and nodded.

"Use your words, Vivienne. Did the Son take out his frustration on this sweet body?"

"Yes." My heart raced with acceptance.

"Did he fuck you hard? Did he hurt you?" He slipped his thumb along the top of my slit, dragging it over my clit until he parted me.

He saw all of me under the bright overhead lights, more so when he used his other hand to widen my pussy.

I shivered, lifting my gaze to stare across the room. "No...no, he didn't hurt me."

"Good." He leaned close, pressing that bloodied face to my slit. "Very good."

He licked, pushing his face lower. "Leg over my shoulder, Vivienne."

I obeyed instantly, resting my knee over his good shoulder, giving him the access he wanted. His tongue was so warm, so soft, licking my clit in feathered touches before he gripped my hips and pushed his face against my slit, driving the tip of his tongue into the core of me. I dropped my head backwards, slowly thrusting against his mouth. I needed this. "Jesus, London...I'm going to..."

"No, you're not." He pulled away, staring at my pussy as I clenched. "You're not going to come until I say, do you understand me?"

I opened my eyes, but all I could do was swallow hard and nod, even as my body quaked. He pulled away, unclipped his vest, and let it fall to the floor with a *thud*. His weapons were forgotten, even his busted hands didn't make him wince. Instead, he couldn't look away from between my legs. London St. James was occupied by something far more interesting...to him at least.

He rose from the floor and moved closer. "No coming now, pet," he urged, sliding his fingers in deep. "Understand? No. Fucking. Coming."

I bit down on the inside of my cheek as that hunger rose. My hips were fixed in position. I didn't dare move. A slight shift, a tightening would be all it took to send me over the edge.

I could fuck Carven and Colt all night...

Still, they never affected me the way London did.

They didn't make me melt.

His singleminded obsession and filthy mouth made me weak at the knees. He was so powerful. So...*in control.*

"You won't come until I have my fill of you. Do you understand me?"

My response was an inhuman whimper. One that made him chuckle as he lowered his head and breathed again my neck. "I want to hear you moan my name, pet."

I grasped the holster, held on with all I had, and whispered, "London."

His deft fingers stroked and pushed in, only to slide all the way out as he thumbed my clit. "Now, you can do better than that," he chastised.

My knees trembled. "London," I forced through clenched teeth.

It took every ounce of my willpower not to succumb to those drugging waves until he pulled away and unbuttoned his pants with slow, careful movements. I gripped the holster and looked down. His cock pushed out of his boxers, the head flushed and ready, making me part my thighs even wider.

He lifted his gaze, met mine, and pressed his body against me. One hard thrust and he was inside. "Do. Better. Pet."

He filled me, stretching my pussy until I rose on my toes. *"London,"* I moaned, arching my back.

"That's the way," he grunted, sliding out, only to drive all the way in. "Again."

"Lon-don," I moaned.

"Again," he demanded, his voice husky against my ear.

"London," I panted. *"Jesus Christ, London."*

He thrust so hard he made me jolt. This was the second time tonight I'd been fucked ruthlessly.

"Tell me..." he gasped, driving deeper...*harder*. "Tell me you love me."

My pulse sped as a pang tore across my chest. "Not love," I moaned against his ear. "It's not...*enough*," I wheezed. "Obsessed, controlled. *Owned*....that's what I am. I'm owned by you."

"As." *Thrust.* "I." *Thrust.* "Am with you pet."

I gave myself over to the power of his passion, to the way he smelled like death and blood and danger...and the way he loved me. The way he hungered for me.

"I...need..." I moaned, spreading my legs as wide as I could. "Christ, I need."

"Come for me, Vivienne. Come all over my cock."

I closed my eyes and dropped my head forward as my body tightened and clenched while jolts of electricity tore through my core.

"Fuck," London mumbled. "You feel so goddamn good."

With a deep, carnal sound, he stopped suddenly and spilled deep inside me. I held on, one leg wrapped around his ass, driving his softening length deeper inside.

"Jesus," I breathed.

"Not the first time I've done battle with him tonight," he growled and turned his head, meeting my gaze. "Nor will it be the last."

That unflinching sound in his tone made me scared. "London?"

"It's nothing." He pulled away, slipping free, then stilled and met my stare. "Really, it's nothing."

He glanced down at my parted pajamas. "It's late. You should be asleep."

"I can't."

"Can't?" He eased my foot to the floor, then reached up and untangled my hands until they dropped free.

I shook my head, unable to tell him about how empty and cold my bed was.

"Do you want to sleep on the sofa while I work?"

I weighed the options, a kink in my neck opposed to a night spent tossing and turning. "Yes, thank you."

He fixed his trousers and reached into his pocket to tug my panties free. "But you don't get these back."

A hint of a smile tugged the corner of my lips. "Fine."

One brow rose. "Fine."

He grabbed his vest from the floor and secured it on the rack, then held out his hand. "Come on. Let me get you settled."

I took his hand and followed him to the study. He flicked on the light, dulling the glow as I sat on the sofa, watching him. The rush of gas hissed before the fireplace came alight.

"This will soothe you," he murmured.

"*You* will soothe me."

He turned, giving me a sad smile. "Only you would say that."

I tried to stifle a yawn and pulled my bare feet underneath me as he reached behind the sofa and pulled up a cushion and a large, soft throw. "Head down." He gave a nod.

I complied, knowing it was useless to fight him, even if I'd wanted to. And I didn't want to. The soft gray cashmere settled over me as I eased my head onto the cushion and closed my eyes. Footsteps sounded as London moved around the room and finally settled in his chair, the creak of leather drawing my focus.

But it didn't linger long. The soft crackle of the fire and the shuffling of pages lulled me. London's dangerous tone came sometime later.

"I don't care what you have to pay, I want Hale found..."

I sank lower, safe knowing that if anyone would find Colt, I'd be London. He'd raze the city to the ground to do it as well. Just like he'd do that for me. *Because we belong to him.*

I drifted into the darkness, surrendering myself to that bleak emptiness...where there was no Colt.

A *clink* woke me later. I cracked open my eyes, feeling him beside me.

"Sorry," London murmured next to me. "I didn't mean to wake you."

Through my slitted eyes, I found him sitting on the other end of the sofa with a glass of Scotch in his hand. He looked from me to the fire, torment sparkling in his stare. One he kept from me as he glanced at the flames flickering in the fire.

I shifted against him, letting him pull my feet over his lap. His hand ran up my legs, his fingers splayed over my thighs. "I've done things tonight...things I'm not proud of. But they were necessary. You understand that?"

I didn't know if he was talking or confessing. Either way, I nodded. "Yes."

His big hands slid down the backs of my thighs, still kneading, as though the movement eased him.

"I blame myself," he murmured. The brush of his thumb grazed my skin. "There were opportunities to take out the major players." His warm hand slid over the curve of my ass, then brushed my slit.

He moved, brushing his chest against my curled knees on his lap. The soft cashmere blanket shifted with a gentle tug and cold air moved over my body. Fingers sank through soft lips, making me catch my breath.

"I would've killed them if I'd known. You have to believe me." He pushed his thumb along my slit. "You do believe me, don't you?"

The question pulled me away from the sensations of his fingers. "Yes." I managed. "Yes, I believe you."

He turned his head, those dark eyes finally meeting mine before they dropped. My pussy clenched, gripping tight, even as his fingers slipped free. But I didn't have to wait long. He gripped my leg and eased it to the side, making me shift my hips flat against the sofa.

"If I'd known what they were planning, that Hale had already given your contract away, I would've killed him then and there." It was so wrong to speak of murder as he eased my legs wider and looked down. So fucking wrong, and yet that was how London loved. He schemed...he *destroyed*. He slid his thumb down my slit, then inside. "I would've killed anyone before they laid a hand on you. I want to kill Killion all over again. I want to kill them all."

I tried to stay with his words, but my brain wouldn't focus, not when he slipped his thumb free and sank two fingers inside. "Sometimes we make alliances with those we have to. You realize that, don't you?"

The crackle of the fire.

The stroke of his fingers.

I bit my lip and nodded.

"But it doesn't change our purpose. It doesn't change those who we explicitly trust. I need you to understand that."

He spoke in riddles...and I was lost to the way he drove inside me, unable to stop my body driving down against his touch.

"You are mine. You always have been and always will be. From the first moment I knew about you on that DNA report and for always. You were my weapon...now you're my salvation. Never forget that, pet. Never *ever* forget that."

I reached over my head, driving down on his fingers. "I won't," I moaned. "I won't just, for Christ's sake, London, I need your mouth. I need you to lick me."

He gave me a soft, devious smile, then lifted the remaining Scotch above my pussy and tipped. Liquid dribbled down my slit before he pushed upward, then leaned down. "Whatever you need, lover. Whatever you damn well need."

I needed this, arching up from the sofa as his mouth connected with my body.

My hand went to his thick, dark hair. My fingers clenched, fisting the strands as I lifted my leg higher, driving his face hard against me. "Oh...*fuck.*"

A dangerous snarl came from him as he opened his mouth, sinking lower to suck and probe. It sent me over, toppling into that seductive lull of delirium. He ate like a man starving, tilting my hips upwards as he surged above me.

One hand lowered to his trousers, undoing his button.

He was inside me, sinking into that swollen heat.

"Use me," I groaned. "God, I want you to use me."

He gripped the armrest of the sofa with one hand and slammed his hips against mine, driving all the way inside. "You will be pregnant with my baby, Vivienne," he grunted. "I will have every goddamn inch of you."

And the image of that filled my mind.

I gripped his body, feeling his powerful muscles flex under my grip.

And unleashed a cry, coming hard.

SIXTEEN

Carven

"Use me." Wildcat's desperate plea reached me as I stood at London's study door. "*God, I want you to use me.*"

My balls tightened as a flicker of dangerous rage rose. Still, underneath that strangling hold came a charge of excitement, a need to see what they were doing.

"You will be pregnant with my baby, Vivienne," London grunted, his hips rising as he drove into her.

Flames flickered, dancing across London's back as he thrust. I took a step inside, listening to her breath hitch before she moaned. This wasn't like watching her with Colt. It wasn't so *familiar*.

No.

This was...carnal.

She unleashed a groan, arching her back. Her brow tightened and creased as the man who'd raised me fucked her. Until she sensed me. Her eyes opened, meeting my stare, as London drove his hips down so hard he pushed her head against the armrest.

"Good girl," he grunted as his hips slammed into her. "You're taking it so good. You make me so goddamn weak. You know that? So fucking weak." He dropped his head and his groan was filled with breathless urgency against her ear. "I will have you, pet. I'll have every *goddamn inch of you.*"

My cock twitched at the ruthless snarl as I watched London thrust hard, then groan.

He came. Filling her all the way. Just like I had.

Jesus...

Vivienne sucked in hard breaths, holding my stare over London's shoulder. But there was no surprise in her stare, no fear or desperation. Just pure fucking need. She wanted this... she wanted *us.*

The thought of that only made me wanted to fuck her again and again.

But I didn't. Instead, I watched London as he pulled out, fighting the desperate need to fucking look at the mess between her legs. I wanted to see his cum dripping, imagined the look on her face as I ran my fingers through his seed and pushed it back inside.

London wanted a baby in her belly...wanted her big and round.

I wanted that for him.

My cock twitched and grew rock fucking hard. The idea of fucking her when her belly was swollen with a child did things to me I wasn't prepared for. So, I turned around and headed for the door.

"Carven?" London called.

But I didn't stop, just headed back to my room and climbed into bed, hating this feeling of isolation. I closed my eyes, still seeing the look of ecstasy on Vivienne's face. That image stayed with me even as sleep pulled me under.

Dreams plagued me, with screams of terror and pleasure.

Use me.

Colt.

London.

I tossed and turned with Vivienne's voice resounding in my head, waking at first light with my eyes stinging. I shoved the covers aside and strode to the bathroom, blasting my body with the searing spray as I scrubbed before turning it ice cold.

Cold enough to shock me back into my body.

And my hate.

I dressed, then walked out into the kitchen before the sun rose. It was early. A perfect time for a home visit. I grabbed an energy drink and stopped at the armory on my way out. Guild was there, waiting.

He leaned against the door jamb, his arms crossed over his chest. "Want some company?"

I shook my head as I pushed past him and into the room. "You don't want to ride along for this, believe me."

"I don't like you going out on your own," he said as I grabbed two Glocks and three fresh clips.

I shoved one into the waistband of my jeans at the small of my back, then palmed the other and the magazines before turning. "Then find my goddamn brother."

It was as simple as that. Give him back to me and I'd do whatever they wanted. I pushed past, headed outside, and climbed into the Explorer London had driven last night.

You're shit at roundabouts, you know that? My own words hit hard as I climbed in and started the engine. What I wouldn't give to hold on for dear life as Colt made one 'more go around' at the damned things. Headlights splashed against the side of the house as I backed out of the drive and headed for the first address on my list.

It was a long list.

But I was scraping the bottom of the barrel and I knew that.

Everyone of importance to The Order was long gone, leaving the collateral damage behind. Houses were deserted, offices cleaned out, or they'd simply left, not bothering to give any excuse at all. I pulled into a quiet residential street. Family station wagons and kids' play areas peppered the front lawns. I glanced at the number on my phone, then pulled up outside a two-story stucco.

Two kids' bikes sat outside, one on its side as though it'd been cast aside in a hurry. I felt that sense of urgency as I climbed out and eased the driver's door closed behind me. Nolan Parks, personal assistant to Doctor Harmon Rivers, one of the more 'silent' partners in The Order, but certainly not the kindest. I walked along the sidewalk, heading to the back of the house. Harmon Rivers liked them young, the younger the better for the sick fuck. He was the first one there when they brought the

Daughters into the orphanage, giving them a *thorough examination*.

Now the bastard had disappeared, leaving good ol' Nolan to pick up the pieces. I walked around to the back, making sure he didn't have some massive fucking hound for me to deal with before I stopped at the back door.

One twist of the pick and I was inside.

My intel said the wife and kids were away.

Fled two days ago, leaving Nolan at home alone.

I clenched my jaw. He wouldn't be home for long.

I turned the handle and stepped inside, scanning the shadows as I made my way further into the house. Scents still lingered, burned popcorn and something sweet...and citrusy. I glanced toward the right, then upstairs. Following my instinct, I climbed, stepping out onto the landing.

The kids' bedroom doors were open, leaving only one door closed at the end. I made my way toward it, glancing into the empty rooms. Drawers were open, clothes were strewn on the floor. Whatever happened to Nolan's family, it happened in a frenzy. I stopped at what had to be their bedroom door, before I turned the handle and stepped inside...finding the bed empty, and still made.

I glanced around the room, then stepped into the closet and stared at the obvious gap in the hanging clothes. The wife was gone, with the kids, it looked like. I spun around, pissed the fuck off.

This was a goddamn waste of time.

I walked out, then back down the stairs, stopping at the bottom. My senses flared as the hairs on my arms stood on end. Instinct pulled me toward the garage at the front of the house. The moment I opened the door, I knew instantly, as the fetid stench of death hit me.

One flick of the lights and I found Nolan swinging. "Goddamn gutless bastard," I snarled, lowering my gaze to the note on the concrete floor underneath him.

Please forgive me.

"Forgive you?" I muttered, finding his bulging eyes as he hung from the rope. "Not a fucking chance."

FUCK! I turned around and clenched my fist, desperately holding back the need to drive it through the goddamn wall. But I didn't. I left that house, climbed back into the Explorer, and went to the next address.

Only I found the same thing there.

Empty cupboards in discarded houses.

All the major players were gone.

Leaving gaping holes behind.

They played it well, setting it up to look like suicides. But it wasn't. The Order was cleaning house and making sure they didn't leave a damn crumb behind. By the time I crossed off the last address on the list after not finding a goddamn thing, I was fucking dangerous.

I drove along the darkened city streets, hunting. I needed just one fucking person, someone I could break. I clenched the steering wheel. *Fuck, I needed to break them.* My brother's face haunted me as I pulled into the same alleyway I had been in before when I was lured there by the Sons.

I scanned the rear-view mirror, then pulled into the alley. The hairs on the back of my neck rose when I climbed out. I scanned the shadows, sensing nothing but vermin in the trash cans and loitering outside the side entrance of the rave as I neared.

One flick of the same card that was left for me by the Sons the last time, and the security guard stepped aside. Right now, I would've stepped into a lion's den if it obtained me the information I needed. Anything as long as it gave me back my brother.

The throbbing noise filled my ears the moment I stepped inside. I flanked the dancers, keeping to the outer edges of the room, and made my way to the rear of the club where another bouncer stood outside a secret door. I didn't have to stop, or slow. One savage glare and he stepped aside. Only the moment I stepped through, I knew something was wrong.

The place was...*empty*.

I stopped just inside the doorway as my phone vibrated in my pocket. With a snarl, I snatched it out, scanning the empty seats around the bar before I looked at the screen.

Beep.

Looking for someone?

I slowly glanced behind me, then left and right as my phone vibrated once more.

Nothing has changed. We want the Daughter. So we propose a trade.

I barely had time to read the message before an image followed the message. Dark, grainy, barely more of an outline of a man tied to a chair with a black hood over his head. "What the fuck?"

Beep.

Still want Rivers?

That same chill I'd had outside swept through me. One that told me I was being watched. Still, I didn't lift my gaze, nor did I make a move to leave. If they wanted me dead, then they would've killed me by now...*wouldn't they?*

My gut clenched in warning. Still, I stared at the name. Harmon Rivers? I typed out a message: *Where?*

Beep.

We'll be in contact.

"Sonofa—" I started, and typed.

No, we meet now.

And pressed send.

I waited, standing there in the middle of the empty bar and waited...seconds turned into minutes. They weren't going to fucking respond. I clenched my jaw, glancing at the empty table where the Ares assholes had sat before I turned around.

And I couldn't take the risk of going there alone. I glanced at the message. "Nothing has changed, my ass. This has retribution all over it."

I didn't trust them. That only meant one thing. I needed backup wherever they wanted to meet. That meant I had to talk to London and tell him everything. This entire thing was going to hell...and it was about to get a helluva lot worse.

I PULLED the Explorer into the driveway, found the Raptor parked in the drive, and parked next to it. The lights were on inside. I bet they were waiting. The image of London and Vivienne came rushing back as I climbed out, locked the four-wheel drive and headed inside.

The thought of them together didn't piss me off like I thought it would. Instead, I felt...*weird*.

I didn't like it.

I liked having to go to him about the Sons even less. *Doesn't matter. Nothing matters. Not while Colt is out there.* I lifted my gaze, punched in the code for the back door and headed inside.

"We train tomorrow." London's careful tone reached me in the hall. "You need to learn to protect yourself. You're all rage, pet, all fire. You need to learn to control it. To use it. To *hone* it."

I stopped outside the study, my pulse booming in my head.

For a second, I didn't want to move.

Because if I did, if I unleashed this anger and hunger inside me, especially now, things would change.

I closed my eyes. I knew they would.

"Carven?" Vivienne called.

I opened my eyes, sucked in a breath, and stepped inside.

London leaned against his desk, his arms crossed over his chest as he glanced my way. "Anything?"

I shook my head. "You?"

"No." He pushed off the desk and strode around. "They're gone. Every single one of them, they're all gone."

"Not all."

He froze, then turned. "Explain."

I glanced at Wildcat, then turned to him. "The man who attacked Vivienne outside the restaurant wasn't part of those who shot at us."

He scowled. "How do you know?"

"Because they were Sons."

His breath caught as panic flared. "Tell me everything."

I told him about the orphanage, then the warehouse, and by the time I got to the attack outside the restaurant, London was pacing the room. "You're not going," he snapped.

"Not alone, but I will."

He spun. "No, *you won't.*"

"*It's been three fucking days, London!*" I roared, stepping closer. "Did you know that? *Three fucking days!*"

He stopped pacing, looking at me with pure desperation. "I know."

"Do you?" I snarled, moving closer. "*Do you really? Every goddamn minute he's out there, they're fucking torturing him! They're fucking beating him, London. They're KILLING HIM!*"

London flinched as though I'd slapped him.

Vivienne lunged, stepping in between us. *Use me...use me...use...me...*

I reacted before I knew it, turning on her in an instant. My hands were around her throat, fingers clenching hard enough to shock her...and me. Instinct and pain were in the driver's seat as I drove her backwards. Still, she never fought me, even when her head hit the wall with a thud.

I stared into her eyes. My breath was a panicked rush.

"*Carven!*" London roared.

But Wildcat just shook her head, flicking her eyes to London. "It's okay." She sucked in panting breaths and turned back to me. "He's not going to hurt me."

She never made a move to react. Not even to save herself. That alone triggered something deep inside me. All I saw were those times Colt had taken those beatings meant for me. He'd been just a kid. We'd both been just kids. Still, he'd stepped in front of me time and time again when they came searching for someone in their anger.

He never fought.

Never screamed.

Just stood there until they'd punched him to the ground.

I saw that same look in her eyes now. That same *devotion* that echoed both in my brother and her. *Use me...*those words echoed as I lowered my head and kissed her. Her mouth parted, opening wide. *Use me...*I pushed against her, my hand still gripping her throat.

A moan tore along her throat, raw and primal, as she trembled against my touch. I tore my lips from hers, unable to look her in the eyes. "I want to use you." The words were out before I realized it. It was too late now. Too late to hold them back. Too late to tether this rage.

"Take her to the room."

I stilled, then slowly lifted my head.

"Is that what you want, pet?" he asked her.

Those brown eyes were fixed on mine. "Yes."

"You don't have to fight us, son," London urged. "Not here. You need release. Take her to the room. Let her give you what you need."

My words were husky. "You want that?"

She never looked away. "I'll let you do whatever you want. My body is yours. Use me."

Use me.

Those words slammed into me, followed by her look of desire. With a snarl I bent, grabbed her around the thighs, and heaved her over my shoulder. I was heading for the doorway before I stopped. "London…"

"Yes?"

"I want you to come too."

SEVENTEEN

Vivienne

CARVEN SUDDENLY HEAVED ME UPWARDS UNTIL I LANDED over his shoulder. My heart lunged, trapped in my throat as he headed to the doorway, then stopped.

I gripped his arm, holding onto his rock-hard muscles, and lifted my head, finding London behind us.

"London."

"Yes?"

"I want you to come too."

One brow rose as London met my panicked stare. "Of course."

Still, that didn't ease the tension inside me. Carven wouldn't hurt me, that I was sure of...*but he'd never taken me into that room.*

Long strides made me bounce against his shoulder. London was a blur behind us, still he was there, holding my stare, until I couldn't hold my body up anymore and eased my hold. I flopped back down, my hand around his bicep as he headed to the east wing and past our bedrooms.

I hadn't been in this room, not with London, or by myself. But the moment Carven turned the handle and stepped in, the basement in our other house came rushing back to me.

The smell of leather was the same. The cold air made my nerves hum. Lights flicked on, softly illuminating the room. Strong hands gripped my thighs and pulled me down. I slid along his body until he stopped the fall, easing my feet to the floor.

Those blue eyes searched mine. Stark blond hair, an unflinching stare. Carven made even the biggest men I knew uncomfortable by his presence alone. 'The Son.' That name was spoken by a few, but those who spoke it knew exactly what they were. Yet this *killer* stood in front of me now, soft and vulnerable.

He lifted his hand, brushing a strand of hair from my face. "You trust me, right, Wildcat?"

There was that edge in his voice. That *hunger* that always made me hesitate before I answered. I felt that hunger now more than ever. This wasn't about comfort. This was about control, and right now, Carven was spiraling. He needed this, needed to control something for just a moment. He needed to find his way back to himself, and he was going to use my body to do it. I met those deep blue eyes. "With my life."

He lowered his head until he whispered into my ear. "What about your body, Wildcat? You going to trust me with that?"

My pulse skipped in response and my core tightened. I didn't need to reach between my legs to know the impact those words had on me. "Yes."

He gripped my chin, lifting my gaze to his. "Fuck, you're dangerous."

Dangerous...me?

I didn't want to look at his hands, didn't want to see the blood etched into the corners of his nails, or see the faces of those he'd killed in his stare. Yet I held that stare and realized he wasn't talking about me being dangerous to everyone else.

Only to him.

I *was* dangerous to him.

He reached down, snatched my wrist, and jerked it upward as London stepped into the room and closed the door behind him.

"It's about her in this room," he murmured. "All about her. Whatever you're feeling, it no longer matters. Not in this room. Your control comes in her release. Find out what makes her wet. Her body will guide you."

"I *know* what makes her wet," Carven snarled, never once taking his eyes from mine.

"Do you?" London stepped closer, being careful not to touch me.

This was all for Carven.

"Do you know how to crawl under her skin? How to make her wet tomorrow, a week from now, a year from now just remembering what you did to her? I do. You're all raw power, you're all stamina. Look deep into her soul, see what she sees.

Take her, rip her clothes off, pull her hair if she moans, spread her legs...and let her feel why you're the animal she wants and needs. Fuck her, protect her. Be *everything* for her."

My breath caught with those words. I'd never heard London talk like that, never heard him so...fierce. Was that how he felt? I wanted to find the truth in his stare, but I didn't dare move. Not now. Not when Carven's grip was a vise around my wrist.

He sucked in hard breaths, then lowered his gaze to the black shirt I wore. "You want me to tear your clothes off, Wildcat? Want me to be an *animal?*"

"Yes."

There was a twitch at the corner of his mouth before he released my wrist and dropped his hand to his waist. One *flick* and the light bounced off the steel blade.

"How about I cut them off instead?"

He slipped the tip of the blade under the hem of my shirt. One sudden jerk and the fabric split, slicing all the way. Panic ripped through me. My heart lunged, slamming against my ribs.

"Still trust me?" he asked, using the tip of the knife to flick each side of the ruined garment aside, exposing my pink bra.

"Yes." My voice was husky.

"Liar," he whispered, pushing the tip of the knife up the valley of my breasts, just under the lace.

He reached up and grasped the bridge between the cups, gripping it as he jerked the knife toward him and yanked me forward. Cold air rushed in and my nipples tightened from the icy whisper of air and excitement. My clit throbbed. I didn't understand my emotions. If it was anyone else, I'd be terrified. But not them. Not *my* men.

Carven yanked, tearing the shredded shirt and bra free before casting them aside. I didn't dare look to London as Carven lowered his gaze to my jeans. "Want me to cut those off too?"

I shook my head. "Why don't you take me to the bed?"

There was a hint of a smile before he bent and grabbed me around the thighs once more, only this time with one arm. He carried me to the massive bed. London's machine waited at the foot, the steel gleaming. Wind buffeted my hair as I was flung backward, hitting the bed with a bounce.

My boots were yanked free and tossed to the floor. The button on my jeans popped, and the zipper was yanked low before I even realized. I shoved my jeans over my hips, lifting my ass. In the blink of an eye, I was in nothing more than pink lace panties.

Carven loomed over the edge of the bed, staring down at me, the knife still in his hands. "What makes you wet, Wildcat?" he asked, before he slipped the knife in between his teeth and lunged, grasped both my ankles, and pulled me down the bed.

I thrashed in his grasp, my gaze riveted to that blade in his mouth. He reached up, took it in his hand, and lowered it between my legs. "Is it fear?" Cold steel pressed against my skin, the tip gently dragging along my slit.

I didn't dare move. I pinned my lip with my teeth, closing my eyes at the fine pressure.

"Open them," he demanded. "Look at me."

I did, finding that icy stare. He said I was dangerous. But Carven was the deadliest male I knew. He killed without thinking and with little to no remorse. He strangled, he beat, he stabbed and shot. He unleashed that never-ending pit of fury through his hands and yet as he lowered his gaze to the tip of the knife he pressed against my clit, I also knew deep down he loved just as savagely.

"I love you," I whispered. "I love you with everything I have."

He jerked his gaze to mine. Panic flared for a second before that darkness rose to snatch it away. It was that darkness that called to me. That darkness I craved.

"That's good, Wildcat." He eased the tip of the knife to the side and pressed, slipping it under the elastic at the side. "Good for the both of us. Because I love you too, and my love is forever." I jerked as he sliced through the lace. His fingers traced the cut, yanking the rest of the lace out before he cut the rest of the way through. "Now, let's see if I made you wet, shall we?" His finger slipped into the crease and slid all the way down until he pushed inside. "Look at that."

He eased his finger free, lifting it to shine in the light. "How's that, London?" He looked at the man who'd raised him. "Was I animal enough?"

London just cleared his throat. "Do you want the machine, pet?"

I shifted my gaze to him at the foot of the bed, watching as he pulled the case free of the machine, then extracted the dildo and connected it. My core clenched at the sight, leaving Carven to slide his fingers back inside, feeling the slick. "Christ, I think that's a yes."

Snap.

The attachment slid into place. I lifted my arms over my head on instinct, giving over to them.

"Move her over," London commanded.

Strong hands slipped under my back and thighs, dragging me across the bed. Carven reached up and grasped my throat gently as the whir of the machine started, making me catch my breath.

"You like this, Wildcat?" he asked, staring deep into my eyes. "You like giving yourself to us?"

"Yes."

His smile tugged. "Anything I want?"

"Anything."

He glanced over his shoulder and gave a nod. The sound of the machine came closer, but I couldn't look. The look on Carven's face gripped me as he watched the dildo press against my core and slip inside. I released a moan as the cold silicone drove inside me, then eased back out.

Carven glanced back at me. "Again?"

I nodded, and the pressure came again, only this time it didn't pull all the way out before it drove back in again. The Son gripped the inside of my thigh, widening my legs as he watched. "Jesus fucking Christ," he growled, slipping his finger along my slit as I was invaded. "I'm fucking hard just watching this."

A memory tore through me.

Him standing at the end of the sofa last night, watching us. Him, me, and Colt together was one thing. But he'd never shown an interest in...this.

"Harder," Carven demanded, sliding his fingers either side of the intrusion.

I bucked as the dildo rammed all the way inside. "Oh, fuck." I slammed my eyes closed, screwing them tight.

I couldn't stop that drugging wave from rising inside me, and pumped my hips upwards.

"Turn on your side, Wildcat," he urged, his voice strange as he fumbled with his jeans.

I did when the dildo slipped all the way free. Carven gripped my ass and leaned in close before he spat. Wetness hit the crease of my ass. He dragged the slick down, then pushed inside the opening.

"Again," he demanded.

I panted as I clenched around his finger. He gripped my knee, holding my leg up, watching as it invaded me once more.

"Oh, fuck," he moaned, his finger deep inside me. "I can feel it."

I closed my eyes, my hips thrusting. "I can't stop."

"Then let's not make you wait, baby," he urged, sliding his finger free before he spat once more.

I pushed back against the head of his cock, feeling the dildo slowly slide in.

"Breathe, pet," London urged, his tone silken.

I exhaled and, on the brink, felt Carven push against me.

"Stretch for me, Wildcat," he grunted.

My pussy clenched, that edge coming closer, so close I could...

"Jesus," Carven moaned as he slipped the head of his cock inside.

They worked together, pushing me to that edge of oblivion. Colt's face filled my mind as I cried out, fisting the silken sheets of the bed. "Not yet, baby." Carven gripped my leg, slowly pushing all the way inside.

I thrashed my head, unable to stop my body from giving in.

"Come, pet," London growled, standing over me. "Come."

I met those dark eyes, crying out as my pussy clenched around the dildo, flutters slammed into me, and my body bucked in response.

"Oh...*fuck*," Carven growled, driving into me.

The machine whirred, and the dildo slipped out, leaving a trail of slick heat behind. One push and I was face-down on the bed. Carven's hands gripped my hips, pulling me up to my knees. "Open your knees, baby. That's the way."

I turned my head, finding London as Carven pushed all the way in.

"Look at that perfect ass stretch," London murmured, glancing from Carven's cock to my eyes. "Such a good girl for us. Let us use you. Let us take what we need. Look how good you're doing."

I panted, moaning as my body shuddered and shook. Deep spasms rocked my core as Carven drove deep inside and gave a grunt, stilling deep inside me. My knees clenched together as I clamped around him. Warmth filled me, until exhaustion hit me, leaving me to slump against the bed.

"Jesus." Carven slid out, collapsing on top of me. "That was fucking intense."

"Take care of her tonight." London leaned down, brushing his curled finger down my cheek. "She's done so well."

"You want that, baby?" Carven murmured against my back. "Want to sleep with me? Let me take care of you?"

The truth echoed in London's stare.

This is what the son needed.

Not just sex. But someone to look after. Someone to care for.

I slowly nodded while keeping London's stare. "Yes. I do."

One hard groan and Carven's weight lifted from me. I turned as he slid his hands under, lifting me to his chest. My arms wrapped around me.

"You're so goddamn beautiful," he whispered as he headed for the door.

London opened it and stepped aside. We were out in an instant, making our way into Carven's bathroom.

He jostled me against him when he hit the light.

"You can put me down," I said, smiling.

He was so damn sweet and awkward, giving me a grin. "I'll get the water going."

I let him wash me. Let him dry me. Let him dress me in one of his oversized shirts before he pulled me to his bed.

Claimed

"You're not going to hit me in your sleep again, are you?" I muttered, sliding between the familiar sheets.

"Probably." He gave a chuff. "But I give you full permission to hit me right back."

Look out...was that actually a *joke?*

I said nothing, slipping down beside him.

"You liked that tonight?" he asked, pulling me down to rest my head against his chest, his arm wrapped around me.

"Yes," I answered. "Did you?"

He didn't answer for a long time, then carefully, "Yeah, I think I did." He sighed, closing his eyes. "Doesn't mean there'll be any sword crossing, so get that out of your head. I'm not fucking my father."

I have a soft chuckle. "I'm sure London will be heartbroken."

"Asshole," he muttered as sleep filled his tone.

But he kept true to his word, holding me all night. In that moment, our world wasn't filled with desolate sadness. For a second, we held onto each other.

"She's not going to like it." London's voice echoed from the study as I neared.

I YAWNED, still feeling heavy with sleep as I neared the doorway with a steaming cup of coffee in my hand. But my mind was already turning to where we were searching today. These torturous days blurred into one.

We searched. We hunted. We threatened, but still we had nothing.

But those words stilled me cold. *She's not going to like it?*

I scowled as I stepped into the doorway, watching as the powerful male jerked those dark eyes to me, then mumbled. "Okay, leave it with me. I need to go."

"What's *she* not going to like?" I asked as he lowered his phone.

He averted his gaze. That was *never* a good sign. "London?"

He gave a hard sigh, then turned to me. "You know I told you we make alliances when we need to?"

My stomach dropped. All I thought about was those men who'd held me down on that desk in Killion's study. If he meant relying on any of those...

"Helene King is coming in to help us coordinate." The words were rapidly out of his mouth.

I flinched. My frantic thoughts of Killion and his buddies froze. "Helene King...you mean?"

London rose from his seat. "Your biological sister."

Ryth filled my head. *She* was my sister, the only one I knew. "She's coming here?"

Tires crunched outside in the driveway, the faint sound drawing my gaze as London answered. "Not coming, pet. She's here."

"Who's here?" Carven muttered behind me.

I turned, glancing over my shoulder. "My sister."

He froze, scowled, then stepped into the doorway. "What the fuck, London?"

London just rose from his seat and stepped past us to stand just inside the doorway before he stopped. "This changes nothing."

Changes nothing? I glanced at Carven, watching as a savage flicker of rage passed through his stare. Helene King was the one person who'd given London what he'd wanted all this time. She'd given him her father...*no, our father, remember?* So if she was here, if we were suddenly making 'alliances' with her, did that mean...*London has already met my father, Weylen King?*

I flinched as the locks to the back door snapped open and London's low voice echoed along the hall. My pulse thudded. Suddenly, I was self-conscious, brushing down the freshly washed strands of my hair. Black jeans and a black t-shirt weren't what I'd imagined wearing when I met my sister. But I wasn't here for a family reunion, no matter how awkward that would be. I was ready to search abandoned houses and empty buildings for the man I loved.

Footsteps echoed along the hall. I lifted my gaze the moment London entered, and she followed behind him. The woman who looked exactly like me. Heat flooded my cheeks. I was aware of everything, the way she strode into the room, scanning the study...until those brown eyes settled on me.

"Vivienne," she murmured carefully, taking a step toward me and reaching out her hand.

Until Carven moved, stepping in front of me. "I don't think so."

A flash of anger tore across London's face, then disappeared. Carven turned to her, but still stood in front of me as he met Helene's stare. "I don't trust you. I sure as hell don't fucking like you. You make a move toward Vivienne, and I'm going to take that as a threat. You feel me?"

She lowered her hand; her gaze flicking to me before she turned back to Carven. "I understand. You're still sore about what happened in the boatyard."

"Sore?" he snarled, then took a step closer. "You almost cost me her fucking life. Do you get that?"

She flinched, her face growing pale. "Yes, that's why I'm here." I'd give her one thing, she was ballsy meeting that savage glare from the Son without flinching. "We're on the same side here."

"Where have I heard that before?"

She didn't rise to the bait, just gave a soft nod. "I need to earn your trust. I get that. I'm here, ready to join forces to search for your brother. Every second we stand here arguing about alliances is a second too long. You know that. I know that. I don't have to remind you what kind of hell he's enduring right now."

Carven moved closer, until he was nose to nose, his tone chilling. "No, you don't."

"Good," she answered, turning to London. "I have new intel coming in any day now. So how about we get to work?"

EIGHTEEN

Colt

"Are you fucking dead yet?"

I cracked open my eyes as a snarl reverberated in the middle of my chest. But it wasn't my chest, nor was it my growl. It was *his*, the *beast*. He snapped his head upwards as heavy boots sounded in the dark room. Trembling muscles flexed as he drove our body through the dark. His hand reached out, clawing the air as though there should be talons on the end of the bleeding stubs.

But there weren't...there weren't even nails, not after they'd ripped them off.

There was only pain.

The beast lunged, desperate to snap and savage and run. *God, he was desperate to run.* Until the chain snapped taut and the shackle around his throat snapped us backwards, slamming us to the cold, filthy floor once more.

Laughter came from the male. Sick, abrasive laughter.

It spilled like acid all over me, snatching the last traces of warmth inside me.

No. Inside him. The beast.

The scrape of boots ended. In the gloom, the beast saw him, dark eyes scanning the damage he'd done. There was a wince before he lifted his hand, covering his nose. "Christ, you're disgusting."

"Fuck you." The words rumbled through our chest.

I felt those words. I *said* those words. Still, they sounded like him. Coarse, husky, his throat bruised from the steel cinched tight.

"It seems your...*father* and your brother are causing me some problems."

The beast stilled, sucking in a hard breath. Memories drifted in the darkness of his mind. Faint memories. Faces he couldn't quite understand.

I've got you, son. The deep male voice rose. *Hold on to me, Colt. I've got you.*

Colt.

Blue eyes replaced the darkened stare. Blue eyes, he knew. *Brother.* The word slammed into me, making my pulse boom. Brother. I knew him. *We protect him. We. Protect. Him.*

"They've torn apart half the fucking city." The man in front of us spat. In the murky light, the man's lips curled. "But they won't find you."

He stepped closer, so close the beast could almost...

Chain links gnashed. A swipe through the air went unrewarded. *Hate. HATE!*

"They can burn all the fucking buildings they want. They can torture, they can kill. They can howl and kick and scream like a wailing child as much as they want to. But it'll get them nowhere."

He lifted his gaze, meeting the beast's. "They won't find you until it's too late. I'll enjoy watching them fall apart, them and that *bitch* you fuck. Wildcat...more like used cunt."

Wildcat?

A roar unleashed, bloodied and blistering, ripping through my throat as her face came to me. Her face. Her *beautiful* face.

I strained against the end of the chain so tight I felt the beat of my heart in my face. *Thud...thud...thud.* Veins popped, stinging as I drove harder, until the steel clamped around my throat choked me. I snarled, baring my teeth, the words a hot rasp. "Touch her and you're fucking dead."

The male never flinched, never backed away.

Just stared at me like the beast I was.

My chest was on fire.

The kind of fire that burned all the way down. I swallowed hard and tasted blood.

"I would say goodbye, Son, but there's nothing good about it." He took a step backward toward the light spilling in through the cracked open door. "Enjoy your last days in this cell. Maybe in your next life you'll do well to stay away from the likes of me."

Then he turned.

I flinched with every step until the howl of the hinges made me whimper.

Then slowly my legs shuddered and gave out.

Thud.

I hit the cold floor and collapsed; the shackle digging into the flesh of my throat. How many days had it been now? Days...*weeks?* I didn't know. What I did know was, I wasn't going to make it. I knew that, knew from the hot coals burning somewhere in the middle of my chest. I wasn't going to see them ever again. I wasn't going to see her...

Wildcat.

The name stayed with me as I closed my eyes. But there were no more tears. Nothing but the sting.

Until the squeal of the door came once more. Only this time the steps were slower and heavier.

Buzz...

A hitch ripped through my chest as I opened my eyes to the arc of neon light...and the face of my tormentor.

"Now, how about we speed up that end a little, huh?" The bastard smiled. "Time to dance for me, big guy."

NINETEEN

Vivienne

O̲h̲ G̲o̲d̲.

I rolled over in bed, closed my eyes, and swallowed.

Then I swallowed again.

And again.

I was going to be sick.

I wrenched open my eyes and shot out of bed, stumbling for the bathroom. Acid hit the back of my throat as I shoved my head over the toilet and gagged. My belly clenched, upending what little there was...it was mostly air. But even expelling that felt better.

Did I eat something bad? I lifted my head, swiped the dribble from my mouth, and slowly straightened. My days were a blur of rage and desperation. Empty house after empty house, desolate building after desolate building. That's all I remembered. I could hardly think about which assholes connected to The Order we'd beaten and threatened, let alone what I'd eaten last night for dinner. Still, I tried.

Some kind of steak and vegetables Guild cooked for us? I think... or was that the night before?

No...

No, that was definitely last night.

Maybe that was it? Maybe the meat had turned.

But as soon as the thought entered my head, I shook it away. There was no way Guild would serve up foul meat for us to eat. That man was careful in the most excruciating way while looking after us. Even after the chef had left and never came back, we'd never eaten a single unhealthy or imperfect meal.

Guild made sure of that. Even if he cooked with a gun on the counter.

My belly tightened again, making me wince. I jerked my head to the side and slammed my hand on top of the cold ceramic tank as I retched. *Jesus, whatever it was...this was bad.*

I heaved and heaved, burping and coughing, until at last the roller coaster in my belly slowed, finally letting me rise to go to the sink and reach for the faucet. Even the cold water tasted weird as I washed my mouth, swished, then spat. I lifted my gaze to the mirror, then grabbed a toothbrush and toothpaste and scrubbed.

It was the stress. That's what it was.

The stress of everything.

How many days had it been now?

Not days. I froze, the brush pressed against my molars. It was weeks.

Weeks without him. Weeks without knowing if he's even alive. I closed my eyes, rocking on my feet. My belly swished, then settled. Even nausea took a backseat to my fucking heart ripping in two.

We were still searching. Still hunting, day after day.

But the nights…the nights were the cruelest of all.

My body clenched. My breath caught.

Even my pulse sped, remembering how many times we'd fucked.

It wasn't love, what we were doing. No matter how many times I wanted to tell myself it was.

How could it be when our hearts were gone?

No heart. No love. There wasn't even air when Colt was gone.

I closed my eyes, gripped the sink, and bowed my head. *Please, God, give him back to me.*

Tears welled and slipped free. I'd give anything, do anything. I'd *suffer any pain,* just to hold him once more. To feel those hands on my skin and his lips on mine. Throw me back in that dark dungeon at The Order. Throw me to the guards for all I cared. It wouldn't matter. I'd go gladly.

But this…

This not knowing.

This *emptiness* was killing me.

No. It was killing *us.*

I lifted my head, pulled the toothbrush free, and rinsed. Maybe that's all it was? Just stress. Just a broken fucking heart. I stepped to the towel bar, grabbed the plush blood-red fabric, and wiped my mouth, hitting my breast as I straightened. An ache bloomed, making me wince.

Oww.

I looked down, dropped the towel back on the bar, and gently cupped the swell of my breast. Fuck, that hurt. I yanked up the top of my pajamas and looked down, searching for a bruise. But there was none. I cupped my other breast and caught my breath. That was just as sore. Almost like I was getting my—

Period.

I froze. My pulse booming. My damn period. I tried to count the weeks. It had been weeks. *Lots of weeks.* Panic filled me as I tried to remember how many exactly it'd been since I'd had my last one. The one where Colt had thought London had hurt me.

It was over a month...

It was over two weeks now that he'd been gone.

Six weeks since my last period. *Maybe even more.*

Gonna put a baby in you, pet. London's growl pushed into my head. *By the time I'm done with you, they'll know...they'll all fucking know. Who. You. Belong. To.*

They'd been just words to me. Just desire. Just his consuming way of possessing me. But now. Now, they felt real. I clenched gently, finding that deep tender ache. Still, I couldn't say anything. Not now. They'd treat me differently. London would. Carven would, for sure. I needed to be the same for them. The same hunter, the same *Wildcat*.

Even if I *said* nothing, I had to be sure.

But how? It wasn't as though I could ask either of them to run to the drugstore, and there was no way London was letting me near any of his cars again. So, what? I walk there. It can't be over ten miles to any kind of store and I sure as hell can't call an Uber.

I needed someone I could trust. Someone who would get me what I needed. I needed...

Guild. Guild would get it for me.

But would he go to London? He was loyal to him, that I knew. Loyal to a fault. But he also wasn't a lapdog. He might...he might help me.

With no other options, I would take that risk.

I left the bathroom behind, dressed in what was becoming my usual attire of black jeans and a long-sleeved black top, before I pulled on my boots and headed out of my bedroom. Nausea followed, especially when the bitter stench of coffee hit me.

I winced, bit down on my lip, and headed into the kitchen, to find Guild standing over the machine. He lifted his head, glancing over his shoulder as I strode into the kitchen. "Fresh brewed. Ready for a cup?"

I winced, shaking my head and earning myself a scowl.

"No?"

I stopped at the edge of the counter. "No, thank you. I can't..."

He turned abruptly, concern in his eyes. "You okay?"

My pulse spiked, making me tremble. I held my breath, glanced over my shoulder at the doorway of the kitchen, and strained to hear London or Carven before I turned back. "If I asked you to do something for me, could I trust you not to tell London or Carven?"

He scowled. "It would depend on what you're asking me to do. Is there someone causing you problems?"

"What? No," I whispered, my mind drifting to that little bean inside me. If I was indeed pregnant. "I mean, not really. I just..."

This wouldn't work. I couldn't be sure. Not *really* sure. "You know what?" I murmured. "Never mind. Forget I asked."

I turned away, my stomach sinking.

"Hey," Guild growled softly. He grabbed my arm before I knew it, easing me around to face him. His dark brown eyes searched mine. "What's going on?"

Stupid. Goddamn. Tears. They blurred his face. "It's nothing." I tried, my voice husky.

"Doesn't look like nothing to me."

I shook my head. The words I was desperate to say sat rock hard in the back of my throat.

"Tell me."

I shook my head.

"Vivienne."

I met his stare. "Can I trust you?"

I was pushing him into a corner. One where I was asking him to divide his loyalties.

"Will this piss London off?" he asked.

I gave a shrug. "Probably."

"Could this be dangerous to you if I don't do it?"

I thought about that, about the buildings we invaded and the men we fought. One punch to the stomach, that's all it'd take. I answered the only way I could. "Yes."

"Then I'll do it. Pissing London off is one thing, but if this could cause you harm, then I won't have that. What do you need, honey?"

I held his gaze and, using all the courage I had, whispered the words I was terrified to use. "I need a pregnancy test."

His eyes widened before he lowered his gaze. *"Preg—"*

I slammed my hand over his mouth, muffling the words. "Shhh." My eyes darted to the doorway as I listened for any sound in the hall. "Not so loud, okay?"

He gave a nod, his breath hot against my fingers before I removed them. Here was a man easily twice my size, who probably had more kills than I'd had hot dinners to his name, letting me shush him.

"You need a..." He started slowly, keeping his voice low.

"Yes."

"Now?"

One brow rose. "Well, the sooner you get it, the sooner I can know for sure."

I'd never seen him move so fast, turning around to stride from the kitchen in a heartbeat.

"Guild?" I heard London call from his study. *"Guild!"*

"I'm busy! I'll be back soon. I need a...*a turnip!*"

I didn't dare move as the creak of London's chair came before the heady thud of his steps. "What the fuck?" His growl reached me in the kitchen from the hallway. "I don't even like turnips."

How long did a damn trip to the drugstore take?

I paced the floor of my bedroom, casting glances toward the door. I'd avoided London by telling him I wasn't feeling well. It wasn't a lie. I just didn't elaborate.

The heavy thud of footsteps out in the hallway drew my gaze. They were too fast to be London's...unless he'd found out.

Oh, shit.

I steeled myself for the onslaught as the handle of my bedroom door turned. But Guild stepped in with a brown paper bag clutched in his hand and closed the door behind him. I let out a pent-up breath, feeling myself deflate.

"They looked at me strangely," he offered. "So I had to tell them it was for my wife."

"Your wife?"

He gave a shrug, his cheeks turning bright red. I thought of Guild saying those words for someone he truly loved one day and my chest swelled with pride. I hoped one day he had that.

"Thank you." I moved forward and grasped the bag from his hand.

But he just stood there, looking awkward.

"What?"

He gave a shrug, then glanced toward the bathroom.

"You want to wait?" I hissed.

I could see in his eyes he was dying to know. But then he shook his head. "Be safe, Vivienne." He turned and went to the door, then stopped with his hand on the handle. "Just know, whatever you need. Whatever that costs me, you can always come to me."

Damn if that wasn't the sweetest thing he'd ever said to me. With my heart in my throat, I gave a nod and watched him leave the room. When the quiet *thud* of the door came, I turned for the bathroom.

My hands were shaking as I pulled the box free, then the test from the packet. Reading the instructions, I tugged off the end, adjusted myself over the toilet, and aimed for the end.

Seconds felt like hours. I placed the test on the basin, unable to stop my hands from shaking. I didn't pray, because I didn't know what to pray for.

Negative.

Positive.

It didn't matter. But as I stood there watching the faint line on the test, I knew I was lying.

It mattered.

It mattered very much.

TWENTY

Vivienne

D<small>ING</small>. T<small>HE ELEVATOR DOOR OPENED.</small>

"Vivienne," London murmured, staring straight ahead. "Behind me, pet."

I stopped with my gun in my hand as London stepped out of the elevator on the twenty-sixth floor of a building in the middle of the city. One filled with powerful men in expensive suits just like the one London wore now. But he didn't look like the stuffy assholes who'd glared at us as we'd walked through the foyer downstairs. He looked like violence wrapped in black Ferragamos.

Polished boots hit the gleaming tiled floor of the foyer with a *thud*. Perfectly cut trousers pulled taut around powerful thighs as he lengthened his stride. Three other men flanked him. Paid mercenaries dressed in black cargos and tight t-shirts, leaving me to follow.

It wasn't just fresh intel my sister, Helene, had given him. It was a whole other level of aggression, one London took to very well. He never once looked nervous as he headed toward the frosted glass doors on the top floor of the building. Ones etched with *Harmon Inc.*

No, he looked like a shark hunting...and he didn't just smell blood.

He smelled a massacre.

Harmon Inc. was one of The Order's newest and biggest financial backers...the chairman, Julius Harmon, was, as of now, one of Hale's latest best friends, and was helping him escape the city.

Over his dead body, where the words London muttered as Helene handed over all the information she had on Julius Harmon. While Carven, Guild, and Harper led teams that raided various parts of the city, we'd waited for the intel Helene had orchestrated to finally come in. Three days of strategic planning later, and here we were.

London pushed through the glass doors, leaving one mercenary to catch the swing and hold it open for me.

"Sir?" The receptionist rose behind a high gleaming glass desk. Her eyes widened, taking in London, then the three massive males, before those wide eyes settled on me.

She swallowed hard, then fumbled for the telephone in front of her.

One of our men stopped in front of her desk. "Uh-uh," he murmured, reaching over the counter to place the handset in her grasp back down. "Let's not do that, shall we?"

We left him behind and followed London as he headed down the long hallway to the closed office door at the end. He was past the point of discussion now, well beyond anyone capable of seeing reason. He lifted his leg, unleashed his boot at the edge of the door and kicked it in with a *crack!*

"Julius Harmon," he said coldly, swinging that deadly stare through the room. "Let me introduce myself. My name is London St. James...and you have information I want."

"What the fuck?" One of the men burst out, his gaze moving to the two other men flanking the table.

But it was the two bodyguards standing at the front of the room they focused on. The men reacted. One reached into his jacket for a weapon as the other one rushed forward, charging one of the armed men. London moved so fast I barely saw it.

Bang!

The crack resounded before the bodyguard in front of him pulled his gun. Blood bloomed in the middle of his forehead before he slumped to the floor.

"What the *FUCK IS GOING ON?*" Julius Harmon roared, shoving to his feet so hard his chair toppled to the floor.

"Like I said, you have something I want and I'm here to get it."

I gripped the gun, my focus on the mercenary and the other bodyguard as they collided with a sickening *crunch*. I swung my gun, my focus on the threat in front of me. I didn't hear the soft creak of the connecting door at my back.

"Don't fucking move." The low growl came from behind me.

London swung his gaze around as the man behind me lifted a gun and pressed it against my head.

"No hasty moves," he murmured in my ear. "Don't want to see the bitch's brains splattered all over the room now, do we?"

If it'd been at any other time before Colt had been taken, I might've been terrified enough to do exactly what he demanded. But like London, I was past the point of fear, steeped well in rage.

"Easy," I whispered. "I'll do anything you say."

I lowered my hand and aimed the gun straight down before I slipped my finger around the trigger and fired.

Bang!

The asshole behind me screamed, shoving me hard. I shoved my hands out, frantically trying to stop the blow. Still, I slammed into the edge of the table so hard a moan ripped free.

"You fucking bi—" The gunman behind me started.

Bang!

He never finished before London shot him, striding around the long boardroom table in the middle of the room. *"Want to keep going?"* he roared, swinging the muzzle of the gun around the room, stopping on the piece of shit who had to be Julius Harmon.

Because the bastard turned a weird shade of ash.

"You okay, kitten?" London captured my chin, turning my gaze to his.

He searched my eyes for the truth. I winced, but gave a nod. My hands had taken most of the impact, my hips the rest as I'd turned at the last minute, shielding my stomach from the blow. "Yes."

He gave a nod, then turned on the others. "Any more surprises?"

The other four men sitting at the table gave frantic shakes of their heads.

"Good," London crooned. "Very good."

A chill swept along the nape of my neck at his tone. I'd seen him in action before, seen him dangerous, seen him deadly even. But this...this was a whole new level of chilling as he lifted his boot and rested it on Julius Harmon's armrest, his gun dangling down.

"I don't want to kill anyone else...but I will." He narrowed in on the object of his wrath. "I will do whatever it takes to protect my family, as I'm sure you would. Isn't that right, Julius?"

The piece of shit in front of him opened his mouth to speak. "What the fuck are you saying?"

London just gave a shrug, pulling his phone from his pocket. "Just what I said. After all...family is *everything.*" He pressed a button, listening to it ring on the other end before Carven answered it.

"Carven." London stared at Julius. "Please show Mr. Harmon how serious we are?"

Muffled moans came through in the background. I glimpsed dark shadows before the camera panned around.

"Katie?" Julius barked.

The gagged woman tied to a chair came awake in an instant. Her eyes bugged wide.

Moans came from Julius. Gasps of utter terror from the other four men around him were simultaneous.

"Now, we let her know you'd be late getting home tonight," London murmured, then lifted his gaze to the other men. "All of your wives..."

"What the fuck?" one asshole barked.

"Veronica Andrews, red-haired, five foot six, drives a black Range Rover, license plate number—"

"*Enough!*" he roared, gripping the armrest beside him. "Just enough!"

London met every gaze of the men sitting around the table. "They won't be harmed, not your wives or your children, as long as you do what I say."

"Motherfucker." Another stared daggers at the man who wouldn't blink twice at ending their miserable fucking lives. But he wouldn't touch a hair on their wives' or their children's heads.

Now, Carven.

Carven was a whole other matter.

"Now that we're well acquainted with each other, I'll tell you why I'm here," London murmured.

"I know why you're here."

London turned on him, staring into Julius Harmon's eyes. "Good, I was never one for pretense. Now, tell me where and when you're getting Haelstrom out of the city."

There was a curl of his lips. Hate seethed in his stare. "You'll never get away with it."

London leaned down, so close he could almost breathe the same air. "If you think I give a fuck about what happens to me after this, you're dead wrong. I want Hale...and you're going to give him to me, otherwise I'm going to make a call...and you can listen to my son kill everyone you've ever loved."

"He'll be gone before you even scream his name."

London's lips curled. "Try me."

Rage burned in both their stares until, with a snarl, Julius spoke. "Edgemont crossing."

Surprise claimed London's stare. "The river? He's escaping by boat?"

But Julius leaned back in his chair. "I've told you what you wanted. Now let us go."

London glanced at me, then grabbed his phone. "What time?"

Julius was silent.

"I said WHAT TIME?"

"Nine p.m." The answer was a mumble as he stared daggers at the man I loved.

I clenched my fist around the gun in my hand, consumed with the need to put a bullet in his skull. "Don't fucking look at him like that."

London stopped typing on his phone, lifting his gaze to me.

But I couldn't stop the wall of anger that slammed into me. I lunged across the room, grabbed that foul, fucking excuse for a man by his crisp white shirt and yanked him toward me. He smirked at my outburst. I knew I was letting him get to me, but

Claimed

I couldn't stop it. *"You don't look at him like that!"* I screamed in his face.

"Pet?" London said carefully.

I sucked in hard breaths, trying to come back down from the rage. They didn't get to look at him like that. Like he was the monster here. Not after what they've done. "Do you even know what they did to us?" I whisper. The rage hadn't left me, but this wasn't the blistering burn. No, it sank deeper and as it did, it grew colder. I glanced at my fists, clenched tight around his shirt, then met the amusement in his stare. "Did you know they used to force us into that room? Down into the dark and the cold. Down where the rats waited. Did you know they hurt us there? That they made us do vile things to them and each other? Did you also know that's where we found them?"

"Vivienne," London warned.

But I was past the point of caring. I wanted this *man* to know exactly what they did there. "All the Daughters. The women your new friend Haelstrom Hale created to traffic and abuse. They forced them down into that room and they made them stand against the wall. They would've been terrified, crying, holding onto each other as the man you think so highly of had his guards lift their guns and murder all of them."

That smile faded on his face.

"We found them still clinging to each other," I whispered. "Their faces barely recognizable from the bullet holes Hale's men left behind."

There was no more amusement now. Not even a hint of the sneer he'd carried seconds ago.

Instead, he swallowed, his voice a croak. "You're mistaken. Haelstrom wouldn't do something like that."

"You have no fucking idea what Haelstrom would do," London snarled, finishing typing before he rose. "He's using you. Just like he uses everyone. He has no loyalty. He has no soul. He cares for only his sick, twisted needs, and you..." He glanced around the table. "Almost helped him escape."

London lowered his boot and straightened. "Never mind all that now." He glanced toward the men we'd come with. "My men here will stay and keep you company. After all, we can't have you making any calls and disrupting Haelstrom's desperate plan to escape justice."

He glanced my way, then lifted his hand for me. "Pet?"

I released my hold, shoving the piece of shit back against his seat. "You need to choose your friends more wisely." I looked down at him. "Or the next time we see each other I might give you a firsthand taste of the depravity your buddy likes so much."

Something dangerous slithered across his stare.

Something that made me flinch. Maybe Julius Harmon knew exactly the man Haelstrom Hale was? Maybe he more than knew. Maybe he was one of The Order? My pulse raced at the thought and my mouth turned dry.

"I'll be watching you," I whispered, even if fear made my voice tremble. I forced myself to turn my head, meeting every stare. "I'll be watching all of you."

London's outstretched hand waited, leaving me to take it.

"You'll see they remain here until this is over?" London asked one of his men.

"Yes, sir," the mercenary replied, giving me a careful stare.

But it wasn't me they should be wary of. My thoughts drifted to Carven, and then like they always did, to Colt. It was those men like Julius should be careful of. Men who were bred to hunt and destroy but who now had a conscience. Thanks to men like London.

I gripped his hand as he led me out of that boardroom, leaving the others behind. The mercenary standing in the reception area gave a nod as we walked past. But then we were out of there, heading to the elevator.

My knees shook, locking and unlocking as I stumbled for the elevator doors. But London was there, letting go of my hand to grasp me around the waist. "Easy," he murmured, frantically stabbing the button for the elevator's doors. "I got you, kitten. Learn on me."

I did, clawing hold of his shirt, barely keeping myself upright before I lunged into the elevator and collapsed against the wall. As the doors closed, London rushed me, sliding his hands under my arms to lift me up. "Vivienne?"

I sucked in hard gasps, watching the lights in the elevator darken then grow neon bright. "I'm okay," I said, mostly to myself. "I'm okay."

My legs grew steadier, holding my weight more easily.

"What the fuck happened?"

I closed my eyes, unable to meet his gaze. *No...this isn't the time.* "Nothing," I answered.

Still, he grasped my chin and tilted my head up. "Look at me."

I squeezed my eyes closed.

"Vivienne."

There was that tone again, the deep, authoritative growl I was helpless to deny. I opened my eyes, seeing the desperate concern in his. "You okay?"

My belly dropped as the elevator stopped at the first floor. I gave a nod, steadying myself as I let go of the elevator wall. "I'm fine."

"You're *not* fine," he disagreed.

But it was too late to answer, too late to tell him the truth.

No, I wasn't fine.

I wasn't anywhere near *fine*.

I held a secret, one I was keeping from him.

One that would change everything if he knew.

"Vivienne." He called my name as I stumbled from the elevator.

The bright foyer lights and the afternoon sun were blinding, still I stumbled for that door.

For the fresh breath of air...and the desperate, fleeing seconds I needed to pull myself together.

I'm fine, I told myself as I remembered the thin white test I'd left on the counter in my bathroom.

A test that was undeniably *positive*.

TWENTY-ONE

London

"V*IVIENNE*."

She kept walking, headed to the Raptor parked in the lot next to the building, and stopped at the passenger side door before she mumbled, "Just unlock the car, London."

Exhaustion was etched deep in her tone, but there was something else.

Sadness. That's what it was. My Vivienne was sad.

Agony ripped through my chest. I pressed the button, letting her climb in. I did the same, sliding in behind the wheel, but I didn't start the engine. Not yet.

"Talk to me," I tried, turning to her. "Please, kitten."

I caught the shine of tears in her eyes before she averted her gaze to stare out the window instead. "It's nothing," she said, "just drive, *please*."

My pulse boomed. My jaw clenched.

She was keeping something from me.

That thought nagged me as I leaned forward, stabbed the button, and started the engine. I cast glances her way as I pulled out of the parking lot. I should look up at the windows on the top floor of the building, focused more on the men I was keeping hostage that very moment. But I couldn't even think about them.

Not even thoughts of Colt held my attention as I followed the marker on the GPS to a part of the city I'd never been to before. Blue water glinted in front of us, stretching out like a stunning oasis. But I barely looked at the view. Vivienne was my single focus, sitting silent in the seat beside me. Her arms wrapped around her middle like she was trying to hold on.

I'd never seen her snap like that.

Not in all the time I'd known her.

She was a fighter, a protector, and a lover.

She was the glue that kept us from sinking into this maelstrom of hate and rage, the only good thing in our goddamn miserable fucking lives. I ground my teeth and shook my head. Right now, she was changing before my eyes, turning into someone just like us, someone tainted by this goddamn world.

Someone filled with uncontrollable rage.

Just like...

Carven. That's what this was about. I knew it'd been a bad idea letting her go with the Son.

The red marker on the map blinked, the voice commands telling us we'd arrived at our destination. I turned the wheel and pulled the four-wheel drive into a darkened driveway shrouded with what looked like a damn rainforest on the outskirts of the city. I barely had enough time to scan the towering house nestled against the canopy before she stabbed the seatbelt and was gone.

"*For Christ's sake!*" I roared, punching the brakes and skidded to a stop as her feet hit the driveway.

Thud.

The door slammed behind her. She was gone, heading to the mammoth double doors at the front of the house as they opened. Helene stepped out, her focus fixed on her younger sister as I killed the engine, grabbed the large black bag in the back seat and, followed.

Helen shot me a look as I neared. "What happened?"

I just watched Vivienne disappear through the doors behind her. "Hell if I know."

I stepped inside, barely looking at the place as I searched for her. "Vivienne?"

"Come on." Helene strode past. "She can't be far."

I found her, standing in the darkened living room, staring at pictures of herself, Ryth, and Helene. The pictures were taken at different times and in different places. But standing here, staring at them, you could see they were blood.

"You never came to me." Her words were barely audible. "All these years, you stayed away."

"It wasn't safe," Helene stated.

"Oh, yeah?" Vivienne swung around, anger sparkling in her eyes. "For who, you?"

But Helene never flinched from the bite in her tone. Instead, she stepped closer. "For you."

"Where have I heard that before?" She shot me a glare.

"You think Hale would've treated you like the others if he knew you were Weylen's daughter?"

"Oh, that's right." Her words carried an edge of hysteria. "Tell me, where is Mr. King? I'd really like to meet him. You know, seeing as he is my blood and all. WEYLEN!" she roared, scanning the house behind us. *"HEY, MR. KING! IT'S ME, YOUR FUCKING FLESH AND BLOOD!"*

"Vivienne," Helene said carefully, never once taking her eyes off her.

But Wildcat never missed a beat as she stepped past us to head deeper into the house. *"DON'T YOU WANT TO MEET ME?"*

"Vivienne," Helene said once more.

My kitten spun, her hair wild. *"What?"*

There was a sad shake of her sister's head. "He's not here."

Vivienne threw her hands into the air. "Of course he's not. I mean, why the fuck would he be? It's not like I've *never laid eyes on the man.*"

Helene said nothing for a second, then slowly. "How about I make us something to eat? I've seen you hardly peck at your food."

In the blink of an eye, Vivienne crossed the room. Her tone was deadly as she held her sister's gaze. "Let's get one thing straight, shall we, *sister*? I'm here for Colt and *only* Colt. The moment we find him, I'll expect you to fade into the background and disappear, just like you've always done."

I winced at the icy tone.

"I'm sorry you feel like that," Helene said carefully. "I hope one day you might see things differently."

Vivienne never missed a beat as she answered coldly. "Not. Fucking. Likely."

The sound of an engine drew my focus. I was almost relieved when Helene gave a slow nod, pulled her phone from her pocket, and touched the screen. "It seems your boyfriend is here."

The *thuds* of car doors followed as Helene headed for the foyer. The moment she was gone, I stepped closer. "Vivienne."

"What, London?" she muttered bleakly. "What more could you possibly want from me?"

I stared, dumbfounded, as the front door opened and Carven strode in, followed by Guild and Harper. All three instantly noticed the icy chill in the air. My two best friends said nothing, but Carven was never that tactful.

He glanced from me to Vivienne, then back again, only this time his face was full of anger. "What the fuck happened?"

I wished to God I knew. But I didn't say that. I just shook my head.

"Food and fresh coffee are in the kitchen," Helene started as the sound of cars on the driveway sounded again. "The intel room is downstairs in the basement."

She glanced around the room. Everyone but Carven and I met her stare. There was only one woman I wanted to speak to, only one woman who held me transfixed. As Helene moved to the door to meet the rest of my team, Carven glared at me. "What the fuck went down?"

I shook my head, replaying the moment it had started. "There was an additional bodyguard, one we weren't expecting."

One brow rose on the son.

"He grabbed her from behind," I continued, watching her. But there wasn't a reaction. She stared at the floor, not once flinching, not even when I said, "But she handled it, acted like she was lowering her weapon, and shot the guy in the foot. He pushed her."

My pulse beat harder, remembering how he'd shoved her toward that desk. It had been just a push. I lowered my gaze to her hip as the others left, following Helene toward the kitchen.

"Wildcat." Carven took a step closer and brushed his finger along her cheek as he stared deep into her eyes. "Want to tell me what's going on here?"

Her cheeks instantly heated as she shook her head, avoiding his stare. "Nothing. I'm just…I'm just pissed off, that's all."

Carven smiled. "Pissed off is good. Pissed off is something we can use. But being unhinged, that shit will blow up in your face. Feel me?"

She gave a slow nod as she slowly glanced my way. "I'm sorry."

The words were a fist to my chest. I quickly closed the distance and brushed my thumb across her chin before tilting her gaze to mine. "You have not a goddamn thing to be sorry about. None of it. This rests entirely with me."

Her brow creased before she shook her head. "London, no—"

But I didn't need to hear her make excuses for me. "How about we join the others downstairs? We can plan this interception and I can show you how to move if you're grabbed like that again."

"Sounds like she moved just right, shooting the goddamn bastard. It was lucky I wasn't there. I would've cleared that boardroom table in a second."

He would've, too...but then so had my bullet, but with a lot less bloodshed.

"Coffee?" I asked as the sharp scent filled the air.

But Vivienne turned gray, shook her head, and covered her nose. "No. Jesus, no. Just water."

I scowled, then gave a nod.

"Let's go," Carven muttered, scanning the house. "I want to search every inch of this goddamn place."

I let him lead her away, watching them disappear before I headed for the others in the kitchen. Guild was waiting for me with a careful gaze. I searched, finding an empty cup placed on the counter. "What's that look for?"

He opened his mouth, about to say something, then shook his head. "Nothing," he muttered before he turned and headed after the others.

What the fuck was going on?

I followed, making my way down a set of steel stairs to the rooms underneath. This wasn't just a bunker. It was an entire goddamn facility.

Harper whistled in astonishment, staring around at the same hi-tech set up we'd found in that deserted house hunting for King. This moment had been years in the making. I'd dreamed about this moment, hungered for this moment. I'd *killed* for this moment.

Yet as I stepped down the last stair, followed Vivienne across the massive room that spanned the entire house, and headed for the furthest point away from everyone, I couldn't...give... two...fucks.

"Pet," I called, following her. I surged forward and grabbed her arm. "Hey."

She didn't fight me. That was good...*that was real good.*

I was aware of the others as they gawked and asked Helene a million different questions. All except for Carven, who stood there watching us. I glanced over my shoulder, finding his stare, then turned back to her. I needed to change tactics, needed to find a way for her to talk to me.

"The balls," I muttered.

"What?" she asked, confused.

I stepped around her to stand at her back. I was careful, so damn careful not to trigger her as I brushed my finger along her jaw and whispered against her ear. "Easy now."

My forearm went across her throat, tight enough to drive her back against me while I grabbed her other hand. "In this position, he is as vulnerable as you are."

She stiffened.

"If you don't have your gun, you still have your hands." I gently tugged her arm, urging her to reach behind, then flattened her hand over the bulge in my pants.

"I'm not giving you a hand job," she seethed.

The thought of that set my nerves on fire. Still, I murmured, "As enticing as that sounds, pet, I'm showing you how with one hard twist, you can drop the bastard behind you to his knees."

She clenched, gripping tightly enough to make me catch my breath. "Like this?"

"Yes," I grunted. "Just like that."

I tightened my hold, my senses flaring out behind me, making sure we weren't the object of their focus as I stroked my hand down and cupped her breast. "You being pissed off at me only makes me want to fuck you even more."

She moaned, but it wasn't one of desire. It was one of pain. Instantly I eased my touch and stepped away. "Vivienne, what's wrong?"

She shook her head, cupping her breasts against her chest, groaning softly. "Nothing."

My phone vibrated in my pocket, making me curse. I yanked it free, dividing my focus between the caller ID and her. *Benjamin Rossi.*

Panic flared at the name, but I could see her pulling away from me. The fleeting fucking flare of amusement that she had fewer detesting thoughts was disappearing, but leaving an empty, wounded look in her eyes once more.

Fuck.

I took a step away, punching the screen. "What?"

"They have Ryth and the Bank's boys." Those words made my blood run cold. "Dante Ares, the Caines, and others I'm not sure of yet."

"The Mafia? How? Why?"

"They see them as an advantage, one they can use. They know King is involved somehow, they also know The Order is splintering. So, they want to use them."

"As fucking bait?" I forced through clenched teeth.

"Bait and weapons," Ben said coldly as the engine of his truck roared in the background. "But we won't let that happen. Lazarus and I are on our way to intercept them. I expect there will be lines of our own drawn tonight. I just wanted you to be ready."

I lifted my gaze to Vivienne. "Whatever you need, all you have to do is say the word."

"I'll let you know as soon as we have them."

"I appreciate that," I answered, then hung up the call.

But I couldn't move, for a second. My mind raced with a tornado of thoughts, all centered around her. All I could do was replay that moment in the boardroom today, the moment she hit that desk, twisting her body at the last second to hit her hip...and not her stomach.

Not her stomach.

I glanced at the way she cupped her breasts, protecting them like they were sore.

My heart hammered.

The world tilted and stood still.

Jesus.

"Problem?" Vivienne cast a careful gaze my way.

I stepped closer, holding that terrified stare. "Well, pet, that depends." I lowered my gaze to the way she cupped her sore breasts against her chest. "Are you going to tell me when was the last time you had your period?"

She flinched, and her eyes widened.

I saw it then.

Saw the truth raging in her eyes.

She was pregnant.

TWENTY-TWO

Vivienne

He took a step closer, inciting terrifying panic inside me. "Well, Vivienne? When was the last time you bled?"

Tell him.

Tell him right now.

And everything will change. *Everything. Will. Change.*

"*London!*" Helene called from across the room, tearing her gaze from her phone and shattering the moment. "We have new intel on a possible location for Colt."

Heads snapped her way. A pang ripped across my chest as I turned. Everything changed at that moment. London left my side, striding toward her. "Where?"

"They don't know yet," she answered, glancing from London to me. "We could finally extract some information from one of the IT chips from the Vault."

"The Vault?" London searched the room. "You have information from there?"

Only then did I finally look around, to the screens and screens of information flickering across what looked like glass walls. But they weren't walls, they were some kind of monitors.

"Yes." She moved to one of them. "And have for the last three years. I've had countless IT guys on this, but we've never been able to break the code...until now."

"What changed?" Harper asked.

She answered, reciting some coding information I had no idea about. Still, whatever it was, it rocked Harper where he stood.

"The information," London growled, bringing them back to the real reason we were here.

"There's a list of condemned buildings that were purchased by The Order. They range from old slaughterhouses to closed down import/export warehouses. I have three teams working through them now."

"How long?" he growled.

I stepped closer as she answered. "Five, six hours tops."

He shook his head, mentally calculating the difference between capturing Hale or hedging our bets on information that may or may not turn up anything. Because we'd been here before, hadn't we? We'd had information they swore was where The Order was holding Colt. Intel that'd been wrong. Could we risk it now? Right when we almost had Hale?

I glanced at London as he scanned the others, stopping at Carven. "We get this done. Drag Hale back here and extract the information we need, then we'll know. We'll know for sure."

There was relief in Carven's stare.

Relief I felt to my core.

My hand lowered to my stomach on reflex, drawing my focus.

Soon, I whispered inside my head.

I SHIVERED in the blistering cold, huddled hard against Carven as we waited in the back of the Raptor for the signal to move in. I scanned the darkness outside the vehicle, then glanced at the clock on the dashboard. 8:55.

Five minutes.

"We need to move," Carven growled.

"Not yet," London answered. "Not until we get the signal."

"The timing is critical," Guild said in front of us in the passenger seat.

"You think I don't know that?" Carven snapped. "This is my brother's life hanging in the balance. If we miss this...if we—"

I squeezed his hand. "We won't." I met London's stare in the rear-view mirror. "We won't miss this."

"There's movement." Harper's voice cut through the moment, bringing a whole new level of tension. *"Headlights are coming this way."*

I turned my head, catching the faint glimmer through the trees lining the river's edge in front of us. *Now?* I turned back to London. *Do we go now?*

"You have your gun, pet?" London questioned softly.

I met his stare, those dark eyes dangerous. Still, I gave a nod.

"Then we move," London finished.

"Finally." Carven yanked the handle and shoved out of the car. I slid after him as both London and Guild opened their doors.

Until Harper's voice came through the two-way once more. *"Wait."*

We froze.

Red and blue flashed.

The police?

More lights followed...*a lot of them.*

"What the fuck is happening?" London barked into the handset.

"Hell if I know," Harper responded. "Standby."

Standby? STANDBY?

My pulse was racing. My nerves were shot to hell. I gripped the gun at my side.

Seconds.

That's where hell waited. In those moments while we waited.

"London..." Harper's voice cracked through.

London raised the two-way to his lips. "What is it?"

"You're not going to fucking believe this," Harper growled. "There's a fucking news van."

What?

"That's it. I'm coming," London snapped, glancing at the others.

Slowly, we all holstered our weapons. Guild walked around to the rear of the four-wheel drive and opened the door before shutting it once more.

"Here," he muttered, handing out black windbreakers. "The last thing we need is more attention."

We all took the jackets, heading to where more headlights filtered through the trees. The bitter cold wrapped around me as I followed Carven between spindled trees with weapons for branches. Headlights burned brighter, but my focus was drawn to the red and blue neon glare that made my panic rise to new heights.

A dark blur headed toward us until Harper's face came into view. "There's someone down at the water. The police are here and it sounds like the coroner is on the way."

"The coroner?" London jerked his gaze to Harper. "What the fuck for?"

"Sounds like they found a body in the water."

London glanced around. "Jesus fucking Christ. Hale is supposed to be here any goddamn minute!"

"I know."

London turned away, scanning the cars and the vans that now crowded the edge of the river. He raked his fingers through his hair. "This is a goddamn bust."

"Not yet," Carven muttered. "Not while we have those bastard's Hale needs in our grip."

But we couldn't hold them hostage forever. London knew that.

"There's a body!" The faint words reached us from the riverbank. News crews snapped to attention. The red and blue lights sent sparks in my eyes as that faint voice cried out. *"Oh, my GOD. It's HAELSTROM HALE!"*

"What. The. Fuck?" London's eyes bulged.

We all moved, striding toward the growing commotion. They seemed to come out of nowhere, more news vans, more people.

"Move!" London barged a cameraman out of the way as he readied himself for the story of a lifetime.

"Hey!" the asshole responded.

But none of us cared, stepping down to where the dark water lapped the high river edge. Faint red and blue lights bounced off the surface of the dark water in a moody kaleidoscope. The sight froze me to the spot as the four police officers crowding the edge pulled something toward the bank.

"This can't be happening." The words slipped from my lips as they hauled a very bloated body from the water.

All my rage.

All my hate.

Directed at one man alone.

Now I felt...*cheated*.

"*No fucking way!*" Carven took a step forward before he turned to London. "*So that's it? HE'S GONE?*"

Heads turned toward us.

I clenched my fists, my body shaking with uncontrollable rage. I wanted to launch myself toward them and slap that body across the face. *Wake up! WAKE THE FUCK UP!* He's not dead. He can't be...

"That's it. It's over," Carven whispered. "He's gone."

I waited for someone to respond, for them to say '*the fuck it is!*'

But no one did.

"*It's Hale!*" A woman cried out behind the detectives as they loaded the body onto a stretcher and hauled it up the embankment. "*It's Haelstrom Hale.*"

I didn't want to look at the body as they came closer, didn't want to see that same fucking face that haunted my nightmares. But as the two officers headed past us toward the white coroner's van, I found myself unable to look away.

Not him.

Not him.

I stared, finding the same face I'd seen so many times before. It *was* him. It was *Haelstrom Hale*. I turned away as my stomach clenched tight, driving acid all the way into the back of my throat.

No.

I lunged, tearing away from them, and stumbled forward in the dark.

"Vivienne?" London called.

But I couldn't stop. I had to get away from them as fast as I possibly could. Acid burned in the back of my throat. I fell to my knees, stiffening my arms on the cold ground as I retched.

"Vivienne?" London was right beside me, dropping to rub my back. "Easy now."

I shook my head as tears came once more. Why the fuck was I always crying? I didn't want to cry. I wanted to shoot Haelstrom Hale in the head and beat his stiff corpse until my body was as numb as my mind.

Beep.

London's phone vibrated.

"Fuck's sake," he snapped, pulling it from his pocket and answering it. "What now?"

The sharp catch of his breath made me wipe my mouth on my sleeve and turn toward him. London didn't breathe. He didn't blink. He stared at me, then said. "You found him? Where?"

My heart lunged. I shoved against the ground, pushing up.

"Jesus," London croaked and closed his eyes. *"Tell them NOT to go in until we get there! DO YOU HEAR ME?"*

My emotions plummeted as London turned from me to the others, lowered his phone, and called out. "We have him! *WE HAVE COLT!"*

TWENTY-THREE

Colt

T*HUD*.

Thud.

Thud...thud...thud...thud...thud.

My eyes cracked open at the sound.

Hinges squealed. Darkness moved in.

A savage sound ripped from my chest as I lifted my head.

The echo of footsteps surrounded me until there was a *click*. Harsh light blinded me, forcing me slowly to my feet, before I lunged.

Kill them.

Kill them.

KILL.

KILL.

KILL.

The shackle snapped taut, strangling the sound. I clawed the air, desperate to reach them. *KILL—*

Until a soft choked sob came from somewhere in front of me.

"Jesus fucking Christ," someone barked.

Another moaned.

But it was that first noise I narrowed in on, finding eyes shimmering with tears.

"Colt?" a male called.

I stilled, sucking in hard breaths as the male stepped closer. The tang of blood bloomed in the back of my throat as I unleashed a warning sound. *I will...I will kill...*

But that wounded, feminine sound, that's what I wanted.

"Colt," That male came once more. "It's me. It's your...brother."

Brother?

I lunged with a roar, clawing, grasping, *desperate to rip and shatter. Get out of the way! I WANT HER!*

"Jesus fucking *Christ!*" The one who called me brother jumped backwards.

"Get back!" A deep booming voice rebounded. *"Everyone get back, now!"*

I swung my gaze toward the movement. I will kill...*I will KILL!*

"Baby," her voice broke through.

Baby?

Through the gloom, movement came, stepping from between the others. I stilled, swallowing my rage, transfixed by the sight of her.

"Fuck *no!*" That deep snarl bellowed as he stepped in her way.

"Stop, *Vivienne!*" The one who'd called himself *brother* moved in from the other side.

Both guarding her...*from me. They were guarding her from me.*

"Get *out of my way!*" She fought them "That's *my Colt.* He needs me...HE NEEDS ME!"

My eyes darted from her to the two other men, then back again. Desperation tightened my chest as she shoved their hands away and rushed past, her tear-filled eyes burning with anger.

Wildcat.

The name was branded in my mind.

"It's me..." she murmured, her focus solely on me. "You remember me, right?"

Movement came to my right. I swung toward it, unleashing a warning.

"*Hey,*" she snapped softly.

I jerked back to her instantly.

She shook her head, taking a slow step forward. "Over here, big guy. You don't need to worry about them. That's it, look at me. You remember me, right? I'm your Wildcat."

"Cat." The word was a hoarse snarl.

"That's it," she murmured, taking one step closer. "*Your* Wildcat."

They all watched her, every male in the room. For a second, I didn't like that. Get your eyes off her. *Mine...*

That movement came again, hedging closer at my right. But I didn't look at them...all I saw was *her*.

"You remember that night you watched over me?" she murmured. "While the storm unleashed over our house."

My heart boomed like thunder, an ache filled my chest.

Pressure came at the shackle around my throat, pushing, fumbling. I wanted to turn, started to, until fear widened her eyes.

"You must've been so scared yourself." She took a step closer. "Still, you sat there watching over me. My protector, aren't you? My big, strong, protector."

My nostrils flared, breathing her in. She was so close now, so close I could—my tongue snaked out, licking my lips. I wanted to touch her. I wanted to—

"I can't get the bolt free." The male that fumbled with the steel around my neck grunted.

"Get that fucking thing off his neck."

I jerked my head toward the deep growl. I knew that growl. I knew *all of them*. But the beast still claimed me. The beast was all I felt. *Kill...kill...you...*I tried to find that deadly hunger, but I couldn't.

These men sounded different.

They sounded...*familiar.*

Click.

The pressure around my throat fell away, the steel hitting the hard floor with a *clang*.

"Easy now," the male beside me urged, taking a slow step backwards. "We're not here to hurt you."

That bestial sound rumbled in the back of my throat as he stepped closer, lifting his hands. "Easy now, son...it's just me. It's Guild."

Guild?

I shook my head as he reached for me, that low, threatening sound rumbling deeper.

"Careful." That voice echoed. *Brother. Brother.*

I sucked in a hard breath, tasting blood. But underneath that foul, metallic tang came something else. A...*sweetness*. A scent that was familiar. Pressure came at my neck, but I was transfixed by that scent and by the...*by the...name. Brother.*

Snap.

"Easy now." The male beside me urged. "Your feet." He sounded nervous. "I just need to..." He sank to the floor beside me. I followed the movement, looking down at him. My lip trembled, curled and tight.

Snap.

The shackles fell away with a dull clank.

"Come on." That deep growl came from deeper in the room. "Let's get you the fuck out of here."

Are you dead?

Are you dead?

Those words resounded, booming, as the shadows shifted and moved all around me. This was too much. This was...

Are you dead?

I flinched at the words in my head. My heart was pounding. That...that voice in my head was screaming. That voice that knew *something*.

Brother.

Brother.

Brother...

I lunged, charging for them. A cry came. Softer, different as the roars descended.

"DON'T HURT HIM!" That deep roar rebounded off the walls in the cell.

I sucked in that sweet scent, drawing it down with the burn as I slammed into a body, sending it flying. A hard *grunt* followed. *Boom...BOOM...BOOM!*

Fight.

Fight.

Get out of here.

Gotta get back to...

"*Wildcat!*" That roar came as I lifted my fists, ready to rip and tear, ready to *destroy*.

I lowered my head and charged, watching as a dark blur rushed me, slamming into me hard.

Wildcat...

WILDCAT!

That name slammed into me. Blue eyes shone in the dark in front of me. Stark white hair. There was something familiar about him. Something...I shifted my gaze to the shadows behind him. To the faint, murky light that barely reached her, caressing her face.

Dark wide eyes grew impossibly wider. "Colt," she moaned. The sound made that booming in my chest seem even louder.

Fire burned deeper as I took a step, but the blond male stepped in front of me.

"No..." He growled and shook his head. *"You don't hurt her. She is ours. She belongs to us."*

Belongs to us.

Belongs to...me.

I closed my eyes, squeezing them closed, then I snapped them open and stepped forward, shoving the male aside. He stumbled, righting himself with a dangerous growl of his own. But I didn't care about him. All I cared about was *her*.

Agony ripped through my hand as I reached out and my bloodied fingers sank into gloom. I stepped forward, but she stepped back.

"Colt," the blond snarled. "Don't make me take you down, brother."

I whipped my gaze toward him as hate burned deep inside me.

"Easy now." That deep rumble came from the other male. "He won't hurt her."

"Yeah?" the one who'd called me brother snapped. "How the fuck do you know that?"

"Because if he wanted to, he would have."

I left that male behind, turning my attention back to *her*. She trembled, her breath trapped, as she took another step toward the door. The sight of that triggered me. The rest of the room blurred as I pushed forward, slamming into her and driving her against the wall.

A cry was snatched from her.

The choked sound was barely audible. But I heard it.

Wildcat...

Wild...cat.

I closed my eyes, pressing her hard against the wall and leaned down. One hard draw of that cold, dank air in the dungeon, and I swallowed her down.

I swear to God, Colt. You bark, wince, or gag and I'll NEVER show you anything again.

Her words came roaring back to me.

But *this* wasn't me. *This* was the beast. The one who wasn't capable of kindness. Only rage.

NO! That voice roared somewhere deep in my head. But I wasn't him...I wasn't...

"Colt?" she whispered.

I jerked my head upwards, hate spilling through every cell of my being and drove her spine against that dank wall.

"Wildcat." Her name was thunder in my chest. I closed my eyes and leaned down. With every breath, I tasted her. With every exhale, I craved her. *"Mine."* The beast staked its claim.

I ran my nose along her neck, licking her skin, triggering a primal, seductive sound in the back of her throat. Underneath the pain and burn, my body responded. I pressed against her, thrusting my hips before I gave one hard lick, then pushed away and stumbled through the open door of my cell.

"Colt!" The call came behind me. *"COLT!"*

They called.

But there was no Colt here.

There was only the beast.

TWENTY-FOUR

Vivienne

"*COLT!*" Carven roared.

All I heard was the *boom...boom...boom*.

But I didn't know if it came from my heart or Colt's fading footsteps. They all ran out, every single one, leaving me behind. I lifted my hand to touch the slick from Colt's tongue on my neck as it cooled against my skin and tried to understand what the fuck just happened.

"*Vivienne!*" London roared.

Thunder sounded once more, then he was there, filling up the doorway of the cell where we'd found Colt.

"Pet?" London gasped, and reached for my hand.

I met his stare, gave a nod, and finally moved, following him out of there. He held me as we ran, following the others along the dark, dank hall of the slaughterhouse until we came to the metal stairs we'd descended minutes before.

It felt like hours...days, almost. Days in that cold and the dank and the smell...*oh, God.* The smell.

My stomach clenched. Blood and death crammed my nostrils as I gripped London's big hand and raced up the stairs a step behind him.

"*Colt!*" Carven screamed, his voice booming through the space. "*COME BACK! WE WANT TO HELP YOU!*"

We ran between the filthy, empty pens that once held animals for slaughter, bursting out from the cracked open doors to stop dead in the middle of nowhere.

"Where the fuck did he go?" London growled, scanning the trees and the darkness.

"Hell if I know." Guild sucked in hard breaths as he pressed his hand to his shoulder and winced in pain.

London swivelled, meeting my gaze. "What the hell happened back there?"

He bellowed at me as though he wasn't right in the damn room himself. "What do you mean?" I shook my head, pulling my hand from his. "I tried to help him. I tried to—"

With a pissed off snarl, London started walking toward the trees surrounding the abattoir.

"I dunno what you all saw. But that...*that was not Colt.*" Guild shook his head as Carven appeared from the trees, striding toward us.

"Yes," London answered with his back to us, his tone grave. "It was."

I shook my head, remembering the pure lunacy in Colt's stare. *My Colt...MY COLT.* He was the man who'd held me, who'd loved me...who'd kept me safe. But that man...that...*that didn't look like him.*

"Maybe he's gone home." Carven shook his head as he strode to where the cars waited with engines still running and open doors.

Headlights spilled along the dirt outside the slaughterhouse. I followed the others, climbed back into the Raptor, and yanked the door closed barely a second before the four-wheel drive shot forward.

"He's alive," London muttered, scanning the trees as we drove to where Helene and her men waited parked by the side of the road. "That's the only thing that matters right now."

We stopped long enough for London to lean out the window and tell Helene briefly what had happened.

"We're heading back home," he finished. "If you hear anything else..."

She shifted her gaze to me sitting in the rear seat, and our gazes collided as she answered. "Of course, you'll be the first to know." She scowled, looking at me as though she wanted to say something.

But she didn't, just turned away at the same time I did.

Damn her.

I clenched my jaw, drawing my focus from the ache that seemed to rise when I looked at her. I didn't like her. I didn't even know her. The images of those photos came back. *But she seemed to know me, though, didn't she?*

That wasn't fair.

Because she was the one who'd wanted it that way.

Tires spun, kicking up stones to blast the underside of the Raptor as we sped away and raced for home. I scanned the trees as we passed, searching for movement. Carven did the same, his gaze on the darkness.

We have him!

We have Colt!

London's roar still resounded in my head as we drove. We stopped every few minutes, climbing out of the car, calling for Colt as we searched the trees between the slaughterhouse and the city. Still, there was no sign of him. The last hour was a blur, coming from the lowest lows then soaring to the highest of highs. I still felt that choke hold that had gripped me as they'd carried Haelstrom Hale's body past us to the waiting white can.

I'd thought it was over.

I'd thought we'd lost, until London said those words which changed everything.

We have Colt.

I pulled my attention from the past, forcing myself to focus. But did we? Did we really have Colt?

I wasn't so sure.

We headed back to the house. The moment we pulled into the driveway, Carven was out, calling his brother's name. I clawed the handle, desperately running after him. But as we raced along the hall to his bedroom, I couldn't help the thoughts from racing through my head. What the hell was going to happen when we found him?

Boom!

Carven threw open the door to his bedroom and raced inside. I hit the hallway, London and Guild a step behind. But as we all raced inside the darkened room, we knew he wasn't here.

"Where?" Carven spun, staring at London. "Where else would he go?" Torment was etched in his mesmerizing eyes as he shook his head. "The old house. He'd go there, right?"

"We can try," was all London offered.

We headed back out, climbed into the four-wheel drive once, and drove through the city to the other side. My mind raced, unable to shake the nagging feeling that it didn't matter how many houses we searched. Colt wasn't there.

Cat...

That hoarse sound Colt had gasped rose as we parked out front of the house I'd once lived in. Car doors opened and closed. That sound was a man clinging to sanity. A man beaten and tortured. A man lost...

"Vivienne?" London called my name, standing outside the car with the driver's door open.

I jerked my gaze to his.

"You can stay here."

"No," I answered, but my hands refused to move.

My scalp pulsed, the memory of my abduction roaring back to me. London opened my door and held out his hand. But it was all too much. Everything. All the desperation. All the longing. I just wanted...peace. Was that too much to ask? *"I just want some peace."*

"What?"

I shook my head, crashing back into reality. "Nothing," I answered, and climbed out, following London back into the house I both loved and loathed.

Moonlight filtered through the shrubs, casting shadows along the footpath to the house. I froze, letting London walk ahead. My mind replaced the murky spill with blood. This was where it had happened, where I'd changed forever.

"Pet?"

I nodded, forcing myself to follow him inside. My gaze instantly turned to the stairs and the bedrooms above as Carven strode along the hallway and headed back down the stairs. "He's not here." He raked his fingers through his hair. "I don't get it. He's hurt, probably bleeding internally. Where the fuck would he go?"

"He doesn't know anywhere else." Guild stepped into view, coming from the rear of the house.

"Yes," London answered. "He does."

We all looked at him as he added. "The one place he shouldn't want to go."

"No," Carven growled. *"No."*

My stomach clenched. I tried to swallow the acid in the back of my throat. But I knew...we *all* knew, even if we didn't want to believe it. He was going to the orphanage.

No one spoke as we left the house and climbed back into the Raptor.

"You sure about this?" Guild cast London a glance as we pulled out.

"No," he answered, his focus on the street as he accelerated hard. "But we have no choice."

I reached for Carven's hand in the dark, but the moment I touched him, he pulled away.

"I just need to get him back." His voice was husky as he stared out the window. "Just gotta get him back."

I swallowed that fist in the back of my throat, driving it all the way down into my chest. Tears shimmered, blurring the fading lights of the city as we left it behind, heading back to the place of my nightmares.

I closed my eyes.

Despair and torture have a certain...flavor about them, as you well know. London's words floated to the surface of my mind. I tried to remember now, gathering together all the things he'd said. *The house was so quiet...so very quiet for one filled with children.*

I remembered now. Remembered that night, he'd taken me all too well. The looming presence of the orphanage was terrifying enough, but that was nothing compared to what waited inside. *Inside.* I closed my eyes, and a tear raced down my cheek. *Please let Colt not be there. Please let him not be in that place.*

Even as I prayed, London's words from that night came roaring back.

You were taken before they could do too much damage and placed with a couple who raised you. They didn't hurt you. I made sure of that...

Daughter.

It wasn't the first time I'd heard the Sons call me that. But it was the first time I truly understood. I'd thought it was used to demean and hurt. But it wasn't...it was *who I was.*

Daughter.

Daughter.

And they were his sons.

The moment we turned off the highway and down that long narrow dirt road, I knew in my heart this was where he was. This was where a broken Colt would come. My hands never trembled as London handled the four-wheel drive, skidded around the corner, and raced toward that chained gate.

He never slowed, never stopped. Just slammed the front of the Ford into the steel, watching as the chain snapped and the gates flew back onto their hinges. Then we were hurtling toward that monstrous, towering place. Dust kicked up everywhere. I was already yanking the handle and shoving the door open wide.

I was out before anyone else...

Even Carven.

I looked up as I raced for the stairs. The front door was open, the boards torn free.

"*VIVIENNE!*" London roared. "*STOP! IT'S DANGEROUS!*"

I knew that.

The floors were rotted.

The rusted nails still sharp.

But I couldn't think about any of that now. I pushed all thoughts of this place aside, grabbed what was left of the wooden door, and yanked, then slipped past the splintered wood and plunged inside.

Darkness, that's all I saw. I prayed to God he was with me and stepped forward.

The pungent scent of dust and terror filled me. I swallowed the air as my eyes adjusted to the gloom. "Colt?" I whispered, taking a step of faith, then another.

Dark shadows yawned on the floor in front of me. I followed the lighter tone, stepped around the fallen away floor, and kept moving. My gaze went right as I pushed further into the house.

"*Vivienne!*" London snarled, pissed off behind me. "*Come back!*"

I couldn't. I hoped one day he'd understand that.

I hoped one day he'd forgive me.

I lowered my hand, cupped my belly, and pushed deeper, turning my focus toward the rear of the house. I left that room with the scratches inside the door behind.

"Here!" Guild called.

A grunt followed the slap of something against a hand before a *click* sounded and the bright shine of a flashlight illuminated the all but destroyed floor. I glanced over my shoulder toward the three men waiting.

London took a step and listened to the beams creak underneath before he spat a stream of obscenities, then fixed those dark eyes filled with desperation on me.

"Stay on the beams, pet," London cautioned, shining the light in front of me. "Follow the light."

I used the bright glow to scan the house in front of me, taking step after step until the glow faded, and I stopped at a doorway that led to stairs above. My heart hammered as I looked back and found Carven's gaze fixed on me. "I have to go up."

"Here," London murmured, turning the flashlight in his hand. "Take this."

Then he cast it through the air toward me. My heart lunged as I lifted my hands and caught it.

"We'll look for another way in," London urged, standing in the dark. "Be careful, pet."

His gaze lowered to my belly, looking like he wanted to say more. But he didn't. Carven turned and left. I shone the light toward them, helping him navigate the ruined floor until he was gone.

"Find my son," London whispered desperately. "Bring him back to us."

I gave a slow nod, then turned to the stairs and aimed the light higher. Footprints were embedded in the thick layer of dust. They looked fresh...*very fresh.*

The light bounced, trembling in my hand as I took a step. I didn't know what drew him back to this hell and not home. I wished to God I understood, but as I gripped the banister and climbed, I realized it didn't matter.

None of it did.

Fresh blood shone on the banister in front of me. I jerked my gaze upwards. It was him...it had to be him. That thought made me surge upwards. The stairs creaked. One gave way, leaving me to cling on for dear life to the filthy banister.

Still, I climbed, stopping at the first floor and aiming the flashlight higher. The marks in the dust continued, so I resumed climbing. The further up I went, the colder it became. I glanced below, my stomach sinking, before I focused above me, until I passed the second floor, then the third.

Until there was nowhere to go.

I shone the light along the footprints, following them until they stopped at a set of stairs that led up into the attic. I froze, the light bouncing against the missing rungs on the ladder. There was no way I was going up there. No way I could even...

The jagged edges of the rungs looked like weapons. Still, I didn't know if it was really Colt up there. *What if it was someone else? What if it was...*

Cat.

That guttural sound still gripped me, along with the desolate look in his eyes. It had to be Colt. It just *had* to be. I inhaled deep, trying to still the damn shake in my body, and stepped up, grabbing the sides of the ladder and clenching the small flashlight in my mouth, until a sound stopped me. One so terrifying it made me flinch.

Guttural. Savage. *Warning me.*

Don't. Come. Closer.

I lifted my gaze to that sound. This was Colt. This was just Colt.

My boots slipped, but I found purchase where I could and pushed toward the opening in the attic. My hand slipped and pain flared across my palm. I hissed with the sting as I twisted my head to shine the light against my hand.

A sharp sliver of wood stuck out of my palm, allowing blood to well and spill down my wrist. I lifted my head and kept going, using my other hand to grip tighter until, with one more heave up a missing rung on the ladder, my head was inside the attic.

I slammed my lips closed, desperate not to suck in the inch-thick filth, and caught the outline of a hunched figure in the middle of the attic. Fear punched through me, making me freeze.

Someone was there.

Someone was right...there.

My heart hammered. I didn't dare move. Seconds felt like hours. Inch by inch, I lifted my hand, took the flashlight from my mouth, and aimed the beam against the side of the attic. The place was beyond filthy. Cobwebs clung to the roof, cascading like a spindled blanket. Something scurried in the corner of my eye. I bit the insides of my cheeks to stop from crying out.

Still a sound escaped, low, terrified.

"Don't," Colt's low, throaty warning came. "Don't come closer. I'm not...*me*. I'm not me right now."

He shook his head, fighting his own personal demons.

"I'm not going to hurt you," I whispered, both terrified to have found him and relieved.

"It's not you I'm worried about."

That sounded like Colt. Like the one I knew, at least. My thighs burned, my knees trembled, still perched on the ladder which could crumble any moment underneath me. I was trapped, unable to stand here, and yet... I lifted my gaze to the shrouded figure. I didn't want to frighten him.

"I'm going to step up, okay?" I murmured.

I had to take the chance. I had to...*risk everything*.

Because that's just what he would do.

I rose carefully, then stepped out of that hole in the ceiling and onto the thick wooden beam.

Chains rattled. I jerked my gaze toward the sound. Light from the torch spilled over him. There was a shackle in his hand, red and rusted. *What the hell...*

I aimed the light lower, finding a bolt in the middle of the floor. A heavy chain was piled around it. I followed the links to the shackle in his hand. One too small to be around his neck...one almost big enough to fit around a—

My stomach clenched.

My breath stilled.

Ice plunged all the way into the center of me.

"C-Colt." My voice trembled as I glanced at the shackle, then at the bolt once more.

"They used to keep me up here."

My eyes widened. I couldn't even speak.

"She did, I mean," his hoarse voice was so faint I had to strain to hear.

I moved without realizing it, taking a step forward to the next smaller beam.

"She laughed when they ripped me away from Carven. She liked that bit—tearing me away while he screamed and clung to me—almost as much as she liked to watch them beat me. I had to kill her, Wildcat. I had to—"

"You protected yourself," I whispered, taking another step.

"She was my mother." He turned around, his deep blue eyes almost black. "Did you know that?"

Surprise slammed into me. *Mother? HIS MOTHER?* I shook my head, unable to believe it…

Only I did.

I did believe him.

I closed my eyes, rocked to my core. "That wasn't your mother," I whispered as a flutter came from somewhere deep in my belly. It wasn't the baby. I knew that, still it drew my focus to that pregnancy test sitting on the edge of my bathroom vanity.

I opened my eyes. Hate and love and desperation collided inside me. I took a step closer, watching his eyes widen. "She might've given you life, but that woman was not your mother, Colt. She was a cruel, manipulative, soulless, spiteful *thing* that occupied a body. What you did, you did in selfdefense." I searched his eyes, seeing the torment he held inside. "She wasn't part of you, and you weren't part of her. You are part of us. *We* are your family."

I stepped again, watching his top lip quiver as he fought for control.

My heart was in my throat, thudding violently as I lifted my hand and brushed my thumb along his cheek. "Family is the one you choose. The one you fight for. The ones who fight for you."

His brow pinched. Heavy breaths made his big chest rise, drawing my gaze. I stared at the blood and bruising...then the bloodied stub on his hand where his thumb had once been.

"Family is the ones who want you, who need you." That lump choked my words. I tore my focus from what they'd done to him and took a step closer. "That part of you who killed also protected you."

He shook his head. "A beast."

"A beast you needed," I whispered, staring into his eyes. "A beast *I* needed. I needed him to keep you alive. But I need him to bring you back to me now." I reached out, watching him flinch as I touched his hand. But I tried again. This time, he didn't pull away as I guided his hand to my belly. "Because we're going to be a family of our own. You, me, Carven, and London...and..." I held his stare. "And our baby."

His eyes widened. Deep breaths sucked in all the air before he whispered, "Baby?"

"Yes, my protector...our baby."

TWENTY-FIVE

London

"Up there." Carven stared at the shattered second-story window in the goddamn place. "It's the only way in."

He stepped closer, grabbed a thick wooden post rising from the veranda, and heaved himself upward.

"Careful." I winced as I heard the thing creak and groan under his weight.

The siding gave way under his grip, splintering until it fell. My heart boomed with the collapse, making me step closer. We'd circled the place, trying to find a way inside. The shattered window on the second floor was the only possible way.

"Fuck!" Carven snapped, then tried again, this time finding a better grip to heave himself upwards.

We wanted in.

No. We *needed* in.

I stood there, watching my son risk his goddamn neck to find his brother.

"Wait," Guild called behind me.

"Not now," I muttered, flinching as Carven's foot slipped, but still he inched toward that window.

"*London,*" Guild growled again.

Anger seethed. I snapped my gaze toward him, then slowly turned my head, sensing movement as Vivienne walked out from the front of the house with Colt's hand in hers. "Carven," I yelled.

"Not *now*," he snarled, reaching higher toward that shattered window.

"*Carven.*"

He jerked his gaze toward me, then slowly shifted it to Vivienne and Colt. His foot slipped on the rusted, ruined siding. From the corner of my eye, I watched him as he jumped and landed hard on the ground next to me.

"Brother?" He brushed dirt from his pants and took a step toward them.

We couldn't look away as Vivienne gave us a tortured look then slowly shook her head. But he was alive, and he was here. He limped when he walked, and flinched as Vivienne opened the rear door of the Raptor and helped him climb in. Still, he was wired as fuck, his wide, fixed gaze looked like a man who was holding onto the last, thin thread of sanity.

We all knew that look, as we strode to the four-wheel drive.

"I'll sit next to him," Carven muttered.

I gave him a careful nod and rounded the front, pulling my phone from my pocket. A swipe of the screen and I punched out a message to Doctor DeLuca.

I need you at the house asap.

Then I opened the driver's door and climbed in. Car doors closed around me with careful, muffled *thuds*.

Beep.

I scanned the message.

DeLuca: Who is it this time?

I winced as I caught Colt's panicked gaze in the mirror before I answered.

My son.

The engine started with a growl. I tried my best not to panic him anymore than he was, making sure the tires didn't spin this time as we drove away. My headlights glinted off the busted open gate. I cast careful glances at Colt, sitting in the middle of the back seat, flanked on one side by his brother and Vivienne on the other, his hand grasping hers like grim death.

Easy.

I aimed the four-wheel drive back to the city, mentally calculating how the hell he'd gotten here from the slaughterhouse. He'd have had to run clear across the thick forest to get here. It was no mean feat...but it was doable. *If you were desperate enough.*

One look at Colt and you knew without a doubt he was. I turned, skirting the outside of the city, and tried to get home as fast as possible, pulling into the driveway beside the house.

"With me, now." Vivienne held his stare. "Okay?"

Colt scowled, his focus fixed on her as he gave a slow nod. Guild was out of the passenger seat in an instant, carefully opening the door beside her. But the moment he grabbed her arm to steady her, Colt unleashed a savage snarl.

"Easy," Guild murmured, instantly releasing his hold and lifting his hand.

My son wasn't himself in that moment. The wildness in his stare told you that.

"He's not going to touch her." I watched him in the rear-view mirror.

Guild stepped away, allowing Vivienne to step out of the car, still holding Colt's hand. He followed her, never once glancing at us.

"Jesus fucking Christ," Carven groaned, staring at them as Vivienne punched in the code for the back door and headed into the house.

My son glanced my way as I turned to watch the door close behind them.

"This is bad, London."

"I know."

"This is really...*really* fucking bad."

I winced as he climbed from the car and followed them inside. I had no choice but to follow, wondering how the fuck I could keep us together now. How could I fight the demons that raged inside my son's head?

I didn't know. But I had to try.

I followed Carven and Guild inside and headed to our wing. I didn't even say anything as Guild invaded our space, following Carven to Colt's room. He couldn't leave us, even if all he did was stand outside.

Carven lingered outside the closed bedroom door, listening to Vivienne's almost inaudible murmur as she coaxed Colt into the shower.

"What if he...what if he hurts her?" He glanced my way.

I didn't know.

No one did.

Where was the goddamn doctor when I needed him?

"I'll make us some coffee," Guild offered as he turned away.

"Don't think I don't know about Vivienne coming to you, either," I muttered, my tone dangerous.

Guild stopped in the middle of the hallway.

"Before this night is over, you and I are going to have a conversation, my friend. One I don't think you're going to enjoy."

"I can't fucking wait," he answered carefully, then walked away.

I sucked in a hard breath. The moment she'd winced and pulled away when I'd touched her in Helene's basement, I knew something had happened. But it was that careful glance from Guild which sealed the deal.

Vivienne was pregnant.

And Guild had known before I did.

That twitch came in the corner of my eye.

I wanted to know why.

I turned around, listening to the water rush from inside Colt's bathroom. They were in there now. Him and her. I could imagine how gentle she was...and how fucking on edge he was. I wanted to see him. I wanted to protect her. Both were needs I couldn't fulfill, not now at least.

Beep.

I looked down at my phone.

DeLuca: Pulling up now.

"About goddamn time." I gave one last glance at the closed bedroom door before turning away and heading for the front of the house.

Headlights flared. I waited for the *thud* of the car door before I opened the front door wide, watching him haul the massive black pack with him.

"This is becoming all too fucking regular," he snarled as he pushed past. "How many more visits will negate your threat on my life?"

"As many as I fucking need," I answered as I closed the door and started walking back to Colt's room.

The doctor followed without a sound, meeting my gaze only when I stopped outside Colt's room and placed my hand across the door, blocking his way. "I want to make it perfectly clear what you're about to see in here is very much my son. So, I'll expect you to treat him accordingly."

He scowled. "What's that supposed to mean?"

I leaned close. "It means he is..." my mind raced, trying to work out how the fuck to convey what he was about to find. "He's fragile. That's what it means."

He glanced at the door, steadied himself, then gave a slow nod. "Understood. Now, let me do my job. Let me help him."

I fucking prayed he could, pushing away from the doorway and taking a step back. "I'll be right here."

"Fine." He turned the handle, then stepped in, closing the door behind him.

I hovered, making sure Colt didn't kill anyone right off, then turned and headed for the kitchen. The smell of fresh coffee was sharp and pungent as I filled my lungs with a deep breath.

Guild was waiting for me, just like I knew he would be. He stood beside the counter, nursing a steaming cup of coffee which he pushed away as I neared.

He thought I was going to hit him. I winced, guessing I deserved that. But as hurt as I was about this whole fucking thing, I was also desperate to keep us all together. A family divided was a family in danger and right now...that was the last thing I wanted.

I poured a cup and turned, meeting his stare. "Want to tell me what happened?"

He gave a shrug. "Depends. Am I going to get punched in the face for it?"

I scowled, then shook my head.

"Good. She came to me as a friend, and as her *friend*, I helped her."

"And you couldn't come to me?"

"And betray her trust? No, London. I couldn't."

Anger flared, making me push off the counter. The thought of her going to any other male but me or the sons made me feel violent. I clenched my jaw, meeting his stare. He held his breath, waiting for me to react.

I lifted my hand and gripped his shoulder. "Thank you for being there, even though you knew it'd piss me the hell off."

"Do you even want to know what she asked for?"

I met his stare, then gave a shake of my head. "No. When she comes to me, that will be good enough."

"Jesus," he exhaled hard. "Who the fuck are you and what have you done with London?"

I gave a chuckle, dropped my hand and turned to grab my coffee. "Keep that up and you will get socked in the jaw."

He let out a grunt of distaste, one I knew accompanied a shit-eating grin. I left him, making my way to the study. The moment I stepped inside, any fleeting hint of amusement left me...because now I had my family back, my attention turned to the new nagging problem.

Haelstrom Hale's dead body.

I placed the cup down and sat behind my desk.

Beep.

I looked down.

Baron: Did you hear the fucking news? Hale is dead? Tell me this is true.

Footsteps came before I even responded. I lifted my gaze as the doctor hesitated in the doorway, peering in before entering.

Beep.

Beep.

Beep...beep...beep.

I pressed the button, switching it off. I didn't need to read the goddamn messages to know what it was. It seemed word had gotten out. The soulless bastard was dead. My gut clenched as I narrowed in on the doctor. "How is he?"

"Like a man who's been beaten and tortured for almost three weeks," he answered, meeting my stare.

I didn't like him, didn't like how he seemed to have grown a pair of balls in our short but violent interactions.

"Apart from that," I forced through clenched teeth.

"I checked his wounds. The ones I could see, anyway. There's internal bleeding, a fair amount, if I'm honest. How much, I won't know until I do an ultrasound...and this time I *will* do an ultrasound. The stub of his amputated thumb has been cleaned. I can offer the name of a brilliant plastic surgeon to assist with the scarring on that and the multiple lacerations the man has endured. But none of that will matter a damn if you don't take care of the pressing issue."

"Which is?" I didn't have to ask. But something compelled me to hear it.

DeLuca stepped closer, gripped the edge of the desk, and leaned down. "He needs a fucking psych consult," he growled. "And now. That man...that man is a goddamn danger to everyone else around him."

Vivienne.

I shook my head.

"He's barely holding on, London. Christ if I don't understand how he isn't psychologically destroyed after what they did to him. All it's going to take is one wrong fucking move and there will be dire consequences."

I met his stare. "Take a look around you, doctor. Our entire existence is living with ticking time bombs. You think my son is going to be any different?"

"But he *is* different. You *know* that."

I shifted my gaze to the now quiet phone on my desk, knowing by now there'd be at least ten, twenty missed calls and messages. "Whatever my son needs, we will provide."

DeLuca muttered under his breath. "Goddamn unbelievable. I should've fucking known." He turned and headed for the door.

Still, I stared at the silent phone. This feeling in my gut was more than a hunch, more than goddamn denial. I didn't care that they'd dragged what looked like Hale from the goddamn river. I knew it was a fucking lie.

"Wait," I commanded, watching him stop in the doorway without turning. "I need you to do one more thing for me."

He spun, glaring. "What the fuck is it now?"

"I need you to get me into the morgue...as fast as you can."

TWENTY-SIX

Vivienne

He didn't even look at me, just stood under the spray of the shower. I couldn't stop staring at his massive hand braced on the wall...the one now missing a thumb. Burned, seared flesh was now a stump. The sight alone made me feel nauseous.

We must've been in here for an hour. In all that time, Colt hadn't said a word. He just stood there, letting the hot water cascade down his strong back onto the cuts and bruises marring his body.

This will help with the pain, the doctor muttered as he pushed the needle into his flesh. But Colt never even noticed, just stared with that catatonic stare. One that still held him transfixed.

"Colt?" I whispered, taking a step closer. The spray hit my arm as I reached out to trail my fingers along his arm, drenching my shirt. But I didn't care. My focus was only on him. "Maybe we should get you out of the shower, huh? You must be exhausted."

All I saw was that filthy fucking kill room where they'd held him, the one stained with terror and blood. My hand shook and my fingers danced on his skin. The tremble seemed to wake him enough to lift his head. I reached past and hit the faucets, ending the spray.

"Let's get you dried, okay?" I grabbed the towel, carefully brushing it over his arm before I dared to move closer.

His hard muscles quivered, making my pulse race. The last thing I needed was for him to lash out and hurt me. So I put my trust in his love. Because he loved me…deep down…under whoever this person standing in front of me was.

I brushed the towel across his shoulders, then moved to the other side. He didn't move, just let me touch where I needed, wiping the water from his arms, then moved to his torso. A deep purple hue covered most of his stomach, bulging out at the side.

Internal bleeding. That's what the doc had said. Although he was sure it wasn't life threatening, not anymore, at least, as it would've already killed him. I didn't need the doctor to say the words. I saw it all in the mangled marks in the shape of fists. I swallowed the lump in the back of my throat. I didn't know how he'd survived. By DeLuca's stare, he didn't know either.

"I'll get you into bed in just a minute," I assured Colt as he shivered.

I ran the towel over the marks on his chest. The small punctures were the same everywhere, all over his chest and stomach, even on his back. I stared at the two-point marks as I gently dried his back. They were almost like bites. I scanned the rest of his body as I knelt to run the towel down his thighs and his legs.

He was clean, as clean as I could get him, anyway.

It'd take much more than an hour standing under the water to scrub away what they'd done to him. Still, it was a start.

"There, all dried," I urged, gently pulling him toward me.

He followed me into the bedroom and just stood there as I pulled a soft white t-shirt over his head and eased him against the bed. Sleep shorts were next. I heaved his heavy feet upwards one by one until I gently pushed him down on the bed and worked them up as high as I could.

Cold rippled through me. My sodden sleeves clung to my skin. I needed to change, put on something warm.

"Stay." The word was a husky plea.

I glanced at his eyes as they closed, then at the bedroom door. "Okay." I pulled the covers high up to his neck. "Whatever you need, but I need a shower first."

He reached behind him and tugged the covers low on the other half of the bed as I kicked off my boots, pulled the wet shirt over my head, and hurried for the bathroom.

Get it off...the stench and the filth of that place were like a brand I needed gone. I scrubbed hard, using the last of the hot water to wash cobwebs, grime, and the sickening smell of that kill room off me until the water ran cold.

The bedroom was quiet, not even a shift under the covers. *Hurry.* I washed, then stepped out grabbed the towel, and dried before heading back into the bedroom.

He was still awake, still...*unresponsive*. I slipped on a pair of panties I'd left here earlier, then one of his massive black t-shirts and climbed in. Fear made me hesitate as I reached for him, so I curled my fingers, then pulled away and tugged the covers up high instead.

He just lay there, unmoving, with his back to me. I didn't know if he was asleep.

I wished to hell I could sleep, but every time I closed my eyes, I saw that room.

That *fucking* room where they'd held him.

I shifted my gaze, watching his big chest slowly rise and fall with every deep breath. He was asleep...*good.* I lay there, staring at the ceiling, fighting back tears. *That's really good. You sleep, baby. You sleep and let me stand guard this time.*

My attention moved to the door, and the sliver of faint light out in the hallway. Carven and London were out there somewhere, maybe even asleep themselves. I glanced back as a wave of exhaustion slammed into me. Right now, I felt lonely, with the weight of my thoughts ready to take me under.

I tried to stay awake by opening my eyes and my mouth wide until the corners of my mouth stretched.

Still, that heaviness waited. My eyes drifted closed. No...I opened them once more. *Gotta stay awake...if...he...needs...me—*

THE BED SHIFTED BESIDE ME. Still, I stayed under, sinking deeper into that heaviness, until a hard blast of a breath battered against my cheek. I cracked my eyes open, saw a shadow looming above me, and for a second my mind didn't understand. "Go back to sleep, Colt. It's too early."

A low, guttural rumble followed, loud enough to drag me back into reality. *The kill room...Colt chained there. Colt...a savage be—*

I snapped my eyes wider, finding him on all fours, hovering over me. That threatening rumble like thunder in his chest making my pulse spike.

"Colt?" I croaked.

He lowered his head, his heavy breaths scattering my hair.

"Colt, what's wrong?"

"Not. Colt." The blunt snarl followed.

Not Colt? I flinched as he moved, placing one hand on either side of me and leaned down to sniff the back of my neck. I fisted the sheets, my gaze directed at the wall of the room and away from the door. But I didn't dare turn my head. Not when he—

That snarl grew deeper and his breath was hot against the side of my neck, before he *licked*.

It was the same thing he'd done earlier, right before he ran from the dungeon where they'd held him. Would he run again? I winced as his tongue came once more. I couldn't let him run again, couldn't do anything to *scare him*.

"If you're not Colt, then who are you?" I dared to whisper.

"Beast."

I swallowed hard as he moved down my body, swiping the covers aside roughly. I flinched, turning to look at him, until his hand landed on the back of my neck, squeezing hard enough to frighten me.

"Colt," I croaked, too terrified to move.

"Told you," he snarled, leaning down. "Not Colt."

My pulse was thundering as he pressed his face against my hair, then bit.

Pain flared, sharp...terrifying.

"Oww." I fought, pushing upwards, but I was no match for his grip around my neck, pinning me in place. "Stop...*Colt.*"

He was scaring me now. I thrashed, trying to turn my head, and opened my mouth to scream for Carven...until I froze, playing out what would happen in my head. The bedroom door would fly open and Carven would launch himself across the bed, taking his brother out.

It'd be bad...*really fucking bad.*

Fists, blood. Screaming and roaring.

Hearts would shatter all over again.

I closed my eyes as he shoved my face harder against the pillow. The movement couldn't be more bestial. *Don't move,* it said. Every savage draw of a breath, every dip in the bed, I felt it all as he pressed his face against the back of my neck and bit once more.

I flinched, wincing.

But it didn't hurt as much this time. Instead, it was careful, more controlled. Was he trying not to hurt me? "It's okay," I whispered, praying he understood me. "I know you don't want to hurt me."

He moved down my body, pawing at the over-sized t-shirt I wore. He pressed his nose against the fabric and into the middle of my back, drawing in a hard breath.

A rumble followed, almost like a purr in his chest. Did he like that I wore his shirt? Did he want his scent on my skin? Christ, I hoped so.

"It's you." I tried. "It's always you."

His warm hand pawed my ass, then shoved upwards, driving his t-shirt high. "Don't...move," he warned.

I swallowed hard, trying to stop myself from fighting. I clenched the sheets, my breath warming the pillow pressed against my face as he pressed his hand against my ass.

That sound came again, threatening, predatory. Teeth scraped the flesh of my ass as he bit the sides of my panties. I clamped my mouth shut, biting down on the insides of my cheeks to stop from crying out. One thrash of his head and the thin lace ripped.

"*Wildcat*," he snarled. "*Mine.*"

I stilled, trying to catch my breath as he lifted his head, those dark blue eyes searching for mine. I dared risk shifting my head, meeting them.

There was a tortured look that pinched his brow as he growled. "Won't hurt you." He turned away, lowering his head to my ass.

Pain flared as he bit the soft flesh. I cried out with the sharp sting making me buck. But that growl came again, desperate and needy this time. *Don't move.* I sucked in hard breaths, gripping the comforter with all I had as he licked.

Soft, wet...followed by the hard press of his face into the crease of my ass. Warmth followed as he licked again, his tongue taking my mind away from the aching throb his teeth had left behind. A moan tore free, pain and pleasure taking over as he pressed his face harder in my crease, then moved down.

"Colt," I whispered. "*I mean...Beast.* Don't you think..." His tongue pushed into my core, making me squeeze my eyes closed. "Don't you think you need to rest?"

He eased back, turning his head to nip the inside of my thigh.

"Okay," I yelped, writhing. "Whatever you need...*Christ, whatever you need.*"

Hard fingers gripped my torn panties and yanked, lifting my hips from the bed before the ruined panties completely ripped free. He cast them aside, then shoved the inside of my thigh, widening my legs. I had no choice but to let him do what he wanted.

He wasn't in his right mind. He wasn't in any mind. That thunderous purr came again as he pressed his face against my pussy. "Mine."

"Yes." I arched my back as he licked, driving my hips higher, giving him all the access to me he wanted. "I'm yours." His hand was still clenched around the back of my neck, holding me down as he took what he wanted. "All yours."

It didn't matter he wasn't the Colt I knew right now. All it mattered was that it was *him*.

He eased his hold against my neck, lifted his head to grab my hips and flip me over...like I weighed nothing at all. He shouldn't be able to do that, not without screaming in agony.

But he did...

He did and looked savage and wild and dangerous doing it.

I bounced against the mattress, jerking my gaze to his as he knelt on all fours, towering above me. That wild stare captured mine before he looked down at the t-shirt I wore. With a snarl, he reached up, gripped the neckline and jerked, ripping the garment straight down the middle.

Panic punched through me as that animalistic stare found what it wanted. My nipples tightened in response, puckering as he lowered his head.

"Just..." I whispered as he took one in his mouth, his teeth grazing sensitive flesh. "Don't hurt me."

He lifted his head. Somewhere in that bestial stare was the man I loved.

He dipped once more, dragging his teeth across the tip, making me buck, which only drove my nipple deeper into his mouth. Pain. Softness. He nipped and licked until I couldn't tell the sensations apart. By the time he nuzzled the shredded shirt aside to expose the rest of me, my breast was throbbing, shooting the sensations all the way to my clit.

Panting breaths caught as danger mingled with desire. I shouldn't be allowing this. Not while he was in the state he was, but as he lowered himself further down the bed, I knew this was what he needed.

He needed me.

The points of his teeth pressed against my clit as it throbbed. "Colt," I whispered. "I want Colt."

"No Colt..." he growled. "Not yet."

Pressure. Suction. He shoved my legs wider, sliding his hands under to tilt my hips to his face. "Not until I have my fill," he insisted.

"Oh, *fuck*," I moaned, looking down.

This wasn't Colt. Not the sweet, protective, soft man I knew.

He dipped, that guttural sound rumbling in the back of his throat as he opened his mouth wide and speared his tongue inside me. I threw my hands up, holding on as my nipples pulsed, driving the throb deeper. "Oh, God," I cried.

He lifted his head, his lips glistening with my desire. "Not God. A beast."

He wasn't a beast. He was a tortured, damaged man. Still, he felt like hunger as he licked and sucked, drawing that terrifying, delicious feeling closer.

"My kitten." He rose, shoving his boxers down. One swing of his arm and he tore the shirt I'd dressed him in free. "My *Wildcat*."

I couldn't stop myself from wanting this, lifting my knees, opening wide for him to settle between my thighs.

"I love you," I moaned as he thrust, driving his cock all the way inside. "I. Love. *You*."

He was a savage, holding nothing back as he unleashed all that anger and that pain on my body. My body jolted, driving higher in the bed with every thrust.

I wanted more. Anything he could give me.

"That's it," I moaned, reaching for him. "Fuck me. Fuck me and take what you need."

I grabbed his arms, lifting myself as he drove that hard length all the way to the hilt. But I wasn't ready to stop fighting, not the way my protector needed. I slid my hand up, gripping him behind the neck and snarled, "You fuck me, then you give me back Colt."

There was a curl of his lips. Rage and desperation burned in his stare. But he was so focused on his hunger. So desperate to fuck that he didn't fight. That gave me all the hope I needed.

He yanked his cock out, then shoved me to the side. I moved then, knowing instantly what the beast wanted.

He wanted to mount.

He wanted to rut.

I braced myself on all fours as he thrust back in. His hand moved to grip the back of my neck. I lifted my head as his fingers entwined to grip the strands of my hair.

"That's. It." I urged, my elbows buckling with the strength of his thrusts. "Fuck me."

He unleashed a growl and thrust harder...faster. The sound rebounded from the walls to slam into me, making my core clench. I rode that dangerous, terrifying edge of euphoria until, with a brutal slam of his hips, I tipped over.

I throbbed and swelled, crying out as he came hard inside me.

My arms gave way, letting me fall to the mattress. I couldn't think, couldn't move. Couldn't do anything but feel the quakes his possession left behind.

His grip on my hair eased, his huge hand heavy as his arm drifted down to encircle my waist. One yank and he wedged my body against his.

"Every kitten needs a beast," he murmured, his tone thick with exhaustion. *"Now you know yours."*

TWENTY-SEVEN

Carven

THE LOW HISS OF THE SHOWER SLIPPED UNDER THE DOOR, finding me as I stood in the hallway, listening. I'd stepped out the minute the doctor left, knowing they were both in there. My brother...alone with Wildcat. My jaw flexed, clenching. But it was that nagging voice in my head that wouldn't leave me alone.

Because you know who he is now.

I shook my head. No. I didn't. He was my brother who'd just survived almost a goddamn month of being beaten and tortured.

He's not in his right mind, and you're scared. You're so fucking scared, you're prepared to stand here all night. That's the truth, isn't it?

It wasn't. I was...concerned. That's all.

Oh yeah? Then tell me, dickhead, why the gun?

I flinched, my breaths deepening as I looked down.

The Sig was in my grip, finger on the slide, muzzle pointed down. An ache flared across my chest. That panicked feeling threatened to return. The one that'd render me helpless. One I'd had before Vivienne came into our lives.

When you were a kid, right?

Being ripped away from your brother.

You knew what they were going to do.

You saw that savagery in him.

That...wounded fucking animal in his eyes when he returned.

You knew...that's why you're fucking terrified. Tell me, champ. If he hurts her...what are you going to do?

I shook my head, wincing as that band cinched tighter across my chest. My brother...or the woman I loved. The woman we *both* loved. If Colt was in his right mind, if he could speak to me, I knew exactly what he'd say.

Whatever it takes, brother. Whatever it fucking takes. You protect her, you fucking bastard. You. Protect. Her.

I could hear his voice in my head. Feel his fucking desperation like it was my own. *Because it was, right?*

I loved her.

I fucking loved...her.

Fear filled me, turning my attention to the shower as I fought the need to go in there. What the fuck were they doing, anyway? It had to be a goddamn hour...until silence came. Empty fucking silence. Was she hurt? Was she dead? I could see it now. Her neck snapped, her body slumped against the cold tiled floor. Eyes wide, staring at my brother standing over her dead body.

Christ. That's it. I turned, grabbed the handle, and bore down... but the indistinct sound of her voice stopped me. She was alive and coaxing him into bed. I eased my hold, letting the handle bounce back as I pressed against the door.

"There." I heard her murmur through the door. "All dried."

"Stay."

That husky plea was the first time I'd heard him speak since we'd found him. Just one word, given to her. *Stay.*

"Okay. Whatever you need, but I need a shower first."

I jerked my gaze to the door. She was coming out...going to shower in her room. I'd follow her in, tell her he was dangerous. *Thought you said he wasn't? Thought you said you weren't worried?*

"Shut the fuck up," I mouthed and took a step back, but the moment I did, the sound of my brother's shower came again.

She wasn't coming. Of course she wasn't. She was going to say there, watching his every goddamn move. Because that's what kind of woman she was. I closed my eyes. We didn't deserve her. We didn't fucking deserve to be in her goddamn sphere. That's how fucking incredible she was.

I took a step away, turned, then slowly sank to the floor. The shower stopped running. I tracked the sound of her steps to the bed...before nothing.

Was my brother asleep? I hoped so.

I leaned my head against the wall and closed my eyes until sometime later the heavy thud of London's steps headed my way. I opened my eyes and stood as he stopped in front of me.

"Is she okay?"

I gave a nod.

Relief sagged his shoulders with a heavy breath. "Thank Christ for that. I don't know what I'd do if we lost her or the baby after everything else tonight."

Baby...my mind spun.

London's gaze went to the gun in my hand before he met my stare. "Our baby, son. Our. Baby."

I couldn't move.

Couldn't react, not even when he placed his hand on my shoulder, took one last look at Colt's bedroom door, then turned and walked away, disappearing into his own room.

A baby?

The hallway swayed. I winced, slamming my hand against my chest. She was fucking *pregnant*? Colt had had his hand around her goddamn throat and shoved against the fucking wall in that slaughterhouse. And she'd fucking launched herself across that rotted-out floor like it was nothing.

It wasn't *nothing*.

It was *everything*.

She's pregnant. She's pregnant.

What if I was the father?

My knees shook. I gripped the doorway, trying my best to steady myself as the world spun. I stood there for I didn't know how long, staring at the goddamn wall while I replayed every time I'd fucked her. Christ, don't let it be that first time…the time when I'd been such a bastard.

I was so transfixed by the thought of that, I didn't realize that sounds were coming within the room, barely audible murmurs, savage guttural sounds.

"If you're not Colt, then who are you?" Her husky voice slipped under the door.

I moved, pressing my hand against the wall, straining to hear as my brother answered. "Beast."

Beast…

I shook my head.

"Oww," she cried out. I snapped my gaze up.

Don't do it! I roared inside my head, my hand clenched around the gun. All I could think of was that life inside her. The family I'd never thought we'd have.

"Stop…*Colt*," she barked.

Move! Move…now!

My fucking hand trembled as I reached for the door handle.

"It's okay." Her voice trembled, but it was stronger, full of determination. "I know you won't hurt me."

He wouldn't, would he? Because if he wanted to, he'd already had plenty of opportunity.

The deep, animal grunts came once more. But they weren't a warning. No. They were a *claiming*.

"Wildcat," he murmured. *"Mine."*

Anger flared. Jealousy seethed inside me. I shouldn't feel like this. Not with the one person I'd shared my entire life with, but I couldn't stop that searing hunger. My cheeks burned. My breaths were a strangled fight for air.

I wanted her.

I fucking wanted her.

I stayed there for too long, torturing myself with the sounds of my brother fucking her like an animal, before I left. But I couldn't go to my room, couldn't force myself to sleep in the bedroom next to Colt's. Instead, I went to the gym, hit the lights on, and grabbed the wrapping for my hands.

I wanted to hit something.

I wanted to tear it apart.

Anything to stop me from charging back to that room and listening to whatever that *thing* which possessed my brother was fuck the woman I loved. I neared the punching bag. Memories flickered.

Reach up, grab the bag.

My own hunger was so close to the surface. I could almost hear the rattle of the chains as she'd arched her back. I'd fucked her here...fucked her while those bastards did their best to kill my brother.

Oh, my God. That's Haelstrom Hale.

I reached out and grabbed the bag as that woman's cry filled my head. They'd tried to kill my brother. They'd tried to kill Vivienne, and now he was what? *Fucking dead?*

I pulled my hand back and drove it through the air, straight into the leather. The bag bounced, then again as I slammed my other fist home.

"You motherfucker." I unleashed, swung my body around, and whipped my leg into the air with a roundhouse kick. "You *goddamn, motherfucking bastard!*"

My fists were a blur.

The bag was bruising as I used my knees, slamming them into the side over and over again. Every cell in my body screamed in agony. But it was my mind that drove me, my mind that howled for justice…and wrath.

He was gone.

They were all gone.

We had *nothing* but the destruction we'd left behind.

That wasn't enough. It wasn't *anywhere* near enough.

TWENTY-EIGHT

Vivienne

I was fine until I moved, then that gnawing ache spreading through my body exploded in bright, blinding clusters. Pain tugged at different parts of me. My nipples stung, and the insides of my thighs were tender. I unleashed a soft moan and opened my eyes, trying to come to terms with what happened last night.

It was a mess. A whole terrifying, elated, cruel mess.

I turned my head, wincing at the ache at the back of my neck as I found Colt lying beside me, his eyes closed, his hand wrapped firmly around my arm.

But was it Colt?

Or was it *the beast?*

I closed my eyes as a low moan gathered like a storm in the middle of my chest. Only I didn't let it free. I kept it down there, trapped and rumbling, desperately quiet so I didn't wake him. I didn't want to wake him, and it wasn't just because he needed to rest. No. Because the truth was...I was scared.

The more I thought about last night, the further sleep slipped away.

I was awake...*very awake,* remembering *everything.*

Not Colt.

The words resounded and a new ache flared, one in my heart. My body clenched as the heaviness in my bladder tugged my focus. I needed to get up...and pee. I swallowed my breath, gulping it down as I shifted my gaze to his once more.

Lips together.

Eyes closed.

Still fast asleep. He won't even know I've—I rolled my arm and gently pulled. His eyes snapped open, the blue so dark it was almost black. But he didn't look *at* me. He looked through me, like I wasn't even there. Panic punched, making my pulse skip.

"Colt?" my voice squeaked.

Then in an instant, he blinked and came to life. The deep blue brightened a little. There was a quiver at the corner of his mouth. "Wildcat?" he spoke, his voice husky and raw.

I smiled, pushing up to brush my fingers across his hard, bristled cheek. "Hey there, it's me." He tried to smile at me, but I saw the panic, the doubt. "You're okay now. You're out of there. You're here with me. See?"

I touched his cheek and grazed his jaw before leaning close to kiss him. But his lips barely moved. I pulled away, desperately trying to think of how to ease him. He winced, growing pale.

"Are you hurting?" I shoved upwards, biting down on another moan, and pulled the sheets away from him. He was naked and in the faint spill of sunlight between the blinds, I saw the damage more clearly.

He wasn't just black and blue...he was *all black*.

All of his stomach.

All of his chest.

The tread of a boot was stamped clearly into his check.

Revulsion gripped me, making my stomach clenched. Acid surged into the back of my throat.

"Vivienne?" he croaked as I slammed my hand over my mouth and shoved from the bed.

I couldn't stop, and launched for the bathroom, even when the ache flared deep with every step. The burn spilled out, splashing against the sides of the bowl. Heavy steps came behind me.

"Vivienne?" Colt croaked as he stumbled into the doorway.

I shook my head, my eyes blurred with tears. "I'm okay. I'm okay...I—"

"What the fuck happened to you?" he growled as he lurched closer, holding onto his chest with one hand and the doorjamb with the other.

He yanked me hard, spinning me around until he could take a good look. The panic in his stare didn't get any better. "What the fuck bit you?"

I swallowed hard and looked down. Red, swollen, bruised. I knew it'd be bad, but this...this was too much. I yanked from his hold, covering myself. "It's nothing."

"It doesn't look like *nothing* to me. What the fuck bit you like that?"

I hurried for my clothes and snatching the shirt up from beside the bed, only to stare at the shredded fabric.

"Oh, God...*oh, Jesus...*" he cried, coming closer. "I did this. I fucking *did this.*"

"No." I spun around, glaring. *"You* didn't. Not the you I know, anyway."

But he shook his head and clenched his fist. "I did this...I—"

Smack!

His fist thudded onto his cheek, throwing his head backwards.

I lunged and grabbed his fist as he swung again. *"Stop! Colt, STOP!* You didn't know what you were doing. You—" I stopped. "You were someone else last night. Someone—"

Beast.

The name reverberated inside my head. "You were someone you needed. Someone who protected you. Someone—" I stepped closer, touching his cheek softly. "Someone who kept you alive."

"I need to be tied up." His voice was bleak as he turned from my touch and scanned his bed.

I knew instantly what he was looking for, the thick leather shackles he'd used to chain himself to the bed when it stormed. Only now I knew why.

"No." I shook my head. "No fucking *way* am I letting that happen. Not after what you've just been through. You didn't hurt me. *Hey! Look at me.*"

He jerked back to me.

"You didn't hurt me. You just needed to learn to be gentler."

"It shouldn't have ever happened." His eyes were darkening, growing distant. "I didn't want you to ever know."

I lifted my chin. "Well, I'm glad I do. I want to know all of you, the good and the bad. I don't regret a second and you shouldn't either."

"Did I...did I rape you?"

I think that would've been the last straw. If he thought that's what had happened, Colt would put a gun to his mouth and he'd be dead before we knew it.

"No. You didn't," I answered. "And that's the truth. You were..." I grazed my lip with my teeth as that heady rush came back. Pain and pleasure. The sting was so fucking good. I swallowed hard. "You were perfect."

He scowled, staring at me. "No. That's not—"

"*He* was perfect for me. Rough at first, but then he seemed to understand." Christ, I was talking like it was someone else in the room with us last night and not Colt. "He won't hurt me. *You* won't hurt me. I know that."

"But if he—"

I captured his face, holding his stare. "He won't hurt me because you won't allow it. I will heal, Colt. I will heal and the next time that other part of you rises to the surface, I'll be ready. *If* he ever comes back."

Fear moved into his stare.

He didn't think it was an *if,* did he?

He thought it was a *when.*

Fuck.

His knees shook so hard he stumbled backwards, falling onto the bed. I lunged forward and grabbed his shoulders. His arms clasped across his middle were all I needed to know he needed help. "Wait right here." I whirled to the door. "I'll be as fast as I can."

I threw open the door and raced for my room, bursting in to fling myself into my closet. I threw on anything: panties, jeans, and a t-shirt with no bra. My damn nipples were too sore anyway. So I grabbed a jacket and my socks and boots and raced out.

"London!" I called from the hallway as I ran. "LONDON!"

The sound of a chair scraping came from the study. He was in the doorway in an instant, his eyes wild. "What is it?"

I sucked in a hard breath. "He needs the doctor. He's in pain... way too much pain."

"Fuck." London grabbed his phone, swiped, and pressed the screen. It was answered fast as he turned away and growled, "He's in pain. How fast can you get here? What? *What the fuck do you mean, he needs more?"*

I didn't like the sound of that. I liked it even less when London scowled. "Those scans would be where? He's not going to any fucking hospital, so you can get *that* out of your head." Silence. I hated silence. "Yes, I know it. It's private, and you can keep the records out of his file?" He leaned his hand on the end of his desk. "I'll expect you to be attending there. Yes...yes, I'll have him taken there and yes...I'll see you tonight."

Tonight? What was tonight?

He hung up the call and turned to me. "He needs scans. I'll call Guild, get him to drive you."

"No."

I spun at the low growl. Colt was there, his skin almost gray as he leaned in the doorway, but he'd somehow pulled on sweatpants, a t-shirt, and sneakers. "I'll drive myself," he muttered.

"No fucking way." London winced when he looked at him, then stepped past me and out into the hall. "You can barely stand up, son." He placed his hand on Colt's shoulder. "Let us help."

Colt met my gaze, then shook his head.

He was pulling away from us, too scared to be around those he loved. "I'll take the Raptor. It's automatic."

"It's not the goddamn gears I'm worried about." London shook his head, following Colt's stare to me. "What am I missing here?"

"Nothing," I answered a little too fast. "You missed nothing."

Colt stepped away and pushed past me into the study to grab his keys from London's desk. "I need a phone," he muttered. "Text me the address."

"I'm coming with you," I answered.

He stopped as he began to walk past and back out into the hall. "No, you're *not*."

"It's *not negotiable*," I insisted.

He spun, agony and desperation all over his face. "You're that goddamn desperate to get yourself killed?"

That was the actual fear. Movement at the corner of my eye drew my gaze as Carven approached. He looked pissed off... really pissed off...but stopped to cross his arms over his chest and lean against the wall, enjoying the goddamn show.

I thought if anyone was going to help me make Colt see reason, it was the one person he loved the most. But one look at that cold, bottomless stare, and I knew I was wrong.

"You know how dangerous I am," Colt added. "You *know* I could be violent at any minute."

"Yes, I do." I took a step closer. "I also know that even if you do...become not yourself, I can handle it. I know what I'm dealing with."

"And the baby," Carven snarled, glaring at me. "Are you prepared to risk the life of our child, as well?"

Warmth drained out of me. The baby...

Carven knew?

"The baby?" Colt croaked. "Jesus, that's right...you're pregnant."

Carven pushed off the wall and strode toward me. "Any of us could be the father.

I scowled, turning around to face London.

"Oh, *Jesus fucking Christ,*" Colt looked like he was about to pass out.

"So how do you *know* if Colt lashes out, he's not going to hurt you?"

I froze...my heart racing. I prayed to God I was right and the mental calculations I'd made were correct. "Because I'm about ninety-nine percent certain Colt is the father."

TWENTY-NINE

Colt

You're the father.

You're the father.

I clenched my eyes while the wand moved over my belly, pressing down until a sickening wave of agony washed through me.

Let me out, that low voice demanded in my head. *I want out now.*

"No," I whispered.

"Am I hurting you?" the young nurse asked beside me.

I shook my head, unable to even speak. Quakes ripped through my body and it wasn't just from the pain. It was from fear.

I want her, the voice rumbled. *Give her to me.*

I knew that voice wasn't really there. This was all just a figment of my imagination. A shattered part of my conscious mind I'd created as a child to keep me safe. This wasn't real. *He* wasn't real.

Still that low snarl reverberated in the back of my throat as clear as anything else I'd felt.

"Oh, God. I'm so sorry," the nurse cried. "I'll try to be more careful."

I snapped my eyes open to find her eyes shimmering with tears. That sound died away in the back of my throat. He was clawing to the surface, fighting to get through. I gripped the metal railing on the bed, missing thumb and all, and heaved myself upwards. "Are we done?"

The nurse just nodded, unable to take her eyes from my bare chest. "I know we're not supposed to ask." Her voice was small. "But I have to know. What happened to you?"

I looked down, white scars were almost neon against the deep purple bruises and gouges their boots had left behind. But it was the marks from the stun gun I stared at as I clasped my chest with one arm and slipped from the bed. "A car accident."

The young nurse rushed around to grab me as my knees buckled. "Jesus." She took my weight as I crumpled, steadying me. "It's a miracle you survived."

A miracle? Not a miracle, that was me. You need me, the beast growled. *I can give you all the strength you need...just... let...me...out.*

"No." I forced the word through clenched teeth. *"No."*

The nurse dropped her hold instantly and stepped away. "I'm... I'm sorry." She whispered. "I'm so sorry."

I yanked my t-shirt over my head. "It's okay. I just..."

"Not sure if that's your girlfriend or your sister waiting out there, but if you...if you need someone to look after you," she breathed, "I get off at six."

That snarl came again, only this time it wasn't desperate. It was pissed. This...*bitch* was trying to come on to me when the woman I fucking loved waited out there for me? This woman didn't love me. She *couldn't*. She looked at me like I was broken, like I was something she could *fix*. I didn't need fixing. I needed...*Wildcat*. Cold plunged through me as I narrowed in on that panicked stare. *"Get the fuck away from me."*

Her eyes widened. "I'm sorry!" she burst out, then turned and hurried from the room.

I both hated and loved the sound of those panicked steps. They triggered that hunger inside me. The one which wanted to hunt and destroy. I yanked my shirt down and pushed away from the bed, following her out of the room until I stopped.

Vivienne sat outside the room, taking up the closest seat as she waited. Her brow rose, turning from the nurse as she frantically hurried away. "Everything okay?" she asked as she stood.

My nostrils flared. I couldn't stop myself from scenting her. "Yes," I answered, but the threatening tone said otherwise.

Vivienne took a step, scowling as she placed a hand on my arm. "Easy," She urged.

Desire slammed into me, speeding my pulse. I need her...*I need* —I lowered my gaze to her lips, then lower to the line of her neck. I knew just how soft her skin was there, how her thready pulse danced on the tip of my tongue when I licked her.

"Colt?" she whispered.

My cock tightened, thickening in my pants.

Let me taste her, the beast demanded. *I want between her legs, my tongue in her pussy. Her come sliding down my throat right before I drive my c—*

"Baby?"

I wrenched my arm from hers. The bright overhead light buzzed and brightened as I slammed my hand against the wall and stumbled away. I had to get out of here. I had to get—

I can still taste her blood, licking the grazes my teeth left behind.

A sound ripped free.

"Colt?"

I raced from the treatment rooms, desperate for the sun and the air on my face. I sucked in deep lungfuls as I stumbled outside, staring up at the dusky pink hues that filled the horizon. It was already late, already night. I'd lost too many days down in that hell. Too many...but it wasn't the days I wanted.

It was the nights.

With her in my bed.

Her hand clasped my arm. I closed my eyes, suppressing a shudder as she said, "Talk to me."

Mine, the beast demanded. *Give...her...to...me.*

I spun, drove her against the side of the four-wheel drive, and slammed my hand against the window, boxing her in. "You don't get it, do you?"

Her eyes widened. Still, she didn't look away, and she didn't flinch. She wasn't like the goddamn nurse, terrified of a hint of that *thing* inside me. She was goddamn defiant, facing whatever *this* was head on. It's what he wanted, what he craved.

I'd known it the first time I saw her. The first time London carried her kicking and screaming over his goddamn shoulder to throw her on the foyer floor in front of me. The beast wanted her then…and that hunger had only grown. "You think last night was a one-time fucking deal?"

She scowled, trying to understand.

"He *wants* you," I growled, pressing harder against her, then I glanced down. Christ, I could even scent her, the heady scent of her perfume and under that, her desire. "He fucking wants you, Vivienne. He wants you and I can't fight it. I can't fight *him*. Knowing I'm the…" I met her stare. "Knowing I'm the father only makes him want you more. He wants to mark you, he wants…" I licked my lips, lowering my gaze.

My body moved before I realized it. Curled fingers skimmed the swell of her breast. The feel of her fucking soft nipples roared into my head, how they'd tightened under the graze of my teeth. My cock hardened with the memory as I pushed into her, pinned against the car. I knew he was pushing to the surface, desperate to devour her.

"I needed him," I started. "Needed him in that place. He was the one who fought for me. He is the one who kills. But he doesn't just want that anymore." I met her stare. "He wants to *claim*. He wants to claim *you*."

The muscles of her throat worked as she swallowed.

She knew what I was saying.

She'd already had a taste of the sick, twisted hunger he had for her. But that was *nothing* compared to what he wanted. *I'd fuck her against this car, have her jeans pushed low and my cock driving inside her before she even knew it. My hand around her throat, my teeth grazing her neck as I bowed her back against me. I want in...I want in that cunt. I want...I want...I WANT.*

I unleashed a moan and shoved away from her, stumbling backwards.

"Colt!" She lunged, grabbing me as my knees trembled, shaking uncontrollably.

"*No!*" I tried to shove her away. "You *don't understand what he wants.*"

She was everywhere, her hands on my arms, her touch like a fucking brand I couldn't escape. I lowered my head, burying my face in her hair. "I'm not strong enough to stop him."

"Then don't," she whispered. "I can take it."

I shook my head. "No. Not this, you can't."

She stilled, her grip easing. "Then we make it so I can."

I lifted my gaze to hers.

She licked her lips and my rock hard cock spasmed. "If he wants to fuck, then we make it on my terms," she murmured. "Only you won't like it."

Relief hit me hard. It was only a matter of time before he clawed his way out once more. The bruises and marks on her skin from this morning were burned into my mind. I couldn't fight him. Not the way I was, at least. Next time she might not escape so easily.

"Try me," I whispered. "Right now, I'd do anything just to have you."

THIRTY

London

Hale is dead?

HALE IS DEAD?

I lifted my head from the constant barrage of messages on my phone. Curiosity gripped me as I opened Facebook and searched his name...

Bad move.

He was *everywhere*. Images of the police dragging his waterlogged body from the river was the first thing you saw. He was certainly working hard to make it well known he was no longer a threat.

But that was just like him, wasn't it?

A liar.

A strategist...

And very much a threat.

I closed down the app, then opened my messages.

I'm on my way. I'll meet you there, I typed, then hit send, not waiting for a response before I rose from my seat and left the study behind.

It was time to know for sure. To look that bastard in the cloudy fucking eyes and ease that clenched fist in my gut. The one which told me Hale was more dangerous right now than he'd ever been…

I pulled on my jacket over my shoulder holster and strode out of the house, hating I was leaving my family behind. But this had to be done.

Beep.

I lifted my phone as I pressed the button and unlocked the new Audi I'd had delivered. Gleaming black paintwork, brushed black steel wheels. It was stunning. I'd better keep it away from Vivienne. But I didn't linger on the thought as I climbed in and read the message.

Rossi: *We need to meet.*

"What the fuck now?" I muttered and typed out exactly that.

Rossi: *We have a problem.*

When didn't we? I glanced at the time and winced. I didn't have time for this. Not now at least. I typed…

Give me an hour.

It was barely a second later.

Rossi: *I'll be at our warehouse.*

I knew the one. A refrigerator trucking company on the outskirts of the city. What was so goddamn important? Whatever it was, it was big. But right now, I had other very dead matters to attend to. I started the brand new car and put it into gear, backing out of the driveway.

By the time I turned onto the highway, the night was already darkening. Twilight, a perfect time to view a body. At least it wasn't midnight.

Beep.

I ground my teeth and glanced at the screen as the message scrolled.

DeLuca: There are no major injuries. Internal swelling, but the scan shows the bleeding has stopped. It's a fucking miracle, but Colt's going to make a physical recovery. My most pressing concern is his mental state. He needs a full psych workup, London. I know you—

I leaned forward and pressed the button to end the voicemail. He didn't need a goddamn shrink. Not one I couldn't control, at least. He needed family. He needed...

Her.

His Wildcat.

I worked the gears, speeding hard as my pulse raced and I fought the need to turn the car around and look for her. Fuck if we didn't all crave her. Especially now that she...

Colt's the father.

If she thought I'd be upset by that, then she'd be wrong. I wanted her now more than ever. The thought of her belly swelling and her breasts growing larger did something unexplainable to me.

"Jesus," I groaned as I reached down and tugged the crotch of my pants.

She might carry his now.

But one day, she'd have mine.

I'd fuck her day and night until she did.

The thought stayed with me as the sky grew darker and I turned onto the off-ramp and headed for the main mortuary in the city. I'd put many in there, but a place like that was never on the top of my list to attend…until now.

Now it was a necessity.

I pulled into the street and caught sight of headlights flashing before I parked near the black Range Rover. The doctor climbed out at the same time as I did. Boots crunched on the asphalt.

"DeLuca," I muttered.

"Let's get this over with, shall we?" he grumbled, turning to the square concrete building.

I followed, saying nothing when he walked in, showed his ID, and filled out a document handed his way on a clipboard by a middle-aged woman who watched me from behind thick black-rimmed glasses. I didn't meet her gaze, just stared at the empty waiting room until DeLuca handed the clipboard back and thanked her.

"Come on," he directed, leaving her behind.

I followed him, pushing through a set of double doors that led along a hallway. His pace was punishing, but I kept up, moving in close. "What did you tell them?"

He shot me a glare. "Does it matter?"

No. I guess it didn't. Still, I wanted my name out of it.

"Don't worry." He stopped, pressed his ID to the sensor, and pushed through the locked doors. "You weren't on the paperwork."

"Good." I followed him through the doors, then we turned.

The pungent scent of antiseptic hit me. I winced, hating that my pulse was already speeding. It wasn't the dead I was scared of...only the truth. DeLuca pressed his card to the scanner on the second set of doors, but I fixed my gaze on the stainless steel bank of refrigerated drawers on the other side of the doors.

He pushed through, and I followed. For a second, I couldn't move, frozen by my own racing thoughts. *What if it was him? What if it was Hale...what would I do then?*

There were more of them out there.

More Hales...

Some who were worse.

Years, that's how long it'd taken Helene to crack the information on the chip she'd taken from the Vault.

Years.

I couldn't wait that long.

Always watching.

Always waiting.

For them to take what's mine.

It was the image of Vivienne big and round, her belly full of life, that drove me forward. I stepped into the room, scanning the stainless steel tables as DeLuca grabbed a clipboard hanging from the wall.

"B13," he muttered, then placed it back. "I hope you're ready for this. There was some degree of decomposition from being in the water."

I ground my teeth, clinging to the image of the woman I'd make my wife and answered. "Let's get this over with."

"Suit yourself," he sighed, tugged on a set of gloves, and strode toward the drawers.

One yank and a hiss of air rushed out.

It's not him.

It's not him.

DeLuca reached in, grabbed the handle of the slide and pulled, dragging the black body bag with it. *Hale,* said the name tag attached to the side. I winced at the sight. Water sloshed inside as DeLuca tugged on the zipper, pulling it all the way down.

Gray wrinkled skin.

The room sucked out all the air.

I stared as the doc pushed the sides apart.

Dark hair plastered against puffy flesh. I stepped closer, peering at the man who looked like the man I hated most in this world.

"Do you remember if he has any distinguishing marks or scars you remember?"

I tried to think.

He picked up the hands, peering at Hale's trimmed nails, then turned his hands over. "Huh, that's interesting."

I jerked my gaze upwards. "What?"

"The pads of his fingers have been burned."

That band across my chest cinched tighter. "What?"

He twisted the wrist as far as it'd go. "Someone has burned his fingerprints off with acid by the looks of it."

"His teeth, they'll confirm identity with that, won't they?"

He scowled, then strode back to the folder, leaving me alone with the corpse. *I hate you.* I wanted to scream the words to his face. *I wish your death belonged to me.*

"According to the records, he has a full set of dentures, so that rules out dental."

I jerked my gaze to him. "What did you say?"

DeLuca held up the folder. "A full set of teeth."

I left the body and took a step toward him. "No, that's not true. He doesn't have all his teeth. I know because I knocked one of them out, lower middle molar on the left."

But DeLuca just shook his head. "Not according to the paperwork."

A mole on his left shoulder. "And he has a mole on the back of his left shoulder," I added as the memory of him with a Daughter at The Order came rushing back.

She was crying.

He was fucking.

I stood there, staring at the corpse while my stomach churned and my soul died a little more. "It was dark, raised."

"You sure?" DeLuca was interested now.

"I'm fucking positive."

He walked over, stepping to the left side this time, tugged the bag lower, and reached inside. I followed as that fist of desperation drove deeper into my chest. The bag creaked as the doc yanked an arm out, then reached under, gripped the body tightly, and lifted.

The entire thing moved, but only a little. He grunted, straining as he lifted again. "A hand would be good," he growled.

No...no fucking way.

He jerked his gaze to mine. "You want to see the mole or not?"

"Goddamn it," I grumbled as I unbuttoned my jacket and pulled it off. Revulsion rose as I yanked the sleeves of my shirt and rolled them up.

The pudgy flesh was cold. My fingers sank in as I gripped the body around the back of the neck and yanked.

Crunch

I winced, grunting as the body suddenly shot upwards. But I didn't care about that, I was too busy looking at the gray flesh of the shoulders.

There was no mole.

There was no fucking mole.

"It's not there." The doc searched the smooth skin and shook his head.

I met his stare as we let the body fall back down. "I knew it. The sonofabitch is still out there."

I WATCHED the red lights of the Range Rover flare once before the four-wheel drive turned and disappeared around the corner. A shudder tore free as I gripped the wheel, taking a deep, sudden breath. The heady scent of the brand new car invaded to fill my lungs, overpowering the stench of the dead.

He's still out there.

Rage burned inside me, making me strangle the wheel. Was he watching me...laughing because his plan worked. It was a smart plan...for someone like him with no backbone. I leaned forward, stabbed the button, and started the engine.

Only now I had a bigger task on my hands. *How the hell did you track a dead man?* I didn't know. But I'd figure it out. I'd find the bastard who'd betrayed me and almost killed my son, and when I did...

When I did...

I'd look in his eyes, smile, then shoot the bastard in the head myself.

The engine of the Audi growled into gear and pulled forward, eager to be rid of the mortuary. My thoughts turned to the warehouse on the outskirts of the city and the Rossis waiting for me. I tried to think what it could be, but my thoughts kept drifting to Vivienne.

I glanced at the phone, fighting the urge to call her.

She's pregnant.

My breath moved a little deeper with the thought. We'd need to do more than find Hale and the rest of the now splintered Order. My days and nights were soon to be busy, hunting, killing...and getting ready for our baby.

The image of that consumed me. By the time I turned into the sprawling industrial compound, I'd almost forgotten why I was there. *The Rossis...that's right. Something so damn important that it couldn't wait.*

I slowed the car and turned into the driveway, to find the bright lights of the trucking company still in full swing. Trucks were being loaded. *Rossi Haulage* was printed on the sides of gleaming trucks. But the gates to the compound were still closed. I pulled up next to the darkened guard hut, scanning the otherwise empty compound, and swore under my breath.

"You'd better be fucking here," I muttered.

Then a sharp knock on the window jolted me.

I jerked my gaze to the guard standing outside the door, peering at me. I stabbed the button to wind down the window.

"Mr. St. James?"

"Yes," I forced through clenched teeth, watching him scan the rest of the car. "Looking for something?"

He didn't answer, just stepped back and turned his head. I followed his gaze, seeing movement in the hut before the gates in front of me opened.

"You can drive in, sir." He motioned toward the main building. "Mr. Rossi and Lazarus are waiting for you."

"He'd better be," I muttered, moving from being annoyed to seriously pissed off.

What the fuck was going on? I pulled the car in, parked it under the glaring exterior lights, and switched off the engine. Benjamin had better have a good reason to drag me all the fucking way out here, then check me over like a goddamn schmuck. A real good reason.

I closed the door, not bothering to lock it, and strode to the closed massive roller doors, focusing on the small door to its side. The regular-size door opened as I neared. Blonde hair, blue eyes, a savage hunger in his stare. You could almost mistake Lazarus Rossi for a Son if you didn't know better... lucky for me, I did.

"Laz." I glanced toward the front of the compound. "Want to tell me what's going on?"

"Better we show you. Dad's waiting inside."

I stopped outside the door, searching his stare as that nagging voice in my head warned *steady*. I peered inside, finding nothing more than shadows. I didn't like this. Not the dangerous glint in his stare, or the clipped way he spoke. These were dangerous times and Hale was still out there, or was he here, maybe holding them hostage?

The memory of that boardroom where I'd had Hale's brand new buddies held hostage returned. They were free now, being observed. Still, you couldn't be too sure. "How about you tell me here?"

Laz shook his head and took a step backwards.

My pulse sped. My mind raced.

I was putting a lot of trust in the Rossis here.

My gun was under my jacket. Still in a situation like this, anything could happen.

If they were in danger, then we were all fucked. I stepped in, waiting as Lazarus closed the door behind me.

"Can't be too careful," the Mafia son muttered, striding through the gloom toward the rear.

The faint sound of a TV came. Screams, cheering. It wasn't until I caught the words, *"The Kings are heading to the finals!"* that I understood.

"Sounds like the Kings won," I commented, earning myself a cutting glare.

"Didn't expect them to lose."

Lazarus was insanely savage about his hockey, and none more than the Crossfell City Kings. The door to the rear office opened and Freddy, their right-hand man, stepped into view. That warning in my gut only grew louder, sending a stab of fear through me.

I rarely got scared. But this had my body tightening.

Until the hitman moved aside and Benjamin Rossi was there, pushing up from leaning back against a desk.

"What the fuck is going on?" I demanded, stepping inside.

The door closed behind me as Ben shook his head, then glanced over his shoulder. "It seems the hitman we spoke about heading out of the city wasn't just any hitman. It was Cerberus."

"Cerebus?" I repeated, that nagging voice in my head growing stone cold.

Cerberus wasn't just any hitman. It was actually three... working for any ruthless bastard with deep enough pockets. Someone just like Hale.

From the corner of my eye, the door to the rear of the office building opened...

My heart was pounding as all four of them stepped out, moving toward me like a river of wrath. Three towered in front, crowded by a very pregnant young woman.

My mind raced, trying to figure out the implications of this. "You were supposed to stay gone."

"Oh, yeah?" Tobias Banks glared, his lip curling in a sneer. "Tell that to the bastard who bombed our fucking house and abducted us."

THIRTY-ONE

Vivienne

I hated this. Hated the way his arms were stretched high over his head, the muscles taut and the tendons strained. But it was the wide leather shackle wrapped over the already bruised, raw skin that was too much. My trapped breath burned as I focused on the buckle in front of me.

"Tighter," he demanded, his voice a low, savage snarl.

My fingers trembled so hard I stopped. "I can't." I sat back on my heels next to him on the bed. "I'm sorry. I thought I could do this, but I can't."

He said nothing for a moment, just lowered his gaze. "I understand."

I shook my head, jerking my gaze to his. "I can't hurt you. It's just not in me and this...this is hurting you." I reached out, stroking his cheek. "You've been through too much already."

A vein at his temple pulsed. He was sweating in January. But it was the flinch of agony I focused on. There was no ending for him, was there? No going back to the man he'd been. He was trapped in this tortured existence that occupied somewhere I couldn't reach in his beautiful mind.

"I have to leave," he finally whispered. "It's not safe here."

"What?" I murmured. "No."

He met my stare, his helplessness was a void, a gaping, desolate hole inside him. "I can't put you in danger. And me being here is exactly what that will do. The doc...the doc wants me admitted for some kind of psych workup. I'm going to find a place that's as far from here as I can and I'm going to go."

The room spun, taking my stomach with it. "No." I shook my head. "No, Colt. I won't let that happen. I can't let that happen."

Colt lowered his free arm, reaching for the one already trussed against the steel frame of the bed. "It's the only way."

"I'll do it." I grabbed his wrist, stopping him as he tugged at the bonds. "I'll fucking strap you to this bed and draw the beast to the surface. I'll make him a deal he can't refuse. I'll give him what he wants."

He met my gaze. "Are you sure?"

"No," I answered. "But we've run out of options, haven't we?"

There was a savagery underneath the empty stare as he nodded. A *beast* that hovered too close to the surface, darkening his already deep blue eyes, until they were almost black. It was that beast I focused on now. That *beast* which made me lift his free hand to the railing on the bed. The thick leather strap hung loose, waiting for me to restrain the man I loved like a damn animal.

A low, throaty rumble came as I leaned across him. Colt dropped his head, pressed his face against my underarm, and inhaled. I tried to focus, cinching the strap softly.

"Tighter," Colt urged, his tone throatier, not sounding like him at all.

I yanked harder, making my body jerk. His face nuzzled my breast, softly at first, then insistent, until his mouth sought my nipple.

"No." He jerked away, shaking his head, trying to stop himself from being like that. "Gotta stay in control, gotta make him understand."

But as I pulled away, I saw it was too late. The bulge in his gray sweatpants told me that. Hard, straining, his cock tented the fleece. I couldn't stop myself from touching it.

He jerked his head up, and that desperate animal warning came. *"Wildcat."*

Shadows moved in, making his cheeks look sunken and his eyes hollow. He was changing right before me. The Colt I knew slipped away second after second.

"Please," he growled.

My gaze was captured by the predator. By the way he tilted his head, animalistic eyes regarding me like prey. But I wasn't prey. I was someone he needed to obey. Because I had something he wanted.

My heart hammered as I slowly slid from the bed. His nostrils flared, his calculating eyes tracking my every move with ravenous hunger. The first time I'd seen him like this, I was terrified. The second...when he'd fucked me, I was frozen for most of the time…but here—I glanced at his hands straining against the bonds—here I could explore this bestial side of him.

"Do you know who I am?" I asked as I slowly kicked off my boots.

He didn't answer, just watched me.

"Tell me."

"*Wildcat*," the beast growled.

"That's right." I grabbed my shirt and tugged it over my head.

He stiffened, drawing in a sharp breath as he stared at my body. *Scenting the air.*

"You and I are going to come to an agreement, aren't we?" I reached around, grasped the clasp of my bra, and unhooked it. "Beast."

He jerked his head upwards, that savage glare meeting my eyes.

"*Aren't we?*" I demanded. There was a twitch in his lip, a curling. The beast was used to getting his own way, until now, that was. Now, he'd learn that you only get when I gave it, *or else*. I slid my bra down just a little.

"Yes." The word rumbled like a warning.

But it was a start. "Good," I murmured, slowly lowering my hands.

His brow creased as he licked his lips. "Closer," he urged.

Goosebumps coursed through me. I did as he demanded. "Is this what you want?" I asked, cupping my breast until I moaned. I still ached from last night. But it was an ache I was learning to like. "Your teeth marked me last night."

He yanked the bindings desperately, as that ravenous rumble came once more.

"*Stop.*"

He flinched, freezing instantly.

"That's better," I crooned, taking a step closer. "You want me, and I want Colt." I grazed a finger along his cheek, meeting that stare which wasn't quite sane. "So, we're going to try this carefully. You bite me and it's over, you hurt me and it's done. Do you understand?"

There was a second before he nodded.

"Good." I lifted my leg and climbed onto the bed.

Thump.

The bindings slapped against steel as he jerked forward. But I ignored it, rising upwards to lean closer, so close he could—

He jerked his head to the side and latched on to my nipple. But there were no teeth this time. I closed my eyes, stolen by the warmth of his mouth. It looked like the beast was learning.

"That's the way." I lowered my hands to his shoulders.

Tight muscles, trembling with the strain as he nuzzled and licked, drawing my nipple into his mouth. He wanted me...*Jesus, he wanted me.* Pain pinched, wrenching me away from the moment. I looked down, finding my nipple pinned.

"*Hey!*" I snarled.

He snapped his gaze up.

"Less teeth."

He said nothing, just held my stare and gently licked.

I gave into that sensation. "That's better," I moaned.

He licked more, then eagerly turned his head to seek my other breast.

"That's so much better. Good, beast."

He purred. That deep rumble vibrated in the back of his throat. "More," he urged. "I want to move down, want you on my face."

I pressed harder, listening to that bestial rumble turn dangerous.

"Wildcat, I need."

Hard breaths consumed me. I pulled away, trying to focus. "Are you sure that's not going to tip you over?"

He yanked the bindings. "I'm about ten seconds away from tearing these straps and destroying the entire fucking room to taste you. *You decide.*"

My heart stuttered. I looked at the strained leather straps, then back down at him. "Okay."

I eased back, watching him shift his ass down, his gaze lowering to my jeans. "Take them off."

I unbuttoned my jeans, knowing once I did this there was no coming back. Only the alternative was no Colt, and that I refused to accept. I tugged the zipper and pushed them low, taking my panties with them. That bestial keening sound grew louder as they fell to the floor.

He shifted his ass lower, his focus on me as he slid lower on the bed, as far as he could go, at least. I still wasn't sure about this, not with his arms stretched so high. I met his gaze. "If you want to do that, I'd need to loosen the straps. Are you going to behave if I did that?"

His answer was a panicked nod of his head. I wasn't so sure about this...not with the gleam in his eyes. Still, all I could think about was him leaving. That was what drew me to climb back onto the bed and straddle him once more.

He kept my gaze as I worked the bindings, leaving his hand to fall to the pillow before securing it once more. He didn't move, just watched me until I finished the second one. But this wasn't Colt. The moment I bet that menacing stare, I knew.

That bloodcurdling rumble resounded in his chest as he shifted down under me until his head lay flat. "Now," he demanded, looking down at my body until his gaze stopped at the juncture between my thighs.

I shivered under that predatory gleam, my voice trembling as I whispered, "Don't...don't hurt me."

He scowled, his nostrils flaring, before he shifted right under me. That carnal stare stayed as he lifted his head, pressed his face against my crease, and licked.

Soft. Careful.

My breath caught as he moved deeper, holding my focus. My pulse raced, just from staring into this male's eyes. He wasn't Colt, and yet he was. He was a part of him that had been hurt so badly, he'd shattered. He was *still* the man I loved, still the man I *wanted*.

"Jesus," I whispered as he sucked, drawing my clit gently into his mouth.

That throaty growl came once more, pulsing in the back of his throat, sending vibrations against my body. Heat flared, making me slam my hand against the bed. My hips thrust on their own. That sensation was fucking...*delicious*.

"More." I was the one who demanded this time. "*More.*"

The beast complied, dipping his head until that feral sound sent vibrations through my core. My orgasm slammed into me, rising from nowhere. I dropped my hand, slid it behind his head, and thrust against his mouth.

Sparks erupted.

Blinding, until I unleashed a growl of my own.

One that echoed underneath me.

He dragged that savage part of my nature to the surface, forcing it upwards with every lick. I clenched my jaw and gripped his head as I ground myself against him as I came crashing down. Hard breaths burned like fire as my pussy pulsed and pulsed and *pulsed*.

It wasn't the beast that was consumed with the frenzy...and it wasn't the beast whose lips curled. It was me. That hunger consumed me. I pushed away, my legs trembling as I moved down. I was the one who held *his* gaze now as I tugged the waistband of his sweats.

"Is this what you want?" I forced through bared teeth.

He gave a slow nod, his cock bouncing free as I yanked. Fuck, he was hard. The head was flushed, the eye beading. I watched that bead well with every pulse of that thick vein as I settled over him, then dropped *hard*. That enormous length drove all the way inside, making me throw my head back and moan.

"You will not hurt me, do you understand?" I didn't wait for him to answer as I ground my hips, riding that delicious feeling. "You *will* give my Colt back to me."

I opened my eyes and looked down, finding that bestial stare fixed on me.

A hard thrust and he yanked his head upwards, snapping the leather taut. The movement was so fast I didn't have time to react. But he didn't hurt me...just thrust underneath me, driving himself deeper as our bodies collided. The hunger in his glare now was something else. Something that looked like desperation...something that could look like love.

"Wildcat," the beast grunted as his cock twitched. *"Mine."*

I ground my body down hard, consumed by that wave as it rose again. My body clenched as I clamped down on what I needed. "Yes," I whispered, giving in. *"Yes."*

THIRTY-TWO

London

The roar of the crowd blasted through the TV's speakers, filling the room. "The Crossfell City Kings have done it again!" the narrator screamed, fighting to be heard over the deafening cheers of the hometown crowd. "Let's cut to the rink and hear what the captain of the team, Kalon Rathbone, has to say!"

But I fixed my gaze on Tobias and on what he'd just said. "What the fuck do you mean, abducted?"

Lazarus turned, grabbed the remote from the desk behind him, and switched it off, instantly ending the ruckus.

"Just what he said." Nick stepped around his hotheaded younger brother. "The bastards came for us, destroyed everything we'd built for the last six fucking months, and took us hostage."

I narrowed in on how big they were now, with lean, hard muscles and careful stares full of disdain. It looked like life in the mountains had suited them, until now.

"Including everything we had for the baby," Tobias snarled.

Jesus, he was fucking *pissed*.

Ryth hadn't said a word the entire time, just stood there, dwarfed by the three men around her. Her dark, sunken eyes looked shell-shocked, adding even more shadows to her gaunt cheeks. Thin fingers peeked out from the sleeves of her oversized sweater and rested on her massive bump. While her brothers seemed to have grown in size, she seemed to have shrunk. The baby seemed to have taken more than it should have out of her. No wonder they were so protective.

That could've been Vivienne. That thought only made me feel…dangerous.

I turned to Benjamin. "Do we have a bead on those Cerberus bastards?"

"I'll do you one better," he growled, shifting his focus to the doorway behind me.

Heavy steps sounded like deep claps of thunder echoing through the warehouse behind me. I turned slowly, my focus instantly moving to the two Sigs strapped across my chest as a mountain filled the doorway. At six foot seven, the towering male ducked his head to step inside, but once he was in, his focus was directed fully on me.

Nick and Caleb moved as one, taking a protective step in front of Ryth. But it was Tobias that lunged forward, rushing the massive male, until he was stopped by Lazarus' hand on his chest.

"Easy," the Mafia son urged.

"London St. James," Ben muttered, his frosty glare tilting up at the big bastard. "Let me introduce Alvarez Cross, one of the three Cerberus brothers."

Jesus fucking Christ. The man was a walking felony. His thick shoulders were barely contained in a black open-collared shirt which was crisscrossed by the thick webbing of his shoulder holster, one that had to have been custom made. You couldn't buy them that big.

"Mr. St. James," the deep voice rumbled as he stepped closer, offering a massive paw. "Been waiting a long time for this moment. It's a pleasure to meet you."

I arched a brow, glancing at Ben for a moment before returning my eyes to Alvarez. Rossi was walking a fine line putting the Bankses they'd kidnapped in front of them. The tic in Tobias' jaw, and the way Lazarus angled himself between the two of them, spoke volumes about just how fine the line was. Frankly, I was surprised the hotheaded Banks brother was restraining himself so successfully, he was well-known for his violent impulsiveness. But he was far from the level of violence my own family would go to.

"I wish I could say the same." I stared at the hand. "Now what the fuck do you want?"

He flinched at my coldness.

I had no time to deal with extortion, which this obviously was.

"I was told you weren't one to bullshit," he muttered.

"Understatement of the fucking year."

A careful smile tugged the corners of his mouth.

"It's not what you think." Benjamin took a step forward. "Alvarez here wants to do business."

"Diamond business," the hitman added with the hint of a smile. "The expensive kind."

I stiffened. "The Lawlors are some of my oldest friends. What makes you think I'll even allow you in the same goddamn room as them?"

The brute just turned his head, those unflinching eyes fixed on Ryth and her brothers. "I can think of four already."

Goddamn *bastard*.

My fingers twitched, fighting the need to pull my gun right now and put a bullet through his thick fucking skull. If there was just him, I might've done it. I might've blown a neat hole right through his forehead, then hunted down whoever had paid him to attack a pregnant woman and exacted revenge from them. But there wasn't just one of him, was there? There were three. Three fucking hitmen to hunt down and take out. As if we didn't have enough to fucking contend with right now.

"I want us to go into business together," Cross smiled.

I glanced at Ben. "You've got to be fucking joking," I snapped, glancing at Ryth, hidden behind her glowering, protective males. But the Mafia bastard was no help. His jaw clenched with seething anger. "He doesn't want my money. He wants connections, I kind I can't help with."

I sucked in a hard breath, my mind racing. The Lawlors were dangerous in their own right. There was no way they'd let some two-bit fucking thug muscle in on them. Not a hope in hell.

"Fine, you want an introduction? I'll get you an introduction. But that's all." I turned to the walking steroid. "But I want assurances you are who you say you are before I'll even make a call." I took a step toward the bastard, narrowing in on that gleam of hunger in his stare. "I want details of your fucking brothers, your wives, your family all the way back to your fucking great-great-grandparents, for that matter. If I suspect you've lied to me, the deal's dead. If I suspect you've threatened the lives of Ryth, the Bankses, my family, or anyone else in this room, the deal's dead. The Rossis included." I met Benjamin's widening stare. "Because if there's a deal to be done, they're in this as well."

The head of the Rossi family just gave a shrug, then jerked his head toward his son. "This is all Laz now. I'm retiring."

Retiring my ass.

The Stidda prince never flinched as I fixed my gaze on him. "Well, Lazarus, looks like we're in bed together."

"Fucking perfect," he muttered.

"You want the information?" the towering hitman muttered. "Then it's yours."

I met that calculating stare. "Just be aware that the information will be kept by me and if at any time I feel you have contributed—" I glanced toward Ryth, "in an attack on those who I consider blood, then not only will the deal be dead." I turned back to him. "You and your entire family will be, as well."

There was a twitch in the corner of his eye. I was sure the Cerberus brothers weren't used to such a direct threat. But then that twitch settled, and he gave a slow nod. "Understood."

I followed with a dip of my own head. "Then we're on the same page."

But it was Ryth who drew my focus as she pushed Nick aside and stepped around them. Tobias moved at the same time she did, driving himself forward to not only match her stride, but push ahead until he was between her and Alvarez Cross.

Hate raged in his stare, which never moved from the big bastard in front of him. One glance at the two of these men and you knew blood was going to be spilled. But Ryth never once looked at the hitman.

Instead, her focus was directed at me. "Now that your business is done," she started, her voice husky as she directed those big blue-green eyes on me. "I want you to do something for me."

Surprise filled me. I glanced at Tobias and the fucking tic in his jaw that felt too much like the countdown of a timebomb and turned back to her. "Whatever you need."

"Good," she whispered. "Then I'd like you to arrange something for me. I'd like to finally see my sister."

PANICKED THOUGHTS FILLED my head as I drove back home. They were about Ryth mostly. Ryth and her tiny fucking body and swollen belly. Ryth and her haunted fucking eyes that stared right through you.

Ryth and her desire to meet the woman I loved.

That fear boomed like thunder in my head. The two women Haelstrom Hale wanted more than anything in the same damn place?

It wasn't just a bad idea.

It was suicide.

The Bankses were now more dangerous than ever. That, I didn't goddamn need. But I couldn't stop thinking about it. Ryth, Vivienne…would Helene come to the meeting, as well?

Vivienne didn't trust her.

Ryth didn't even know her. I wasn't sure she even knew *of* her.

All three of King's blood right there for the taking.

If I was Hale, that's when I'd strike.

Take them all…

Hold them for ransom.

I clenched my grip around the wheel.

Over my fucking dead body.

None of this should've happened. Ryth and her damn stepbrothers were supposed to stay hidden while I ripped apart the goddamn Order, unearthing the sick bastards behind the sickening trafficking ring. The moment I found they'd stolen King's DNA was the moment I knew this started as a way to control him.

Who would want to bring one of the world's richest and most powerful men to his knees? Haelstrom Hale, that's who.

What better way than his own blood?

Breed from his bloodline, use them to take apart his legacy.

At the very least, draw King out into the open…which is exactly what I'd tried to do.

By using Vivienne...

I swallowed hard. But that was before. Before the pain in the ass spitfire clawed her way inside my fucking heart. Now she didn't just howl and scream within those soft, bleeding walls... she fucking belonged there.

Christ, this was a goddamn mess.

I hadn't meant to love her, hadn't meant to want the fucking wildcat. Now we all did. Now she belonged with us. Now she was ours. Red and blue lights flickered in the rear-view mirror far behind me. I left them, shifting my thoughts back to the woman who carried King's DNA.

The moment I found the records of her lineage, I was stunned, then riveted. Hale had always told me there was a purpose to The Order, for him at least. A desperate, obsessive, controlling purpose to unearth the man known as King. Once I found out how he planned to do that, I had to control it.

Only, when I found Vivienne, that all changed.

Now I just wanted to control her.

My pulse sped, narrowing in on her. The way she smelled. The way she touched. The way she moaned underneath me. I wanted it all...now that she was pregnant with our baby. Just like Ryth was with the Bankses'.

The red and blue hues grew brighter as I turned onto the off-ramp.

I focused on the flashing lights that came again. Two cop cars this time.

King and his bloodline faded into the background as the two police sedans raced around me, turning up ahead onto a familiar street.

"What the fuck?" I slowed, glancing at the road in front of me. My house was not far in the distance. I tapped the brakes, slowing the Audi to a crawl.

The two cop cars parked behind the two EMT vans parked in the driveway of the towering mansion. If it was anyone else's place, I would've kept driving. But it wasn't, was it?

It was the Areses'.

In the washed out red and blue hues, a man stood on the front lawn talking to a paramedic as they wheeled not one covered body on a stretcher, but two. I stared hard, recognizing Silas Ares as he turned his head toward me as he stood on the lawn.

I eased my foot off the brake and lett the car roll past, before I grabbed my phone and sped up. One swipe of my thumb and the number on the other end of the line rang.

"Yeah?" Harper's voice was heavy with sleep.

"Two bodies are being wheeled out of the Ares house as we speak. Any idea what's going on there?"

"Two?"

"Two."

"Jesus." Sounds of the bedding shifting under him came in the background.

I turned onto my street, my house blissfully darkened. "Find out what you can," I muttered as I pulled into the driveway.

"Will do," he acknowledged, and ended the call.

This looked bad, real fucking bad. I parked the car, then climbed out and made my way into the house in a hurry. My fingers could barely punch the numbers in fast enough before I yanked the door open and flew inside. I raced past the study as my phone rang. I swiped the screen as I strode into the private wing of our house and growled, "Talk to me."

"Two bodies; one male, age forty-two, deceased. One female, age forty, deceased," Harper murmured as I stared at the closed bedroom doors of my family.

I stopped outside Vivienne's bedroom door, listening. Emptiness came from inside her room. I glanced at the bedroom doors belonging to my sons. She was in one of them, wrapped up in powerful arms, sleeping. I turned away, heading toward the study. "Find out what you can. I need to know if this is going to touch us."

"I'm already digging. London…"

"Yeah?"

"This looks bad."

I winced, pushed open the study door, and flicked on the light. "I know."

THIRTY-THREE

Vivienne

My stomach lurched a second before the hot acid spilled into the back of my throat.

My eyes snapped open. Terror punched through me as I threw aside the covers and lunged for the bathroom. That burning was in my mouth, slipping out to splash on the toilet seat as my stomach clenched again...and again...and again.

A growl came from behind me. Colt was just a towering shadow. Through the tears, I caught his wide eyes filled with panic as he stood in the doorway. But I didn't have enough strength to worry about him right then. Instead, I clutched the seat and held on for dear life.

I tried to keep quiet as I retched, but the sounds that came from me sounded inhuman. I whimpered, held on, and retched again.

The bedroom door flew open, hitting the wall with a bang!

"Wildcat?" Carven called from the bedroom.

I swiped my hand across my mouth and gripped my stomach. Colt spun at the invasion and shoved an arm across the doorway, blocking the way.

"Hey!" Carven snarled.

Until that sickening warning sound rumbled in the chest of his twin. Someone shoved first, then the other shoved back, until shirts were yanked and Carven was slammed against the wall.

"Stop!" I cried out and shoved to my feet. "That's your brother."

Colt whipped his gaze toward me. Those almost black eyes told me all I need to know. I lifted a trembling hand, my knees shaking with the effort. "Easy, now."

"What the fuck is going on?" Carven whipped his gaze from his brother to me and punched his twin's hand from his shirt. "What's gotten into you, asshole?"

"It's not him." I shook my head. "It's the..."

"I know who it is," Carven snapped, straightening the creased neckline of his shirt. "You think I don't know my own blood? I know Colt, know him better than anyone. But this." He waved a hand toward his brother, who just looked at him like a rival. "This isn't him."

Colt's answer was to take a step forward, his top lip curling.

I lifted a hand. "No—" I barely got out before another wave of nausea slammed into me again, making me clutch my stomach and moan.

"Are you supposed to be this sick?"

I winced, swallowing hard as that urge to retch came back. "I don't know."

Fear gripped me. What if there was something wrong? My hand trembled. "I need my phone," I requested as I stepped back into the bedroom.

The hostility in the room didn't ease as Carven searched the floor, grabbed it from amongst my discarded clothes, and handed it to me. But he didn't come closer, just eyed his brother as I pressed one of the few contacts I had stored.

The phone barely rang before it was answered. "Vivienne," the soft male voice said. "Everything okay?'

In the background, I could hear chaos. Multiple orders were barked around the beep and squeal of machines. It sounded frantic. Still, the doctor had answered my call.

"I'm pregnant," I rushed. "But I'm vomiting a lot and I feel like I've been hit by a train."

"How far along?"

I lifted my gaze to Colt, who still glared at his brother. "Not long. Four to six weeks."

"It's normal to be sick in the mornings. How is your health? Have you had any...recent trauma?"

He knew the kind of life I had, and what we'd been through. "Not the best."

"I'm sending you the name of a specialist. She's one of the best gynecologists in the city. She'll look after you. And Vivienne..."

"Yeah?"

"You need to protect yourself now more than ever." He gave a grunt, lifting something as he spoke. "You have another life to think about now. I need to go, but please keep in touch."

"I will. Thank you, Lucas."

"You're very welcome."

He was gone, leaving me holding the phone as my belly clenched again.

"Well?" Carven glared.

I don't know," I said. "He's given me the name of a doctor who'll see me." I closed my eyes, fighting the urge to stumble for the toilet. "I need someone to take me."

The bedroom door opened slowly and London stepped in. His dark eyes missed nothing as he scanned the room before settling on me.

"I'll take you," he declared, then met Colt's threatening stare. There was a flinch before he stepped toward him. "You need to get ahold of yourself, son. We need you, do you hear me? We need you to come back to us."

A flicker of confusion rose in Colt's eyes. The blue brightened a little, leaving the dangerous glare of the beast behind. But it was only a flicker before the darkness returned.

"If you send me the details, I'll make the call." London offered, glancing my way.

I nodded, my fingers trembling as my phone beeped with the doctor's details. I did as London asked, sending the information. "I need to shower," I muttered, going back to the bathroom and leaving them behind.

How the hell were you supposed to look after yourself when your world was a goddamn mess?

I didn't know. But I had to try.

"LET'S get you up on the table for a scan." Juliet Sharpe smiled as she rose from the chair and waved toward an exam table in the corner of the room.

She was everything Doctor DeLuca had promised. Smart, kind, and very, very thorough as she took down all my details. London, on the other hand, was his normal demeanour; cold, quiet, and dangerous. He said nothing, just sat there with his legs crossed and an unflinching stare.

"Sure," I answered, and glanced London's way before I rose.

Juliet moved to a machine. "It's quite early, but I use a cutting-edge ultrasound that allows me to detect the baby even at this stage."

My breath caught as I focused on the black screen on the machine that came to life with a flick of a switch. "So, we're going to be able to see it?" I kicked off my shoes at the base of the bed. "The baby?"

She just smiled. "That's the plan."

My pulse sped as I glanced at London. But he said nothing. Actually, he said less than nothing, just levelled that empty glare on the same monitor.

I ignored him, just climbed up and lay back, tugging my shirt up as Juliet unbuttoned my jeans and tugged them down a bit.

"A little cold gel," she murmured, squeezing an upended bottle until a thick, clear substance squirted on my abdomen.

But I was fixed on that black screen as she pressed a wand to my belly and pressed. Sounds came through the speaker, sloshing and distorted, until she shifted the wand and bore down...then there was a racing, fluttering sound.

"There we go." She smiled and glanced my way.

I stared at the blur on the screen.

"It's very early...about eight weeks, by the looks of it. This is the baby's heart right here and there—"

She stopped, scowling.

I searched her face. "What is it?"

Juliet just shook her head. "That's...strange."

She grabbed the bottle and squeezed more gel onto my belly before pressing down once more. From the corner of my eye, I saw London uncross his legs and lean forward a little. My pulse sped, thrashing in my ears as I met his stare.

Now there was life.

And worry.

He pushed up from the chair. "What is it?"

She didn't look at him but focused on the screen, and that thrashing sound came once more. "You're...um. You have another baby."

"Another baby?" I whispered. "What do you mean, another baby?"

She pressed harder into my belly. "This is so strange. Another placenta, another complete sac. This baby is more developed, about twelve weeks, by the looks of it."

Twelve weeks? My eyes widened as I fixed on London.

He knew...exactly what I was thinking.

"This other baby. Could it be by the same father, or another father?"

The doctor winced. But she knew our living arrangements, had made sure she took down all the details of London, Carven, and Colt, including our very active sexual conditions.

"It's possible. Extremely rare, but possible. It's called heteropaternal superfecundation. Two compete babies, fathered by two different men."

Two babies...

By two different fathers.

I was already doing the calculations in my head, already resurrecting the three months before, when it had just been Colt...and a lot of London. My breath caught, and the room tilted. *A whole lot of London.* Twelve weeks ago, it was us...all the time.

"London," I whispered.

"I'm the father," he murmured, sounding a bit dazed.

THIRTY-FOUR

London

THE TINY THRUMMING HEARTBEAT FILLED THE SPEAKERS. I felt that flutter...all the way to the center of my chest. "I'm the father."

"You're the father," Vivienne whispered, her eyes wide.

My knees trembled. I clutched hold of the side of the bed, staring at the tiny black and white image moving on the screen. I wanted to be happy...I was *desperate* to be happy. I was, for a fleeting second, until Vivienne turned her head and looked away.

"What is it?" She just shook her head, but I saw the tremble of her chin. "Hey." I reached around and brushed my finger along her jaw, gently turning her back toward me.

There was a shake of her head, but there were tears in her eyes, shimmering against the brown. I tried to stop from sounding desperate as I urged. "Talk to me."

"What if it..." she started, then swallowed once, twice. That thick huskiness made my chest hurt. "What if it's a girl? What if they're both girls? How can we bring our daughter into this world when there's...when there's..."

When there are men like Haelstrom Hale.

That's what she meant.

Soft curls, a button nose. The same splattering of freckles as her mom. But dark, intense eyes...ones that looked exactly like mine. That's all I could see. *Jesus fucking Christ.* Our daughter.

I tilted her shimmering gaze to mine, swallowing my rage until my chest was a wall of damn fire. "That's for me to worry about, pet. I promise you, on *my goddamn life* I will *never* let anything or anyone hurt you or our children, son or daughter. Your safety and well-being are my *only* purpose now and forever."

There was that swallow again.

I pulled her into my arms, pressing her head against my chest.

It was pure self-preservation.

Because I couldn't let her see the savagery I felt inside.

My body quaked with the need for blood.

Because her fears were real. *Very fucking real.* Hale was out there. I knew that with every fiber of my soul. He was plotting, scheming, watching my every goddamn move. My gaze shifted to the monitor and the still image of the two little blips on the screen.

He was just waiting for an opportunity, and right now I was looking at two.

Two babies.

Two of our *babies.*

Haunted eyes, gaunt cheeks. A belly that was far too big for her frame. The image of Ryth blazed in my mind. She was worn down by all the running, a shell of herself. I couldn't let Vivienne end up like Ryth. I *refused* to allow that. Always in fear. Always waiting for the hand around your mouth and the needle in your neck. Always waiting for men like Hale to take your entire world from you. Always vulnerable.

The sons and I wouldn't let that happen.

We'd find Hale.

We'd find them all.

And tear the world apart to do it if necessary.

"That will not happen," I whispered, that fire now in the back of my throat. "I give you my word."

WHAT IF...WHAT *if it's a girl.*

Those goddamn words haunted me as I pulled into the driveway and stopped the car. Vivienne had barely spoken on the drive home, just stared out of the window with a numb, shell-shocked stare.

"Carven's inside waiting and Guild has your favorite hot chocolate on standby."

She turned her head toward me, giving me a ghost of a smile. Fuck, it just looked sad. I reached across the seat, captured her face in both my hands, and drew her closer. Her soft lips met mine. She grabbed my arm, clinging to me tightly.

I wanted nothing more than to take her inside and make slow, consuming love with her. I wanted her mindless and quivering under my hands. I wanted her empty so I could fill her again.

So she might taste the malice I had inside.

So she would know the lengths I'd go to just to keep her safe.

But none of that mattered. Words were pointless.

Action was *all* that mattered.

I eased my hold, letting her pull away. "I'll be back as soon as I can," I whispered.

She stared into my eyes and nodded.

In the space of a breath she was gone, shoving open the door and stepping out, closing it behind her with a soft *thud*.

I swiped the screen on my phone, watching her stride toward the door. But it opened before she even got there and Carven stepped out to meet her. He glanced my way and gave a slow nod. I shoved the car into reverse as the call was answered.

"I'm here," Harper stated, his voice clipped.

"The Priest," I answered. "Has he spoken?"

"Unfortunately, no. But his brothers are circling and, by the carnage they've left behind to find him, they're pissed. But it's done, the tracker's inserted. So when they come, and it's only a matter of time now, they should lead us all the way to Hale and the Order."

"Good." I hit the end of the driveway, then stopped the car and put it into gear. "That's exactly where I want them."

"Everything okay with Vivienne?"

What if it's a girl, London?

"Looks like we're having twins," I answered, still numb.

"Congratulations, brother." The lilt in his voice echoed through the speakers. "You're going to be the very best father. You all will...even Carven."

"Yes." My focused shifted to the twins, but it wasn't Carven I worried about, it was Colt. "Even Carven."

"Have you heard any more about the Ares murders?" he asked.

"I'm heading there now." I turned the wheel and pulled into the street, remembering the red and blue flashing lights of the emergency vehicles last night. "I'll let you know."

"Hale has to be connected, London," my friend growled. "Because that...that was far too brutal to be anything else."

"I agree," I answered, braking to a stop outside their house. "I'll call you the moment I'm out."

This morning we're rocked by the tragic and horrific news about one of our shining stars in the corporate world. In the wake of the terrible news of Haelstrom Hale's death, we have two more. Corporate mogul, Dante Ares and his wife, Meredith, have been found deceased in their luxurious home. First reports are of an unconfirmed murder-suicide, but we will have more on this shocking incident as the investigation unfolds.

"Murder-suicide, my ass," I muttered as I killed the engine.

Hale was behind this.

I needed to find out how.

I climbed out of the car and took a second to lift my gaze to the expansive house as I adjusted my jacket. But why? What would Hale gain by taking out one of the most influential, connected Mafia families? I shifted my thoughts to Cerberus. According to Ben and the information obtained thanks to our new alliance, Dante Ares was the main instigator involved in the abduction.

If that was the case, was this the Banks brothers? They were all capable...especially Tobias. But to do something like this took a degree of carefulness, and that's something Tobias wasn't. He was a hothead, wired to shoot and keep shooting.

I stepped up to the door and pressed the button. No, something like this took skill and cunning. Something like I did. Heavy steps came from inside before the door opened and Silas Ares stood there, those unflinching eyes meeting mine.

He stepped to the side without saying a word, letting me enter.

Clack.

The locks sounded before the eldest son turned and headed along the hallway to the sitting room. I scanned the house as I followed. Empty. Cold. Our steps echoed like they had in the damn morgue. That's exactly what this place felt like, a morgue. I inhaled, tasting the remnants of carnage, and suppressed a shudder as Silas led me to the same sitting room I'd been in before.

My focus moved to the same leather sofa where Dante had sat, which seemed like only yesterday. Silas gave a wave of his hand. For someone whose parents were just brutally murdered in the same house we sat in, he was terrifyingly calm.

I remained standing. Instead, I offered my hand. "I'm really sorry for your loss, Silas." My gaze automatically shifted to the closed door at my right and the bright yellow police tape across it. The same study where it had all happened. "Do the police have any information?'

He didn't grasp my hand, just stared at the very expensive Rothschild rug under our feet before he lifted his gaze to mine. "You mean, if it's true? If my father—" A nerve twitched in his cheek. "If he...if he murdered my mother..."

I didn't react, just searched his eyes. Because none of this felt *right*. Memories of the last time I was here slammed into me. The way Dante had looked at his wife told me he wasn't just a man in love. He was fucking smitten. There wasn't a hint of trouble under the surface, certainly not the kind that spilled blood.

"I don't believe that, and I know *you* don't either."

There was that tell again, making his cheek tremble as the eldest son of the Ares empire settled that dangerous fixed stare on me. "It's what everyone says. So it must be true."

"Your father is not the man who'd..." My words stuck in the back of my throat.

"Blow a hole in my mother's head, then turn that same gun on himself?" His voice was so quiet, I barely heard it.

Still, I didn't need to, did I? It was written all over my face as I glanced at the study once more. "I need to know." My own sense of desperation roared inside me. I hated this, hated how I was pushing him. "I need to know it was your father."

He suddenly turned and strode across the sitting room before he ripped the police tape aside and threw the door open wide.

"I dunno...does that look like my father's fucking brain matter to you? I can't fucking tell."

The room was chaos, upturned chairs, blood splattered across the desk. My eyes were drawn to the bright pink markings on the floor in front of the desk. The ones in the outline of a body.

Blood pooled underneath, dark brown, bits of white amongst the mess. *His mother...it had to have been.*

Desperation drew me closer. I shot Silas a panicked stare, but it was the hitman in me that mapped out the room. I glanced at the door, searching for markings.

"No forced entry," Silas muttered, standing in the doorway with his back to the room.

"Windows?"

He glanced at the towering panes of glass, ones I knew would be fitted with magnetic switches. The moment they were opened or smashed, an alarm would be triggered. Silas gave a shake of his head. Then, in an instant, his gaze whipped to the right.

From the corner of my eye, the sitting room door opened and Angelica Ares stepped in. If I thought Silas was cold to her before, now he was damn well frostbiting. His top lip curled as she lifted her head, froze, then met his stare. Something passed between them; hate, desperation, pain. She glanced my way, those intense green eyes brightening until they shifted to the open study door.

Her throat muscles worked, as her breath caught.

Silas unleashed a low snarl and took a step forward, making her flinch. The tension between them was terrifying. She whirled around, grabbed the door handle, pulled, and disappeared once more.

"Is there something I need to know here?" I turned to Silas.

"It's a family matter," he growled.

Whatever was going on was dangerous...for her, at least. My gut clenched. *I've seen her...at The Order.* Vivienne's words resounded. She not only knew the Ares daughter, but she'd seen her with The Principal. The same bastard I wanted to lead us back to Hale. I fought myself not to get more involved.

But I couldn't.

I already had enough on my own plate.

Whatever was happening here wasn't my problem.

The door closed, leaving Angelica Ares to slip away...like a gazelle bounding away from a lion. I turned my head, seeing that deadly stare fixed on the door—for now, at least. How long she avoided the menacing Ares sons was another matter altogether.

"You'll contact me if you need anything?" I offered.

He didn't look away from that closed door. "I appreciate the offer. But we take care of our own."

A chill raced along my spine, so I gave a nod and headed toward the door.

He didn't follow, just continued to stare at the door where his adopted sister had left like he was contemplating spilling a little more blood. I shook my head as I yanked the front door closed.

The Ares daughter wasn't my problem.

God knows I had enough of my own.

Beep.

I grabbed my phone, swiped my thumb across the screen, and looked at the message.

Caleb Banks: Ryth isn't well...she wants to see Vivienne. Make it happen, London.

Make it happen.

I strode toward my car in the driveway, knowing I'd avoided for long enough telling Vivienne her sister was back. "Shit," I grumbled as I yanked open the driver's door and climbed in.

I typed out a response:

I'm on it.

THIRTY-FIVE

Vivienne

LONDON WAS THE FATHER...

I stared at the kitchen counter, replaying the moment it had hit me. My pulse skipped, then raced. *Twins...as in two babies were inside me. Two babies. Two fathers. How in the hell had that happened?* The water sloshed in the glass in my hand.

"You okay?"

I jerked my head upwards, finding Carven standing in the doorway staring intently at me. I forced a smile. "Fine."

He scowled, then shook his head, moving around the counter toward me. "Can't lie to me, Wildcat."

I shook my head, then stopped. I guess there was one thing I couldn't do with the men I lived with and that was to hide my feelings. "I'm numb, if I'm honest."

He stopped in front of me. "Why? Has it got two heads or something? What did the doc say?"

He didn't know.

"I—I'm pregnant," I started.

"That we already know, Wildcat."

"With two babies."

He froze, his mouth open, before he slowly spoke. *"Twins?"*

I shook my head. "No. Not twins." I saw the fear and excitement as I took a step closer. "Two babies by two different fathers. Conceived at different times."

"Two babies, Wildcat." He grinned, totally missing the point. *"TWO BABIES!"*

With a rush, he lunged forward, grabbed me around the waist, and lifted my feet from the floor. "Two babies," he beamed, pulling me close until he nuzzled his face against my neck... then froze.

A low, deadly sound echoed in the air.

Threatening.

Careful.

I slowly lifted my head, to find Colt standing in the doorway. Only it wasn't Colt, was it? It was the savage part of his nature that had splintered from his mind, the beast. Carven eased me back down as his own twin brother slowly rounded the counter, turning his attention from me to Carven.

"You've been through a fucking brutal ordeal, brother," Carven declared as he stared at Colt's missing thumb. "But you need to leash that fucking monster, or he and I are gonna come to blows."

Just like that, Colt stopped in the middle of the kitchen. His dark eyes brightened. There was a shake of his head before confusion set in. One look around, and Colt...*the real Colt* settled on us. "Vivienne? Carven?" he whispered, his voice husky.

Carven stepped forward, carefully at first, before he grabbed his brother around the shoulders and pulled him into his arms "Good to see you, buddy. That other part of you is a real asshole."

Tears welled in my eyes at the sight. I swallowed the water in my glass and felt it move around the hard lump in the back of my throat. Colt lifted that haunted gaze to me. Dark circles swelled under his eyes, but still they softened as they settled on me.

"Babies," he whispered.

My lips trembled as I nodded. "Yes, babies."

He left his brother, and moved slowly toward me. Carven shifted, observing his brother carefully. But I wasn't afraid, not of him, or the animal part of his nature. I lifted my hands as Colt stepped into my arms. His strong, trembling muscles seemed to release under my touch.

"That's the way," I urged, sliding my hands along his powerful shoulders. He lowered his head to my shoulder, curling his spine into me. "Two babies and you're father of one of them. London...London is the other."

They both jerked their gaze to mine at that one. I didn't have all the answers. I'd barely come to terms with any of this myself. *"Familia est omnia,"* I whispered, the words coming from nowhere.

"*Familia est omnia*," Colt murmured, his voice husky in my ear.

"*Familia est omnia*," Carven repeated.

Beep.

His phone chimed, breaking the moment. But it didn't matter. We were together and family...and that's all that mattered. I breathed in the heady scent of Colt, losing myself in the comfort of him. Desire ignited, coming to life as I exhaled.

"London's on his way here," Carven said, drawing my focus to him. "He wants to talk to us."

Instantly, I lifted my head. "Is everything okay?"

He just gave a shrug. "I guess we're about to find out."

My chest tightened as Colt took a step away, then bent down to kiss me softly. *Oh.* I melted into that kiss, opening my mouth to take every gentle brush. I ached for that, desperate for something different. These men were always so hard, so demanding...and this...this wasn't anything like that.

Colt took my hand and lifted it, placing it flat against his chest. The strong beat of his heart vibrated under my palm as he broke the kiss and lifted his head.

"I love you," I whispered, catching the faint sound of London's car turning into the drive.

He held my stare, those blue eyes darkening for just a second as the beast tried to push through. But Colt...*my Colt* held on. "I love you," he repeated, his tone deeper, sounding almost like that darker part of his nature. So deep I wasn't sure if it was him or that dangerous entity inside him who answered.

I gave him a smile, watching his eyes brighten.

A car door thudded outside.

Carven glanced toward the doorway. "This can't be good," he muttered and headed for the hallway.

Colt followed his brother, leaving me last. London strode toward us, his focus directed at me as he slowed at the doorway, waving me back inside toward the study first.

"Okay," Carven muttered. "Hit us with it."

London unbuttoned his jacket and tossed it over the back of the chair before he took his usual stance, leaning back against the desk. His shirt strained as he rolled the sleeves and crossed his arms.

"Well?" Carven snapped. "Don't keep us in suspense."

"My gut is telling me the Ares murders are connected to Hale somehow," he started, glancing at me. "But it's not an outward attack, not from what I've seen."

Surprise hit me. I shook my head. "It's not?"

"No." He settled that careful stare on me. "I think it's exactly what they said it was...a murder-suicide."

A murder-suicide. In my head, I saw the way Dante and Meredith Ares had looked at each other in that sitting room. They were in love, that had been so damn obvious. Blinded by their obsession, they barely saw anyone else. That wasn't a couple at war...not one that ended in both of them dead.

Then Angelica slipped in...

Angelica, with her quiet, careful demeanor.

Angelica, whose gaze was fixed on me, because she knew.

She knew I'd seen her in that place....

With the Principal.

"The wife was scared." Colt shook his head. His deep voice was huskier than it was before. "She knew Ophelia was coming after us and she wanted to be as far from that as possible. Because she was scared of Dante finding out what she was up to. Maybe he did. Maybe he found out and he didn't like it one bit."

My body trembled as a chill tore through me. The idea of that was terrifying. This had The Order written all over it. The repercussions of that vile place would be neverending. "I don't like this," I whispered, meeting his dark stare. "I don't like any of it."

"I don't either. But right now, we have enough to deal with..." he winced, choosing his words carefully. "Seeing as how Ryth and her stepbrothers are back."

My breath stopped.

My mind raced.

"Ryth's back?" I glanced at the others. Carven wasn't showing any hint of surprise, but Colt was.

"Yes," London answered carefully. "And she wants to see you."

My chest swelled as my lips curled. "Yes...now? Can we go now?" I started moving toward the doorway.

"No, pet." His answer stopped me cold. "There are things you need to understand. Things you need to prepare yourself for."

I spun, finding that same careful expression fixed on me. "What things?"

He pushed from the desk and strode across the room. "Things haven't been easy for her. I need you..." He glanced at the others. "*We* need you to prepare yourself."

Things haven't been easy? What the hell did that mean? "Tell me," I demanded.

"She's pregnant..." He lowered his gaze to my stomach. *"Very... very pregnant.* And it looks like the pregnancy hasn't been easy. She's going to watch your every reaction, every flinch, every stutter. It's all going to matter to her. The Banks boys are protective enough already."

Then it hit me. I stepped closer to him. So close he automatically reached for me, pulling me against his muscular body. "She was supposed to stay hidden. Why is she here?"

He looked down. "It seems Dante and the other heads of the families didn't like that they were hiding. They wanted them where they could see and use them."

I flinched as it hit me. "Did they kill the Ares'?" As soon as the question arose, I knew it didn't sound like them.

"It's possible."

"But you don't believe they did."

He shook his head. "No."

"So I can see her, then. I can see my sister."

He didn't like the thought of that. One glance around the study and I saw none of them liked it.

Except for me.

"As soon as I can make sure it's safe," London answered.

I fixed my stare on him. "Then make it safe, London. Make it safe and make it soon. Because it sounds like my sister needs me…and I need her."

THIRTY-SIX

London

"Any word from the Alpha team?" I murmured to Harper, tearing my gaze from the black and white image on the screen in front of me to the bank statement splayed out on the desk.

So much money. Hunting Hale was a slow damn death, bleeding me dry financially.

"None as yet, although tonight they found Konstance Lane's premises empty and his prized Maserati gone. All of his bank accounts have been cleaned out. Three billion and change."

"They're all running."

"They're all running," he confirmed. "All we need is one of them to lift their heads and we have them. I promise you, London. I will have them before they even know anyone is watching. I'll track them back to Hale and we'll have that bastard before he even knows what hit him."

I closed my eyes. All I saw was that steel table and the cold, clammy skin of the body they'd pulled from the river. "He's not dead, Harper. I know it in my gut, he's not dead."

"Then you keep listening to that and we'll be there to do whatever it takes to find the bastard and bring him and this whole foul fucking Order to the ground."

I'd never felt so thankful to have my friends and family. Never been so thankful to have them alive and breathing and under my roof. Silas Ares' haunted eyes pushed into my mind. There were others out there not as lucky, others left trying to figure out how to pick up the pieces and move on. I didn't want that. *God, I didn't want that.*

An ache ripped across my chest. My senses sharpened, forcing me to open my eyes as a shadow spilled into the doorway. Then she was there, biting her lip, hovering like only Vivienne King could hover. Those big brown eyes wandered across the room before settling on me.

Fuck, she made me feel dangerous.

"Keep me updated," I directed.

"Every damn step of the way."

Then he was gone, leaving me sitting there with the phone against my damn ear, nervous as hell. I don't *get* nervous, only around her. I slowly lowered the phone and waited. She walked in, those hips sashaying, and I was transfixed by the movement. Just wait until her belly was big and round and full with my—

"You don't want us to meet, do you?"

I didn't need to be psychic to know what was running through her mind. "No, I don't."

She didn't flinch, just held my stare. Christ, she was tough now. So goddamn tough...and mesmerizing. I rose from my seat, fighting the urge to look at the black and white images from the gynecologist that had held me transfixed for the last two hours.

I rounded the desk and stopped in front of her. "If I could hide you away forever, then I would." She crossed her arms, looking up at me as I brushed my fingers across her cheek. "If I could just have us..." I looked down at her stomach. "I would keep you hidden forever. Even if you hated me for it. Even if you... refused me. I would gladly accept that."

"Why?" Her stare bored right through me. "Why go through all that?"

I scowled. "Why?" She still didn't get it.

I lowered my head, my voice husky against her ear. "Because I'd do anything to keep you. I've killed for just the idea of you. I've strangled. I've stabbed. I've murdered men in their sleep and men staring into my eyes. I've ended men as they begged and as they've raged. And I've done it all because you and our children and my sons are my *everything*. You want to know why I don't want you even in the same city as your sister, and I'll tell you. The *only* thing Hale wants more than my head on a damn pike is Weylyn King. Hale not only wants to bring the man he once thought of as a mentor to his knees, he wants to destroy him *and* his bloodline, even if it's a bloodline he created. He stole the man's DNA just so he could create women he could use. You and Ryth are that bloodline, the *only* way Hale can get to King. The man has faked his own death, just so he can disappear. He's never been more dangerous than he is right now. So, if it takes keeping you away from Ryth to protect you from Hale and The Order, then that's what I'll do... even if it..." I winced. "Even if it hurts you."

Tears welled in her eyes.

She was fighting them, swallowing the hard lump in the back of her throat. I closed my eyes and pulled her against me, wrapping my arms around her tight. "I love you. I love you so fucking much it scares me. I don't want—" *Jesus.* "I don't want to lose you, *any* of you. I almost lost Colt. I almost lost *my son.* I can't go through that again."

She trembled, holding her composure for a second before she broke, wrapping her arms around me and burying her head against my chest. Her heavy sobs were fists against my chest. Still, she said nothing, just wept until there was silence.

"You can hate me," I reassured her.

There was a shake of her head before she lifted her gaze to mine. "I don't hate you, London. I could *never* hate you."

I wiped a tear from her cheek. "But you should. You should hate me very much and my sons, as well."

"Never," a voice came from the doorway.

I glanced toward the sound, finding Carven standing there, his piercing blue eyes fixed on mine. He moved to her other side.

"You are the only reason we're alive, the *only* reason I have my brother." He glanced at Vivienne. "The only reason we have the woman we all love. *Familia est omnia.*"

"Family is everything," I whispered huskily.

"Family *is* everything."

I met her stare, knowing exactly what she was thinking. Family was indeed everything, and she was being torn apart because of it. Blood. Heart. I was forcing her to choose. *No,* I was making the choice for her, which was worse.

"I'll do it." I scowled. "I'll make a way you can see your sister. I'll keep you safe."

Her eyes widened. "Really?"

I brushed her hair behind her ear. "Really."

That sad, beaming fucking smile made me feel like a bastard. I lowered my head, tasting those salty tears on the edges of her lips, before I took her mouth deeper. She responded instantly, not a second of hesitation as she wrapped her arms around my shoulders and pulled me harder against her.

Fuck if this wasn't something worth dying for.

She was worth dying for.

I speared my fingers through her hair, pressing her ear against my hand, holding on as I deepened the kiss, until she broke away. I lifted my head and looked at Carven next to her. He cupped her jaw and turned her head until he could kiss her.

My pulse thundered.

My breath stilled.

Watching my son with the woman I loved.

It was wrong. I *knew* that. But the booming in my ears drowned out any nagging worry as Carven took a step and pushed her against me. *Love her,* he was saying. *Touch her.* I reached up and gently gripped her throat as their kiss deepened until her cheeks were flushed.

Fuck, I loved that.

Desire hit me hard, making my cock harden.

In an instant, this turned into something else. Something more desperate. Something *carnal*. She unleashed a moan. Her hand wrapped around my wrist as she leaned against me. Carven turned desperately, breaking away from her mouth to lift his gaze to mine.

His look said it all.

Can we?

I'd shared her with Carven before, but that'd been different. That'd been all fire, all desperation, when we'd been mindless with worry, searching for Colt. But this...

This felt real.

"Do you want this?" he asked the both of us.

"Yes," she answered instantly. "I need this."

She needed it. I thought about the implications for *us* together. My son was all fire...and I was stone. The last thing I wanted was to hurt her. "Are you sure about this?" I questioned.

She nodded, reached up to grasp the back of my neck, and drew my mouth to hers. I kissed her, my pulse beating a thousand miles an hour. A low moan echoed in her chest, sending the vibration through her mouth and into mine.

Jesus.

My body responded, a little too fucking eagerly as my cock punched against my zipper. My hands were all over her, then I grasped her head to turn her toward me.

I fought my own hunger to break away from her mouth and murmur. "Colt?"

"He's in the gym," Carven answered. "Has been for the last two hours and will be all night by the way he was looking."

I met her stare. "My bedroom, then."

Her cheeks flushed. One careful nod was all she gave before I reached down, grasped her around the hips, and lifted. Her legs wound around me as I turned and headed for the door. Voices from the guards came from outside. But I ignored them, sliding my hands along the backs of her thighs as we headed past the kitchen and toward the private wing.

Clang!

The sound of weights echoed along the hall.

CLANG!

Carven followed, barely a step behind, as we headed for my bedroom. My steps slowed as I took her weight with one hand and opened the door. Then we were inside, sinking into the gloomy shadows. She'd barely spent any time in here, occupied with Colt and Carven. That was the way it should be, the way I *wanted* it to be.

I stopped at the edge of the bed, staring into her eyes.

"You sure you don't want to take me to the room?"

CLANG!

"No." I shook my head, seeing the black and white images of our children. "No, not while there's a chance of hurting you...or the babies."

She frowned, a furrow between her brows deepening. "Hurt the babies?"

I eased her down until her feet hit the floor. "So we just take it a little easy," I murmured, brushing my curled fingers along her jaw. "Until all three of you are out of danger."

Carven closed the bedroom door behind him and crossed the space, stopping at her back. She lifted her gaze to me as he reached around and worked the buttons of her blouse. "Pet," I whispered, watching as her blouse opened, then slowly fell away.

"Yes, Daddy?" she answered.

My cock twitched at the word.

Only she could make me feel like this. My lips curled as her bra was unhooked and discarded. Her breasts were full and round, the soft peaks of her nipples tightening under my gaze. I brushed my thumb across the peak of one. "Christ, you're beautiful."

"Show me how beautiful I am," she breathed.

Carven did all the work, easing the zipper down at the side of her slacks until they dropped to the floor at her feet. I risked a glance over my shoulder, listening to silence from outside the bedroom.

"London?"

She drew me back to her, to the way her full lips waited for me to devour them. I was fucking weak with her. I surged forward, grabbed her jaw with one hand, and worked the buttons of my shirt with the other. Carven undressed, too, tearing his t-shirt free before unzipping his black jeans and kicking off his boots...

Until the door to my bedroom opened with a *boom!*

Wood splintered under the force.

The door handle embedded deep into the wall.

Colt stood in the doorway, eyes blazing with rage as he settled that bestial stare on the three of us.

"*MINE!*" he bellowed, his lips snarling, before he lunged.

I was hit from behind by a brick wall, lifted, and thrown clear across the room. They were a blur as I hit the wall with a *crack*. I'd never been hit that hard before, not even by men who ate steroids as a main meal.

I shook my head, lifting my hand to grasp onto the dresser.

This was no man.

This was what The Order had created.

"*No!*" Vivienne stepped forward, placing herself between me and that...bloodthirsty male. "*Beast!*"

He whipped that cold, killing stare toward her.

But this was too dangerous.

Far too dangerous for the precious babies she carried.

"Stop!" I pushed upwards and took a step toward her, but that only drew Colt's deadly focus. "*Over here,*" I urged, desperate to draw his attention. I risked a glance toward the doorway. I needed to get Vivienne out of here. "Over here, son."

I moved forward, fully drawing the beast's wrath.

In an instant, Colt's hand was around my throat, squeezing tight. *FUCK!* I grasped his wrist and drove it upward, trying to break his hold. But it was like fighting a goddamn bear. He wasn't my son in that moment. One look at that distant stare and I knew the son I loved was no longer there.

"Get the *fuck off him!*" Carven slammed into his brother.

But all that did was piss Colt off more...or the *beast,* whoever this fucking was. Dark midnight blue eyes were fixed on Carven as that grip around my throat tightened. I tried to breathe, tried to think. My mind drifted to the gun hidden under the edge of the headboard of my bed for a second before I pushed it away.

No.

Stars danced behind my eyelids.

If this is how it ends, then I'd be happy. Happy it was him. Happy it was—

"PUT HIM DOWN NOW!" Vivienne roared.

The grip released around my throat, letting me slump to the floor. I grabbed my throat, sucking in hard breaths.

"I can't...London, I'm so—" Colt cried.

I shook my head. "It's not your fault. It's..."

A savage sound ripped from him as he thrashed his head. His eyes blazed with ferocity until Vivienne stepped between us.

"Hey!" she called, snapping her fingers in front of his nose.

The woman...standing naked in front of him, snapped her goddamn fingers!

"You will get control of yourself," she demanded.

"Wildcat," he hissed desperately, then slowly lifted his gaze to me and his brother.

"Carven," she spoke carefully." I need you to go into Colt's room and get the wrist ties around his bed.

"Fuck." He was already shaking his head. "You sure about this?"

She never once looked away from Colt. Instead, she moved even closer.

He visibly fought that beast inside himself, wrestling like it was his own personal demon. In a way, it was. One who could take control.

"Yes," she answered Carven. "I am."

The beast stared into her eyes as Carven left the room and returned moments later. Thick leather straps were in my son's hand, ones I had had especially made for the nights when the storms hit. Now it looked like the storm raged all day and night.

She took one strap and lifted it. "Beast, hand please." My son obliged instantly, watching her as she cinched it tight around his wrist. She held out her other hand. "The other."

Like a well-trained animal, he lifted his other hand for her to strap it tight.

"To the bed," she commanded.

He turned his head toward me. That dangerous, possessive gleam rose swiftly, making him turn his top lip up and growl.

"Don't you worry about them," she urged. "They will not hurt me. You need to understand that. You need to learn to... *share*."

He swung his gaze back to her.

"It's that or nothing." She laid down the rules. "So it's up to you."

One wave of her hand toward the headboard of my bed and he flinched, shaking his head, wrestling with the idea of that. For a second, my mind went to the gun under the edge of the headboard. All it'd take would be one wrong move, and we'd all be dead.

Murder-suicide.

I shook my head. This was a bad idea...a really bad idea.

Until, with a clink of steel, the creature that occupied my son turned and, like a good puppy, climbed onto the bed and lifted his hands for her to secure him to the headboard.

Jesus...this was happening, wasn't it?

I swallowed hard. Fear moved through me as she secured one wrist and then the other until both arms were outstretched tight.

"London," she called, turning her gaze toward me. "It's all or nothing."

I had no choice here...not if I wanted to keep my family together. With a desperate snarl, I strode forward. "Pet...you're dancing with death here."

"We all are," she answered, and lifted her hand for mine.

THIRTY-SEVEN

Vivienne

London dropped his shirt onto the floor, then kicked off his shoes. "Carven," I murmured, turning back to the beast. "The other side of the bed."

"Jesus," he muttered. "My brother's gonna tear us apart."

I turned to the beast as he strained against the bonds around his wrists to get to me. "No, he won't."

I moved closer and reached up, spearing my fingers through those thick curls I loved so much. Any other time, I'd be gentle with Colt. Any other time I'd be soft, caring. I'd kiss his bruises and lick his scrapes. I'd ride him slowly, letting him take control and tell me what he needed.

But this—the beast growled softly—this wasn't him.

I burrowed my grip in the strands of his hair, fisting them taut, and yanked until his head snapped backwards.

"Fuck," Carven groaned behind me.

I ignored him, my focus on the beast...and the beast alone. Corded tendons pulled tight along his throat. "You will do what I tell you to do, won't you?"

There was no room to be gentle here.

No room to allow the beast any kind of control.

I had to be dominant. The one he obeyed.

I yanked harder, leaning in until my breath bounced off his firm jaw and licked that rough five-o'clock shadow, leaving a warm trail along his skin. *"Won't you?"*

A keening sound rumbled from his chest before he gave a desperate nod.

"Good boy," I encouraged, watching the spark ignite in his eyes. "My beast." I looked down to the thin tank top straining over his rock-hard muscles. "My beautiful, powerful beast. You're going to stay there and watch while Carven and London fuck me."

"Pet," London murmured behind me. "I hope you know what you're doing here."

The beast's top lip curled at the sound of London's voice.

I slowly released my hold on his hair. "If you want me?" I whispered as I reached down to the top of my panties and slid my fingers inside. "You will be good."

My pulse was racing. Fear made the desire simmer. None of us were really into this, not anymore. But this was the only way forward, the only way the beast saw London and Carven weren't a threat. Those dark eyes narrowed in on me. Nostrils flared, drawing in my scent as I turned to London. "Kiss me."

One panicky glance at Colt and he stepped forward. "London, trust me."

He didn't want to do this, and it had nothing to do with him being scared. One hard swallow and he looked at Colt once more. He didn't want to hurt him. I knew that. But the alternative was a lot worse.

"All or nothing, London," I whispered.

He swiveled that dangerous stare my way, understanding this had to be done. "Fuck it," he muttered, then he surged forward, grabbed me around the waist, and yanked me against him.

I slammed against his hard chest, my hands going to his shoulders.

But my focus was on the beast, on every soft snarl as London kissed me and the strain of those leather bonds as Carven joined us.

Colt's brother ran his hands down my body until he was the one who grabbed my panties and yanked, sliding them down my thighs.

That low, warning sound grew louder.

"Ignore him," I whispered, turning to Carven and sliding my hand around his neck to pull his lips down to mine.

He gripped my jaw, his cruel fingers clenching as he took my mouth with such ferocity it stole me away from where we were...and what we were doing.

I unleashed a moan as London lowered his head to lick my nipples.

Jesus...

I wasn't into this before...but now, now that desire came rushing back.

"Push her to the bed," London ordered. "I want to see your cock in her mouth."

My hair fanned out as Carven eased me down until my head hit the bedding.

"That's the way, princess." London lifted my hips tugged my panties off, and threw them to the floor before he slid my legs apart. "Open up, pet."

Carven reached down, one hand fisting his length, and leaned forward. Colt drove his body forward, bowing his arms behind him, straining to get to me. But I didn't meet that desperate stare, just turned my attention to Carven and reached up to grasp his cock as I eased it to my mouth.

"Wider," London commanded.

But he wasn't talking about my mouth.

He gripped the insides of my knees and pushed them further apart.

"You like to control my brother." Carven slipped his hand behind my head as I opened my mouth. "I can see, you enjoy it."

The smooth head of his cock slipped along my tongue and sharply pushed inside, driving all the way to the back of my throat. "But we, Wildcat...we control *you*."

Panic flared, making me suck air in through my nose. I fought the fear, staying calm. One tiny flicker of desperation and who knew how the beast would react. Carven looked down at me with those intense blue eyes, not well he thought.

"We control you," he repeated. "Now suck."

I did as he demanded, drawing back a bit as my tongue flicked along the pulsing vein under his cock.

"Good girl." London ran his thumbs along each side of my slit, pushing gently against my clit. Heat raced, making me grip Carven's cock harder, driving him all the way to the hilt.

"Oh fuck," Carven moaned as London massaged the lips of my pussy against that sensitive nub.

"She likes that," London urged, his voice deep and husky. Cool fingers met my warmth as he pushed inside me and fucked. "Carven's going to lie down and you're going to straddle him, okay, pet?"

I nodded, opening my knees wider as he dragged his fingers from my slit and ran them each side around my ass. That desperate growl echoed, drawing my focus from that surge of hunger inside me. But my body was a beast of its own, blooming with need.

I wanted to fuck all the time now.

Fuck and vomit...

Then fuck some more.

I whimpered, clenching my ass, driving my hips upwards as London lowered his head and licked. He opened my slit wider, then spat. "Now, son," he urged.

Carven obeyed, pulling out of my mouth to fall to the bed beside me. I lifted my head to watch London grip my ass and drive his mouth against my pussy, sucking hard.

Throb.

"Oh, God." I threw my head backwards.

Throb.

Throb.

"On Carven's cock, pet," London demanded as he pulled away.

My body was slow to move, still desperate for his mouth. I pushed upwards and grabbed London's neck to kiss him. Colt snapped forward, driving his mouth toward mine. But it was the salty taste of my desire I hungered for.

Beep.

London's phone chimed.

"Don't you fucking dare," I warned.

London grabbed me and gripped my throat gently, showing me exactly who was in control here. "This is happening. Now climb onto Carven, pet. I want to watch you ride."

He kissed me again, forcing my mouth to stretch until the corners burned.

I still felt that burn when he broke away, leaving me to turn to Carven. He sat upwards and grabbed my hips to steady me as I threw my leg over him.

"As hard as you want, Wildcat," he urged.

I reached down, grabbed his length, and positioned myself over him. I wanted him inside me...*as forceful as I could get*. With a brutal slam, I dropped, feeling the push as I rocked, grinding him deeper.

"Jesus fucking Christ." He gripped hold of me and closed his eyes. "You're gonna make me come like a fucking teenager."

The big, warm hand at my back urged me forward. "Not yet, you won't. Leash it..." London pushed against me, running his hand down my spine to my ass. "We're not done until she's a trembling mess, isn't that right, kitten? Are you going to quiver for us?"

My pussy clenched, making me push forward and brace myself on my hands.

"Normally your ass is mine." Carven gripped my waist, driving his cock deep. "But right now, I can't get enough of this perfect pussy. Fuck, you're soft." He closed his eyes. "Soft and full of our babies."

"Just wait until you're big and round," London murmured against my ear. "I'm going to enjoy filling every goddamn hole, pet. Now, lean forward."

I did as he asked, my ass clenching with the brush of his fingers as he ran them along my slit to that ring of muscle, then pushed them in.

"Christ, I can feel him inside you," London growled.

He leaned down, spat, then aimed his cock at my entrance. "Breathe, baby. Deep breath."

I inhaled.

"That's the way, relax for me."

My knees trembled and my thighs strained as I lifted my ass, sliding all the way along Carven's length. The head of London's cock made me stretch, but he was always so fucking smooth, pushing in with barely a thrust.

"So fucking good," London praised. "Look how well you take us."

He moved with me as I sank, pushing against Carven's balls.

"You're going to be dripping by the time we're done, Wildcat," Carven forced through clenched teeth.

London's hand settled on my back, bracing as I rocked forward. "That's the fucking way. Christ, look at how well you ride. Such a good fucking pet, aren't you? A good pet who needs to be fucked."

I whimpered and closed my eyes, my core quivering. Need slammed into me. I moaned, panting hard as I rode faster.

"We've been neglecting you," London murmured. "Not anymore. Ride him, pet. Ride him hard."

Colt unleashed a savage snarl as I cried out and slammed forward, testing the bonds to get to me. I lifted my head and met the wild stare in his eyes.

"Mine," I moaned, grabbing hold of Carven's arms as I drove down, buried him deep inside, and climaxed.

My body clamped down, quivering and blooming, making London groan until he pushed in. "Again," he commanded.

I closed my eyes, shaking my head at the aftershocks, panting. He chuckled, sliding that big hand up my spine as my body broke out in goosebumps.

"You've got one more in you, pet."

"I—I can't," I whimpered.

But he was merciless, reaching up to grip my throat and pull me back against him. Only, I stared into the bottomless, demented stare of the beast.

"You can," London grunted, rising on powerful thighs to drive in deep. "And you will."

I moaned at the same time as Carven. He raised his upper body, wedging me between both of them. "One more clench, Wildcat," he forced through gritted teeth. "One more fucking clench and I'm gonna nut inside you."

My pussy squeezed on reflex alone.

The beast unleashed desperate, savage moans. His hands were almost white from the strain as he tried to reach me. But I was too far gone, even inches away from him. Carven let out a growl as desperation filled me, then floated away as warmth filled my pussy.

Colt's lips parted and he breathed in the hard rush of my air as I groaned.

"That's it," London urged, grabbing hold of my hip with one hand, the other still wrapped around my throat. "You're going to be so full of us...so fucking full," he grunted, driving my body down on him.

Impaled by his cock, I whimpered.

And that carnal need to be owned rose once more. "Use me," I cried out. They were the same words I'd used when we were falling apart, now I used them to bring us back together. *"Use me, London. Use...me."*

He grunted, gripping me as he thrust in an unforgiving frenzy.

All I felt was his cock.

All I saw was the beast as he whipped a savage, frantic glare at London. He pulled harder against the bonds, desperation burning in his stare as his arms stretched out behind him. But there was a flicker of sadness there, knowing this was how it had to be. It was all of them or nothing, and now the beast understood. I bowed my spine as I clutched at Carven and climaxed hard.

One low moan and London grunted.

Hard, panting breaths filled the space as I fell forward, caught by Carven alone.

That tormented keening sound came once more.

"I think—" London gasped. "I think he got the point."

I couldn't answer. I could hardly breathe. But I forced myself to nod and lift my head. "Undo him."

"Wait." Carven shook his head, easing out from underneath me. "We need to think about this."

But one look into the beast's eyes and I didn't need to. The longing in that stare was almost cruel. "Undo the bonds, Carven. Let him come to me."

The beast opened and closed his mouth, desperate to find mine. Both Carven and London eased backwards, slid from the bed, and reached for Colt's hands.

"You want me?" I lifted my arms. "Then come."

They'd barely undone the buckles before he lunged, slamming into me and driving me back against the bed. I hit the pillows hard as he pressed his nose against my neck, his tongue licking the spot where London's grip had been.

He was all over me, moving down, sniffing my breasts, licking my nipples, before he sank low and nuzzled my legs apart with a shove of his chin. "Oh, God," I whimpered as his tongue hit my pussy.

Beep.

London's phone chimed once more, but I barely heard a thing as the beast gripped my ass, tilted my hips, and devoured my pussy. My clit pulsed, making me lift my head to watch the beast move upward, flicking that dark, animalistic stare to me as he drowned out the scent of his brother with his own.

"Looks like he's settled in," Carven muttered as the beast nuzzled that sensitive nub, making me whimper. "Christ, he's going to be there for hours, isn't he?"

I arched my back, opening my legs wider. "God, I hope so."

Beep.

London swore under his breath and yanked on his clothes. "Carven, you're going to need to stay here tonight. I don't want her left alone."

Carven yanked on his jeans, but left them unbuttoned, and crossed his arms. "Oh, I'm not going anywhere. I'm quite enjoying the show."

I fisted the sheets as that drugging charge ripped through me, making my back arch. The beast dipped low to lick my ass with one rough drag of his tongue. He reached up, grabbed my hips, and flipped me over, until I was face-first against the sheets.

"Where," I managed, still clenching the bedding. "Where are you going?"

London stepped closer. Only this time, the beast never paid him any mind, just yanked my hips upwards until I was on my knees, my ass directly in his line of sight.

"Taking care of business, pet. You just lie there and enjoy yourself."

I shook my head as the beast speared his tongue inside me and my pussy clenched, milking another climax to the surface. "It's torture."

"It looks like it," London answered. "Now, be a good girl and come all over his face."

I dropped my head, rocking back and forth as that desperate wave rose once more.

I didn't feel London leave.

Felt nothing other than that slick warmth pulling out, and the cool air...a second before Colt dipped lower and slid that delicious tongue over my clit once more. Then I was falling apart, being driven backwards, pushing against his mouth, and unleashing a cry of release.

THIRTY-EIGHT

London

BEEP.

I looked down.

Helene: He's almost at the warehouse. You need to get here, London, ASAP.

I let out a curse as I lengthened my stride, tucked in my shirt, and tightened my belt. I barely stopped at the study long enough to snatch the keys from my desk before I headed for the weapons room. There was no time for jackets, or pretense now. The Principal knew the kind of monster he was dealing with.

I stopped at the weapons room, slipped my shoulder holster on, and holstered my guns before pushing out the back door and heading for the Audi. Seconds later, the headlights were on and I was backing down the drive. I glanced at my phone, grabbed it, and braced my hand against the wheel as I brought up the cameras around the warehouse and peered into each one.

The place was quiet...so far.

I pushed the Audi harder toward one of Harper's excavation equipment warehouses at the edge of the city and pulled up along the side street before killing the engine.

I'm here. I typed out a message then closed the door and locked it behind me.

A flash of headlights and doors opened to the familiar dark sedan. Helene was a blur of shadows heading toward me. I met her at the gates, punched in the code, and unlocked the door. She followed silently, slipping in behind me, and headed along the path.

My jaw clenched. I didn't know if it was because of her presence or what I was about to do. I stopped at the small side door and rapped my knuckles against the steel door, fighting the sound of music playing from inside. The choking stench of dust and grease billowed out as the door cracked open and the hard beat of AC/DC bellowed out.

I met Percy's stony stare and gave a nod. "It's time."

"Finally," he muttered, glancing at Helene behind me.

There was the hint of a smile. His eyes brightened and his teeth shone. But that didn't last.

"Can we get this romantic moment over with?" she muttered softly as she pushed past.

I watched her for a second, hovering in the shadows, out of The Priest's view. *We have a Plan B.* Her words surfaced. I wondered what Plan B actually looked like. Her gaze never moved from The Priest, strapped to a chair in the middle of the warehouse under blazing overhead lights.

"When Riven gets here, I want it to just be us," I commanded.

"Took him long enough to find us," Percy muttered.

"Yeah, well," I responded, my voice turning cold as I stepped forward. "He's been busy getting rid of dead Daughters."

Rage burned inside me as my gaze settled on the betraying bastard. He looked worse today than he had two days ago—I clenched my fists, still feeling the aches of the beating—he should. I'd worked him over hard enough. I licked my lips, still tasting Vivienne as her sister flanked the bright light like a damn vampire.

She never went near him.

Not even close enough for him to hear her voice.

Got you by the Balls pumped through the speakers. The music was her idea. Anything to muffle the sound of her voice. I scowled, narrowing in on the way she watched The Priest. It was almost like she knew him. A chill raced along my spine at the thought.

I took a step forward just as my phone buzzed.

The sound echoed in Percy's hand.

He looked down. "We're on," he murmured, then lifted his head and raised his hand, giving a signal to another of Harper's men across the space.

I pulled my gun as the music ended abruptly and made my way toward the pathetic piece of shit. "Looks like it's time for a family reunion."

He lifted his head, his one good eye fixed on me. "Good," he croaked. "I can't wait to watch my brother put a bullet in your head."

I gave a chuff and lifted the gun. "That, Father, will *never* happen."

It wasn't my head he needed to be worried about. I sniffed, wincing at the stench of blood and sweat. He still wore the same clothes I'd taken him in. Only now they were a little worse for wear.

Crack!

The faint sound of a gunshot echoed in the night. I scanned the shadows, finding Percy and his men gone, until movement stole my focus. Helene lifted her head from her phone, then took a step backward as the far door of the warehouse opened with a *bang!*

I clenched the Priest's shirt as Riven Cruz strode in, his shirt and face covered with a splattering of blood. I scanned the doorway behind him, searching for his brother...but he wasn't there. Just *The Principal,* striding his way toward me.

"Riven," I murmured, shifting my hand with the gun.

I met the bastard's stare, remembering all the fucking things Vivienne had told me about him. My finger eased inside the trigger guard. "That's far enough."

He jerked his focus from his brother to me. "You *fucking bastard.*"

I didn't move. "Desperate times."

His lips curled, but he said nothing.

"Where is he?" my demand echoed.

I watched his reaction, searching that stony stare for any hint of panic. But there was none. None because he was a stiff piece of shit, icier even than me, frozen all the way to that rotten core. Because Riven and his fucking brothers were rotten, there was no denying that.

I yanked his brother's head back and raised the gun. "Where the fuck is Hale?"

"Haven't you heard?" Riven snarled. "It's all over the news. Hale's dead."

But he wasn't dead, was he? Because *Riven was still fucking here.* That nerve twitched in the corner of my eye. "You know I'm not that fucking stupid."

"I don't know." He spat. "Hale seemed to have the upper hand for a long time there. I was thinking you'd given up on finding your son. He is your son, isn't he? Your son with Ophelia, right?"

Twitch.

He smirked. "That's right, not your son. But one you wanted, right? Just like you want King's bitch."

My breath caught.

He glanced at his brother for a second, then at me. "You think I don't know about that? You think I don't know about both those fucking little sluts?"

My pulse was booming as my mind raced with all the implications of Riven and his brothers knowing about Vivienne and Ryth.

"I don't care about them," Riven declared, glancing at his brother once more. "You can fuck as many of King's little whores as you want. All I want is my brother." He took a step closer. "Give him to me and I'll go away. You never have to look at me again. You can leave this place. Hell, with your money and connections, you can make a life anywhere. Why stay? Take your little bitch and your sons and just go."

Fuck, it sounded tempting.

There was no Ophelia now.

No real reason I had to remain here. My gaze drifted to the shadows where Helene King had stood. The Daughters and the Sons...the entire fucking Order wasn't my problem, was it? Not really...not anymore.

I had what I wanted.

I shook my head. That desperation collided with reality. I was trapped between what was right in front of me and what all my years of wading in the filth of Haelstrom Hale had taught me.

This wasn't over.

I ran now and not only would I be running forever, but I'd lose all the ground I'd fought for. This would've all been for nothing.

"No," I answered, meeting that killing stare. "You *will* tell me where Hale is."

"Fuck you," The Priest grunted, wrenching against his cuffs. *"Fuck you to Hell."*

I inhaled hard, that savage part of my nature rising to the surface. "Now, is that anyway for a priest to talk?"

He unleashed a roar, throwing himself forward, until I grabbed hold of his hair and yanked him back. *"YOU WILL TELL ME WHERE HALE IS!"*

I jerked my gaze up to his brother, lifted the gun, took aim, and squeezed the trigger.

Crack!

Screams erupted. Piercing screams that echoed in the space. Blood bloomed in his thigh in the exact place I wanted it. Maximum pain. Minimum damage. All nerves and flesh. Still, it had the impact I wanted.

Riven's eyes widened. There was a flicker of fear as I pressed the gun to his brother's temple. *Don't fucking test me.*

Riven shook his head. The panic was all too real now as he bellowed. "*I don't fucking know!*"

"Lie."

He stared at the muzzle pressed against his brother's temple as The Priest's howls died to low, guttural moans. "It's the truth," he spat. *"I don't fucking know!* All I heard was what was on the goddamn news. No one has contacted me. No one has told me a goddamn thing!"

Bullshit.

He was lying. He had to be. There was no fucking way Hale was lying on that stainless steel table in the city morgue. *He couldn't be.* Because this wasn't over. Not by a long shot.

"And how do I know you're telling me the truth?"

Riven reached up, raking his fingers through his hair as he wrenched his gaze to where Helene King stood. The Priest's moans quietened to brutal gasps for air as he tried to ride the waves of pain. But Riven's focus was fixed on that spot in the darkness. He couldn't see her, nor could he sense her. Still, his brow furrowed like he felt *something*.

"Because I'm just as fucking desperate as you are," he finally answered, swiveling that chilling stare back to me. "You think you're the only one who has blood at stake here?"

He shifted his focus to his brother.

The Priest shook his head. "No, Riven. Don't…"

"You think you're the only one who has *everything* on the fucking line?"

I'd never seen Riven desperate, not as The Principal, or as Hale's fucking lapdog.

"Then we both want the same." I yanked the Priest's head back and drove the hot muzzle against his temple. "And now you understand the implications if you betray me."

There was a flinch before that stony stare met mine.

"I want Hale," I urged, lowering my gun. One brutal shove and The Priest stumbled forward. "And I want him now."

Riven never moved when his brother hit the filthy floor at his feet. Just held my stare. "The moment I find out something, you'll be the first to know."

"I'd better be," I answered, finding the hateful glare of The Priest as he swung his gaze to me. "Because the next time I come for you…I won't be seeking a negotiation. Just revenge. Always revenge."

The corner of my lips twitched, curling as Riven bent down, grabbed his brother by the arm, and dragged him upwards. He glanced to that darkened spot where the third King daughter lingered before he heaved The Priest with him as he headed for the door.

I waited until they were gone, and Percy and his men moved in, closing the door.

"Any casualties?"

"One," Percy answered. "Took him out before we even saw the bastard. He's dangerous, London. He's real fucking dangerous."

"Aren't we all?" I answered, swinging my gaze toward the movement as Helene King stepped from the shadows. "Want to tell me what the hell is going on?"

She just gave a shrug as she glanced at the door. "Let's just say I've been preemptive."

"What the fuck?" I whispered as the pieces fell into place. "You know him?"

She shook her head. "Not Riven, no. Not yet, at least. But I will…" Her hard stare swung back to me. Christ, it was hard to look at her and not see Vivienne. "I'll do whatever it takes to make sure my sisters are safe and bring The Order to the ground."

That renewed sense of determination hit me.

She met my stare, her true feelings raw and bleeding in front of me.

Helene King loved.

She loved so much.

Like me, she just didn't show it.

I lowered my gaze to the scar on her arm, remembering the mass of ruined flesh on her stomach. A remnant of just how deep that love was. It was a pity Vivienne didn't see it. Maybe she didn't want to. Maybe this was her way of protecting her heart. God knows, we'd bled enough in this chaos.

Helene turned around and headed for the door.

"Wait," I called, stopping her.

She glanced over her shoulder.

"I need to ask a favor...for your sister."

Her brow rose. "Vivienne?"

I shook my head. "Ryth."

There was a flicker of sadness before she answered. "Anything."

"She wants to arrange a meeting with Vivienne. Somewhere safe, somewhere we can protect them."

Pain cut across her face. "Consider it done."

"You'll be there?"

A soft chuff followed. "I think Vivienne has made it perfectly clear she wants nothing to do with me."

"I don't care." I took a step closer. It didn't matter what she said, they were family, for fuck's sake. "I want you there."

A sad smile moved in. "You're going to keep pushing us together, aren't you? Even if she hates me."

"Even if she hates you," I answered. "The woman doesn't know what's good for her. But I'll teach her. I'll teach her just how deeply she can love...even if it's the last thing I do."

Helene just smiled. Fuck if that wasn't her saddest expression of all. "I'll be in touch," she answered. "And London?"

I waited.

"Thank you."

One slow nod and she was gone, yanking open the side door and slipping into the shadows where she seemed to belong.

Thank you.

Those words didn't seem to belong here, not amongst the stench of blood and rage. But there they were, ringing in my ears as I murmured, "Keep on him, Percy. I want to know the moment Riven and his brothers make a move."

"Of course," he answered. "You'll be the first to know."

I gave him a nod and left, making my way back to the Audi. My hand stilled on the handle. I wouldn't put a bomb past the bastard as an act of retaliation. My senses sharpened before I yanked the handle and climbed in.

A bomb wouldn't be Riven's style.

He was the sort of bastard to look you in the eyes right before he killed you.

But I had to be more careful now. Maybe more than ever.

I started the engine and pulled out of the side street. Headlights flared behind me as I pulled onto the on-ramp and headed for home. I kept watch, speeding up to let them fall away. But there was a nagging feeling at the nape of my neck, a whisper of a warning.

I was on alert the entire way home, making sure I took back streets before I pulled into the driveway and parked. *Thank you.* Those words lingered as I climbed out, hit the lock button, and went to the house.

Claimed

My footsteps echoed along the hall. I didn't even stop to remove my holster, just headed for our bedrooms as an overwhelming sense of desperation hit me. I needed to see her, to make sure she was safe...to make sure she was here. My damn hand trembled as I grabbed her door handle, turned it, and pushed.

But her bed was empty.

I swung back and headed for Carven's room. He moaned, swearing at me as I stepped in and scanned the darkness.

"What is it?" he mumbled.

"Nothing. Go back to sleep."

He shoved his head under the pillow, grunting as I left. But Colt's room felt empty as I neared, leaving my gaze to shift to the last bedroom. Mine. I neared, opened the door, and stepped inside before I stopped.

They were both there. Colt was curled against her on his side, and Vivienne lay naked, with her arms outstretched over her head. I took a step closer, watching her in the faint light. Her chest rose and fell rhythmically. My gaze shifted to the sheets pulled high, but it was her belly that held me transfixed. I lowered myself to the bed, still fully clothed.

"London," she murmured, her voice full of sleep.

"I'm here."

One eye cracked open as she reached for me. "Good, come back to bed."

I lay down, leaned backwards, and she burrowed under my arm in an instant, snuggling against me. *Jesus*...I sucked in a hard breath, my chest tightening. Only she made me feel like this, terrified and dangerous all at the same time.

"I love you," she whispered.

"I love you too, pet." I curled my arm around her and allowed my eyes to close. "I love you more than anything."

I didn't want to rest.

I couldn't rest.

I had too much at stake here and there were too many wolves at our doo—

HALE.

Hale was here.

His face morphed from the shadows, that hateful fucking glare pinching as he smirked.

I'm coming for you, London, he whispered. *I'm going to rip apart everything you've ever loved. Are you ready? Are you ready for me? BOO!*

I jerked awake, and my hand flew to my chest. Cold steel met my palm as a low, savage rumble came from beside me. But I was aiming for the darkness in front of me, the darkness where Haelstrom Hale stood.

Boom.

Boom.

BOOM.

My pulse was deafening. I sucked in hard breaths, scanning the emptiness. But he wasn't there. He wasn't there. I glanced at Vivienne, fast asleep beside me on the bed, then at Colt as he stared at me, then at the doorway, that same threatening snarl rumbling in the back of his throat.

"He's out there," I whispered. "He's out there...and he's coming for us."

I waited like that, my gun pointed into the darkness. My senses were on alert, until that sickening fear pushed all hope of sleep aside.

"Stay here," I urged Colt. "Stay with her. Protect her with your life."

I slipped from the bed, the grogginess from lack of sleep burning my eyes as I left them behind.

There was no time to sleep.

Only to protect.

And if I had to...to kill.

THIRTY-NINE

Vivienne

Where is he?

I jerked awake with the bitter tang of acid trapped in the back of my throat. Those words resounded, booming in my head as I turned, finding the other half of the bed empty. *I thought he...I thought he'd come back to me.* A soft pang of pain filled my chest. But he mustn't have. I reached out, because the sheets were cold.

A sharp inhale on the other side made me turn my head. Dark eyes found mine and held me transfixed. But as I lingered in that animalistic glare, the darkness brightened.

"Colt?" I whispered.

He blinked, scowling. "Yeah?"

"Just checking."

He lifted his head, glancing around the room. "Where the hell are we?"

"London's bedroom."

"Oh." He dropped back down, closing his eyes once more. "Wake me in the morning."

My stomach clenched. I still tasted that bitter tang of morning sickness. "It is morning," I groaned ad I pushed upwards.

My stomach rolled with me, swishing and swirling as I swallowed again and again. "I need my bathroom," I moaned, and slid my feet from the bed. He was naked, his arms stretched upwards. Vague memories of him moved in before, in a rush, it all came back to me.

I lifted my gaze to the leather bonds still wrapped around the top of the bed, as I remembered the way the beast had strained to get to me. Then he did. My core clenched, swollen, aching, reminding me exactly what we'd done.

"Jesus," I whispered, reaching down and tugging the top sheet, whipping it from Colt's naked body.

"Hey!" He snapped his eyes open.

They grew pitch black for a second, narrowing on me.

"Mine," I demanded.

Then with a slow stare, the beast retreated.

"Fine." Colt rolled over, his powerful thighs flexing as he pulled his knees to his chest. "Take the damn thing."

I tugged the ends around me and headed for the door, each step re-igniting that ache between my thighs. But the moment I was out in the hall, breathing in the cool air, my stomach settled. I shuffled to my bedroom, slipped inside, and tugged the sheet off as I went into the bathroom.

I wanted a shower…and food.

I brushed my teeth, then enjoyed the time in the shower before I stepped out. The taste of the mint toothpaste drove that vile bitter taste away, letting my stomach settle as I dried off and headed for the wardrobe. Soft denim jeans, one of Colt's shirts, and a sweater later, and I was striding out of my bedroom.

The house was quiet and felt empty. I glanced into the kitchen, but found the place empty. I headed for the study. In my mind's eye, I saw London there before I even stepped into the doorway, hunched over, working on tracking Hale down, his eyes brightening when he saw me.

That image stayed with me as I stepped in and found him in the same position I'd imagined.

"Morning."

He didn't lift his head, didn't meet my gaze. There was dried blood splatter on the rolled sleeves of his white shirt. But I'd learned not to ask questions. Mostly because I'd be sickened at the answer. Still, he remained focused on the spreadsheet in front of him.

"I said, morning."

"I heard you."

Oh, okay. Pain bloomed like a deadly rose. I swallowed down its foul scent and glanced at the spreadsheet. It was bank statements, lots and lots of bank statements. "Anything I can help with?"

"No."

"Fine," I muttered, and turned, feeling pissed off. But the moment I stepped back into the doorway, he spoke.

"The meeting you wanted...it's tonight."

I froze, the words resounding as I spun. Had I heard right? No, I must be imagining things, just like I'd imagined him smiling at the sight of me. "What?"

With a hard, slow exhale, he lifted his head and repeated. "The meeting you *wanted* is happening tonight."

"But I thought you said no?"

He eased back in his chair. "I changed my mind."

Panicky, elated thoughts slammed into me. He could be as moody as he wanted. I was about to see Ryth. I was about to see *my sister*.

I lurched forward, then flew across the room and flung my arms around him. *"Thank you. Oh, God."* I closed my eyes. "Thank you, London. I know you didn't want to do this."

He gripped my arms, then pulled me close. I buried my head against his neck and inhaled. He smelled like exhaustion and gunpowder. Both made me ache for him a little more.

"I...I want you to be prepared." His words were strained. I lifted my head, meeting that dark stare as he continued. "Ryth is tired and her stepbrothers are...nervous, as expected."

He searched my gaze as he spoke, and a heavy feeling dropped into my stomach. There were things he wasn't saying, things he was holding back from me. Was that the reason for the icy reception? Because he was worried about Ryth's brothers?

"As we are with you," he finally added, his gaze moving down to settle on my stomach.

It hit me then. He was scared. He was so fucking scared I was going to lose the baby...

Babiesss, remember?

He was scared I was going to lose our babies.

Then, in a smooth, flawless movement, he slipped from the chair until his knees hit the floor. His hands went around me, sliding up the backs of my thighs until he cupped my ass...and he gently pressed his face against my stomach.

"We're so close, Vivienne. So damn close. I can't let anything happen now. I can't let anything happen to you."

I looked down at the deadly, ruthless male on his knees for me and saw his fear as clearly as I saw him now. "It won't." I lifted my hand, sliding my fingers through his gray-flecked black hair. "It won't."

He said nothing, just pressed his face against me. A shudder ripped through him, one so violent it jerked me forward. I'd expect nothing less from this man. I caressed his head, my heart pounding in the back of my throat.

I'd seen him violent.

I'd seen him bloody.

But this silence.

This trembling, choked silence.

This was terrifying.

Movement came from the hallway. Like the deadly killer he was, Carven was silent as he stopped in the doorway, watching us.

"Nothing will ever happen to me," I whispered, holding Carven's stare. "Because you won't let it."

FORTY

Vivienne

London flicked a dangerous stare toward the doorway. Carven paced the grimy workshop, past a chair that looked like it was bolted to the floor, treading all over the fresh blood splatter beading in the inch-thick dust.

I tried not to look, remembering the blood splatter on London's crisp white shirt this morning. What I didn't know couldn't come for me, right? I winced and looked away. Not in our house.

Colt stood in the shadows, trying his best to leash the beast, watching me as he inhaled deep, sawing breaths. But it was Guild who jerked his gaze to London and snapped, "This is taking too long, London. They should be here by now...*where the fuck are they?*"

That wasn't like him.

Not even in the slightest.

The tension was a hard, throbbing lump in the middle of my chest.

I brushed my hand across my belly, London's warning blazing in my mind. *Ryth is tired...Ryth is...tired.*

What if...what if Ryth didn't want to see me? What if she really was as fragile as London said? This could be dangerous...for her and her baby.

I jerked my gaze at London as he scowled. All it'd take would be the stress of this and she could go into early labor. Worse, she could collapse.

I couldn't let that happen...not even to see her again. It was just...*too much.*

"Call it off." I shook my head. "It's too dangerous. Call it all off, London."

He jerked a glare my way and opened his mouth to speak.

Beep.

But the message on his phone's screen stopped him as he snatched it up. "It's too late, they're here," he muttered, then looked toward the door.

The handle turned, then the door was pushed in. Dark eyes, savage glares, as three massive men strode through the door into the warehouse. They scanned every inch of the open space, drifted over Carven and Colt, then London, before settling on me.

I barely recognized them.

They were harder, colder. Even Nick, who'd always been kinder, was stony as he strode through the door. Caleb followed and nodded to London. "St. James," he acknowledged.

Then a small...shrunken figure stepped through. Her belly was the first thing I saw. Then her eyes, her dark, sunken eyes and a haunted stare that seemed to pass right over me as though I wasn't even there...

I flinched, fighting to swallow past that hard lump in the back of my throat.

Then rage walked in.

In the form of Tobias Banks.

His top lip curled as his gaze settled on Carven, then whipped my way. A shudder tore through me. He'd been a bully before, but now he looked downright terrifying. How the hell did Ryth survive him, let alone the three of them? But there was a warning in his stare and a desperate pleading as he shifted his focus to the woman in front of him...my sister. His gaze softened instantly, turning to desire.

So that's how.

He looked at her the same way London and the sons looked at me. Maybe we had more in common than I'd realized. She looked around the warehouse, cringing.

"It's a fixer-upper," I muttered, drawing that terrified stare with a sweep of my arm toward the chair. "We're going for that freshly tortured, grungy vibe. What do you think?"

She let out a bark of laughter, then lunged.

"Baby," Tobias reached for her as she stumbled.

But she was already gone...as was I.

I tore across the space, ignoring the panicked stares from Carven and Colt and, with a cry, slammed into her. Warmth pressed against me, clinging onto me for salvation.

She was so small, *tiny* almost. Nothing more than skin and bones. My arms went around her shoulders. In my head, she was the same feisty woman who'd helped me break into The Principal's office, then played bait as I knocked out the nurse when we'd fled that goddamn hell.

Only now, that seemed like a lifetime ago.

All we'd had was a few frantic messages from London's encrypted connection, fleeting moments to make sure we were both still alive. It hadn't been enough, not anywhere near enough. I closed my eyes, pulling her against me until my body bowed around her belly. "Fuck, I missed you."

She clung to me. "Me, too," she whispered, her voice thick. "So *very* much."

Deep baritone voices echoed all around us. I felt the weight of their stares. But none of that touched us at that moment. It was just her and me, holding onto each other, until I slowly relaxed.

There was no need for conversation.

No revealing our pain.

We knew exactly what it'd taken to get us here. The desperate need to survive and love...the love of those we belonged to.

"*Familia est omnia,*" I whispered.

"Family is everything," she agreed, gripping me tighter.

Slick, warm tears trailed down my cheeks. I buried my face against her, breathing in the faint scent of smoke in her hair. Awkward silences were all around us. But I couldn't worry about how awkward this was for them.

I had my sister.

"I fucking love you." I pulled away and grasped her small face, looking at her through the blur of my tears. "You hear me? *I fucking love you.*"

She raised those big blue eyes to mine and fresh tears slipped free. "I love you too, Viv. I really missed you. I missed you so much it hurt."

I yanked her close again, turning my head to find London. "I missed you too, kid."

The sound of the door opening behind me intruded. But I pulled away, looking down at her once more. "We stay together now, okay? No matter what, we stay together."

She nodded, desperation roaring in her eyes before they shifted to the door behind me. I turned around, to find Helene King. She glanced at Ryth, the corners of her lips trembling in a nervous smile.

The need to step in front of Ryth surged up. I didn't know this woman...after what she'd done to Carven, I certainly didn't *trust* her. That possessive flare of anger grew.

"Ryth." She took a step forward and held out her hand. "It's so good to finally meet you."

On reflex, I shook my head, stopping Helene instantly.

"Pet," London warned.

A nerve twitched in the corner of my eye. I didn't know who I was angrier at, *her* for turning up here...or London for belittling my distrust.

"*London.*" I whipped my gaze toward him.

They all stared at me, even the most possessive one of them all: Tobias. Confusion flickered and heat rose, melting my icy sting.

"She's Ryth's sister too," London urged, shifting nervously. "Maybe you could give her a chance?"

"Just don't give her your back," Carven muttered. "She's likely to knock you out."

There. At least Carven was on my side.

But it was Caleb who stepped forward, cutting across me to hold out his hand. "Caleb Banks."

Helene shook it. "I know who you are," she admired as she glanced at the others. "Nick. Tobias. I'm really sorry to hear about your father and your mom, Ryth. It was a shock to us all."

Father.

Just the mere mention of that word swept me back into dangerous territory. "Was it?" I asked. "A shock, I mean. I just assumed you knew everything. After all, you are your father's minion, aren't you?"

"*Vivienne,*" London snarled, only more insistently this time.

"What?" I snapped, shooting him a glare. "It's the truth, isn't it? She and her father are the reason we're here in the first place?"

"And the reason you're still alive," London added, scowling at me.

I hadn't seen him this angry...not since that first night when he'd forced me into the car and driven me to the orphanage. But he was angry now, and disappointed. Pain cut through my chest.

"Yes," Helene said. "When you put it that way, he is."

Surprise flooded in.

"But he's also *your* father, too," Helene added, before she turned. "And Ryth's."

My sister just shook her head. "No, I already have a father. There's no room for another one."

Helene shook her head, opening her mouth to speak. But I didn't want to hear what she had to say. Ryth's mind was made up. She had a dad and by God, Helene needed to respect that.

"The baby." I swiveled around, ignoring the woman who claimed she was my kin, and focused on the only one who mattered. "Tell me all about it?"

"It's a girl," she beamed.

The floor seemed to drop out from under me. My heart hammered and my mouth went dry. The fear I harbored engulfed me like a deadly storm. I glanced at London, but he was already striding across the space toward me.

Tobias shot us a glare, scanning the warehouse. "What is it?"

I tried to swallow as London's hand settled protectively against my back. "We're so happy for you, Ryth," he spoke calmly while I fell apart in front of him. "I heard you have a place now. You can rest assured your daughter's aunt here is going to spoil her as well as any aunt does, right, sweetheart?"

He turned to me. I couldn't speak...

My breaths were racing. My mind was screaming.

"What is it?" Ryth whispered, her faint smile fading.

I shook my head, swallowing my fears. *What if it's a girl, London? What if it's...*

I couldn't tell her that. I couldn't ruin what little happiness she had. "Nothing." I forced a smile. "I'm just so happy. We..." I glanced at Colt, then Carven. "We have a bit of a surprise ourselves."

"You're not?" Ryth whispered, her eyes widening.

Just like the terror that consumed me had left her alone. "Two of them," I whispered. "By two different fathers."

Nick shot Carven a sideways glance.

"We're going to have babies at the same time?" Ryth burst into tears.

I looked down at my flat stomach, the bump barely visible. "Well, not exactly. But it'll be close eno—"

She threw her arms around me, crying and jumping as much as her body allowed. "Oh, my *God*. We're going to have babies together! I can tell you all about it. Morning sickness is the *worst.*"

I smiled and nodded. "Yeah, I seem to have that part down pat."

"But the sex is good," she added with a wink. "So...so good."

Tobias coughed, choking on a gulp of air. Nick slapped him hard on the back. "Easy now, brother," he muttered, grinning hugely. It was the first time I'd seen anyone else smile.

Even London smirked. "Yes, well, we have that to look forward to."

"Hey." I shot him a glare. "You don't go without, buddy."

London froze. "Buddy?" he muttered. "Huh."

His distaste only made me laugh. I moved closer, sliding my arm around Ryth's shoulders and leading her away. "You can tell me all about it." I gave her a wink. "You know, sister to sister."

I was so busy being happy, I didn't hear the door open once more. It wasn't until heavy steps echoed, drawing Ryth's gaze, that I turned. But as I did, I caught the shadows in front of me, hiding behind the large machinery, move.

"Dad?" Ryth whispered.

I scowled as I glanced toward the door when Jack Castlemaine stepped in. He looked at Helene until she shook her head, then turned to us.

"Baby," he beamed as the shine of a gun came in front of me and three men stepped forward. Three men I'd never seen before in my life.

Ryth was too busy looking at her dad to notice. But I saw.

Empty, cold stares fixed on us.

They were exactly like Carven and Colt had been...

They were Sons.

"Just as soon as we kill the bastard who murdered our leader," one snarled as he swung his gaze to Carven. "We'll take you both back where you belong."

Then they lunged. One grabbed Ryth, tearing her from my grasp, as he lifted his gun and fired.

Crack!

Crack!

CRACK!

The warehouse erupted as another grabbed my arm, yanking me forward.

"*Let go of me!*" I screamed, clenching my fist and driving it through the air.

But all I saw was Ryth as her knees buckled, the weight she carried dropping her like a stone.

"*NO!*" Tobias roared, the deafening sound ripping through the open space.

A gun drove hard into my stomach. I lifted my gaze to the eyes of a killer. "Hello, *Daughter*," he smirked. "We've been looking for you."

FORTY-ONE

Carven

Tobias lunged, unleashing a chilling bellow of rage. There was no booming of my pulse as I watched the Sons drag my Wildcat into the shadows. Just silence. An emptiness I knew would become my world if I didn't move *NOW!*

I palmed my gun, drawing the muzzle high.

Seconds...it wasn't even that.

But fuck, it felt like forever.

My finger moved too fucking slow, *squeezing*.

Crack!

A shot tore free.

Crack!

London's blast came barely a heartbeat later.

Chaos descended as Nick and Caleb both dove forward from the steady stream of returning gunfire. I saw it all...and heard as

I leaped into action. The faint sound of an engine starting outside made my stomach drop like a stone.

They were going to take her.

They were going to take HER!

"The FUCK you are!" I howled, and lunged.

Tobias was hit in the shoulder as he ran. It spun him like a damn top and dropped him to his knees. I caught the sight of blood. But I was already charging toward the machinery where they'd taken her.

"Get the fuck off her!" Vivienne screamed. *"LEAVE HER ALONE!"*

I just knew she was fighting, giving it her all...to protect her sister.

Crack.

Crack.

Crack crack crack!

A bullet narrowly missed me. The muzzle flare, neon in the dark. I aimed for that light and squeezed off a shot as Tobias pushed up from the floor behind me. But as we flew deeper into the shadows of the warehouse, it wasn't Ryth's brother who hit them first.

It was mine.

Colt.

No.

Not Colt.

The Beast.

He slammed into the dark outline of one of the Sons, slamming him back against hard steel. The *grunt* that followed was soon replaced by terrifying screams. Hands flailed as I took aim, desperate to protect my blood...but there was no need, the bullet would be wasted. My brother, *the beast,* grabbed the Son's head in his massive hands and with one sickening jerk, snapped the bastard's neck.

Crunch.

The Son's knees buckled and he dropped to the floor. Only, the beast wasn't done, not by a long shot. He followed the attacker down, slammed him to the concrete floor, and savagely attacked, driving his face into his neck. Sickening, tearing sounds came as he thrashed his head, savaging the male like an animal.

"What the fuck?" Tobias stared, horrified.

Rage flared as I jerked my gaze upwards, fighting the need to aim my muzzle in the Banks brother's face and roar, *LOOK AWAY IF YOU CAN'T HANDLE IT!*

But the truth was, not even I could handle what my brother had become.

Then there was a moan. A soft, fragile sound as Ryth called, "Tobias."

The Banks bastard snapped his terrified stare to a crouched figure in the dark, one that slowly pushed upwards. Cold night air washed in, hitting my legs, and traveling upwards. Goosebumps raced along my spine and the sound of that car's engine grew louder. London raced forward, then dropped to the floor, his feet skidding out from under him as he rolled under the partially open roller door.

"Colt!" I bellowed as I charged after him.

That bestial gnawing ended as I followed our father, dropped hard to scurry under the door, and pushed upwards. Screams filled the night. Vivienne's and Guild's, jerking my gaze to the bodyguard as he stood directly in front of the dark four-wheel drive, bathed in the blinding headlights. The engine of the vehicle revved, blowing gray exhaust fumes against the door I'd crawled under. His gun was in both hands, aiming at the driver behind the wheel.

But the third Son had his arm across Vivienne's throat and his gun pressed against her head. That empty stare found mine. I knew exactly why he'd come. It had nothing to do with reclaiming a Daughter.

He was here for revenge. Pure and simple. I was the one who'd killed their leader.

There was panic in her wide eyes and her lips were ashen. Fuck, that hurt to see. My lips curled as I jerked my eyes back to the bastard's stare as the last moments of the attack outside the restaurant came flooding back.

The leader of this renegade group of Sons had tried to abduct her as we'd fought for our lives. I'd almost lost her then. Hell, I almost lost myself. But we'd survived...and he hadn't. I'd left his body slumped on the ground at that derelict building, and now they'd come for payback.

"There's no way out for you," London said calmly, standing in front of them. "Not alive, at least. Let her go and we'll let one of you live."

In the corner of my eye, Colt rolled under the roller door and pushed to stand. Blood was smeared all over his face. He took a step forward, snarling. But the bastard who had Vivienne whipped his gun toward my brother. "Come closer and I'll start firing."

"*Beast!*" Vivienne cried out as she fought the bastard's hold. "*No...no, you hear me? No.*"

Desperation filled her stare, fixed on my brother.

Even in the face of her own danger, she thought of us first.

Agony plunged deep into my chest like a damn knife.

It was that fucking dressing room all over again. In my head, she lay across my brother with her arms outstretched, putting her own life on the line to protect him. Just like that desperate glare she had for my brother now.

The bastard who had her shifted the gun back to her head. "You." He stared at me. "Gun down and on your knees, or I'll put a bullet through her head."

"*NO!*" she screamed, thrashing against his hold to drive her elbow into his stomach. But he saw it coming and shifted his stance at the last second, narrowly avoiding her blow.

"You won't." I shook my head. "She's a Daughter."

His lips curled into a smirk. "One less won't worry us."

Someone flinched. I didn't know if it was Colt or Guild. But the sonofabitch saw it. He yanked his gunhand backwards and with, a growl, cold-cocked her in the side of her head. Dazed, she stumbled sideways, her knees buckling before the hold around her throat yanked her back.

Ryth tore around the side of the warehouse. Her stepbrothers and father followed, spilling out around us.

"*Stop!*" Jack Castlemaine bellowed, lifting his hands into the air.

Helene King was right by his side, a gun in her hand, aimed at the asshole who had the woman we loved.

"Take me." Jack stepped forward. "Take me instead."

"The fuck?" London glared at the man who had no stake in this fight. Still, the bastard was determined to make it about him as he took another step forward.

Crack!

I flinched as the shot sounded, terror ripping through me. But the bullet landed in front of Castlemaine and bounced off the concrete.

"One more fucking move," the Son warned, breathing hard. "And I will splatter her goddamn brains everywhere." He turned back to me. "Now *move.*"

I lowered my gun and took a step forward.

There was no getting out of this.

And it was okay.

I held her stare and slowly nodded.

It was all okay.

I sank to my knees. The *thud* of the landing tore up into my thighs.

If I had to leave this world, then this was the way I'd want it.

London and Wildcat would protect my brother.

After all, she carried their children.

They would love him and care for him. I fixed my gaze on the woman I loved and knew in my soul...*this was meant to be.* The gun moved from her head to point at mine once more.

"No." Vivienne thrashed, a stream of blood spilling down the side of her head.

"Pet," London murmured carefully.

But I couldn't look away from the dark muzzle of that bastard's gun.

"Exactly how I showed you."

What?

I shifted my gaze as her wide brown eyes fixed on London. She slowly dropped her hand and reached behind her. All I could see was that bastard's finger squeezing the trigger, the gleam of steel reflecting the moonlight, until he suddenly flinched, then scowled. In the space of a breath, the color instantly drained from his face. He dropped his hand and doubled over with a guttural, agonized roar.

Movement simultaneously happened all around me.

London swung his hand with the gun.

Wildcat lunged at the same time my brother did.

BOOM!

BOOM! BOOM...BOOM...BOOM...

The night exploded with gunfire. Guild and London unleashed, shattering the windshield and killing the Son behind the wheel as the beast tore Vivienne's abductor apart. His screams started and never stopped, not when Colt savaged his face, tearing at his lips with his teeth and driving his fists into his face.

There was nothing any of us could do to stop him.

Not even if we'd wanted to.

I shoved upwards, catching Vivienne as she fell.

"I got you." I yanked her against me as London strode forward.

He wrapped his arms around her, pulling her from my arms to check her. "Look at me...*hey. Look at me, baby.*"

He ran his hands over her head as the rest of us stared at my brother.

Wet, gurgling, repulsive sounds silenced the Son's screams stopped. Still the beast ripped, beat, and tore. There was no end to the savagery. Nothing stopped his wrath, not even death.

There were no words this time.

No turning away from what we are.

Even Ryth and her father watched the nauseating display. Eventually Guild walked around and yanked open the driver's door of the SUV. The dead Son fell out as he reached in and killed the engine. In the silence, the stomach-churning sounds were louder.

"Who the fuck are they?" Caleb Banks snapped.

"Sons," I answered, still staring at my brother as he ripped the dead man's throat apart. "Working for someone to abduct the escaped Daughters."

"What the fuck?" Tobias shot me a glare. "Who the fuck is sending them?"

"I have a fair idea," Jack Castlemaine murmured, drawing everyone's gaze.

"If you say King, I'll put a goddamn bullet in the man's head myself," London growled, looking away from Colt's grotesque attack. "Just as soon as I find him."

"You won't have to look far," Helene answered.

"Oh, yeah?" London glared her way. "Why's that?"

She met his stare. "Because he's right here."

FORTY-TWO

Vivienne

King is here? I looked around, my knees locked but still trembling. The echo of gunshots rang in my ears. Still, I tried to understand what Helene was saying…because this was important.

Ryth trembled, her own knees giving way in a rush. Tobias was there, lunging to grab her before Nick and Caleb swept in. All three moved around her as Tobias lifted her in his arms.

"Maybe we should take this inside," Jack Castlemaine urged.

London shot him a possessive glare, then slowly nodded. "You're right."

Ryth and her brothers headed back inside. She turned her head, searching for me before our gazes collided, then they disappeared once more.

"I'll call the cleaners." Guild shoved the driver's door closed and reached for his phone, leaving the four of us alone.

Colt turned his blood-smeared face away.

"Baby." I stumbled forward.

Until he stopped me with a shake of his head. "No. Don't."

I scowled, looking down to the puddle of blood I stood in. It was all around me, splattering the sides of the four-wheel drive, reflecting in the moonlight.

"Don't?" I grabbed his arm. He tried to pull away, but I held on and wouldn't let him. *"Hey!"* My voice was croaky. "Look at me."

He shook his head, swiping the back of his hand across his face, catching the drops of blood that fell from his chin.

"I said. Look. At. Me."

Compulsion, and the beast forced his gaze to mine. Those deep blue eyes were filled with revulsion and horror.

"You saved me," I whispered, stroking his cheek. "The beast *saved me*. You think this is your worst? Well, I'm here to tell you, it isn't. Not by a long shot. This is evolution, pure and simple." I lowered my gaze to what remained of the bastard who'd tried to abduct me. Memories of Macoy Daniels came rushing back. "I love you, Colt, and I love that darker part of you. I thank the beast every day for protecting you and bringing you back to me. You aren't different to me. You're just as perfect as you were before."

He held my stare, then gave a small shake of his head. "I can't control him."

I can, the words whispered through my mind. "Then we'll figure it out together."

He lowered his gaze to my belly. "What if he hurts you, or the babies?"

Carven gave a grunt and stepped closer. "Take a look around you, you big brute. You just ripped two men in half trying to protect her." He gave his brother a slap on the back. "So, I'm pretty damn sure, Wildcat's safe. It's everyone else who has a damn heartbeat I'm worried about, including myself and London."

Colt looked horrified. "I'd never hurt you."

"I know you wouldn't, buddy." He gripped his brother's massive shoulders. "I know."

A car door slammed behind us. I jerked my gaze over my shoulder to find Guild heading toward us carrying London's jacket in his hand.

My teeth chattered as a tremor tore through me. Guild handed London his jacket and he instantly strode forward to wrap it around my shoulders.

"Let's get you inside, pet."

I nodded, jerking a glare his way. "Don't think my near death has made me forget you took Helene's side in our argument."

"I wouldn't dream of it," he murmured, those dark eyes twinkling with amusement. "I expect you'll take it out on me as soon as we get home." He leaned down to whisper against my ear. "In fact, I'm *very much looking forward to it.*"

Heat moved in, stealing away the bitter cold. I couldn't stay mad at him.

Not when he looked at me like that.

Goddamn him.

There was a twitch in the corner of his mouth before he murmured. "Let's get you inside."

Guild hung back, watching our backs as we headed inside the warehouse. London's strong arms wrapped around me as we stepped through the door. Jack and Helene turned around, watching us as we entered.

"How about you finally show us your hand?" London growled at Helene. "You've been lying and evading our questions from the very beginning. If you want to have a relationship of *any kind* with your sisters, then don't you think you need to start with the truth?"

The truth.

That's all we wanted.

Our one hope to escape this nightmare once and for all.

"Well?" London snapped.

She didn't flinch, never even looked away, just held London's stare.

Caleb stepped forward. "We're waiting," he urged.

All of us were, our gazes locked on her.

"Who the hell is King?" London forced through clenched teeth.

Helene barely flinched. But she wasn't the one who answered.

"I am," Jack Castlemaine spoke. "I'm Weylen King."

The entire room froze...until London gave a sharp inhale of breath. "You?" He took a step forward. "You're King?"

Jack nodded, casting a careful glance my way. "Vivienne." He turned his head. "Ryth."

"*No!*" Ryth let go of Tobias and stumbled forward. "You're *not* him! You're not the man who...the *man who*—"

Started this.

She couldn't even say the words. But we all knew.

All the terror. All the blood. London had told me the Order was created by two men...and two men alone. One we were desperately hunting...and the other. The other we'd just found out was *our father*.

"TELL *ME!*" Ryth screamed.

Jack just shook his head.

The betrayal in Ryth's voice was sickening.

"Why?" I hissed, the words blistering in the back of my throat. "At least tell us that? Why did you do this?"

"I—" he started, then stopped, glancing at Helene. "I'd already had Helene when I met your mother, Ryth," he said carefully. "By the time I found out what was happening and tried to stop it, it was already too late. They had my DNA...and they were already using it."

Ryth burst out in tears, which only triggered her brothers, causing them to surround her.

"That doesn't make sense," London snapped, his eyes wide with fear. "You and Hale. I just don't see it. You're not even in his circles. You're *not* like him."

He meant Jack wasn't a sick, depraved motherfucker and he wasn't. One look into his eyes and you saw that. Jack

Castlemaine, or Weylyn King, or whoever the hell this man was, wasn't even in the same world as Hale.

"He doesn't just hate you," London snarled. "He wants to tear your world apart..." He glanced at me. "We need to know why?" He swung back to Jack. "At least give us that."

But Jack scowled, stared at the concrete floor, and in a careful voice he said. "I took something he wanted. That's all I can say. That's all I *will* say." He lifted his head and met my stare. "For now, until I have the opportunity to explain this privately to my daughters."

Me.

He wanted to explain it to me.

London flinched, straightening his spine.

He didn't like that idea at all.

I shook my head, glancing at Carven. But he just stared at Helene.

"That's how you got out of The Order." Caleb gripped Ryth protectively, shooting a glare at Helene. "The explosion...that was you?"

She gave a slow nod. "Yes."

"Jesus." He dragged his fingers through his hair.

"We need to find him, Hale and the others," Jack urged. "We need to find them all before it's too late."

"What the fuck do you think we've been doing?" London glanced toward Colt. "Some of us have had reason to hunt the bastard down."

"Why didn't you just tell me?" Ryth whispered, her voice thick. "Why couldn't you tell me the truth?"

Jack took a step forward, his voice etched with pain. "Because I couldn't trust your mother. That's the truth. That day when I left you...the last time, before our house burned to the ground, I was getting you out." He turned to look at me. "Helene had made plans for the four of us to just disappear."

"Disappear?" I whispered.

"Yes." He met my stare. "You, Ryth, Helene, and me. I would've taken you away and explained it all. But somehow, Ryth's mother found out. The next second, I was being arrested and thrown into jail."

"My mother?" I started. "Who is she?"

There was a tortured flicker in his eyes. "I never knew her. Hale had my DNA and had impregnated a number of women. They didn't survive...only you." He inhaled hard, trying to keep his voice from shaking. "I lost control of the information, only finding you years later. Well, after you were..." he glanced at London. "Monitored."

There was a look of pride in London's stare and the tight twitch of his lips said it all.

I beat you.

Everything with these men had to be a goddamn pissing contest until that gleam faded away. "Now Hale is out there, planning his new attack," London warned.

"I know," Jack answered, turning to Helene. "That's why we're here."

She reached into the back pocket of her jeans and pulled out a set of folded photos, handing them over to her father. *Our father.* The words filled me as he unfolded the images. "These were taken at six a.m. yesterday morning."

My pulse thundered as we all surged forward as one. My gaze was fixed on those images in Helene's hand. They were dark... really dark. A man stepped out of an open car door, heading to another. But he'd turned his head at the last moment and that's when the camera took the snapshot...of Haelstrom Hale.

It was him.

It was really him.

Alive.

"I fucking knew it." London forced the words through clenched teeth. "I knew that bastard wasn't dead."

"Not only is he not dead, but he's setting up a new Order, and he has the power and the money to do it," Jack added. "He will come for us, no doubt about it. He'll come and there won't be a damn thing I can do to stop him. Not this time."

"Where is he?" London's voice was dangerous. He glanced at Carven, who just met his stare with a nod. "Give me a goddamn location and he's dead."

"I can't," Jack answered, folding the images once more. "The moment he stepped into that car, he disappeared and I haven't been able to find him since."

Rage flickered in London's eyes.

"I can't find him in that network," Jack repeated carefully. "But Helene can."

I jerked my gaze to her. She was so calm, so...unemotional. "How?" I asked her, my mind spinning.

"Simple," she answered. "Plan B. The Teacher. The Priest... and The Principal."

Riven Cruz? I swallowed the panic that rose. *No...no fucking way. Not him. Not when he likes to...not when he likes to break you.*

Helene was going to use herself as bait.

"No," I hissed. "You don't understand. Those men...they're monsters." That ache in my chest grew thorns as I stared at the woman who looked so much like me. I couldn't care about her, right? I couldn't care about one more person who could be taken from me.

I just didn't have the strength left.

*Family...*London's words rose. *Is everything.* "They're monsters," I repeated in a whisper, remembering all the things they'd done to me and the others.

Helene held my panicked stare, then moved, slowly crossing the space to stop in front of me. Her brown eyes met mine. It was like looking into a mirror.

She lifted her hand and caressed my cheek. "Yes, they're monsters," she whispered back. "But if there's one thing you should know about me, little sister, it's that I'm very good at monster hunting. Especially for those I love."

WANT MORE of Vivienne and *the Beast?*

I've written a bonus scene for you! Grab your copy here.

Preorder your copy here

Trouble.

I hit it with my car...

Then I carried her home.

Taking care of her wounds with my own dark depravity.

Her scars tell a story, burns, cuts...some old...but there are some wounds that are fresh.

So fresh they tell a dangerous, intriguing tale. One I'm captivated to learn.

When she opened her eyes she didn't recoil like the others.

Instead, she told me her name.

Helene...

There is something about her. About the way she meets my stare. About the way she watches me.

She's not afraid.

And some dangerous part of me wants to keep it that way.

Just this once...

When Halestrom Hale and his controlling fist clenches around me and my blood. I hide her in the only place I know. A place I can control. A place where I can watch her...

The Order.

When my brothers find out, they are furious.

Everything we've worked for. All the lies we've told.

All the sick, depraved things we've done.

Could be all for nothing.

If she tells.

So we make it that she doesn't whisper a thing.

We keep her busy.

Every night...and all day long.

Until we realise this woman isn't in need of saving.

She's the grenade The Order has been terrified of...and I've just invited her in.